Andrew C. P. Haggard

Under Crescent and Star

Andrew C. P. Haggard

Under Crescent and Star

ISBN/EAN: 9783337406530

Printed in Europe, USA, Canada, Australia, Japan

Cover: Foto ©Andreas Hilbeck / pixelio.de

More available books at **www.hansebooks.com**

UNDER CRESCENT AND STAR

Andrew C. P. Haggard

UNDER CRESCENT AND STAR

BY

LIEUT.-COL. ANDREW HAGGARD, D.S.O.

AUTHOR OF 'DODO AND I,' 'TEMPEST-TORN,' ETC.

WITH PORTRAIT

CHEAP EDITION

WILLIAM BLACKWOOD AND SONS
EDINBURGH AND LONDON
MDCCCXCIX

TO

ALL MY OLD COMRADES

WHO FOUGHT OR DIED IN EGYPT.

ANDREW HAGGARD.

Naval and Military Club,
November 1895.

INTRODUCTION TO THE SECOND EDITION.

THE first edition of this book was published without any preface, but the second seems to require an introduction, if only to reply to one or two of my critics where a reply seems necessary. The press has received this record of recent Egyptian history so very favourably that there is not, however, very much that demands notice.

One journal — and only one — a London weekly, animadverted somewhat severely upon my remarks about the Irish Reserve men of 1882, saying—"Now, if all that is set down here be true, our service, as regards its Irish regiments, must be in a bad way, unless — which is not at all probable — the state of things has marvellously altered in the last twelve years. If, on the other hand, there is exaggeration or extravagence about the language used, then a gallant regiment and a fine body of men have been grossly libelled." This is very slipshod writing on the re-enlist annually or join the militia; and indeed their so doing is often winked at by recruiting-sergeants. Thus the nation imagines it has more men available than is really the case. Things being thus, if there is a lesson to be learned by the country from the behaviour of those Irish Reserve men of 1882, it is that the sooner long service, with the prospect of a pension, is reintroduced the better both for the country and the men.

And now, dismissing this subject, I wish to acknowledge with thanks the information given me by a writer in the 'National Observer' of December 21, 1895, as regards the later career of the outlaw Baramberas Yasoos Kella, and his information that my old friend, Barabbas the Robber, instead of having gone over to the Mahdi, is now living at Massowah, a prosperous gentleman, held in high esteem by the Italian General. I also accept from the same source the correction that the Province of Bogos was not annexed for Egypt by an Italian Bey or Pasha about 1871, but by the Swiss Munzinger in 1874.

ANDREW HAGGARD.

NAVAL AND MILITARY CLUB,
March 1896.

CONTENTS.

CHAPTER I.

CHAPTER II.

CHAPTER III.

CHAPTER IV.

CHAPTER V.

CHAPTER VI.

CHAPTER VII.

CHAPTER VIII.

CHAPTER IX.

CHAPTER X.

CHAPTER XI.

CHAPTER XII.

CHAPTER XIII.

CHAPTER XIV.

CHAPTER XV.

CHAPTER XVI.

CHAPTER XVII.

CHAPTER XVIII.

CHAPTER XIX.

CHAPTER XX.

CHAPTER XXI.

CHAPTER XXII.

CHAPTER XXIII.

CHAPTER XXIV.

CHAPTER XXV.

CHAPTER XXVI.

UNDER CRESCENT AND STAR.

CHAPTER I.

LEARNING ARABIC—THE 1ST RESERVE DEPOT—"DEVILS IN HELL" —TOO LATE FOR THE BATTLE—"WE DON'T WANT TO WORK" —"THE DEAR OLD FALSE PROPHET"—THE MOSQUITOS' RE- VENGE ON THE MUSKETEERS.

ALTHOUGH I was always one of those unfortunate people who found it easier to begin learning a language than to acquire it, I shall never regret the noble impulse which induced me, when quite a lad with my regiment at Aden, to commence the study of Arabic.

I was serving with the 2d battalion of the old 25th Regiment, the King's Own Borderers, and the days were hot and the time was long. I had already studied Persian and Hindustani until I was sick of them, and therefore, although my brother-subalterns laughed at me for taking the trouble to learn a lan-

A

guage which they said would never be of any use
to me, I fell tooth and nail upon Arabic—the pure
Arabic of the Hedjaz or Holy Land of Arabia. I
studied it grammatically, learning the verbs with all
their inflections; and I purposely used to go out
day after day with the Arab fishermen to practically learn the proper pronunciation of the gutturals,
which are to many a stumbling-block almost impossible to surmount.

After all, I did not learn the language at all well,
for I never had the time before the regiment sailed
for England in March 1876, and I thought that I
had entirely forgotten it when I went out to the
Egyptian campaign of 1882. But there I was fortunately mistaken. My Hedjaz Arabic came back to
me after a few days in Ismailia, but I soon found
that it was too pure for the Egyptians, who could
not understand a word of it. I found, however, that
it was comparatively easy for me to pick up the
bastard Arabic spoken on the west of the Red Sea,
and to that fortunate fact I owe the Egyptian experiences which have formed the most interesting
features of my life.

My first experiences of Egypt in 1882 were by no
means exhilarating. I had been appointed adjutant of
a body of men drawn from the Army Reserves and
called the 1st Reserve Depot. It was commanded by a
full colonel and officered in every way as a regiment,
but with officers who were volunteers from various
corps. The men did not know the officers, and the

officers did not know each other. The 1st Reserve
Depot was, in fact, a heterogeneous mass which would
have required a certain amount of time to weld into an
efficient fighting machine as one integral battalion with
one interest and one aim.

The original idea had been to send this fine body of
men, numbering some 900 or 1000 strong, to Cyprus:
but this was changed; and, sailing in two vessels, we
made for Egypt direct. The headquarters of the battalion, with which of course I was present as adjutant,
made straight for Ismailia; the remainder, on arrival at
Malta, received orders to go to Alexandria, and there
they remained—we never saw them at all. They had
a colonel in command, and formed to all appearance a
separate battalion at that seaport until broken up and
drafted to different regiments.

The Reserve-men in the ship with the headquarters
were composed half of Irishmen and half of Englishmen. The former were, although they had originally
served in various other Irish corps, all called out
to join the colours of the 18th Royal Irish Regiment
and of the 87th Royal Irish Fusiliers: the latter were
wearing the uniform of the Duke of Cornwall's Light
Infantry—that is to say, the old 32d and 46th Regiments amalgamated.

From their behaviour on board ship, and again on
shore after we reached Ismailia, I can honestly say that
of all the unruly and insubordinate scoundrels it has
ever been my lot to meet wearing the British uniform,
those Irish Reserve-men were the worst. I could easily

understand the feelings of the wretched captain of the 87th who had experienced the delights of bringing these gallant soldiers from Clonmel and Armagh respectively, when he said that they were not men that he was in command of, but that they were either wild beasts or devils from hell. From the relation of what he had gone through during his few days with them before he had got them to Portsmouth, it is really a wonder that his hair had not turned perfectly white. Even on board ship, after we had got them in hand a bit, they nearly tore this officer to pieces one day when, being captain of the day, he was going round the men's dinners. I, as adjutant, hearing a tremendous row between decks, had to despatch a rescuing party of one or two more officers and the sergeant-major to bring the captain of the day safely back to the upper deck, where I was doing some business with the commanding officer. As he emerged from the hatchway he was followed by a band of truculent unshaved ruffians, looking, in the red stocking-like caps which are served out as part of a soldier's sea-kit, more like a group of banditti than anything else.

Each man carried in his hand an enormous plateful of food heaped up high with meat and vegetables, looking enough to keep a starving family for a week at least. Utterly regardless of discipline, they pushed past the officers present, and rushing up to the colonel, held the steaming masses of food close under his nose, vociferating loudly at the same time, "D'ye call that a foighting man's ration, sorr? D'ye call that a foight-

ing man's ration, sorr?" So much noise did they make,
that it was long before the cause of complaint could
be discovered. It was very simple. According to the
scale of food hung up in the soldiers' messes, each man
that day ought to have been served with half an ounce
of boiled split-peas. This had been forgotten by the
cooks. As, unfortunately, the commanding officer was
too good-natured an old gentleman to punish the
scoundrels, we had plenty more trouble with them
before long.

By chance I had happened to be performing temporarily the duties of paymaster of the 18th Regimental
District at Clonmel when a large number of these very
Reserve-men, being called out, had come to me for
payment on being embodied. Most of them had come
to me in rags, and looking as if they had had no other
meal than "potatoes and point" for the preceding six
months. But they had all gone and got drunk immediately, and among other freaks they had performed
at the railway station, many of them threw themselves
down on the rails in front of the engine to prevent the
departure of the train until they had imbibed sufficient
glasses of " the crathur" with their friends.

The English Reserve-men we had on board were a
far quieter and more respectable lot; but although
both the Irishmen and the Englishmen were all anxious
enough to get out to Egypt in time for a fight, they can
hardly be said to have had any great delight in being
called out to rejoin the colours. This is not to be
wondered at, for many of these men had had to resign

situations in civil employment which they knew perfectly well they might not be able to obtain again when the war was over, and many of them had left their wives and families almost destitute. It was a poor look-out for them.

One great difficulty we had was to get reliable non-commissioned officers. The appointments we could make were of course only likely to be temporary; but even when we had selected good intelligent men, and made our acting sergeants and corporals, we often found, to our surprise, that they did not do their work, nor bring to the notice of their officers glaring cases of neglect of duty or of insubordination. The key to this riddle was afforded to me one day by the acting sergeant-major on board. A sergeant had, for no apparent reason, shielded a private soldier who had committed some serious offence, and which had come to light in some other way. Upon making inquiry into the case I found it very simple. The sergeant and the private were both employed in the same works at home, but whereas the sergeant was only a common artificer, the private was his foreman in those works. Naturally the sergeant was afraid to report the private, lest when they got back again, should they return to the same works, the foreman should "have a down upon" the workman. This shows the disadvantage of the Reserve-man as compared to the old long-service soldier.

One day, when we were well past Malta on our way to Port Said, we passed a ship which made us a signal.

This ship was coming from Port Said, and the signal it made to us was, " Gained a victory !" This sent our hearts well down into our boots, for we could not help feeling that we were probably too late. And so we were ; for on reaching Port Said a day or two later, we learned that the victory was the battle of Tel el Kebir, and that the war was virtually at an end.

What made our disappointment the more bitter and galling to us was, that as we entered the Suez Canal we met various transports crowded with troops coming the other way—men returning from Ismailia and being sent back to Alexandria or Malta. These men jeered us as they passed, shouting out to us, " You're too late," " Turn round and go the other way," " Come for the next campaign," and various other facetiæ of that sort. This enraged the men on our transport so much that, could they only have got at the others, there would most certainly have been bloodshed, and that on no mean scale. They could, however, only reply to the taunts of the con- quering heroes by shaking their fists and by howls of execration and curses. Even some of the officers were gained by this feeling of hatred, and I shall never forget the very peculiar gesture of contempt in which a lively young gentleman in the Royal Welsh Fusiliers indulged in reply to the taunts of a passing steamer. However, this young gentleman's decidedly vulgar action, if prompted by anger, was nevertheless so very grotesque that it restored good humour for the time, and caused a hearty laugh among all the onlookers.

The battle of Tel-el-Kebir had been fought on the

13th September 1882, and we did not land on the sandy shores of Ismailia until the 17th, just four days too late for the fair. But if we were too late for the fighting, we very soon found out that we were not too late for the fatigue duties, a business for which our men in their state of temper were not particularly inclined.

There were then lying in Lake Timsah, the large lake in the Canal opposite Ismailia, between eighty and ninety ships of various kinds and sizes, from the largest man-of-war to the smallest merchantman. It was a most wonderful sight to see all these ships, but the worst of it was that they nearly all of them either wanted to land some stores, goods, or animals, or else had already shot enormous heaps of stores, forage, ammunition, and so on, on to the sandy beach, where it was waiting in enormous piles to be removed elsewhere. And no sooner had we got our bell-tents erected on the sand between the stinking fresh-water canal, full of corpses and filth, on the one side, and a long line of squealing and evil-smelling mules on the other, than a request came in for strong fatigue-parties to go out in every direction and work in the hot sun.

The English troops squirmed, and the Irishmen became more insubordinate than ever. But they worked in a kind of a way at first, dragging guns, carrying sacks, and so on, while staggering through the sand. I even heard one man remark to another almost cheerfully as he tottered along under a sack of barley, "Be jabers, Tim, there's corn in Agypt this toime, any way."

When the evening came there were more requisitions

for fatigue-parties, and the men had to be paraded by
the orderly officer and marched off. They began by
being late in falling in, some were missing, they talked
in the ranks, they turned out improperly dressed, so the
adjutant had to be sent for. The adjutant, poor wretch!
who had never sat down for the whole day from before
dawn, and who was just thinking of getting something
to eat, came.

"What is the matter? Let me hear the complaints."

"Oh! if you please, sorr, sure it's the English
sargint-meejor's wronging us entoirely."

"What do you mean?"

"Why, sure, isn't he excusin' all thim Duke of Cornwall's min, an' givin' all the fatague-work to us Royal
Irish?"

"That's wrong, sir," said the sergeant-major; "here's
my list of how the duties are being divided—will you
please inspect it?"

The list is examined by the light of a lantern, and
when it is found to be quite fair and correct, after a
few words from the adjutant to the men more forcible
than polite, the subaltern commanding the party is
ordered to march them off. "And look here, Mr
So-and-so, see that you allow no malingering."

Away they go grumbling, and the adjutant gets rest
for a quarter of an hour, until the quartermaster comes
to complain that the Commissariat people have failed
to deliver the rum, of which a tot has been promised
to every man on fatigue-duty on his return. And
so off goes the adjutant again to hunt up the Com-

missariat officer whose duty it is to issue the rum, and when he is found, another party has to be found to go and fetch the barrels. They return; they cannot carry them. An indent now has to be issued to some one to supply mules to bring the rum; the mules don't come. The adjutant has to go and see the officer who should have sent them; he is asleep: and so on, and so on.

Eventually, just as the adjutant has, without removing his boots or clothing, lain down for a rest, *réveillé* sounds, and his tent door is crowded with quartermasters, doctors, orderly sergeants, cooks, and ration-carriers requiring respectively indents for meat and bread, stretchers, forms on which to make out the various companies' morning-parade states, cooking-ranges, and tin ration-pans.

These matters are settled, and the adjutant once more tries to snatch a sleep. Suddenly some firing is heard. All the troops tumble out and fall in. The sentries on the canal-bank report large bodies of the enemy about. Presently some men come in bearing one or two inanimate objects on stretchers. Some marauding Bedaween have shot some of the sepoys of the Indian Regiment, encamped close by, who have wandered out in the desert a little too far. No more sleep now; the new day has begun in earnest, and the first day's work on active service is ended.

The fatigue-duties at Ismailia became worse and worse as the days went on, and sometimes the Irish-men struck work *en masse*. One night they made

huge bonfires on the sand, and instead of falling in
for fatigue when ordered, went round the fires, sat
down and commenced singing a song, three lines of
the chorus of which went as follows :—

> " While we can we'll shirk,
> For we're all Oirishmen,
> And we don't mean to work ! "

Now it is impossible to try whole companies of men
by court-martial, so after a certain number who seemed
worse than the rest had been confined as prisoners in
the already overflowing guard-tent, bribery had to be
resorted to. I, as adjutant, found it necessary to advise
the commanding officer to authorise the issue of a tot
of rum to the men before going on fatigue-party, as
well as one when returning off it. Then they went;
but I made the prisoners in the guard-room go too,
as they were only too pleased to get off doing their
share of duty by lying snoring on the sand in confinement and doing nothing.

The flies and the smells in that camp at Ismailia
were something dreadful; and then the water we had
to drink, which came from the Sweet-water Canal, was
absolutely poisonous. You might filter that water over
and over again—and we did—nothing would purify it;
so of course, what with the hot sun and the hard work,
there was soon plenty of sickness. Every one had
either diarrhœa or dysentery. It was then that the
characteristics of the good officers came out.

There was one young fellow, Lieut. Walton, who, although himself far more sick than most of the others,

was always ready to take any other man's duty. I have long since lost sight of him, but I shall never forget him and his cheery ways. Even when we found that we were to have no fighting, and that as the medal-rolls were ordered to be closed on 15th September, we, having landed on the 17th, were not even to get what Tommy Atkins calls the leather medal for crossing the frontier, this cheery young fellow was not in the least despondent. "Never mind," he said, "we shall all get our medals yet. There's a false prophet, a jolly old false prophet, who's kicking up a row somewhere up there in the Soudan. We will all go for the false prophet. Good old false prophet! I'm all for the false prophet. You see, we shall all go for him before long." Little did he know how prophetic his own words were to prove, and that the next few years would tell a terrible death-roll owing to the Mahdi, whose name we had not even then heard, including many an honoured name of general and colonel in command, and many a gallant soldier, the loss of whom, even if less known to fame, is none the less deplored by a grateful and admiring country.

It is needless here to dwell longer on the events at Ismailia. Eventually, on the night after the burning of the station in Cairo, when the store shells exploding did so much harm, we all embarked on baggage-trains, and, reclining upon corn-sacks in the trucks, by slow degrees steamed through the deserted lines of Tel-el-Kebir, and so on up to the historic capital of Egypt. And if, whenever the train halted for an hour or two

by the banks of the canal, the mosquitos rose up in
their wrath and descended on us in clouds, almost
dragging us from our nests among the sacks, why
should we complain? Was it not that they too, like
ourselves, were seeking fame; and what is more, they,
more fortunate than we, achieved it. For while the
deeds we would have done, had only the Fates been
propitious, have never been heard of by a disappointed
world, their combined attack upon the foes of Egypt
was crowned with signal success, and the sting of their
deeds of conquest on that fateful night will never be
forgotten by the vanquished.

CHAPTER II.

On arrival in Cairo the 1st Reserve Depot was disbanded, its various component parts being, as far as the men were concerned, drafted off to various corps, while, after a short time, most of the officers who had belonged to it returned to England, I myself being among the number. Crowded as it was with troops, the city of Cairo presented a strange and animated scene. Perhaps the strangest sight of all was to meet at every corner, not only soldiers and sergeants, but officers in uniform with their swords on, riding about the streets, wide or narrow, on that humble animal the ass, while the barefooted donkey-boys ran shouting behind. Just at first there were perhaps more officers riding horses and ponies than asses, for all the Egyptian cavalry horses had been annexed when the troops got into Cairo, and every one who had been lucky enough to find or capture a crock had stuck to it. Repeated orders were, however, issued that all these looted ani-

mals were to be returned, and in spite of all evasions,
most of them were recovered at length. Not all, though,
for some did not bear the Government brand of the
Arabic letter *jeem*. Such unbranded horses, some of
which were perhaps the private property of dead
Egyptian officers, were of course never given up, in
spite of all orders on the subject, but for years were
ridden continually by various officers who remained in
Egypt as part of the Army of Occupation.

With the exception of Shepheard's Hotel, which was,
I believe, only actually closed for a very few days during
the war, most of the hostelries of Cairo had been deserted: the enormous numbers of Greeks, Italians, and
the Levantine population in general which is usually to
be found in Cairo, were also conspicuous by their absence in those early days. Cairo was therefore as
Eastern a city as an Eastern city can be. But beyond
the absence of the Europeans, who were really not
missed, there was nothing whatever to show that the
country had just undergone an enormous political con-
vulsion. The Khedive, Tewfik Pasha, was back again
in the Abdeen Palace; the native merchants still
lounged, smoked, and slept on the *mastabehs* in front of
their little shops in the bazaars; the native ladies, en-
veloped in their black silk *habaras*, were as usual to be
seen riding about on Syrian donkeys, hunched up on
the high saddle in a shapeless form, in a position half
sitting and half straddle-legs; the fair-faced and dark-
eyed Circassian and Turkish women from the harems of
the various palaces, only thinly veiled with white mus-

lin, drove about in the afternoons in their broughams as they were accustomed to do before the war. All this although Tommy Atkins was everywhere to be met with, which shows how great was the sense of security which prevailed among all classes of native men and women alike, from the very first arrival of our troops in the capital.

That that feeling of confidence was well deserved cannot be better proved than by the words used to me by that wise potentate Mohamed Tewfik himself. It was some four years later, when I was having a private interview with the Khedive, and we were discussing together an article by one Monsieur Planchut in the 'Revue des Deux Mondes.' This article abused the British officers and soldiers roundly, and put into the mouth of the Khedive words to their disparagement which I did not for one minute believe he had ever used. At any rate his assertions on the subject were very emphatic.

"It is a lie, I tell you, and the fellow is a liar, Hajjard Bey" (he always pronounced my name in the Turkish style). "I am sorry I ever allowed him into my presence. As it was, he was presented to me, but I scarcely spoke to him, and I give you my distinct authority to deny every word he says that I made use of in abuse of the British troops. On the contrary, although, naturally, I wish that my country was strong enough to go alone, I know that she is not yet strong enough to do so, and I am therefore obliged to have foreign troops in my dominions. But as for my having any complaint to make of your soldiers, far from it! It is very different to the state of things which took place in Egypt during the French occupation at the beginning of the century, when Mons. Plauchut's compatriots were here: then the hareems were broken into, the women ravished, and all sorts of disorders took place. But now your British soldiers are the same as if they were my own soldiers. They salute me respectfully when I meet them, they are clean and orderly about the streets, they never indulge in orgies by which my people are hurt, and during all the years since the first occupation of Cairo, there has never been a single case of outrage on the women."

These were almost word for word the Khedive's own expressions to me, and he further asked me to write an article for some influential English Review, to give the lie on every point to the article in the 'Revue des Deux Mondes.'

It is a strange position to be in, that of thus looking back to the past from what was in that past the future, and of being able to observe how exactly things have turned out as it seemed probable that they would do. The might of Britain looked in 1882 too firmly established in the civilised streets of Cairo ever to leave them again, and it has never yet left them. On the other hand, the attitude of Mohamed Tewfik, who, even in his gratitude to us, seemed in those days helpless in our hands, was so gracious, so welcoming, so kind, that it struck any man who thought about the subject at all that it would be almost a brutal thing if the British nation, having come nominally to his rescue, were to take advantage of the situation to gain possession of his country. I did not think that Egypt would be annexed by England—and she was not; but it seems in these later days more than ever unfortunate that we did not at least declare a Protectorate. This could have been so managed that, while the ruler's feelings were saved from pain, he himself might have been assured in his position; while we, the protectors, being then supreme, could have assumed an attitude entirely free from possible interference from France or any other European State, which attitude could never afterwards have been challenged. *Eheu!* we did not do it then, when we might have done so, without further bloodshed. Now, who that has studied the politics of Europe, who that has more especially noticed the aggressive attitude taken up by France towards us regarding Egypt ever since she refused to co-operate with us in the bombardment of Alexandria, can dare to hope that we shall ever maintain our supremacy in the East without much bloodshedding on the banks of the Nile, or without severe and sanguinary struggles on the sandy shores of the Suez Canal?

Notwithstanding the general state of quiet in the city, officers were always expected to wear their swords,—a necessary precaution; for there were in those days a considerable number of Bedaween camping about in the desert around Cairo, who occasionally robbed and ill-treated Europeans whom they found unprotected and wandering about for the sake of exercise beyond the city limits. One day these Bedaween rather startled me.

Having gone out in an *arabiyeh*, a native victoria, to the Pyramids, another young officer and myself had neglected to take our swords or revolvers, considering that we should find them out of place on the top of Cheops' great monument, as no doubt they would have been. We had made the ascent and were bowling home again comfortably, when at about half the distance between the Pyramids and the Nile bridge of Kasr el Nil we saw men on camels coming towards us. The driver of the *arabiyeh*, turning round, half pulled up and pointed forward, saying at the same time in rather a frightened tone, " Bedaween! Shall I go back to the soldiers ? " For there was a post of Indian cavalry encamped at the foot of the Pyramids; but this was four miles behind us, and had the desert marauders been hostile we could never have reached it in time. I instantly thought, moreover, that to turn round and go back would be such an evident sign of fear that it would be an absolute invitation to the Bedaween to attack us, whereas if we went straight on, we being in uniform, they would probably not have any idea that we were unarmed until we were past them, and perhaps not even then; besides, they might be too frightened at recent events to attempt to molest us at all. Bidding the driver go ahead swiftly therefore, we met them face to face as they came along the narrow road in a string, about twelve of them, on swift dromedaries, one behind the other in Indian file. They were all armed *cap-à-pie* with Remington rifles, pistols, and daggers; but they contented themselves with sternly and savagely scowling at us as they passed silently on. We were uncommonly glad when we had passed the last of them, especially as we both felt that had anything happened to us we should have well deserved our fate for our temerity in venturing unarmed eight miles beyond the Nile bridge into the desert. We both determined never to commit such an act of folly again.

The next day I sent my soldier servant out to see the Pyramids and the Sphinx, several other officers sending their servants at the same time. They mounted donkeys, and off they went in a body to enjoy themselves. When they returned in the evening, I asked my servant, a Cockney whose name was Cane, what he had seen.

"Oh!" exclaimed Cane, joyfully, "we 'ave 'ad a jolly time, sir; we seen it all, that there Spinks—them there perapets, and everythink."

"Them there what?" said I.

"Them there perapets of Chops, sir," retorted Cane, gleefully; "though why they calls 'em perapets of Chops I don't know; we didn't see nothink like a cook-'ouse round there to cook no chops in. Chops or no chops," he added confidentially, "it's a lucky thing that them there perapets at Tel-el-Kebir wasn't as tall nor as thick as them is. If they 'ad a-been, I think the rest of the fellers would 'ave 'ad to a-waited till the 1st Reserve Depot 'ad arrived just to give 'em a leg over."

Poor Came! he was confounding the mighty Pyramids of antiquity with the parapets of field intrenchments; but as he seemed perfectly happy I did not undertake to teach him the difference.

From Cairo, towards the end of October, I went down to Alexandria, where, in its then ruined condition, it was difficult to find any place to put up in which was not too utterly filthy. However, after much trouble I managed to obtain a lodging in a house which had remained standing between two that had been burned and had crumbled to ruins ; and as I was still suffering severely from the effects of the waters of the Sweet-water Canal, I considered myself very lucky in not having to rug down in the street. But after a day passed in that house, I came to the conclusion that the street would have been infinitely more wholesome ; for its insanitary condition was something too awful for words, and it is a wonder I did not get typhoid fever on the top of my other complications.

Alexandria in those days was a sink of iniquity. I cannot say what may be its condition still. Since the advent of British troops to the place, all its scum of European and Levantine inhabitants who had fled to Europe at the time of Arabi Pasha's rising had returned, or were in October 1882 returning daily to the town.

Leaving Alexandria and its ruins, I embarked, with a battery of artillery and some other stray officers, upon a hired troopship. After having had a very jolly stay *en route* at Gibraltar, and a stormy passage through the Bay, during which we lost several horses, we arrived in due course at Portsmouth in the early days of November.

Thus ended the first phase of my Egyptian experiences.

CHAPTER III.

IN the same way that Arabi Pasha fell, so also the battle of Tel-el-Kebir rang the death-knell of the Egyptian army. Such troops as held out in other parts of Egypt for a few days longer surrendered in most instances without firing a shot, and then the regiments to which they belonged became quite dis- organised and broken up. Many of the officers whom we had taken prisoners after Tel-el-Kebir were for a time kept as prisoners by us on board some of the hired transports anchored in Lake Timsah. After a time I know not what became of them; I think they were all released unconditionally, and told " not to do it again." Their names remained on the lists in the Egyptian War Office, but they were nearly all placed *en disponsibilité*—that is, on half-pay.

The country was full of soldiers, but they were

old and worthless; and the first care of England,
after things had become settled, was to try and re-
organise the Egyptian army completely, so as to establish a small force which would at all events be
from the commencement capable of maintaining order
in the interior of the kingdom: that was as much as
could be expected. There were, of course, many
troops, both blacks and Egyptians, still away in the
Soudan, in places like Khartoum, Darfour, Suakin,
Massowah, Tokar, Kasala, Senheit, and so on: these
nobody after the peace seemed to trouble about—
they were away out of Egypt proper; so much the
better! Let them stop away and try to hold the
Soudan for Egypt; but that was an exterior matter,—
they could be considered later. In fact, it was considered just as well to send off as many more troops
to the Soudan as could be spared; and this was done,
an army leaving accordingly for El Obeid under Hicks
Pasha in February 1883.

The troops that still remained of the old army were
converted from regulars into gendarmerie, at least in
name and status, although they remained armed in
every respect the same as before, and wore the same
uniforms. These were placed under the command of
Baker Pasha, late Colonel Valentine Baker of the 10th
Hussars, who had resigned a high command in the Turkish army to come over to Egypt for entirely another
purpose than to command a rubbishy lot of worthless
ex-soldiers who were to be called gendarmerie.

At the invitation of the Government of the day

he had consented to come to its assistance and re-organise the Egyptian army. To establish the *cadres* of the new force, and to arrange a plan by which the new army was to be raised, manned, and officered, and, especially as regards its superior officers, to be officered by English officers on full pay in their regi-ments,—this it was which had caused Baker to earn the Sultan's displeasure by resigning his Turkish com-mand and come into the land of Egypt.

Baker Pasha did his part of the business excessively well; but when all was ready, and the recruits for the new regiments were actually being raised by conscrip-tion among the young men in the provinces—when his lists of officers, both English and Egyptian, were all ready—there occurred a *contretemps* which was to rob him of all the fruits of his toil, and to prevent his becoming the Sirdar or Commander-in-Chief. It was a *contretemps* which had never been expected by the Ministers who had asked him to undertake these la-bours, but it was one for which they should have been prepared and guarded against before putting Valentine Baker in such a trying and unmerited position. It was simply this, that her Majesty the Queen intimated that she would not allow Baker Pasha to be in any position in which he would have English full-pay officers under his command.

The whole thing was at a dead-lock at once. What was to be done? Baker behaved splendidly. Although between two stools he had fallen to the ground—for he could not go back to Turkey, and could not command the new Egyptian army — he handed over all his arrangements unconditionally to the British authorities, and told them to place them in the hands of any other man whom they might select. Another man was chosen in the person of Sir Evelyn Wood, V.C., and he became the Sirdar of the new Egyptian army at a salary of £5000 a-year, while Baker, as before mentioned, was relegated to the command of the gendarmerie, both horse and foot, all worthless troops, as they proved afterwards at the first battle of El Teb.

In this force he had some Englishmen under him, but they were all, with one exception, either officers who had resigned their commissions or else civilians. There were also some Italian officers, and there was one Austrian officer in the person of an old colonel named Mocklyn Bey. Hicks Pasha, who went off to the Soudan never to return, he and all his force being slaughtered in El Obeid, also had Englishmen under him. They were, as far as I know, all civilians, ex-soldiers, or militiamen. I was with a number of his officers at a farewell jollification in Stuart Wortley's house in Cairo the day before they left, but I cannot say definitely, as that is the only time I met any of them with the exception of "Baby" Martin, whom I shall mention later, and who died at Assouan, and Forestier Walker, both of whom returned invalided *via* Suakin. But Walker, poor fellow, was not to escape, as he afterwards died fighting nobly under Baker Pasha at the first battle of El Teb, where he was in charge of the Gatling guns.

From the foregoing pages on the subject of the Egyptian army it will be noted that there were in 1883 many officers, not of the so-called army proper, who were employed in various departments and forces under the Egyptian War Office, under the various heads of army, gendarmerie, or police. Of these there is one of whom I will make mention while I think of him, whom I met in Cairo later on after he had returned from Khartoum, of which he was virtually in command until Gordon went up, relieved him, and sent him down to Cairo. This was an Englishman named Coetlogon Bey, who on his return, after two and a half years' absence up the Nile, was very unfairly treated by the Egyptian authorities, who entirely failed to keep the terms of their contract with him, although he had had much fighting, done splendid work in the Soudan, and virtually preserved Khartoum until Gordon came. It was Coetlogon who organised and carried out nearly all the defences of Khartoum, and indeed placed the town in such an efficient state of defence that Gordon, when he arrived, had but little left to do to prepare it for a siege. And yet, as nobody ever now hears of Coetlogon, who has modestly sat down under a considerable amount of injustice, I, for one, will here put on record the name of a man who has long been deserving of his country's thanks and praise.

When Sir Evelyn Wood took over the formation of the new Egyptian army from Baker Pasha, he also took over his aide-de-camp, Lieutenant Stuart Wortley, commonly nicknamed "Wortles," a smart officer of the

60th Rifles, who, after seeing service in Afghanistan, had been performing the duties of staff officer to Sir Owen Lanyon at Ismailia. Sir Owen, I may mention, was the officer in command at the base at the time that I was there with the 1st Reserve Depot. Another officer on Wood's personal staff was Captain Slade, a gunner, commonly known as "Keggy" Slade. Both of these officers are now so well known in the British army that their nicknames alone are quite sufficient if mentioned in a club or a mess, without the usual appendage of a surname being at all necessary. And that they are both distinguished officers everybody knows, of course.

Among the other twenty-three officers whom the General selected as his staff in the new force, I had the good fortune to be one. Accordingly the end of January 1883 found me on my way back to Cairo. I travelled out with Berkeley Pigott, a young officer who in those days had only four years' seniority, during which time he had been constantly on active service, and had gained four decorations for war service. Pigott had been serving in the Mounted Infantry in the late Egyptian campaign, and had the bad luck to get a bullet through the leg at Kassasin. However, he was none the worse for that, and was, like myself, one of the selected officers for the Egyptian army.

It was on the journey out that I made the acquaintance of the late Duke of Sutherland, and also notably of his late henchman and piper, Alistair MacAlistair, a grand old character. The Duke, of whom I saw

much later on, was once kind enough to a-k me to
come up and stay with him at Dunrobin Castle. The
old piper, who was standing by, evidently did not
think that the Duke's invitation was sufficient; for,
turning to me, he seconded it, "Yes, indeed, Major
Haggart, an' a'm sure I hope ye'll come; we'll be vara
pleased indeed to see ye up at Dunrobin." Alas! when
I did go to Dunrobin for the first time, the old piper
had already piped his last tune, and now the Duke himself has joined his faithful henchman in the world of
spirits. It may be put on record here that the Prince
of Wales, when old Alistair was ill, showed one of
those instances of kindness of heart for which he is so
justly popular. Despite his endless engagements, the
Prince found time nearly every day to pass half an
hour by the old piper's bed until the end came.

In addition to myself, Stuart Wortley, Slade, and
Pigott already mentioned, I will give below the names
of the others who joined the force of the Egyptians
under Major-General Sir Evelyn Wood, V.C., G.C.M.G.,
K.C.B., himself an officer well deserving all the letters
of the alphabet which a grateful War Office has tacked
on to his name.

The remainder of the little band under his orders at
the first start off were as follows: Lieutenant-Colonel
Grenfell and Major C. Holled Smith, both of the 60th
Royal Rifles; Lieutenant-Colonel Fraser, C.M.G., Major
Watson, Captain and Brevet-Major Chermside, Captain
Kitchener and Lieutenant Mantell, all Sappers; Lieuten-
ant-Colonel Duncan, Captain Wodehouse, Lieutenants

Parsons, Rundle, and Carter, Gunners; Lieutenant-Colonel Taylor, 19th Hussars; Lieutenant Sinclair, Indian Cavalry (the only Indian); Captain and Brevet-Major Parr, 13th Light Infantry, who, like Pigott, had been wounded in the leg while serving in the Mounted Infantry in the 1882 campaign; Captain Shakespear and Lieutenant Marriott, Royal Marine Artillery; Captain Owen Quirk, 41st Welsh Regiment; Major A. Singleton Wynne, 51st Regiment; Lieutenant Chamley Turner, 53d Shropshire Regiment; and Lieutenant Davidson, 79th Highlanders.

To this list was added almost at once Veterinary Surgeon Beech, a brave young fellow who, for his repeated acts of gallantry, was a few years later actually transferred from the veterinary to the combatant branch of the British army, and made a captain in the 20th Hussars. Afterwards there were a few army doctors, and by degrees, as the years rolled on, many other combatant officers added to the Egyptian army; and what a stepping-stone to advancement has it not proved to be to nearly all! Could one take the names of all those who have joined the Egyptian army between January 1883 and 1895; could one borrow all the medals and clasps, Khedive's stars, the Osmaniehs, Medjidiehs, and Distinguished Service Orders which adorn their manly bosoms; could one in addition obtain from the lucky recipients the stars of Knights and Commanders of the Bath, the decorations of St Michael and St George, add them to the preceding and pile them up together, what a heap of gewgaws they would make! Heaped all together, they would probably fill a good-sized waggon; while the ribbons of the various grand cordons and medals, if hung in graceful festoons, would form a very elegant adornment for the front façade of that dingy building the British War Office. And then look at the promotions both by brevet and otherwise which have fallen to the lot of these same officers. Let any young subaltern with a turn for statistics get hold of an Army List of 1883, and one of every succeeding year up to date. Let him then get hold of the lists of the officers of the Egyptian army, including the medical branch, and watch their progress in rank from the day they joined it until the present day. Let him see the subalterns who have become full colonels, let him note also the colonels who have become generals. I think that before he has got half through his task he will agree with me that, whether they stuck to it for long or not, to have once belonged to the Egyptian army was a distinct step in most instances on the road to fortune.

Purely from a soldierly point of view, putting all promotions and advancements on one side, what glorious chances of seeing active service have fallen to the lot of the Anglo-Egyptian officer! There is hardly one of them who has joined its ranks during the last twelve years who has not been under fire, while most of them have been under fire many, many times. Yet of the original lot who joined Sir Evelyn Wood at the same time as myself, how many of those still living remain in Egypt and in the Egyptian army? Only two from the first!— Kitchener, who has now been for some years Sirdar; and Rundle, who is commandant of all the mounted troops — that is to say, all the artillery and cavalry,—Wodehouse, who preceded him in that command a year or so ago, having left, with a splendid war record behind him, to rejoin the Royal Artillery in India. Wingate, who joined a month or two later, is a third nearly from the beginning. Parsons, after leaving, has gone back again. Yes; the Egyptian army has, I repeat it, proved a fine field of education and experience for the British officer, and a magnificent field for promotion too.

But we did not know all that lay before us in the days when I joined; yet we were a gay-hearted lot, and all cheerful with the anticipation of hard work, and started with a good honest feeling of *camaraderie* for one another. The terms upon which we entered were also, as regards pay, pretty liberal. The Sirdar got £5000 a-year; Lieutenant-Colonel Grenfell, who was made a brigadier-general, £1200; the four officers who commanded infantry regiments and the one cavalry regiment got £750 apiece. Poor Colonel Duncan—Dunkey Bey, as we called him, and who later became a member of Parliament and died— was paid £1000 a-year for commanding the artillery; two other gunners got £600 a-year as second commandants: each infantry regiment had also a second commandant at £550 a-year, while the nine supplementary officers got £450 apiece.

I started as a supplementary officer, but was very

soon made a second in command, and my first regiment
was the Dortingi Orta, or the 4th Battalion E.A., the
commandant of which was Major Wynne, who had
now become Lieutenant-Colonel Wynne, in the same
way as I became Major Haggard; for we captains and
subalterns were all made field-officers at once on joining,
while those who were already majors or lieutenant-
colonels were promoted a step, or in some cases two,
in rank. We all received our commissions sealed in
the Egyptian fashion by the Khedive and the Minister
of War. If I remember correctly, they were made out
in English and Arabic, and the rank was substantive.
This addition to our former rank, when we became
Egyptians, gave us all a considerable amount of prestige
among our brother officers in the British Army of Occupation; and although for a year or two no notice was
taken of the circumstance, it gave rise to a considerable
amount of jealousy to the little-minded loafers on the
verandah of Shepheard's Hotel, who grudged us our
rank and grudged us our pay, although, if ever men
worked hard for both, from the highest to the lowest,
they were the officers of the Egyptian army in the
first year or two of its organisation.

We were employed through the Foreign Office,
and all had, on joining, to go through the ceremony
of signing a contract with the Egyptian Government,
whereby we engaged ourselves for two years; but
before I mention the terms of the contract, I will
note the terms of the agreement and conditions under
which we twenty-five officers accepted service under

Sir Evelyn Wood. There were the usual conditions for entering the Staff College, also good horsemanship, musketry, signalling, gunnery, and freedom from disease likely to be aggravated by prolonged service in Egypt. Every officer was to be capable of carrying on official correspondence and conversation in French, to pass a colloquial examination in Arabic in six months, and a further examination after twelve months. Officers who should pass the second examination with honours were to receive a donation of £100. I think that little Mantell, the sapper, whom Sir Evelyn Wood used to constitute our examiner, was about the only fellow who ever got this £100. He was employed in the Intelligence Department of the War Office, where he had plenty of time to study; what is more, both he and Kitchener started knowing Arabic well. But no one else—that is, none of the regimental officers—ever had time to learn the language more than colloquially, for every one of them was at work drilling the men almost every available hour of the day.

The terms of the contract signed with the Egyptian Government were as follows: An officer was to be allowed to quit the Egyptian service at his own request after giving three months' notice. The Egyptian Government to have the right of dispensing with the services of any officer after six months, and afterwards, if the officer had qualified in Arabic, he was to receive a gratuity of one year's pay on dismissal. No quarters were to be allowed, and all officers mounted at their own expense; and further, all to abide by the decision of Sir Evelyn Wood, or his successor, and forego any right of reference to international tribunals.

This last clause acted later on very hardly on one of our number, a smart young officer — a very good fellow he was too—whom the Sirdar sent about his business in a most peremptory manner simply because he hadn't paid his tailor's bill in Cairo,—the tailor, who was a Greek, having complained. He was, when spoken to on the subject, perfectly prepared to settle his account at once; but notwithstanding the fact that he was assured there was nothing else against him in any way, and nothing whatever against his honour, he was given no option, but had to go. It is a strange fact, nevertheless, that I afterwards learned from the very best authority that this officer had been complained of by his commanding officer, a fact of which he was never informed. But, of course, if we signed a contract of this nature, and anything of this sort happened to us, it was our own fault; and in this particular case, in saying nothing of any official complaint, the Sirdar was probably only trying to spare the officer's feelings.

When Pigott and I arrived at Cairo on the evening of the last day of January 1883, we descended at that jolly old caravanserai Shepheard's Hotel, where we found a change in the composition of the guests. Whereas a few months earlier the enormous dining-room had been daily crowded at meal-times with officers attired in every variety of fighting kit—only

one lady, Lady Strangford, being present at the table—
we now found plenty of officers certainly, but all decently and decorously attired in mess-dress, while there
were plenty of pretty ladies to vary the monotony of so
many military men. For the visitors from England
and elsewhere had begun to regain confidence, and
were coming to finish the winter in Egypt, many being
relations of fellows who had fought in the recent war.
What a jolly and a merry crowd they all were! Ah,
indeed! Those were cheery days in Cairo, cheery
enough at times almost to make the Sphinx laugh.

After dinner we strolled round to look up Stuart
Wortley in his first-floor apartment in a usually quiet
street in the Ismailia quarter. It was a lovely Eastern
night, and I have no doubt that we should in romantic
fashion have enjoyed to its full the beauty of the scene,
as the crescent moon shed its silvery rays over the
palm-trees in the Esbikiyeh Gardens, had not strange
sounds fallen upon our ears, making us think the devil
himself had got loose at least, or that the Quorn or
Pytchley were running a fox close by. Ringing clearly
through the night air came the sharp sound of a hunt-
ing-horn several times repeated, then, in true Jorrocks
fashion, other sounds—namely, cries as of the huntsman
encouraging his hounds into cover. "Yoicks! over
there, my beauties! Hoick him out there! Hi away
in there, little beauties!" This was accompanied by an
occasional deep-toned note, as though a hound were just
getting on to the scent of a fox. Then came the eldritch

screech of a view-holloa, then another and another
" Whooi ! whooi! whooi !   Gone away ! gone away !—
away !" Twang ! twang ! twang ! went the hunting-
horn, then with a burst of melody from twenty throats,
representing the hounds in full cry, out bounded a lot
of merry fellows through a French window on to a balcony, along the front of it, and in at another window.
Over the chairs and under the tables went the hunt,
merrily, merrily sounded the horn ! and before the fox
was duly killed, with many a whoop and a holloa, we
ourselves had joined in the chase, gaily giving tongue
with the rest of the fellows, many of whom we had
never seen before, and most of whom we never saw
again.   Stuart Wortley was entertaining the officers of
Hicks Pasha's force, who were leaving next day.   And
Captain Candy, late of the 9th Lancers, the well-
known "Sugar," who always was and always will be a
boy, was only just giving one of his famous representations of a fox-hunt to cheer them up before their departure. Well, peace to their manes !—they and we had
at all events "a high old time of it" that night.   I
wonder what the respectable Italians and others in that
quiet European neighbourhood thought of their mad
English neighbours.   But, fortunately for them, Sugar
himself, who had just joined the gendarmerie, where his
career was short and glorious, did not reside in that
part of the world.   And yet that was where he shone
brightly for a while, especially in the cholera season of
the latter part of 1883.   Then, indeed, he showed that

he could do something else besides skylarking; for he did capital and very trying work in establishing quarantine cordons with his gendarmes around the centres of infection, incurring much personal risk.   But unfortunately he could not help mistaking the Egyptian gendarme for a football.   Therefore, sad to relate, when the cholera left us, Sugar departed too!

CHAPTER IV.

ALTHOUGH I have in my possession some few notes by my late great friend Chamley Turner, who was drowned in the Nile, and many daily records of my own, it would make very dull reading were I to set to work to describe in detail how we formed an army of efficient soldiers out of a wretched lot of fellaheen; for be it noted that although we were obliged, at all events in the beginning, to utilise chiefly officers and non-commissioned officers who had belonged to the old army under Arabi Pasha, we started the new army entirely with new recruits, or conscripts as they really were. We formed eight infantry battalions, of which four were under English superior officers, the other four under Egyptian superior officers. The artillery and cavalry I will leave alone; I have already mentioned that Colonel Duncan commanded the former, and Lieutenant-Colonel Taylor, who was an extremely

good fellow, the other. Unfortunately they are both
dead.

Our eight infantry battalions formed two brigades,
Grenfell being brigadier of the 1st Brigade, that with
the English officers, while a charming old Circassian
general, by name Yousouf Pasha Schudi, took over the
command of the other. I had much to do with Schudi
Pasha later on, and can honestly say I never liked a man
better or met a better fellow than that gallant Circassian. He had commanded an army in the Turko-Russo
war with considerable distinction, and when we British
took the direction of affairs he came most loyally to
our assistance. He was not, as are so many Orientals,
our friend on the outside only while secretly doing all
against us in his power, but was loyal throughout.

Our chief difficulty was of course at first the language,
or rather the languages, in which we had to carry on
our work. Our second difficulty was the drill—that is,
to find out the best kind of drill to suit the Egyptians.
As regards the former, we had to talk French to such
of the officers as understood it, and to conduct all our
correspondence in French and Arabic. Secondly, we
had to deal with all the non-commissioned officers
and soldiers in Arabic alone; and thirdly, the actual
words of command, which we had to pick up ourselves
before we could roll them off the chest in fine sonorous
tones to the soldiers, had to be in Turkish, of which the
soldiers themselves understood just about as much as
we did. To tell the truth, it was a very bastard
Turkish that we used in those words of command,

many of which we manufactured for ourselves as time went on; but still the old non-commissioned officers and the officers from whom we learnt it, many of whom were half Turks and Circassians, understood what it was meant for, which was all that was wanted.

As we all worked very hard from morning till night, and as the Egyptian has naturally a wonderful aptitude, or, to be more accurate, a wonderful affection, for drill, we very soon found things going along splendidly. Of course we made some frightful mistakes to begin with, but that did not matter—all pioneers make mistakes. One of the chief of these was that the English officers took it at first in very ill part, when going round the barrack-rooms at meal-times, if the Egyptian Tommy Atkins, who, crouched down on his hunkers, was comfortably guzzling his beans and lentils, did not jump up and stand at attention as the English Tommy does under similar circumstances. It was at such times that our English sergeants, who were lent to us by the English and Scotch regiments, used to wax particularly furious at such a want of respect to a field-officer, and an enormous amount of hustling about and pushing was indulged in accordingly. For, to begin with, all the instructions, given by either the sergeants or ourselves, had to be done by signs, by doing the things ourselves first to show the way, and then by pushing. After a short time, however, we discovered somehow that it is against the ordinances of the Mahomedan religion for a man to stand up when at his food to show respect to another man, as it is considered in that religion as an insult to the Creator, who supplies all food to His humble creatures, and so after that we left them to squat at their meals as much as they liked.

As regards the drill, we had at first two great difficulties to contend with: one was, that the Egyptians seemed absolutely unable to understand the meaning of a straight line, and more especially unable to grasp the meanings of one line being at right angles to another, or of a line being parallel to another. The result of this used to be very funny. Supposing a battalion was drawn up on parade in the barrack square of the old and unhealthy Kishlak el Asfar, the Yellow Barracks, where at first the whole eight battalions were quartered. The adjutant-major, who was a sort of native adjutant, would have collected all the reports and have the regiment in column with the men standing at ease, waiting to receive the commanding officer with due respect by calling them to attention as "the Bey" should ride on to parade. When the adjutant-major had called out "Zenhar" (attention), accordingly, and shouldered arms to his commanding officer, the latter would notice that, although the left flank of every company might be resting on the straight barrack wall, and although each company might be "dressed" correctly in a straight line of its own, the outer flanks of the companies in column would perhaps be five or six paces farther from, or nearer to, one another than their respective inner flanks. In fact, instead of being parallel to each other, one company of a battalion would bear the same relative position to another that the radii of a circle do, supposing an arc of the circle to be divided by as many radii as a battalion has companies. This want of the power of understanding the meaning of straightness caused us many weary hours of vexation and labour; for day after day it was the same thing, and the native officers and non-commissioned officers absolutely could not understand what it was that was wrong. However, we conquered the difficulty at length.

Another trouble was that the soldiers love to squeeze themselves up together in the ranks. Great hulking fellows that they were, from their extraordinary habit of squeezing they would occupy about half the space in line that an English company would if only half as strong, and of course they often squeezed each other right out of the ranks. This peculiarity made such a thing as an advance of a regiment in line almost impossible. To get rid of the difficulty of drilling the men caused by this squeezing up, we therefore designed a new drill, according to which the companies were, even when in line, always to be six paces apart from each other, and after that we managed to get along very well. Sir Evelyn Wood also ordered various other changes, such as always having all the captains in front of the companies, having a guide on both flanks on all occasions, and other alterations, some of which proved beneficial and some not.

These alterations were chiefly originated at the suggestion of Major Wynne, who on arrival from India took over the command of the 4th Battalion, with which

I was serving, and in which I became his second in command. That Colonel Wynne is a very clever fellow in the matter of drill may be attested not only by the modern Egyptian Drill-book, for which he was chiefly responsible, but by much that is good in the later Drill-books in use in the English army also.

Beyond mentioning that the way we English officers taught our men the bayonet and firing exercises was usually by taking a Remington rifle in our own hands and standing in front of them as a fugleman and doing it ourselves, I am now going to dismiss the subject of drill. I will only say that by thus going through the bayonet exercises, with a heavy sword-bayonet on the end of a rifle, half-a-dozen times in the morning or afternoon, I kept myself in splendid health. I also soon learnt from the aching of the muscles of the arms and legs to understand what the soldier feels when worked at it too long, without "an easy," by thoughtless non-commissioned officers, as is so often done. I accordingly ever after in my career as a soldier was especially careful not to allow sergeants and corporals to bully the men, according to their wont, by keeping them far too long in constrained and painful positions without allowing them to stand at ease.

The regiments soon began to look smart and soldier-like in their white uniforms and red fezes, and the suburb of Abbasiyeh, where they were all eight quartered, rang with martial music all day long, as they were alternately being marched out to the drill-plain or marched in again.

The band of each regiment was alike, simply consisting of drummers and buglers, whose bugles had chromatic attachments, and in those early days they all only knew one and the same march-tune, which they invariably played. It was a very well-known air from "Madame Angot," and the officers and men of the various British regiments, who were also quartered in barracks in Abbasiyeh, were simply nearly driven mad with it. Poor wretches! I pitied them; for at times, when not too busy to notice it, it nearly drove me crazy myself. However, nothing used to amuse me more than to go to lunch at the mess of a British regiment, usually the 38th South Staffordshire, or the 49th Berkshire, and while there to listen to the curses and anathemas that the fellows used to hurl at us in particular, and the "Gyppy" army in general, whenever this wretched tune used to begin. As there were four regiments, entirely officered by native officers, who went out to drill at different hours to those commanded by the English officers, there simply never was any peace all day long; for as soon as one lot of "Madame Angot" would be heard fading away into the distance, another lot of "Madame Angot" would be heard approaching. It was devilish! and I will defy any of the English officers of the British regiments who heard it in those days to read these lines without a good solid curse simply at the recollection of the infliction of that music. But the old Anglo-Egyptian officers will only smile; for it was the jealousy with which "the English," as after a time we got to call them, regarded us on Wood's staff which caused a good deal of their cursing at everything Egyptian. And as of course we knew this, and were amused, I don't think we took much trouble about suppressing " Madame Angot," for a time at all events. After a while, however, we got music instructors, who taught our musicians all kinds of marches, which they learnt to play in a most satisfactory manner.

A year or two later, when I was in command of the 1st Battalion Egyptian army at Suakin, I was fortunate enough to get hold of a drum-major of Marines, who took a real interest and pleasure in instructing my Egyptians, who were very quick at learning. He taught them any number of tunes, and made the drums exceptionally good. Indeed I never knew better drums than the side-drummers of my regiment became under his tuition. Owing to this, a year later, during and after the campaign against the Dervishes up the Nile under General Sir Frederick Stephenson, the British troops encamped anywhere near my battalion, instead of hearing the horrid and loathed " Madame Angot," used to be regaled daily at " tattoo" or " retreat" with such plaintive airs as " Take this letter to my mother," or by the then popular " Wait till the clouds roll by."

Apart from the regimental drums and bugles for the different corps, we soon established two splendid bands of trained musicians, one for each brigade. In addition to being able to play the wild plaintive Arabic music, so beloved by the Easterns and which is natural to them, the 1st and 2d Brigade bands could play march

or opera music as well as any European military bands-
men. It is indeed very strange how these peasants
from the banks of the Nile have this extraordinary
facility for acquiring the music of both the East and
the West.

With reference to a remark above, it will be noticed
that we had some reason for talking about "the English" as distinct from ourselves; for we soon had to con-
form to various Mahomedan ways and customs. Firstly,
the Khedive insisted upon our discarding the use of
helmets, and adopting the use of the *tarboosh* or fez,
and of gorgeous uniforms with a crescent and a star on
our buttons. Secondly, we always used the Friday, the
Mahomedan Sabbath, as our day of rest, and worked
away as usual at drill or anything else on the Christian
Sunday; so it was very seldom any of us were seen
inside the English church in Cairo: thus the worthy
padre, Dean Butcher, was justified if he considered us
as of the race of Turks, infidels, and heretics, for such
we were.

The Egyptian army was inaugurated with a considerable degree of *éclat*, and we soon found that we were
the cynosure of all eyes. It is indeed a wonder how
we Anglo-Egyptians ever survived our earlier days;
for so interested was everybody in us and our performances that we were, before we had even properly learnt
company drill, being inspected almost daily by bigwigs of all sorts in both battalion drill and brigade
drill, and in some wonderful manner these parades
always came off all right, being invariably pronounced

a grand success. This was fortunate, for as we were expected to perform prodigies, it would have been a pity if we had disappointed them.

One day it was Lord Dufferin, then on a special mission to Egypt, who rode out with Sir Evelyn Wood to Abbasiyeh to inspect the whole division. Next day it would be some German princes and other officers arrayed in smart uniforms who rode out to see how the trick was done. Then there was a grand review for inspection by the Khedive himself, which review would be witnessed by the whole of the smart folks in Cairo, visitors and residents; and when it was all over, and we had been properly complimented by his Highness, our day's work done, we officers would all ride into Cairo and join the idle throng on the verandah of Shepheard's Hotel, where we would be prettily complimented by all the charming ladies who were then assembled to lounge and chatter until dinner-time.

In addition to the amount of showing off we had to do in the inspection line, we also had to show ourselves good men over the dinner course. For everybody used to consider it the correct thing to do, to invite Sir Evelyn Wood and all the Egyptian officers to dinner *en bloc*; and tremendous dinners they used to be, with any amount of liquor and any amount of speechifying, the gist of all of which was to show what grand fellows the Sirdar and we, his humble followers, had been in the past, how much grander fellows we were going to be in the future, and what wonderful fellows we were in the present. I can remember some of those gorgeous

dinners perfectly well, the most splendid and costly
being perhaps that given at Shepheard's Hotel by the
late millionaire, Sir George Elliot, who, it may be remembered, commenced life as a boy in a coal-pit, and
who was so fond of the ladies. On that occasion the
whole place was turned upside down, the roof and walls
decorated with flags, bands were playing outside, and,
in fact, to use the vulgar slang of to-day, the sporting
old miner "did us uncommonly well." It was a very
long dinner, and I remember well that Kitchener and
I had, just to pass the time, a match with each other,
like a couple of schoolboys, to see who could eat the
most. Alas! for the credit of the infantry, that I
should have to record it, the gallant sapper had far
more staying powers than I had, and I was defeated
hollow, for the Royal Engineer could have easily given
me 7 lb. in a half-mile handicap over the food-course.
Over the liquor course I was luckily more successful, as
I remembered an interesting story which Lord Dufferin
had recently told me of a dinner to which he had
been invited in Iceland, when the Icelanders had
tried to drink him under the table; but he was not to
be beaten. Pulling himself together, the noble Earl
had, according to his own statement, exclaimed inwardly, "And shall it be said that a descendant of
Brian Boru and all the kings of Ireland shall be
defeated by a parcel of half-civilised islanders who
live near the North Pole? Perish the thought!"
And at the end of the dinner it was not the Earl
but the Icelanders who were under the table. The

story struck me as a good one, and I tried, with moderate success, to emulate the noble Earl's example.

After Sir George Elliot's dinner came a horrible and dreary one given us by Taha Pasha Loutfi, who was then Minister of War. It was served in the Turkish fashion on little round brass trays, we were regaled with horrible native music the whole time, and given in the way of refreshment some poisonous claret. It was dreary in the extreme, as the entertainment went on for hours, during which time we were mixed up with a lot of native Egyptian officials, including Loutfi himself, who could talk nothing but Arabic or Turkish, and with whom even those of our party who could understand them, or make themselves understood, had soon exhausted their subjects of conversation. I believe that all the Pasha's beautiful Turkish wives and charming Circassian concubines were observing us the whole evening from behind a perforated *musharabiyeh* screen. I hope they enjoyed the performance of seeing the beasts feed more than the beasts enjoyed the feast themselves. I shall never forget the comical expression I caught upon General Grenfell's countenance as his eye met mine when, with extra politeness, some snuffy old Pasha was handing him, in his fingers, a mutton kidney he had himself just plucked from the juicy joint. From the power of pantomime displayed by that comical glance of resignation, I inwardly determined that although fortune had made the gallant General a soldier, nature had most surely intended him for a comedian.

After Loutfi's dinner came a very much more cheery one in the European style, given us at the New Hotel by our comrade in arms, Brigadier-General Yousouf Pasha Schudi. This was a very jolly affair indeed; and so the days went on—with big drills by day, and big dinners by night.

When this sort of thing had been continuing for some time, the Khedive expressed his wish to have the British officers of his army presented personally to him. Accordingly we all proceeded to the Abdeen Palace, where he received us most kindly. After shaking hands with us all round, he entertained us with coffee and cigarettes, the coffee being served from jewelled cups. It was the first time that I had ever personally met his Highness, and the charm of his manner struck me at once. Although he learned English later, on this occasion he talked to us in French, told us that he was delighted with the progress made by the new army from what he had seen at a review two days previously, and desired to thank all of us very much for our exertions. His manner on this, my first time of meeting Tewfik Pasha, impressed me considerably: there was something frank and honest about his clear brown eye, which made one feel intuitively that he was a man who was completely straightforward and utterly free from any oriental chicanery in his character. Moreover, the quiet urbanity in his mode of greeting us was graceful in the extreme. What a factor this same urbanity of manner is in the lives of those placed in high

position to make them popular or the reverse! What
is it but his urbanity of manner which has ever made
Lord Dufferin, of whom I have just been speaking, so
successful both as Viceroy and diplomatist? Those in
a lesser position like to feel that their betters think
them worth the trouble of being civil to, and no man
is more polite to all whom he meets than the noble
Marquis of Dufferin and Ava. I can recall two instances of his pretty speeches to myself as an example
of this. The first occasion was one day in Egypt when
the hot weather had commenced. I saw Lord Dufferin,
who was as usual, whether in Egypt or India, impru-
dently wearing a high black silk hat, standing at
mid - day out in the burning street talking to some
official. He was there so long that I thought he
would be positively roasted. When I saw that he
was eventually disengaged, I ran down the steps from
under the comfortable shelter of the covered verandah
of Shepheard's Hotel and went to speak to him. I
had on no stove-pipe hat, but was well protected by
the silken folds of the white and gold Arab *kofeeyah*,
which we officers wore over our fezes in the hot
weather. But Lord Dufferin's concern seemed to be
instantly aroused, not for himself, but for me. Grasping my hand and shaking it kindly, he said, just as
though I were conferring a favour upon him, "Oh,
how very kind of you, my dear fellow, to take all
the trouble to come down out into the hot sun like
this to shake me by the hand!"

When again I met him years afterwards it was at

Simla, as Viceroy of India, where, as I was wearing a different uniform, and we met under such entirely changed circumstances, I should not have thought that it would have been worth his trouble to remember me at all. I told him therefore, as he shook hands with me, that I thought he would have long ago forgotten me altogether.

"Not at all, my dear Haggard," blandly replied the Viceroy; " I never forget the face of a friend."

Now the noble Marquis, being an Irishman, may perhaps have kissed the blarney stone; but still, what is all true politeness from the great to the small but the truest and most laudable form of blarney?

My greatest chum among my brother-officers, almost from the beginning of all things, was Chamley Turner. He was an officer of the 53d Shropshire Regiment, who had been present with his corps during the war at Alexandria. Here, as every one knows, a considerable force was kept watching the lines of Kafr Dowar while Wolseley made his dash on Ismailia. Chamley Turner was the *beau idéal* of a soldier. Were I now, as I have occasionally done, writing a novel, I could find no finer fellow to represent all that was plucky in a man, all that was bright and powerful, than Chamley Turner— my chum—to select as a type for a regular slap-dash hero. He was very tall, very broad-shouldered, had a dark face with keen blue, almost jackdaw-blue, eyes. He was downright, devil-may-care, good-natured, hot-tempered, and a splendid shot. He would work all day unceasingly, sit up all night, get out again on parade next morning at five or six o'clock, and work all the following day, and to give his own phrase when he was perhaps a little merry, which he would quote with a stentorian laugh, " Fear! Chamley Turner does not know what fear is." When first he made use of this phrase to me, I thought him boasting. Over and over again afterwards, until his death by drowning in the Nile, I found that his words were absolutely true— Chamley Turner was in this world the one man I have met who positively did not know what fear was. I will give a few instances.

One day when I was with " Baby " Martin, already mentioned, I for fun bought five asps from some snake-charmers, who said they had had their fangs removed. I curled them up, shut them up in a little box, covered it with a paper marked " superfine writing-paper," and the same evening, when the verandah of Shepheard's was crowded, produced the box.

" Chamley, old boy," I said, " I've bought some new writing-paper at Hanna's shop, which they pretend to be real English; do you mind giving me your opinion on it?"

He took the box—opened it. Up came five snakes' heads, all the snakes hissing! Did he drop that box? Not much! Exclaiming, " Snakes! oh, ripping!" he plunged his hand into the box, seized all five snakes at once, and with them curling round his hand and wrist in every direction, and biting him, started around to clear every one off that verandah; which he did in about a minute and a half, or less. When he had

turned every one off the place into the street or the
hotel, he put the snakes back in the box and only then
asked if they were poisonous. That was the sort of
man he was!

Among other feats of his of which no one has ever
heard, was a little reconnaissance he made entirely by
himself into the enemy's lines of Kafr Dowar. He
went alone, got over the parapets among the enemy,
and returned again all right. These were the sort
of freaks he liked.

Very soon after the army was started, Turner was
given command of the Camel Corps; and to see the way
he would, without any previous experience of camels,
walk in among a lot of vicious and snarling dromedaries, all burbling at him at once, open-mouthed and
ready to bite, seize them by the nostrils and force them
into submission, was one of the most extraordinary
instances of nerve I ever witnessed, but it was simply
another of the proofs that Chamley Turner absolutely
did not know what fear was.

CHAPTER V.

WHILE speaking of Chamley Turner I am reminded
of the fact that among other distinguished personages
who were staying at Cairo during that spring of 1884
was the late Duke of Hamilton. He had left his
yacht the Thistle at Alexandria and was staying in
Shepheard's, which was indeed in those days like an
enormous club: it was the general place of rendezvous,
and all Cairo, whether staying there or not, passed a
good deal of time either on the verandah, loafing round
the bar, or lounging on the divans in the passages.
Chamley Turner, being a splendid shot, used particularly to distinguish himself at the pigeon-shooting
matches, and the Duke being also a keen sportsman,
they were great friends from their similarity of tastes.
I myself was also one of his friends, and I can look

back to no pleasanter hours than those which we all
three sometimes passed together of an evening.

We found the late Duke of Hamilton what I suppose
hundreds of others have found him—that is, one of
the most generous minded of men, and I fear that he
himself must have remembered to his last days the
unscrupulous manner in which we used to punish his
cigars. Not only was he generous minded, but—all
the more wonderful for a man who suffered from
gout—I personally found him the sweetest tempered
of fellows. I shall never forget one night when he
had gone to bed ill, and I thoughtlessly stirred him
up very late to ask for one of the famous havannas,
how he would insist upon turning out of bed himself to get the box for me, an act which was under
the circumstances more the act of an angel than of a
man with the gout. As I only once met him since,
and then but for a minute or two in a hotel dining-
room at Monte Carlo, I never had an opportunity of
telling him that I had never forgotten his noble and
Christian-like behaviour upon that occasion.

The Duke's generosity, however, went, as far as Turner and myself were concerned, further than merely
giving us cigars; for he gave each of us a two-year-
old race-horse—that is, he promised to keep the horses,
then yearling colts, for us in his training stables until
the following spring, or whenever we liked to write
for them, when he promised he would send them out
to us to Egypt. Turner and I were looking forward,
accordingly, with a considerable amount of confidence,

to carrying all before us over the Cairo race-course in the coming by-and-bye; but when spring came we were both engaged in far more serious pursuits than racing, being both on active service in the Soudan. So we never wrote for the horses, and then when, shortly after the campaign, my chum Turner was, to my great sorrow, drowned in the Nile, I never cared to remind the Duke of the promise he had made to us mutually. However, if, as I did not remind him, I never got the horse, I had other things to thank him for. Some years afterwards his yacht called at Suakin when my younger brother, Arthur Haggard, was serving there with the Shropshire, Chamley Turner's old regiment, which did a long weary year of garrison duty camping on the sands in that most unhealthy spot. On this occasion the men of the regiment were supplied from the Thistle with quantities of all kinds of fruit and vegetables, which was an inestimable boon to men who did not know what green food meant. These supplies, I believe, in his kindness of heart, the Duke had taken down expressly for his friend's old corps. To my brother also and other officers he was particularly kind.

It is when soldiers are cut off not only from their homes, but completely from the very faintest approach to comfort of any sort or kind, that acts of thoughtfulness like this are most thoroughly appreciated. Perhaps in the future it may fall to the lot of some who may read these pages to be able to perform a similar act of kindness to the British soldiers in foreign lands. If so, they will follow a good example, and may

rest assured that Tommy Atkins will never forget it.
I remember in a similar way, on the 16th February
1885, that Sir Donald Currie and some ladies—his wife,
two daughters, and a Miss Cameron—having arrived
that day at Suakin in Sir Donald's steam yacht Zingara,
went up by train to the Sandbag Camp, and took out
a quantity of vegetables and fruit to the officers and
men encamped there, and that they were most heartily
cheered by the soldiers, as indeed they deserved to be.

The new Egyptian army was getting on very well,
and continuing to make rapid progress, when in the
month of June the Khedive left Cairo and went down
to Alexandria to pass the hot weather in the palace of
Ras el Teen; and I have no doubt that, as he observed
daily the holes in the lighthouse near by which some of
our ships had accidentally made during the bombardment, his Highness had ample time to think what
a very hot time of it the troops of the old Egyptian
army had given him in that same palace less than a
year before. One of the battalions—I think it was the
1st Battalion under Chermside—went down also to
furnish the palace guards.

On the 24th June 1883 we first heard reports of
cholera having broken out in the ports of Damietta and
Rosetta, but we did not think much of it. Two days
later all the superior officers of the Egyptian Force
had to follow the Khedive to Alexandria, although
for the day only, simply for the sake of congratulating
him on the anniversary of his accession. All the
principal officials in Egypt attended this function. It

was a stupid and wearisome business of ceremony, indeed one of the kind which gives rise to the saying,
"Much cry and little wool." We had to go a six-
hours' journey by train the previous evening, get up
very early, dress in our grandest uniforms, and after
getting coffee and cigarettes in an ante-chamber, wait
until it came to be our turn to march past the Khedive
and bow to him. Then we had to repair to another
part of the palace, where we were received by a
poisonous black negro with a squeaky voice and a
huge diamond ring on his finger. This was the chief
of the eunuchs, and he represented the Khediviah, his
Highness's only wife. If I remember correctly, we
were obliged to take the inevitable coffee and cigarettes
again with this worthy, and write our names down in
a book before departing. After this we repaired to
yet a third gate of the palace, where we found another
swell eunuch, another book, and more cigarettes. This
was the part of the palace occupied by the Queen
Mother. We were then at liberty to get back to Cairo
as soon as we could or would. I remember that, after
the cool refreshing breezes of Alexandria, we found
the journey up very hot, and that we had a good long
brigade field-day under General Grenfell early next
morning, so as to make up for time wasted during the
day we were away.

The Fast of Ramadan began that year ten days after
this excursion, on the 6th July, when the weather was
at its hottest; and I observe in an old note-book of mine
a note of that date to the effect that our Mahomedan

soldiery tried all they could to shirk their work in
Ramadan. In making that remark I was writing from
inexperience; for the wonder is that, starving all day
as the men were, they were able to do any work at all
in Ramadan. Utterly without food, drink of any kind,
or tobacco, from the first stroke of dawn until sunset,
the young soldiers were, in the hottest part of the year,
expected by us at first to be able to perform exactly the
same drills and duties as usual. We thought that, because they fed at night and had good hearty meals no
doubt, they ought to be as strong as usual. But far
from it! the month of Ramadan has the effect, to
use a slang term, of "knocking the stuffing" out of a
soldier completely.

There was one good effect it had with our men—it
at all events stopped them from drilling each other all
night long. This habit had been a perfect curse to us
in the 4th Battalion E.A., for we had gone to live out
in some barracks in the desert, consisting of one large
building and many detached ones, called the Polygon,
where, so still was everything, we could hear this drilling going on in the barrack-rooms from tattoo to *réveillé*.
It was useless ordering the practice to be stopped: as I
have said before, the Egyptians loved drilling—you could
never give them too many hours of it. The habit was
therefore encouraged by the native officers, and stimu-
lated by the non-commissioned officers, who would, for
that matter, gladly go without a night's rest so that
they could get in an hour or two's extra drill. The
result used to be that night was made hideous. From

a barrack-room on one side would be incessantly heard such words as *Saghdan-garia-dun, bir, hek, ouch, dort* (Right-about turn, one, two, three, four); while from a barrack-bungalow on the other side would merrily ring out the words of command appertaining unto the manual exercise, such as *Salaam dur* (Present arms), *Huz dur* (Shoulder arms), *Rahat dur* (Order arms); and so on until it was time to get up and go to parade. But Ramadan stopped all that for us, and gave us peace for a time. And with Ramadan the cholera arrived in Cairo—that is to say, it arrived about ten days after Ramadan had commenced. And then, as the sailors say, there was plenty of work for all hands.

The ground selected for establishing camps of observation and quarantine camps was in the desert near the Polygon. The work of getting these camps pitched, and arranging for their rationing and supplies, therefore fell chiefly upon my own regiment, the 4th Battalion E.A., which also had to find the guards to establish cordons of sentries to prevent the healthy from passing into the lines wherein were isolated men returning from leave who came from infected towns. Soon, in addition, we had to establish a regular hospital for the cholera patients, of whom before long there were plenty. The only place we could find for the purpose was a large deserted house situated between the Polygon and an enormous lunatic asylum on the Abbasiyeh side of the Polygon, but still in the desert. This deserted house had in the middle of it an open cesspool; but we were forced to begin using it before the cesspool could be covered in and properly cemented up, a circumstance which might have cost us the life of a very valuable officer, who, however, has since lived to do much valuable work for Egypt. This was Wingate, a young gunner who came from Aden, and who was appointed to the 4th Battalion; for although he belonged to the Artillery, and the 4th Battalion E.A. was of course infantry, it was a theory of Sir Evelyn Wood's that all his officers ought to be interchangeable. Colonel Wynne having gone on leave to England, I had succeeded to the temporary command of the regiment, getting Wingate as my second in command.

Just as Wingate was getting on well with his infantry drill the epidemic fell upon us, and as the English could spare us no doctors at first, we found ourselves in the unfortunate position of having none but Egyptian ignoramuses, who were cowardly, ignorant, and worse than useless. Some of them, however, got better afterwards, when they found they did not die at once, and actually did very good work. In the meantime, however, we combatant officers, and notably Chamley Turner, who invented strange medicines, were all trying our 'prentice hands at doctoring, and were, according to orders, daily and nightly assuming the duty of looking after the native doctors, taking upon ourselves also hospital duties generally, and running the discipline of the place, where the patients were soon arriving in crowds, often dying as soon as they came in. Now dying meant that the dead required burial, and a choleraic patient is best buried quickly, and for this we had no means of making proper arrangements.

General Grenfell. Pigott, Chamley Turner, myself,
and Wingate had given up coming out daily from
Cairo, and were all now living permanently in the
Polygon, so as to be near our men, and we all did our
best. Pigott and myself, for want of any one else to
do it, even took upon ourselves one day to bury a dead
choleraic patient in a fox-hole in the desert; but, as
Pigott remarked, while he calmly lit his cigarette in
the blankets of the deceased, which we were burning
at the time, a little better hospital arrangement was
becoming absolutely necessary.

And this being recognised, young Wingate was appointed hospital superintendent. He was the sole responsible person by whom all requisitions were made,
and he was answerable for everything. And that he
did his work nobly all we living survivors can testify,
and an enormous amount of credit is due to him for
the way he soon got that abominable building clean
and ship-shape, beautifully whitewashed and full of
disinfectants, and in fact something like a hospital
should be. While doing all this, he was, however,
more in the building than any one else, and far more
exposed to the horrible stench exuding from the open
cesspool. The consequence was that, although he did
not catch cholera, he was, after he had got everything
in good working order, attacked by typhoid fever, and
I can well remember how long he hovered between life
and death before he slowly recovered. Unfortunately
an Indian boy, who was his servant, and who attended
him devotedly, caught the disease and died. I am glad

to say that he was presented with the 4th Class of the Osmanieh in recognition of his services.

About this time—until the arrival of English doctors from England to study cholera, amongst them notably a capital little fellow named Theodore Acland, who used to ride my pony and fall off daily—we had to dose the men ourselves, to do which we had to invent medicines, which we varied at will. I had the distinguished honour to be with Chamley Turner the joint inventor of a most successful "corpse-reviver," as we called it, the potency of which was so great that it was bound, as Turner used to say with a roar of laughter, either to kill or cure at 1000 yards. Turner used to sit upon a bed holding up a dying Egyptian soldier in his brawny left arm, with a cup of the corpse-reviver in his right hand. It being Ramadan, we had always the greatest difficulty to make them during the daytime take medicine even which contained brandy; but Turner, whose Arabic was still sketchy, would try to convince them that his medicine was nothing but water. To do this, after his patient had with disgust turned his head away from the cup which he had been touching with his cholera-stricken lips, Turner would put the cup to his own lips in turn, saying, "No! no! *shuff* [look here], *mowya, mowya* [water, water], *quies keteer*" (very good, indeed); and thus at the imminent risk of his own life would he persuade the wretched creatures to drink the remedy.

Notwithstanding his noble behaviour in the hospital, he was the greatest joker in the world at this period, and used, in spite of remonstrance, to eat enormous quantities of unripe water-melons, saying, when told he would get cholera, that he hoped to, as he wanted *to spread the disease.*

He also had an unpleasant habit, which frightened everybody except me, his pal, of suddenly falling down and writhing and twisting on the ground, moaning and groaning as if in fearful agonies, turning up the whites of his eyes, and generally behaving as if in the stage of cholera we call cramps. It was most convincing, and just as the other officers were sending for a stretcher to carry him off, he would jump up from the ground with a roar of laughter, call them all silly idiots, and bawl out for a brandy-and-soda. I saw him once fall down in this way at the door of our quarters at the Polygon, as he and I were getting out of an *arabiyeh* in which we had just driven from Cairo and then from the cholera hospital. He frightened the driver so much that, leaving his horse and carriage, he ran straight off into the desert as fast as he could go. So great, indeed, was the man's terror and fear of infection that he would not return, and soldiers had to be sent off to pursue him. Eventually, nearly at the end of the epidemic, when the cases were not, strange to say, nearly so often fatal as at the beginning, Turner really got cholera himself. Then so great was his confidence in our own concoction, that in the presence of Grant Bey the doctor, whom he disliked thoroughly, he asked me to give him a wine-glassful of corpse-reviver instead of any of Grant's d——d stuff. And he recovered, being very kindly taken by Sir Evelyn Wood to his own house in Cairo as soon as he was fit to move.

I mentioned above the objection that the cholera-stricken Egyptians had to taking spirits. I had an example of this which came under my own especial notice in the case of a fine young Egyptian officer. He was a captain in the Artillery, and a handsome man; and the very day he was seized he was in Army Orders, as being promoted to the rank of brigade-major. He was suffering agonies from cramps an hour or so after admission to hospital, and he begged me to rub his legs and stomach for him. I did my best for the poor fellow, but was utterly unable to alleviate his awful sufferings. I then tried all I could to make him take some brandy, holding the glass to his lips. But he spat out the liquid, saying, "No; it is Ramadan, and I will not touch a drop of anything until sundown." By sundown he was dead, poor fellow.

That epidemic of 1883 was certainly terrible, and the loss of life in Cairo alone something awful. At one time the death-rate was considerably over one thousand daily, and the road leading from the Fargallah quarter of Cairo out towards Abbasiyeh would every morning and evening be covered from end to end with strings of rough coffins being carried along on men's shoulders or conveyed on donkey-carts in batches of from ten to a dozen at a time. The principal Arab cemetery lay to the right of the road in the desert, covering a very large area of ground. Here, owing to the difficulty of getting sufficient coffins, the deceased cholera patients were often taken out of these coffins, buried, and the coffins taken back again for other occupants. So callous did the natives who took the empty ones back become, that I have over and over again seen an Egyptian sitting inside the coffin which he was driving back on a donkey-cart from the burial-ground. They were fatalists, and once they had accepted the fact that cholera was there among them, the commoner sort took not the most ordinary precautions to prevent it spreading. Indeed, just to save the trouble and vexation of certain police regulations concerning giving information of deaths, many thousands of persons were buried beneath the floors of the houses which the rest of the family continued to inhabit.

Among the British regiments in Cairo some suffered severely, and the British military hospitals, in the Citadel and at Abbasiyeh, were soon full of poor fellows, most of whom only required the attention of the doctors and nurses for a very short time. To lessen the risk of contagion, the English troops were marched out into the desert towards Helouan; and, if I remember rightly, some were sent away to Ramleh, near Alexandria. But for some time, wherever they went, the pest went with them, and the death-roll showed no signs of diminishing.

In very sooth, Cairo was in those days like a city of the dead. There was scarcely any movement by day save of hearses in the European quarter, and of people in all quarters alike hurrying to the chemists' shops or for doctors. By night huge bonfires of tar-barrels were lighted in the middle of the streets, filling the air with sulphurous smoke, the flickering glare of the flame and the heavy rolling smoke together recalling to mind the pictures of hell-fire by old masters. But the fire and

the smoke could not stop the plague, and for a long
time the numbers of deaths kept increasing daily.

Before going out to the Polygon, I was, until the
cholera had actually got amongst our men, living at
Shepheard's Hotel, and in the habit of riding or driving
backwards and forwards to Abbasiyeh to my work. I
was therefore often in the hotel at meal-times, where
there remained a good many others who, like myself,
came home to lunch and dinner, at any rate sometimes.
They were all officers, or officials of some kind, either
in the British or Egyptian army, or in the various
departments of State. There were also a few ladies
present, whose courage had prompted them to stay
on for a while in the plague-stricken city. And
the most interesting part of these meals was not by
any means the lists of dishes inscribed on the bills of
fare. Far from it; they were lists of quite another sort
which circulated from hand to hand at the table twice
a-day. These were lithographed returns showing the
number of deaths certified by the police in the different
quarters of the town up to noon and up to sunset respectively; and according to whether these lists were
increasing or diminishing, no doubt, did the appetites
of many increase or decline in a corresponding ratio, at
all events until they got accustomed to it. The lists
would run something as follows, say, for a morning :—

Ismailia Quarter	.	.	.	109
Mouski "	.	.	.	16
Boulak "	.	.	.	83
Old Cairo "	.	.	.	132
Fargallah "	.	.	.	43

And so it would go on through all the different parts
of Cairo, with the grand total added up at the bottom.
It was certainly a strange habit this of handing round
the death reports with our food, and I don't know how
it originally commenced: most probably some of the
principal military doctors, or some of the other heads
of departments, had had them served out to them, and
thought we others should find them interesting. This we
most certainly did, and all alike looked forward to seeing
them. Indeed I well remember that when one day the
lists were not forthcoming, every one's luncheon was
quite spoiled.

A description of the cholera season of 1883 which
did not mention the nobility of the Army Hospital
nurses would be indeed incomplete. Their devotion
and courage were deserving of the very highest praise.
One afternoon I had an opportunity of observing them
at their work. The epidemic was decreasing, and I
and one of the doctors we now had with us up at the
Polygon found that we could take a half-holiday,—it
was Theodore Acland, I think, and he suggested that
we should pass our half-holiday in driving into Cairo
and seeing the way the patients were attended to, first
in the large Egyptian civil hospital, and secondly in
the British military hospital at the Citadel, where we
thought we might learn a few wrinkles. It was not
the first inspection we had made together, and I am
sure, if ever my friend Acland's eyes should peruse
these pages, he will vividly recall the awful experiences
we underwent together when, almost by force, we broke

into the Abbasiyeh Lunatic Asylum and insisted upon opening door after door, only to find men and women, some of the latter perfectly naked and all uncared for, shrieking and dying of cholera in abject misery on the filthy floor. Many of the people in that lunatic asylum in those days were by no means mad, but simply confined there by their relatives, wealthy pashas or beys, to keep them out of the way. The guardian of the asylum stuck to it all the time that there were no cases of cholera, but only a few simple fever cases, in that terrible building, the stench and the awful sights wherein were so terrible that they made even Berkeley Pigott too ill to accompany us on our rounds. Now, when it is considered that Pigott was at that time in our own cholera hospital daily, and that he was a brave soldier, accustomed to face war in all its most terrible aspects without flinching, it must, I think, be conceded that that lunatic asylum, where, by the bye, many of the dying patients were in chains, was something awful indeed. Death is always terrible, but within those dreadful portals everything that the callousness and ingenuity of man could do to make it more so had been done. Thank God! we were the cause of a thorough reformation in that lunatic asylum.

What a change of scene it was to the British hospital in the Citadel! Here, too, death was rampant around us; but as we were being shown round the shaded wards by the soft-voiced, red-cloaked army nurses, we quickly realised that all that could be done to alleviate the dying soldier's last moments before dissolution, these ladies were doing. In spite of many difficulties, and the want of many necessary things, they performed wonders, and one had only to watch the grateful look in the eyes of poor Tommy Atkins, as they approached, to know—to feel the devotion they were putting into their work, while running the gravest peril of their own lives. I do not know when most to admire the hospital nurse—whether it be when, as I have seen her, after a battle, she, a delicate frail girl whose nerves would be thought unable to stand the shock, is, while soundly rating him for his awkwardness, showing some clumsy hospital orderly how to staunch a frightful wound, or when in scenes like this of a terrible epidemic. Under both circumstances she is equally admirable, equally deserving of her country's praise. That afternoon, after going round the wards, we were taken into her own sanctum and given tea by a charming lady who, having already been decorated with the Order of St John for devotion to the wounded in the last war, was now the head of the nurses at the Citadel. It was indeed a quiet retreat she led us into, and her bright and intelligent conversation charmed us both. Poor lady! I only saw her once again; for she, who had saved so many lives herself, was killed in a carriage accident in the streets of Cairo, mourned sincerely by every officer and soldier in the place.

CHAPTER VI.

At first we in the Egyptian army only concerned ourselves with the drilling and training of such soldiers as
the Egyptian authorities supplied to us, without having
time to inquire how they were obtained; but before
long we became aware of frightful abuses in the recruiting, and had to see to it.

Throughout the cholera season, recruits, or rather
conscripts, were still being forwarded to Cairo. These
were of two kinds—fellaheen, or peasants, with brown
skins, who were supposed to be selected for service
on a nominally perfectly fair arrangement, and who
were coming to us for enrolment in the regular army;
and blacks living in Egypt, mostly slaves, who were
kidnapped by force from their places of employment,
put in chains, and sent up under armed guards to
Cairo to be added to the gendarmerie under Baker.

I never knew where the poor wretches were usually
trained, but well remember one large batch which was
raised under the pretence that they were being enlisted
voluntarily by Zobehr Pasha. These men were drilled
at Abbasiyeh, then sent to the Soudan under Baker,
thrashed at El Teb, and the survivors afterwards gave
me plenty of trouble at Suakin. However, our business in those days, before we had begun to raise black
troops for ourselves in the army, was only with the
fellaheen. It was only in the rural districts that the
young men were taken for military service, the two
cities of Cairo and Alexandria being very unfairly
exempt, although by a recent decree passed this year
(1895), in Council under the Khedive Abbas, they too
will have to give their conscripts unless they pay a
redemption of £E20, which is more than £20 English;
but the recruits in my time had to pay a fine of £100
Egyptian to escape service.

When the cholera was about at an end, Sir Evelyn
Wood, the Sirdar, had come to the conclusion that it
was about time that a little supervision and investigation should take place as to the strange old Egyptian
methods under which the *mudirs*, or governors of provinces, were conducting the conscription. Accordingly,
as soon as Colonel Wynne, my commanding officer,
returned from leave, I found myself under orders to
proceed to various large towns in all parts of Egypt
to make these investigations, visiting and making
longer or shorter stays in Tantah, Zagazig, Mansoorah,
and other towns to the north of the Delta; then again

travelling away to Assiout, and to the far-away province of The Fayoum, quite at the other end of Egypt.

It was during these trips that I learned more of the inner life of romance and intrigue which goes on beneath the surface in a population where the women are always secluded, than I should ever have known had I remained simply in Cairo. But although, being young then, I had strange adventures, by which I came into contact and formed friendships with not only Syrian and Coptic ladies, but even with one or two beautiful Circassian slave-girls, this history is not a personal history, nor is it a tale of romance, therefore the details of those friendships will never be revealed further than that some of them have been hinted at in the history of Zuleikha the Circassian in my novel 'Dodo and I,' which Messrs Blackwood & Sons gave to the world some years ago. However, I like to think that there will be among my readers some who are not altogether averse to the idea of a spice of Eastern romance existing in the present day, any more than when they are carried back to the days of the past by the perusal of the delightful pages of the 'Arabian Nights.' To them, then, will I give a hint. The times when beautiful dark eyes flash on the passing cavalier day by day from behind a veil or a window lattice, until love or fancy hath entered into the fair one's heart, are not even yet gone by.

And when once an Eastern woman loves, or fancies she loves, she does not believe in calmly waiting until, in the European way, the object of her young affections tells her that she is adored by him. On the contrary, she promptly finds some means of communicating with the object of her choice. Even should he, fearful of bow-strings and yataghans, seek to elude her, it is of no use; for sooner or later, whether he will or no, he finds himself somehow or other in the lady's presence. She is veiled at first from head to foot, and although her eyes are bright and beaming, he does not know whether the black silk *habara* conceals a face and figure of fifteen or one of fifty. But a female attendant comes in with the little cups of coffee and the cigarettes. It is evident that in order to either smoke a dainty cigarette or to drink a cup of coffee, the veil must be removed by the slave, and a lovely face disclosed.

Oh, my boy! if you be a lover of romance, as you should be, this is the moment when you will thank your stars that you spent so many weary hours in acquiring the Persian, Turkish, or Arabic language. Make, then, the best of your time!

As I muse upon these things, and upon the oriental woman's innate love of intrigue, I think that it is strange how in every part of the world Scott's words prove absolutely correct:—

> "Love rules the court, the camp, the grove,
> And men below and saints above;
> For love is heaven, and heaven is love."

I must now, however, with a parting blessing, leave Cupid for conscription, and romance for recruiting.

Moreover, although women alone can, at all events in the East, never have a really good time without

men, we of the inferior sex when with each other
very often enjoy ourselves to the full. I am bound
to confess, therefore, that I have never had a more
agreeable and interesting time of it than when, a year
after my independent excursions among the provinces,
I went up the Nile on a Recruiting Commission, with
my good friend Brigadier - General Yousouf Pasha
Schudi as its President. It was, in fact, a regular
yachting trip, with plenty of hard work thrown in
to prevent its becoming monotonous.

It had become a recognised fact that there were
endless abuses going on everywhere—bribery, corrup-
tion, and oppression by the sheikhs of the villages—
and a determined effort had therefore to be made to
alter all these things by sending a special Recruiting
Commission to take all the towns and villages on the
banks of the Nile to the southwards—that is to say,
up the Nile towards Assouan.

When Schudi Pasha and I found that we were to be
respectively head and second in this special Commission,
we determined to do it comfortably, and to make the
Government provide us with the means of doing so.
We asked for a *dahabeah*, one of the Nile yachts in
which both rich natives and foreigners every winter
pass many weeks on the most classic of all rivers; and
in spite of several attempts to fob us off with a ship of
inferior size and quality, we would not start until we
were supplied by Government with one of the very
best. Then we went off. In addition to the gallant
old Circassian Pasha and myself, the medical element

was supplied by my late friend Surgeon-Major Galbraith
of the Egyptian army. He was also a great friend of
the Pasha's, and altogether a very jovial and good companion. He was clever at his work, a capital performer
on the fiddle, knew Arabic well, and was altogether up
to Egyptian tricks. He and I had already passed a
year together at Suakin. The rest of the Commission
consisted of an Egyptian major of great intelligence
named Ali Bey Haidar, an officer who, having been for
some time brigade-major to General Grenfell, had improved upon his great natural intelligence; of a smart
lieutenant named Ismail Effendi Ragi; and lastly, of
Mourad Effendi Ghalib, the Pasha's *écrivain*—that is to
say, paymaster and scribe.

The name of our ship was the Cheops. It was in
October that we were to start, a delicious time of the
year for a Nile voyage; but of course when the day
actually came for our departure there were the inevitable delays before we could get off. First of all, it was
discovered that the inventory on board the *dahabeah*
had not been signed. Now red-tape rules in Egypt
quite as much as elsewhere, therefore two of our Commission had to ride back into Cairo, from the place
where the ship lay above the Kasr el Nil bridge, to get
the proper person to come on board and sign it. Then
it was discovered that there was no food on board.
That of course would not do! Hassan, the Pasha's
excellent cook, was sent to Cairo to get food; but as
he never came back, Ismail Effendi Ragi had to go to
Cairo to look for him, and also to get materials where-

with to make an Egyptian flag, bearing the crescent and
the star. For it was evident that such an important
Commission as ours must fly a flag in its own honour.

Eventually everything was arranged, and we sailed
away to the southward, making, with our two enormous
three-cornered sails, splendid progress against the current with a capital breeze. Passing many palaces and
palm-trees on both sides, everything looked beautiful,
so we were all happy. When passing a little island a
splendid view was obtained of the Pyramids of Gizeh.
Here the Pasha, in the exuberance of his spirits, tried
to shoot a vulture with a rifle, but he only succeeded
in knocking out a wing feather. This island is called
the Golden Island, and the land on it is some of the
richest in Egypt, the rental being from £8 to £10 an
acre, as it produces three crops in the year of *dura* or
other grain. Beyond the Golden Island we passed suc-
cessively the little towns of Tourah and Helouan on
the right bank. They are both situated in the sandy
desert, having a background of red barren hills; but
Tourah is well known on account of its convict prison,
which was in those days being so ably reorganised by Dr
Cruickshank, while Helouan has been famous since the
time of the Romans for its sulphur baths and splendid
air. It is even now a very favourite place of resort for
Cairenes of all nationalities for a few days' relaxation,
and is the terminus of the Cairo Helouan Railway.

On the opposite side of the river to Tourah, and
extending beyond Helouan, are thousands of graceful
date-palms. These date-groves extend for miles and

are very valuable, the district being known as Mana-
wat. We stopped our craft the first night at 9.30 P.M.,
and in the usual Nile fashion tied her up to the shore
at a place known as Abukedwan. It is not usual to
sail up the river so late at night, and as we had no
ship's lights, it was a rather dangerous proceeding, as
we might have been smashed by Nile ships drifting
down with the current. On making fast, word was at
once sent to the sheikh or headman of the nearest
village, who thereupon sent two watchmen to take care
of the vessel by night, and himself became personally
responsible for the safety of the ship and all on board
her. A strange custom this, but it was always done when
persons of any importance were travelling up the Nile.

Gaily we bowled along again next day with a spank-
ing breeze, and as we lounged about under the awning
on the deck, life seemed a thing worth living. Soon
we found the Nile becoming very wide. Here in the
distance we sighted the smoke of two steamers ahead
of us which our sailing craft was rapidly overhauling.
We knew it to be the smoke of two steamers containing the Royal Berkshire Regiment, all the officers of
which were personal friends of mine and of Galbraith,
as we had been on service together; and at the pace
we were bounding up against the current, we knew we
should pass them in an hour or two. Hereupon the
gallant old Pasha, who was most excitable in tempera-
ment, became particularly anxious that our ensign
should be completed in time to hoist and to dip to the
gallant 49th Regiment as we passed.

Although we had both sailors and orderlies busily engaged sewing the crescent and the star on to the huge red bunting, it seemed as if it would never be done. At last, just as were overhauling the two steamers, the flag was finished. The Pasha, a man of many languages, rubbed his hands, exclaiming "All right" many times over. But he soon changed his "all rights" to horrible objurgations in French, Arabic, and Turkish, when he found that, although the flag was completed, the sailors were too stupid to know how to rig it on the halyards. Just as we overtook the sternmost of the steamers, however, the Pasha's excitement was too much for everybody. He was determined to have that flag up, and he did get it up! But it was no sooner hoisted than it was discovered that, owing to a knot in the halyards, hauling it down or dipping it was impossible. More expletives! not only in Turkish and Arabic but in German, for German was a language the Pasha excelled in. I dreaded that he would have a fit of apoplexy. Fortunately, the noble Berkshire Regiment never hoisted any corresponding flag on their steamers, probably because they had not got one. This pacified the gallant Circassian general, because it put dipping our ensign out of the question, as the people to whom we wished to pay the compliment could not respond.

Instead of going through that ceremony, therefore, as we passed we sailed close to the steamers and chatted with the fellows. We felt sorry for the officers, for they did not look half so comfortable in their steamers

F

as we in our spacious *dahabeah*. Moreover we felt that, after all the gallant work the Berkshire had been doing in Suakin, they deserved a winter in Cairo instead of in the deserts up the Nile. However, with our enormous lateen sails, the *dahabeah* soon drew away ahead; so we waved good-byes, and before long had left the steamers' hulls down behind us, and at nightfall we made fast to the banks of an island called Geziret Abu Saleh, where we had a merry evening with plenty of music. After piano and violin duets and some songs, we got the crew of sailors and made them give us a chorus of the wild, weird, native music, accompanied by the strange *darabookahs*, or hand-drums, and cymbals. To describe the wild trilling sounds of the Arab singing is impossible, but all Eastern travellers know it well. What amused both the Pasha and myself was to find that Galbraith could do it quite as well as the Arabs, for he was a born mimic.

The next day, as there was no wind, we all went in for sport. Every member of the Commission was out with guns, the native members took pistols also. Everything that moved was shot at. The worst of it was that our Egyptian companions had a horrible habit of leaving loaded guns lying about anywhere on the decks, so as to be ready to shoot if any ducks came along. They would also twist about with loaded and cocked revolvers in their hands in a way calculated to give one the jumps. Galbraith and I, after returning from shooting some pigeons, passed the rest of our morning going round and unloading such weapons as we found charged.

We quite expected, to quote 'Pickwick,' to find something heavy in the bag before long!

A breeze, however, sprang up at length, and we got off and sailed to the town of Beni Soueff before being overtaken by the steamers of the Royal Berkshire. At Beni Soueff we were received by Major Izzat Effendi of the gendarmerie, who was in charge of the prison and some gendarmerie troops, chiefly cavalry. We went ashore and paid a visit to the *mudir*, a most intelligent Turkish gentleman, then made an inspection of the prison and gendarmerie stables. The prison was much overcrowded, but it was easy, for one who knew what these Mudiriyeh prisons had all been a year or so previously, to see what English supervision had done in the way of improvement. There were now English and Arabic forms brought to us showing the crimes, dates of imprisonment, and when the sentences of the prisoners would expire. There were 170 male and 3 female prisoners, of whom the former had a chain round the leg, the other end of the chain being carried in the hand.

At this town our Commission was joined by a Coptic high priest or *komos*. As the Copts are very clever in forging lying certificates to escape military service, the presence of this functionary was perhaps necessary ; but we did not like him, anticipating many lies from him, for very few of these Coptic priests are straightforward, and all are dirty in their habits.

From a visit to the native bazaars of Beni Soueff we found it without exception the very dirtiest place we

had ever seen; it was not at all a nice town, in fact,
but we had plenty to do besides looking out for the
beauties of the scenery. Our first day there was a
Sunday, which was passed in looking over the lists of
men returned as being fit for military service, and com-
paring them with old lists to see that there had been
no fraudulent alterations, also in reading some of the
lengthy petitions which had been sent to the War
Office, complaining of fraud and conspiracy on the part
of all the Government officials, the sheikhs, and the
Coptic priests of the place. The petitions accused everybody excepting the *mudir*. His *vakeel*, or representative, headman, adjutant — by whatever name he
might be called — was accused roundly of fraud all
round.

That same Sunday night the Pasha, Galbraith, Ali
Bey Haidar, and myself, went to dine with the *mudir* in
his palace. His name was Ali Bey Thabit. He gave
us an excellent Turkish dinner of at least twenty courses,
which succeeded each other with the rapidity of lightning. Although these were served on the usual round
brass tray, he gave such of us as preferred it plates,
knives, and forks; nor did he force the food down our
throats by presenting us with pieces in his own fingers,
in a manner already mentioned with reference to Loutfi
Pasha's dinner.

Long before the end of the feast some of the party
began to call out for *el ruz* (the rice), which is always
the last course of all, and to ask for which is a sign
that one has had more than enough. The best of

these Turkish dishes was one composed of the breasts of chickens mashed up with milk-and-sugar and very delicately seasoned with spices. This, however, arrived about fourteenth on the *menu,* so none could do it the justice it really deserved.

The *mudir* introduced us to his adopted daughter, in those days a charming little girl of about six years of age, with fair hair and dark-blue eyes. The little maiden was not a bit shy, and made great friends with me. Her history was as follows. After the bombardment of Alexandria, the *mudir* had found her beside the dead body of her mother, a Circassian, who had evidently been dead several days, the child being almost dead too. The father, a Circassian effendi, had never since been heard of; he was either dead or had deserted his wife and child. The *mudir* having no children, had therefore kept the little girl and adopted her.

After dinner we all went out into the garden, which was illuminated in our honour, and where there was provided enough refreshment of an alcoholic nature to have made the Prophet Mahomet rise from his grave to reprove his unfaithful followers. There were then told some of the most amusing stories it has ever been my lot to hear. Some of the old Arab poets were also quoted with great success, Ali Bey Haidar particularly shining in this line, quoting from the poet Antar several pieces which were deservedly received with considerable applause. I took the trouble to make in verse almost literal translations of a couple of them. The first of these was a spirited verse from a warrior to his mistress; it ran as follows, in pretty imagery :—

> "I thought upon thee when the javelins were flying,
>   My blood dyed the Indian blades, nor was I loath ;
> And I longed to embrace those bright swords, e'en if dying,
>   For they shone like the lightnings of thy smiling mouth."

The second poem was the history of a guitar, which detailed its experiences from the time that it first formed part of the branches of a tree in a garden. It began with Sybaritic advice :—

> "In thy life's early day ever sip from the cup,
>   From her hand whose lips are sweeter than honey,
> Rob the sweetness of life before 'tis used up,
>   For life without pleasure is a purse without money.
> So drink in sweet music, and tell this my story,
>   To the harp's gentle tinklings my love sorrows breathe ;
> Soft tales thou shouldst learn ere thy head hath grown hoary,
>   They to those broken-hearted forgetfulness give.
> Now I am the son of the sweetest rain-water,
>   And the branch which I grew on swayed in the soft breeze,
> Clad in garments of green like a saint's lovely daughter,
>   No houri has raiment to vie with the trees !
> When thirsty I drank from the fresh running brook
>   Which rippled so brightly, as silver itself ;
> 'Twas to me just as wine, for 'tis writ in a book
>   That water's the wine to those without wealth !"

There was much more of it, all equally pretty.

The evening, however, was devoted not only to poetical recitations and tall stories, for there were also given many witty little catch phrases and difficult sayings, much after the fashion of our own " Around the rugged rocks the ragged rascals ran a rural race."

There was one little catch story which especially
caught my fancy. Accordingly I give it as nearly
as I can remember it :—

There was a certain king who had a vizier of whom
the other courtiers were jealous. He was a very clever
man, but had a defect in his speech by which he could
not pronounce the letter r. The most jealous courtier
of all, one who wished to become vizier in his place,
came to the king saying, " How can your Majesty keep
him as vizier ? why, he cannot even read out a letter to
you so that you can understand the sense of it ? "

" Give me a letter," his Majesty replied, " which he
cannot read to me so that I understand the sense, and
he shall be beheaded and you made vizier in his stead."

" That is easy, your Majesty," replied the jealous one,
and he indited the following epistle, of which it will be
noted that almost every word contains the letter r.

" Amr, amir ul umra, bihafr biran ala attarika, lisharb
tiha as sāri wa al bāri."

The literal translation of the above is :—

" Ordered the prince of princes to dig a well on the
road that might drink in it the comers and the goers."

The vizier was called, and the king told him to read
out the letter. He saw the trap ! Without a moment's
hesitation he read out as follows :—

" Hakm, hākim alhukama, bifahat ainan ala assikkah
liyishki tiha al hādi wa al bādi."

Not one of these words contained the fatal letter r.
Every single word in what the vizier read out, however,
was absolutely synonymous with the respective words

in the letter which was laid as a trap. So it was the other man that was beheaded! And this little story may be taken as exemplifying the extraordinary richness of the Arabic tongue.

The following day was the first of the public assembly of the Commission, the duties of which were to investigate and verify the labours of ordinary commissions which had been complained of as being corrupt. Our place of assembly was a large room in the Mudiriyeh, a partially ruined palace which had been built by Said Pasha when Ruler of Egypt. There were still a few rooms remaining in good order. The greater part of the building, however, had been destroyed by fire, and the ruined walls were the haunt of quantities of blue rock-pigeons, which afforded us excellent sport when the court was not sitting. Our most important duty was finally to determine which of the young men of the neighbourhood were to have their names inscribed in the ballot list. It was necessary, therefore, that especial precautions should be taken to arrive at the exact truth in the case of every young man brought before the court.

This being the case, in addition to the ordinary Government officials, sheikhs of villages and religious sheikhs, who were responsible for the ordinary correctness of all proceedings relating to the conscription, we caused four of those persons to be present who had written the petitions complaining of the injustice of the enlistment operations in the district of Beni Soueff. These four men acted throughout as sort of prosecutors and witnesses at once against the rest of the community. Whenever it appeared to the court that somebody was lying, which was frequently the case, or that facts were being concealed, which was constantly, they were appealed to, and they were in many instances the means of our getting at the truth, and showing up sheikhs who had accepted bribes to assist sons of rich people to escape military service by false representations.

The conscription laws in Egypt were in themselves simple enough and fair enough. Roughly speaking, they were to the following effect: All young men between the ages of nineteen and twenty-three were liable to military service for four years, and then to eight years' service in the Reserve. The exceptions were in favour of those who were known as *wahidāni*. This word—from *wahid*, one—means an only son; but for purposes of conscription it had a broader signification —namely, to denote any son upon whom devolved the care and support of an old or infirm father or mother, or of young brothers or sisters, so long as they should remain small or unmarried. A great deal of lying always took place upon these points. Another exception was in favour of all religious pupils, Mahomedan or Christian, of priests or persons engaged as servants in the Coptic churches or in the mosques. This was the great door of escape to the Copts, who produced false certificates. Finally, of all persons engaged in the Khedive's household, and of those medically unfit. In addition, anybody could claim exemption upon payment of £100 Egyptian.

Our first day we began by examining before the Commission about fifty of the young men whose names were inscribed in the lists of the twenty-three-year-olds. The scene outside the court would have been very interesting to any one who had never seen anything of the sort before, as all the conscripts had come accompanied by their fathers, mothers, sisters, and brothers, all of whom were seated upon the ground or on the stone steps of the palace. Many of the females—fellaheen women, of whom the girls were often unveiled and particularly handsome — bore petitions in their hands referring to their sons or brothers. These petitions they presented to us whenever they could fight their way in through the crowd at the door, or managed to get over the scruples of the police by *backsheesh* or argument.

We noticed that upon these occasions the old women were wise in their generation. They thought, apparently, if they had a pretty daughter, that the petitions would be more likely to be accepted from the girl's hands than from their own withered and grimy ones. Therefore, when mother and daughter had both managed to fight their way into the council chamber, the old woman would crouch up against the wall and veil her swarthy features, probably to avert the disagreeable impression which might be caused by their disclosure to the members of the court. She would then thrust the paper into the hand of her lissom young daughter and give her a little push towards the judicial table where we sat. The girl, barely veiling the point of her chin, and with a shy but coquettish manner, would stretch out her shapely arm—and Egyptian women's arms are shapely indeed—with the petition to the nearest of us, with such a beseeching look in her lustrous eyes that it was usually accepted from the dainty fingers. Alas! however, that I should have to record it as a testimony to the want of gallantry of the members of the court, one glance at the petition, and one or two questions tersely put, were generally enough. The statements set out were usually found to be a tissue of lies, and the exit of that mother and daughter was more often than not so rapid that it must have seemed to them like a dream, if indeed it did not take their breath away. For there is one thing in which an Egyptian gendarme can show his zeal—that is, in clearing a court-house or a street when ordered to do so by a pasha or a bey who is looking on to see it done.

Now, we had one pasha and two beys, of whom I was one, on that Commission. Galbraith also was a Hakim Pasha, or head doctor, with a grand uniform, and he was very often the first to have them slung out, although, poor dear fellow, I should be insulting his memory sadly were I to say that he did not love the sight of a pretty face as much as we all do. Partiality, favour, and affection, however, to quote the oath on military courts-martial, were unknown quantities on that Special Recruiting Commission. Had it not been so, I believe that every one of us, from the Pasha downwards, would rather have given back a young man from the jaws of the ballot to a pretty girl than to an ugly one.

That first day Galbraith rejected twenty young men for medical reasons, we let off eleven as being *wahidanis* or only sons, and one Copt was excused as being the son of a priest and also engaged as a servant in his father's church. We knew we were being deceived about the Copt; but the sheikhs had been well bribed, and the four public prosecutors, being all Mahomedans, could tell us nothing about him. I may as well here mention, *en parenthèse*, that the Copts being by far the best educated, and also capital at figures, are always made the quartermaster-sergeants in Egyptian regiments, one to each company. The regimental paymaster is also nearly always a Copt.

The Copts are the old original race of Egypt. I never learned how they became Christians, but I saw from the first that they were more given to the arts of peace than to the arts of war. To look at, they are just the same as the other Egyptians, and this in spite of the large admixture of Arab, negro, and other alien blood in the Mahomedan population. The reason of this is that from some strange climatic reasons, no matter how much admixture of blood there may be, the progeny of a mixed race always reverts to the original Egyptian type as we see it represented on the old frescoes in the temples.

But a hint to those who would visit the Coptic churches. Beware of the fleas, unless you would be driven mad!

The subject of fleas reminds me of a picnic excursion that Sir Evelyn Wood organised in Cairo in our first year of formation. He thought that it would be a grand thing to combine business with pleasure by taking a lot of officers and ladies a few miles down the Nile on a steamer to inspect some empty barracks which he had a thought of taking over. We visited those barracks, the floors of which were deep in dust. The ladies, of course mostly young and beautiful, accompanied us round the rooms on our tour of inspection. We had not been long in the barracks before there were apparent great signs of distress among the fair sex. Do what they would, it was impossible for them to avoid at times stooping down furtively to pull up the hem of the dress and the pretty white garment below to give a vicious scratch at the shapely ankle they concealed. Presently it was worse than this, and any further attempt at disguise being impossible, every lady was rubbing and scratching at herself through her clothes like mad. When their cries of genuine distress brought the men to their sides, it was seen that even the outside of their dresses was literally covered with fleas! As for the men, all officers in uniform, they were wearing long brown boots and white overalls, so of course the fleas could not get inside. The outside of the overalls, however, was as black as though covered with small pepper-corns, and the little hoppers could be brushed off with the hand or a glove by dozens at a time. A stampede was made for the steamer. Here the poor ladies, who were

simply in tortures, had to shut themselves up in the
stuffy cabin, and pass through the partially opened
door all their articles of clothing, that the gentlemen
outside might if possible shake them clear of the
myriads of fleas. The men did their work nobly, and
handed these garments back again as spotless and
white as undriven snow.

Notwithstanding this, the trials and tribulations of
the unfortunate fair ones were not even then over; for
on undressing themselves, many of the little brutes had
fallen upon the floor of the cabin, and as they resumed
their attire they hopped back again to recommence the
campaign. The poor ladies completed that day and
the journey back to Cairo in perfect misery. They
were indeed nearly eaten alive, and not one of them
was able to wear a low dress for a week. In all the
annals of the merry picnic parties of which Cairo can
boast, it is not likely that the celebrated picnic of the
fleas will ever be forgotten. Indeed it was a joyful
picnic for them, if for no one else concerned.

To visit the interior of a Coptic church is to run the
risk of undergoing as much physical discomfort as that
above detailed. But now to get back to the Coptic
conscripts.

CHAPTER VII.

LYING EVIDENCE TO ESCAPE MILITARY SERVICE—VENALITY OF
THE SHEIKHS—DISEASES OF THE EYE AND HEAD AMONG THE
YOUNG MEN—THE PASHA FURIOUS—A WOMAN WITH FOUR
HUSBANDS—VILLAGE GIRLS IN THE CORN-FIELDS—STRANGE
IDEAS OF MODESTY—UNEXPECTED DESCENT UPON BOUSH—
MARAITHS AND KANDALIFTS—THE PRICE OF A FALSE CERTIFI-
CATE—MUTILATION OF FOREFINGERS—FIKIS AND MUEZZINS—
GREAT CHANGES IN THE EGYPTIAN MILITARY SERVICE.

ON excusing from military service the Coptic lad mentioned in the last chapter, we carefully took down from
him the names of all other servants and religious pupils
engaged in his church. This list we found useful
when presently two other Copts appeared, both claim-
ing to be students, and both armed with certificates to
that effect sealed by the Patriarch. By its aid we found
them not to be religious pupils at all, but first-class
liars engaged in other occupations. They were ordered
to be enlisted at once, and one, moreover, to be tried
by court-martial on enlistment. We should not have
enlisted this boy if only he and his father would have
told the truth, as we considered him necessary to the
support of his father and seven sisters. But the farce

of his being a religious student was so extravagantly kept up that an example had to be made. Lying, indeed, was the most notable feature of that day's proceedings. Many prisoners were made among the liars who were found out; but others lied and were not found out, or their lies could not be proved against them. I think the old Psalmist must have been engaged on a special recruiting commission when he said in his heart "all men are liars." I must give a good instance of Egyptian ingenuity in this respect.

A certain man, not too old to be capable of still doing work himself, had three sons, two of them within the limits of age for conscription, the third one small. One of these sons was distinctly liable to the ballot for service, the other might have been excused at the discretion of the court on the ground of his father's age. But what did this clever old rascal do in order to get both his sons off, which he had hitherto succeeded in doing. To the previous Recruiting Commission, that which we superseded, he had presented only his second son. This young man was excused upon evidence being given that he was the sole support of a divorced wife and several small children of that divorced wife. This time the old man presented his elder son, and nearly succeeded in getting him also excused on the ground that he was the support of him, the father, and of his own mother, who was not divorced, and who was produced in court.

Of course it appeared that the old man had been married twice, and that both his wives were living.

But the four public prosecutors soon exposed this fallacy, and proved most conclusively that the old scoundrel had never had any divorced wife at all, or indeed any other wife than the one who had appeared before us in court. *Tableau!* The choleric Pasha, our President, used "language," and that father and son were removed to the black hole of the Mudiriyeh in double-quick time.

The village sheikhs lied horribly on the following day, and half the conscripts whose names were called were absent, being screened by the sheikhs, whose palms had been well oiled, and who explained their absence by a hundred fictitious excuses. Among the sheikhs there was one who came to grief by thrusting himself in unnecessarily. There is an Arab proverb which runs as follows: " Al dabur zann likharb'eshshu" (the hornet hums to the destruction of his own nest). This proverb applied to his case.

A young man's name was called; he did not appear, whereupon a certain Sheikh al Haret, or sheikh of the quarter, without being called upon, made a voluntary statement to the effect that to his certain knowledge the boy had been absent ever since the promulgation of the approaching assembly of our Commission. This seemed likely enough, and some others backed the sheikh up by saying they knew the young fellow had gone off to Cairo. Unfortunately two or three witnesses testified to having seen the youth on the preceding day outside the court-house itself. The sheikh was hereupon ordered to be imprisoned for

the night. Next day a great farce was gone through.
No sooner had the daily train from Cairo arrived at
the Beni Soueff Station, which was close to the
Mudiriyeh, than the young man appeared before the
court, panting for breath as though he had come
from the station at full speed. His father declared
that he had arrived from Cairo in response to a telegram he had sent to summon him, a story we were
expected to be simple enough to believe. However, it
was easily proved that this lad had been present the
day before; that when the Sheikh al Haret had been
imprisoned for false evidence he had run off to Ishment,
the next station, and returned thence by the morning
train as though arriving from Cairo. Two or three
hours were wasted on this case alone. It may therefore be imagined what was the frightful trouble of
investigation when it is stated that there were upwards
of one thousand cases in Beni Soueff alone, all of which
required impartial investigation.

In addition to other causes for the rejection of conscripts, we found that of disease very important; we
had to cast a great many on account of eye diseases.
These were mostly diseases of the cornea, such as ulcera-
tions, nebulæ, and cloudiness, caused most frequently
by pustular ophthalmia. Another very common disease
among the fellaheen which existed then as now was
tinea favosa, a parasitic disease of the scalp of the head
of most loathsome appearance. Loathsome though it
might be, however, the fellaheen often inoculated themselves with this disease in order to escape military

service. It is a nearly incurable complaint, but, strangely enough, the natives also inoculate themselves with it to serve as a counter-irritant to diseases of the eye. They sometimes succeeded in curing themselves of it by washing their heads with petroleum. Another plan was to cut out the top of their *tarboosh* or fez, so as to let the hot sun shine upon their heads. By this method, apparently in some cases the excessive heat killed the parasites.

It must not be supposed that the Commission were always able to carry on their proceedings with that quiet and decorum which usually exist in a court-house; far from it. Alas! there were sometimes very stormy scenes, when half the sheikhs and notables present were all talking at once and screaming at the president, and when the president in return would not scruple to tell the sheikhs and notables aforesaid a few home truths in a voice which did not at all resemble the cooings of a sucking dove. At such times the words *kaddâb* (liar) and *harâmi* (thief) would resound through the lofty council chamber with a ring which perforce carried conviction with it. Playful remarks also did the righteously irate Pasha indulge in, in connection with the Abbasiyeh Military Prison, where various sheikhs were already confined, and of the weight of the chains which were in store there for their brethren of Beni Soueff for offences in connection with the *kora*.

One of the stormiest of these scenes which I recollect was when it was discovered that one of the richest men in the whole district had been lying about his two sons—fraudulently representing them as *fikis* or Muslim Scripture-readers. In this statement he was supported by three village sheikhs and by many false certificates. To get at the truth the Pasha requested the sheikhs to swear, with their right hand on the Koran, three times by the name of God that the man's sons were *fikis*. They could not stand the solemnity of this test, and declined to do so.

For the next few minutes no lion ever roared louder than did old Sehudi Pasha in his rage at the deceit which, under the cloak of respect for religion, those three hoary old sinners were trying to practise upon us. It is hardly necessary to add that the two younger men's names were both enrolled; for we had them both in court, and found that, far from being able, as a *fiki* is, to repeat long chapters by heart, they could only with an immense amount of stammering and spelling read the Koran at all. Had not the Pasha had a thorough knowledge of the people, and had he not been, moreover, thoroughly determined and fearless in his efforts to get at the truth from every one, no matter what his position, the whole Commission would have been a mere farce. For we should never have been able to exercise even ordinary justice towards those of the Khedive's subjects who were not rich enough to bribe the sheikhs, nor, on the other hand, to insist upon those who were rich, and therefore able to supply the necessary palm-oil, fulfilling their duties towards their sovereign and their country.

In the constant effort to escape from military service, we came one day upon a most curious and complicated case, which may be quoted as an example of the difficulties we experienced in getting at the truth. Two brothers appeared before us. They had the same father but different mothers. The mother of the elder had been divorced by the father of both. This woman had previously been married and become a widow; she had then married again and been divorced. Her third husband was the father of the two boys produced in court, and she was stated to be either living with or else married to a fourth man. It was not ascertained for certain whether she was actually married to the fourth or not, although the woman herself was examined, and had also two of her ex-husbands before us to give evidence. The point of the case was this. The father of the two boys claimed exemption for both from military service on the ground of one being necessary for the support of himself, the other for the support of his mother, the ex-wife, the frequently married one. He brought witnesses to prove that the woman had no other sons by any of her husbands, and he swore to it himself. After the most wearisome and infinite pains, it was, however, eventually proved that he and his witnesses were "Ananiases" of the purest water, that the woman had borne other sons, and was to all appearance again married. At the end of it all, her son's name was inscribed on the list of the *kura*, while his half-brother was excused.

On one Friday, although the Mussalman Sabbath, the Commission made an unexpected descent upon a town called Boush. This was an interesting and thriving place, about seven miles away from Beni Soueff. The only roads by which we could ride were much-beaten tracks along the banks of irrigation canals, or leading through the high waving fields of Indian corn or sugar-cane. Here frequently, as we came round a corner, we would come upon a group of pretty fellaheen girls, who would bound with assumed shyness in among the green stalks, only to look out again coquettishly a moment afterwards as we passed by. They only wore one simple garment, a kind of blue shirt called a *gallibiyeh*, which leaves a great portion of bosom, arms, and legs bare. This is a very simple toilet, although, as they usually wear veils also, it is from an Egyptian point of view decidedly modest. It must, nevertheless, be owned that the fellah girl as often as not puts her veil to one side to show her pretty face to a stranger when no men of her immediate male relations are by; and as for their modesty, with them appearance is everything. Apropos of the above remark, I may mention an incident which once occurred to me.

I was riding very early in the morning in Upper Egypt when, traversing some date-palms, I suddenly came by a deep descent through a small nullah or ravine upon the Nile, which, being very low at that time of the year, was perfectly hidden from the banks above. No sooner was I on the banks of the river than

I found myself face to face with a pretty village girl of
some eighteen summers, who, denuded of even the merest
vestige of clothing, was washing herself in the river, in
which, on account of the swift current, she did not
stand deeper than her knees. The situation was em-
barrassing. I reined up my horse; the maiden cast one
irresolute glance at the swiftly running stream behind
her, then another at her clothes on the bank by my
horse's feet. That glance decided her. In a second
she had made up her mind. In a couple of bounds she
had sprung out of the water, and stooping, picked up —
what? her *gallibiyeh?* No; her blue loose chemise was
left lying! It was her veil which she seized upon, and
swiftly covering her face therewith, she calmly walked
back into the water again.

To get back to Boush. Built almost entirely of mud
houses, it stood on a high hill or mound caused simply
and solely by the *débris* of former towns built of the
same Nile mud. It was a curious thing to walk round
the base of this hill, where extensive digging had taken
place, and to notice the various strata of parts of old
walls and successive layers of pottery of different ages.
When we were there the town was surrounded in a
great measure by a lake, out of which sprang quantities
of palm-trees, the lake being simply caused by the in-
tentional flooding of the land by a neighbouring canal
which brought the fertilising mud from the Nile itself.
The effect caused by the waving palm-trees growing out
of the water was very graceful and strange.

At Boush, by our unexpected descent, we discovered

ninety-one young men whom the sheikhs and *omdahs*
had falsely reported to us at Beni Soueff as having
absconded altogether, so it was a very successful surprise party indeed.   Dr Galbraith and I further visited
two Coptic churches, where probably no white man had
ever been seen before.   We were anxious to find out
how many *marattils* and *kandalifts* were habitually employed about the Coptic churches, these being the classes
of young men for whom exemption was always claimed
as religious students.

We had the good fortune to come across, at one of
the Coptic churches, a respectable, clean, and truth-
telling priest named Komos Girgis—that is, High Priest
George.   He told us that one *kandalift* and one *marattil*
were quite sufficient for a church.   And yet at Assiout,
where, although a great Coptic stronghold, there are only
five churches, no less than 160 young men had appeared
before the preceding Commission with certificates signed
and sealed in regular form to say that they were either
the one or the other, with the result that they had all
to be excused military service.   It was indeed time for
a special investigation on a searching scale.

The *marattil*, it should be mentioned, is a sort of
assistant to the priest when officiating; while a *kandalift*
is an attendant kept for the sole purpose of lighting the
kandeels (lamps, not candles) and for cleaning the church.

The result of our inquiries was not only to discover
how many servants were required to be employed in a
church—we also found out how much it cost a young
Copt to get a false certificate.   This was about £18

sterling, and this is how it was disposed of. To the Coptic *kasis* or priest, and to the Mahomedan *sheikh al bilad* or village headman—between them, £5; to the *uskoff* or Coptic bishop, £5; to the *bash-kātib* or head writer of the Patriarch in Cairo, £3; and to the *rakeel* or agent of the Patriarch, £5.

Schudi Pasha was, I am glad to say, the means of getting this *rakeel* dismissed from his very lucrative employment.

Before leaving Boush I must mention that we found it had evidently been a village of malingerers for long past; for we noticed that nearly all the middle-aged men wanted the first joint of the forefinger of the right hand, which had been cut off to avoid military service. The Khedive Ismail Pasha, however, used to be "one too many" for these malingerers, as he had them impressed all the same, and taught to pull the trigger with the middle finger.

We passed the whole of one day in what I may call the practical examination of Mussalman youths who had hitherto escaped service on the pretence of being *fikis* and *muezzins*. The former should know the whole of the Koran by heart, and be able to repeat it in a peculiar sing-song manner, which is half singing, half reciting. When properly done, this "reading," as they term it, is by no means unmusical; but I found that watching the *fikis* swinging their bodies to and fro with closed eyes while drawing out their verses produced a peculiarly somnolent effect upon the listener. Some of those we examined passed with flying colours, after

having sent all the court to sleep, but many were
plucked ignobly by the examining *imaum* or priest.
A *fiki* should be like an Indian *fakir*—poor, with no
visible means of subsistence. Oddly enough, all those
who could not repeat the Koran properly turned out to
be the sons of rich men who had bribed some one to
swear they were *fikis*. Every one of their names was
promptly added to the lists of the *kora*.

If the *fikis* made us drowsy, there was not much
sleeping in court when once the examination of the
muezzins began. As every one knows who has been in
the East, the *muezzin* is the official whose duty it is
to shout from the summit of some minaret the call to
prayer to the faithful five times a-day. So effectually
did the *muezzins*, real and false, wake us up in court
with their shouting that the Pasha was nearly acceding
to my suggestion that we should send them by turns
up the minaret of the nearest mosque, while the whole
court adjourned into the open air to see how they ac-
quitted themselves. He was, however, too suspicious
to let them out of his sight, saying that if frauds, they
would probably be changed for another man, who was a
proficient, while going up and down the stairs of the
lofty minaret. So they went through their calls in
court, a good many more being successful in passing
this ordeal than had proved successful among the *fikis*.
This, however, is easily understood, for it is easier to
learn five verses of the Koran than it is to learn by
heart to repeat the whole book.

It may perhaps seem to my readers rather a hard-

hearted thing to say that the grief of those who came
before the court was sometimes rather amusing to witness, and yet this was nevertheless the case. For the
youths and their fathers and mothers often made themselves very ridiculous both by their speeches and actions—so much so, that however much one might really
feel for their distress, it was impossible to repress a
smile at their antics.

One instance of this was when a boy, who had been
declared fit for service, refused to leave the court, but
remained yelling, " My mother has been divorced for
ninety - two years. By the life of the Prophet, my
mother has been divorced for ninety-two years." He
had to be removed by force; but still he could be heard
in the distance, as the police gently but firmly led him
away, repeating in a melancholy voice his strange statement about his mother. We sent for the lady into
court, and she was made to unveil for a moment that
we might judge of her age. She was not at all a bad-
looking woman of, at the very most, thirty-five years of
age, who must have been married at the age of fifteen
or sixteen. At length it dawned upon the puzzled intelligence of the court that the youth had meant to say
that his mother had been divorced in the year 1292 of
the Hegira—the Mahomedan era: that was eleven years
previously, as we were then in the year Hijri 1303.
This proved to be the case, and as we found the fair
divorcée had got two small daughters under the mar-
riageable age, we excused the son from military service
to act as bread-winner for the family.

have occasionally, when a young man got outside the court, after having been excused from service for some reason, it was an amusing sight to see from the windows by which we sat the crowd of assembled women rush upon him and kiss him; but on the other hand, if it was one who was taken, the woman would greet him with distressing howls and yells of the most melancholy description.

The Egyptian mother was in those days, whatever she may be now, by no means a Spartan mother. Poor thing! until the last few years she never had the chance of telling her son to "come back with his shield or on it"; for, once he had left her to join the ranks, he, in the old days, never came back again to the village of his birth, unless it were as a broken-down old man some forty or fifty years later. Then, when feeble and worn out, he was no longer fit to carry arms, he was stripped even of the uniform he stood up in, and, clad in any rags he could obtain, allowed to find his way home as best he could to his distant birthplace. On arrival there it was no longer a home to him; all his relations were dead, no one knew him. Too weak to work, he had nothing left him but to die as soon as possible, to quit the miserable existence of utter destitution to which he was reduced. Was it to be wondered at that, with such miserable examples before their eyes —for there were at the time I write of many such from the old army present in the villages—the military service did not seem to be a very desirable profession in the eyes of the people?

However, the British nation may now truly say, after thirteen years' occupation of Egypt, "Nous avons changé tout cela"; for the young soldiers of the present army are well fed, well paid, and well clothed. They get a periodical furlough to see their friends; are allowed, in the same way as English soldiers, to travel by train or steamer at greatly reduced rates; are given medals for active service; and if discharged from the service on account of wounds or sickness, they are sent home with a gratuity and a complete set of clothes. This good treatment has already in a great measure been productive of the very best results. The military service is now no longer unpopular, and malingering by self-mutilation has entirely ceased. The young soldiers themselves have turned out well, and have frequently behaved with distinguished bravery in the field, of which I shall give some instances later on.

And now, after stating that before I left the Pasha the regular drawing of the tickets for conscription took place, and that, strangely enough, it was nearly always the sons of rich men, who could have paid the £100 for exemption, who drew the high numbers which excused them from service, I shall bid the whole subject of recruiting farewell. For I was relieved from the Special Commission, and while the Pasha, Dr Galbraith, and the rest went bowling away in the gallant Cheops before the north wind up the Nile to other towns and villages, I bade them all farewell, and returned to Cairo to resume the command of my regiment.

CHAPTER VIII.

EVERY year in Cairo there is a very great religious festival, that of the *Mahmal* or Holy Carpet. This is a carpet which is sent each year to the holy shrine at Mecca, whether as a covering for the tomb of the Prophet or for the floor of the Kaabah, the sacred mosque, I know not; for the carpet was never disclosed to the public eye, but, at the time of the despatch to Mecca, carefully packed up and placed on the back of a gaily caparisoned camel, whose trappings of cloth-of-gold covered with worked inscriptions from the Koran were something wonderful to behold. In addition to the camel carrying the *Mahmal* itself, there was in the eighties always another, upon which year after year the same religious fanatic used, naked, to make the pilgrimage to Mecca. There were also many other camels carrying presents for the priests, men on horseback carrying arms, and a strange tagrag and bobtail of fol-

lowers, chiefly on camels, who all took advantage of the
escort of the *Mahmal* to follow the *cortège* to Mecca,
and so earn the coveted title *El Hajji*, the pilgrim, as a
suffix to their names. The cavalcade starts from a
small mosque in a large open square or plain situated
below the heights upon which is built the enormous
mass of buildings comprised in the Citadel.

The procession used, before starting for Suez by the
desert route, to march round and round this square,
accompanied by the wildest and most delirious strains
of music and the wild shrill cries of thousands and
thousands of people. A large body of troops was required to keep the ground, and to treat the Holy Carpet
with proper solemnity by presenting arms to the camel
and the carpet as they passed.

In either 1882 or 1883, I forget which, such was the
nature of the *entente cordiale* between the British and
the Khedive, that a brigade of British troops from the
Army of Occupation was compelled to be present and to
present arms as the procession passed—a matter which
was the cause of a considerable outcry at home, and
justly so, for why should British soldiers be forced to do
homage to a set of howling savages in the most heathen
rite—in fact the only heathen rite in the Mahomedan
religion? With us Egyptians it was different; we of
course had to furnish a brigade of troops on the
occasion.

Formerly the ceremony of the *Mahmal* very much
resembled the passage of the Juggernaut car, for people
ran in front of the camels and horsemen, cut themselves

with knives, and threw themselves down before the camels and horses in order to get themselves trampled to death. In the year after the occupation of Egypt, however, these barbarous customs had been discontinued, and the most disgusting part of the show was the sight of the enormously fat naked man who sat upon the top of a camel's hump, swaying his huge body from side to side at every movement of the beast, while at the same time he violently beat upon a drum fixed before him.

As a pageant I have never seen anything so wild as the procession of the *Mahmal*. The picture of the rich uniforms of the pashas and officers all assembled in kiosques around the Khedive, and the quantities of thinly veiled and beautiful ladies in carriages in the foreground, was interesting and striking in itself; but what was by far more remarkable was the sight of the mass of the inhabitants of Cairo covering every available point of vantage on the craggy Citadel Hill from base to summit. There must have been upwards of a million people, all clad in brilliant-hued dresses, the men wearing turbans of all colours, of which white and green predominated. Swarming on the cliffs like bees on a hive, they made the whole scene under the brilliant Eastern sun one of the most wonderful pictures of colour which the world can produce. What with the roar of the artillery, the brilliancy of the uniforms, and the masses of colour both on hill and on plain, I have never seen anything like it in my life, and never expect to see anything like it again. To witness this

pageant alone it is worth while to belong to the
Egyptian army, and to be able from the point of
vantage of a horse's back at the head of a regiment
to take the whole wonderful scene in to the fullest
advantage. Beyond doubt, of all Eastern scenes I
have ever witnessed, the festival of the starting of the
Mahmal for Mecca was by far the most entrancing
and characteristic.

There used also to be a very considerable ceremony
at the time of the return of the caravan from Mecca.
Then, as at the time of the departure, nearly all the
Egyptian troops would have to go out to receive the
pilgrims with great ceremony and honour.

Thus, with these and many other State functions, our
young troops were, when not actually at drill, always
kept employed; and so matters passed away quietly
enough until the end of the first year of their enrolment. When I say matters passed away quietly
enough, I must not omit to mention that some months
before the end of the year we received tidings that
there was to be an organised rising of the inhabitants
of Cairo, and that we, with the Egyptians so newly
raised, were expected to quell it.

I was then temporarily commanding the 4th Battalion
E.A., while Chermside was commanding the 1st Battalion, and well do I remember the anxious confabula-
tion held with us by the Sirdar on the point as to
whether the Egyptian soldiers would, if necessary, fire
upon their countrymen. They were getting pretty well
disciplined by that time, and they had just learnt how

to use their rifles; so it was, at all events, determined
to try. We did not, however, tell any of the officers
about it, but, on the pretence of a big skirmishing day
and outpost drill, we took all the available regiments
commanded by British officers to the outskirts of Cairo
on the Abbasiyeh side. When we had skirmished for
a long time through the tombs of the caliphs and all
over the uneven ground of the cemeteries filled with
the scarcely covered victims of the cholera, the men
were pretty tired; so, on pretence of having a rest, we
halted and waited—waited anxiously.

Every one of our men had twenty rounds of ball-
cartridge in his possession, and I somehow think they
would have fired them in the right direction if anything
had happened. Of course they might not, though, and
then these lines would never have been perused.
Fortunately for us, perhaps, the matter was never put
to the test, as the expected *émeute* never took place at
the appointed time. Therefore at nightfall we marched
back to barracks, where we had the ammunition collected
from the troops and returned into store.

About this time, indeed before half of the troops
were properly trained in musketry, Loutfi Pasha, the
then Minister of War, made suggestions to the Sirdar that we should all be drafted off at once to the
Soudan to overawe and fight the Mahdi's troops. In
spite of some pressure, and it must be confessed a considerable amount of warlike feeling among the British
officers under him, Sir Evelyn Wood strongly refused
to allow anything of the sort. And so, as I have said

above, the troops remained in Egypt proper, and got a thoroughly good groundwork of training.

It must, nevertheless, be confessed that all military authorities who knew Egypt continued to look upon an army composed entirely of Egyptians with the very gravest suspicion, which suspicion was not lessened when towards the end of the year 1883 news came filtering through from the Soudan that Hicks Pasha and the whole of his troops had been slaughtered in the province of Kordofan. They were not slaughtered to a man; for report said that Adolph, an Austrian corporal in the service of Major von Seckendorff, was kept alive and had entered the service of the rebels. With the news of this terrible disaster came also to Cairo definite information that the false prophet, now openly called the Mahdi or Messiah, was collecting a large army and marching on Khartoum. And from the date of this announcement the Egyptian policy of the British Government commenced to be vacillating in the extreme; and so it continued for the next two or three years, to the loss of prestige of Great Britain, of blood, and of money also, eventually ending in the loss of the entire Soudan, with the exception of Suakin and Massowah. For although there were good advisers, they were not listened to: it was indeed as the case of the children in the Bible who said, " We have piped unto you, but ye have not danced; " or, to use another Biblical simile, the Government were exactly in the position of the deaf adder that stopped her ears and listened not unto the voice of the charmer, charmed he never so wisely.

Among one of the charmers, whose voice should have carried considerable weight, was the late Sir Samuel Baker, who knew more about Egypt and the Soudan than any one living, unless perhaps Abd-el-Kadir Pasha. I might add Gordon's name to these two; but I do not mention Gordon as knowing so much about the Soudan as Baker, because there is no doubt that Gordon's strong religious views often gave his mind a certain bias with reference to Egyptian affairs which the mind of Baker was free from entirely. Another of those who charmed in vain was our administrator in Egypt in those days, the Earl of Dufferin. There can be, indeed, but little doubt that that clever diplomatist saw from the very first the mistake we had made in not proclaiming a protectorate of Egypt immediately after the battle of Tel-el-Kebir; but as we have now brought matters to the end of the year 1883, we may as well leave the views of Baker and Dufferin to another chapter, when I can quote them both together from an almost prophetic letter which Sir Samuel wrote to the 'Times' on January 1, 1884.

CHAPTER IX.

THE letter referred to as written by Sir Samuel Baker to the 'Times' on the 1st day of January 1884 was strongly against the policy of abandonment of the Soudan which Mr Gladstone's Government had announced. He urged that a railway should be established from Suakin to the Nile, and that the various races of the Soudan should be governed by a just administration. He boldly urged that, as we had gone into Egypt by force, we should throw off all disguise and accept the entire responsibility of government. What he meant most undoubtedly was, that we should even then establish a protectorate, for it was not too late in those days to do so! He was very critical as to the composition of the new Egyptian army, which he declared ought to be furnished with a large backbone of Turks, and was justly irate because his brother, Valentine Baker Pasha, had just been sent off to Suakin with a mass of worthless gendarmerie, who were, as has already been explained, old Egyptian soldiers, while of Turkish soldiers, who alone could be expected to prove of any use in attempting the coercion of those Arab tribes who had recently destroyed three separate detachments of Egyptian troops, he had but a few.

What Sir Samuel Baker stated was throughout so absolutely correct that it is worth while, even after the lapse of years, quoting some of his arguments.

" The military position," he states, " has witnessed a continued series of defeats throughout the Soudan, with a loss of about 9000 men killed, before the late General Hicks assumed the command. Abd-el-Kadir Pasha and Hicks both obtained a success upon the east and west of the Peninsula in Sennaar, but the subsequent destruction of General Hicks's force in Kordofan has aggravated the losses of the Government troops, and has necessitated the concentration at Khartoum of all outlying detachments. By the latest intelligence the garrison of Fashoda has fallen back upon Khartoum, and has raised the strength of the defenders to 4000 men.

" With that number in possession of Khartoum, and Sennaar still occupied, while Berber and Dongola are garrisoned, and the desert routes open for supports from Cairo, both by Korosko and the west of the Nile, I cannot conceive the necessity for raising such a question as the abandonment of the Soudan. Hussein Bey Khalifa, the great sheikh of the Korosko desert, can at once organise an Arab contingent if honestly and

promptly paid. This Arab army will force the passage
of the desert and secure the wells from Berber to
Snakin. If that route is opened, there will be no difficulty in supporting Berber within fifteen days of Cairo
by the Red Sea and desert, and the safety of Khartoum
is assured.

"A British High Commissioner with full powers
should be despatched to Dongola and Berber without
delay to inquire into the grievances of the people.
Why should not Gordon Pasha be invited to assist the
Government? There is no man who would be more
capable or so well fitted to represent the justice which
Great Britain shall establish in the Soudan. That determination upon the part of England would quickly
gain the confidence of the people, and would be more
worthy of her reputation than a cowardly retreat from
the positions, resulting from long and patient years of
enterprise and courage since the days of Mehemet Ali
to those of his Highness Ismail the Khedive."

After much more in the same strain, representing the
numberless evils which would result to Egypt by the
abandonment of the Soudan, especially the increase of
the slave-trade, Baker quotes "the able and exhaustive
report upon the reorganisation of Egypt by Lord Dufferin, where there is," he says, "a sentence pregnant
with the intensity of fact."

That sentence is as follows: "The masterful hand of
a Resident would have quickly bent everything to his
will, and in the space of five years we should have
greatly added to the material wealth and the wellbeing

of the country by the extension of its cultivated area,
and the consequent expansion of its revenue, by the
partial, if not the total, abolition of the *corvée* and slavery, the establishment of justice, and other beneficial
reforms."

Here, I think, we may leave this most interesting
protest on the part of Sir Samuel Baker, whose advice
was not listened to in any single respect except as regards Gordon, and not really even as regards him;
for though Gladstone's Government a little later sent
Gordon up the Nile to Khartoum, they sent him across
the Korosko desert, save for Colonel Stuart, alone and
unaided. He did not go to represent the justice of
Great Britain in the Soudan, but simply with orders to
carry out, in the best way he could, the shameful
policy of scuttle which, *coûte que coûte*, had been determined upon.

In the meantime no notice was taken of Sir Samuel
Baker's excellent suggestion to employ Hussein Khalifa,
the head of the Korosko Arabs, and the opportunity
was lost. Reports came in by telegraph day by day
showing that things were getting worse and worse,
and that garrison after garrison was either surren-
dering or being defeated. There were in those days
telegraph lines all over the Soudan, so there was no
difficulty in obtaining news of the disasters; but at
last, about the middle of January, came news that all
telegraph communication with Sennaar was broken off,
that about 80,000 of the rebels under the Mahdi were
advancing towards Khartoum, and that about 30,000

of the Mahdi's troops held a place called Halfeh, which was on the line of wire along the White Nile. By this time it was generally admitted that things were as bad as possible.

Previous to this there had been much dissension among the foolish and ignorant Egyptian Ministers. Although they must have known that without British help with troops, or assistance in some way, to hold the Soudan was impossible, they still clamoured to retain it. The Khedive, Tewfik Pasha, was not, however, so foolish. He saw that retention was impossible, and frankly going in with the English, said—

"You tell me to evacuate the Soudan. You say you will not help me to retain it. Well, a great part of it is already lost; then for heaven's sake let us rescue as soon as possible all the troops and Egyptians we can, who will otherwise be slaughtered; for if you cannot or will not help me, no one else will."

The native Ministry kicked against him; but Sir Evelyn Baring, now Lord Cromer, who was then, as now, Consul-General in Egypt, had more influence with the Khedive than the Ministers, who had to resign. A new Ministry was formed, with Nubar Pasha, a most enlightened Armenian, at its head; and Abd-el-Kadir was made Minister of War in the place of our old friend Loutfi, who gave us the big dinner which has been described.

One thing was determined on, which was, as the Soudan was to be given up, to offer back to Turkey the whole of the Eastern Soudan, comprising the sea-

ports of Suakin and Massowah, the towns of Sinkat
and Tokar near the Red Sea coast, and the inland
fortresses of Senheit and Kasala on the Abyssinian
frontier. This Eastern Soudan was held by Egypt
from Turkey under a sort of feudal tenure, and Egypt
had to pay a big annual tribute for it; therefore it
would evidently be a good thing to get rid of it as
cheaply as possible by giving it up again to Turkey,
and so getting out of the obligation of paying tribute.

Turkey unfortunately did not quite see the force of
having to throw troops into the Eastern Soudan — a
proceeding which would have cost her money. She
therefore declined the proposed cession. Thus Egypt
had perforce to retain possession of the Eastern Soudan,
where before long a swarthy gentleman of the Hadendowah tribe, named Osman Digna, commenced to give
a good deal of trouble.

In the meantime Gordon Pasha arrived in Egypt,
had interviews with the Khedive and all the English
officials, and started up the Nile for Khartoum, where
he safely arrived in due course about the beginning of
February. On his arrival he immediately commenced
sending down as many purely Egyptian troops and
civilians and their families as possible, and for a long
time these fugitives were being received regularly by
Colonel Duncan of the Egyptian army, who was sent
up to Assouan with some of our native troops, the 3d
Battalion infantry, a battery of artillery, and a squadron of cavalry. Duncan, who received them all in
very miserable plight, did most excellent service in

forwarding on to Cairo these poor wretches, who had
lost everything they had got in the world, and in trying, with some success, to improve their miserable lot.
An enormous number of people passed through his
hands—to the best of my recollection 24,000 souls—
before Khartoum having become thoroughly invested,
no more could leave, and all further escape was
impossible.

Of course it is easy enough for us, who were not in
Gordon's position, to criticise; but looking back after
a period of years, there is one point in his behaviour which does seem open to criticism. It is this:
Since he was so distinctly ordered to evacuate Khartoum, why did he not do it? He safely got off most
of the Egyptians; nearly all those remaining behind
were negroes, whom he imagined it his duty, although against his instructions, to remain to protect.
Now, had he left with the Egyptians, these negroes,
being Mahomedans, would simply have done what the
remainder of them who were not killed have done
since—that is, made common cause with the Mahdi
and his troops; and they would, had they surrendered
without fighting at first, have been none the worse for
so doing. In any case, since by direct orders Khartoum was to have been abandoned, it does seem that it
would have been better to have formed into an army
those who wanted to leave, and to have marched away
northward along the Nile bank with as many as could
march, taking all the boat transport available on the
river to carry what was possible, and as many women

and children as could go in those boats, rather than to
have remained behind on the off-chance of England
coming to relieve a beleaguered city which she had
distinctly declared she would never relieve.

Of course, as a soldier, one can, on the other hand,
recognise the reasons which would make a soldier
under certain circumstances refuse to believe it possible that orders which seemed to him to have emanated
in perfect madness would not sooner or later be re-
scinded.   An indomitable courage, moreover, and, above
all, the knowledge of the advance of an excellent foe,
would, to such a mind, inspire a spirit of opposition
which would make the idea of retreat impossible, and
the determination to resist to the death, if necessary,
paramount.   A soldier might under such circumstances
feel that to disobey orders was a far greater honour
than to obey them; and although the result, if successful, might have been a trial before a court-martial, or at
any rate a reprimand, while failure might bring death
itself, then that death was far preferable of the two
evils from a soldier's point of view.   This, no doubt,
was Gordon's own idea.   Moreover, he believed that he
could by sheer determination force the British Government to come to his assistance and back him up in his
views.   He was right in the end; but he never realised
in time what a thorough mule he had to deal with in
the British Government of those days.   He did not
grasp the fact that the ordinary amount of kicking,
cursing, and even caressing necessary to drive ten
ordinary mules could not start that one stubborn mule

until starting was useless,—could not break him into the commonest of ambles until even a trot was too late.

Whatever Gordon's reasons, and whatever his ideas, he was one of the most gallant men who ever lived, and his fame is imperishable, not only among his own countrymen, but among all those countless hordes of the Soudan, who respected him only less than they dreaded him. He was a born leader of men, and I can call to mind the pride with which a native in the interior of the Soudan once showed me an Arabic letter in his possession which bore Gordon's seal. For in Egypt we all had seals; no one ever signed his name unless to a document for Europeans alone. And well do I remember the trouble it took us at first to learn how to dab the ink on to the seal properly, so as to leave not merely a smudge on the paper, which always had to be wetted with saliva, but a legible name in Arabic characters. I wish now I had retained that letter with Gordon's seal upon it; its owner would have given it me for the asking.

The administration of Egypt in those days was a curious one. It was supposed to be carried out by the Egyptians alone, but was in reality carried out by the English, although by not having declared a protectorate the British officials were always finding themselves thwarted at every turn. When Nubar Pasha came back into office, for he had been in office once before since the occupation, things went better in many ways. His ideas were English, and he worked on our side, though making himself unpopular by doing so.

In January 1884 the state of things on the Red Sea coast was becoming serious. Baker Pasha had been sent to Suakin with his wretched troops, who were embarked almost—indeed some of the blacks absolutely —by force; but there was in those regions no sufficient paramount authority. In consequence, Admiral Sir William Hewett, V.C., whose flagship was the Euryalus, was constituted Governor - General of the Red Sea Littoral. This was distinctly an Egyptian office, but I know not if it was the Egyptian War Office or the English officials in Cairo who conferred this status upon the gallant sailor.

Admiral Hewett was a very kind friend of mine a little later on, when I too became, in the same way as he himself had become a Governor-General, a sort of governor under his orders. Meanwhile things fell about in this wise.

The two towns of Sinkat and Tokar near Suakin were besieged by the rebels. The former fell gloriously under an officer named Tewfik Bey, who, after burning everything in Sinkat, marched out with all his men and met his fate nobly. Tokar held out for a time. It was a small town used as a convict settlement a few miles from a natural harbour called Trinkitat, a short distance down the Red Sea below Suakin. Baker Pasha was ordered to go with his rabble and relieve the place, which, proceeding to Trinkitat by sea from Suakin, he attempted to do. Among the English officers who were with him I can remember the following, all of whom I knew well: Colonels Burnaby and Sartorius; Captain

Hay, then Hay Bey, but now Lord Hay of Kinfauns; Morice Bey, a marine officer and an excellent fellow; Bewley, in the police; Forestier Walker; Captain Harvey; and G. D. Giles. This last was a young officer belonging to the Indian cavalry, who has since become a famous painter of war-pictures, and has, I believe, found the brush far more profitable than the sword.

G. D. Giles and I were great friends; we were also in those days much alike in personal appearance, of which circumstance my chum was thoroughly well aware, to such an extent even that a little later on, when Suakin was thronged with troops who knew not either him or me, he told me one day that he was in the habit, under certain circumstances, of passing himself off for me. He was very fond of singing, and, in the exuberance of youth, of singing at night after dinner, very loudly. If any man asked him his name he would, as he informed me, then reply that it was Haggard, and remarked that I had no idea what a reputation I was in consequence getting as a songster.

In those days I thought that this was all chaff on his part, but a few years later I found out that he had spoken the solid truth. I was walking along Piccadilly when a fellow came up to me and shook me by the hand. I did not recognise him in the least, when he seemed annoyed.

"Come, come! Haggard," he said, "you surely must recollect me. You remember we first met at Suakin that night you were so infernally lively that you would swim across the creek and back, roaring at the top of your voice 'The Girl I left behind me.'"

"You certainly are right about my name," I replied; "but I never swam across the creek at Suakin in my life, I assure you."

"Oh, nonsense!" replied the stranger. "I know that it was you; and as for your name, well, you could not well deny it, for you told it me yourself as I gave you a hand out of the water at the landing-stage."

"Save me from my friends!" I exclaimed inwardly; and hurrying away, I left that stranger for ever to his own convictions. But that my friend "Gilo," as we called him, had spoken the truth, and had really played off on me the trick he had said he did, there was now no longer any room to doubt.

When Baker went up to try and relieve Tokar, he suffered, as all know, a most crushing defeat at El Teb, where were slaughtered of his forces about 2400 of all ranks. Having crossed a heavy morass on the previous day, he started in the early morning of February 5 from a fort he had constructed about four miles inland from the landing-place at Trinkitat. He had about 3500 men in all, consisting of Egyptians, negroes, some small forces of Turkish infantry and cavalry, and some European police under Italian officers.

When the enemy were met with, after firing at them a few rounds from the Krupp guns, Giles was sent to charge them with the Turkish cavalry, as most of those seen were mounted on horses and camels. The enemy fled at first, and the cavalry were soon scattered and

entirely out of hand. Moreover, the Egyptian cavalry
scouts, who had commenced firing at random, killed
a couple of them. Captain Harvey was now sent to
call Giles back, when all the Egyptian scouts and the
whole of the Egyptian cavalry were suddenly seen flying in disorder with some large numbers of the enemy
after them. Colonel Sartorius had been meantime
trying to form the troops into a large square, but they
refused to obey orders, especially the new negro regiment of Bezinger blacks. When at length they did
form up, they did it in such a way that the Turkish
infantry and the Massowah blacks, old men of Gordon's,
the only two bodies of natives who attempted to show
any fight, were prevented from firing properly.

Meanwhile the flying cavalry rode down upon Baker
Pasha and his Staff, who with difficulty could force his
way through them to the square, where all was in
fearful confusion. The gunners of the Krupp gun,
which they had been firing, were unresistingly speared
by the Arabs where the gun stood a little in advance;
and then the enemy, without pausing, threw themselves upon that face of the square which was formed
by the Egyptian Alexandria battalion, the men of which
were employing themselves by firing wildly into the
air with their breech-loading Remington rifles, or else
blazing away among their own friends—anywhere, in
fact, except at the enemy.

As the Hadendowah fuzzy-wigged Arabs fell upon
them they turned, and facing inwards, shrieking and
crying in terror, fell upon the ground or tried to hide

I

behind one another. They made not the slightest
attempt at resistance, and were butchered like sheep,
—Baker Pasha, Sartorius, and the others, while vainly
trying to encourage them, nearly getting killed themselves by the fire of the Massowah blacks, who were
standing their ground.

Fortunately for the Staff, however, they were firing
chiefly in the air, so Baker himself rode along their
whole front with impunity. Forestier Walker, who
had some Europeans with his Gatlings, brought them
into play, and stuck to them like a brave man, firing
steadily; but as the enemy increased in number, so
the panic became even more desperate, and soon poor
Walker was left fighting alone with his revolver.

Although the European officers tried to inspire
courage among their men by the drastic measure of
shooting down a few of them with their revolvers, this
only detained a portion of the cavalry for a minute or
two. And then every native that could possibly fly did
so. Horses, mules, camels, men, all were struggling
together to get out of the square, which had, owing to
the side-faces getting forced in, become one shapeless
jammed-up mass, the enemy by this time hemming it
round on three sides. The fourth side all the time was
melting away in a stream of fugitives. Walker, Morice
Bey, Dr Leslie, and many of the foreign officers, fighting hard, were now being killed, and evidently it was
useless for Baker to remain any longer. He, Sartorius,
Hay, Burnaby, Harvey, and a few more charged together through the rebels. They did not even draw

their swords, but got through them easily. Their foemen's numbers were really not more than about 1000
fighting men altogether, and had the troops made
only the slightest stand, they must have been easily
beaten off, if not defeated. Instead, there was one
general stampede; and, throwing away arms, boots,
even their clothes, the remnant of the Egyptian force
struggled back through the morass down to the shore.
Here, the cavalry soldiers taking the saddles off their
horses and turning them loose, in order not to have
to mount again, all together, men and officers alike,
struggled wildly for the boats and got on board ship.
The surviving European officers alone remained on
shore, and worked at embarking such stores as they
could get on board for the return to Suakin. Such is
the disgraceful history of the first battle of El Teb!

No wonder the English officers in Sir Evelyn Wood's
army were annoyed and disgusted at this horrible
rabble of Baker's being supposed to be a representative Egyptian army; but, as a matter of fact, our
new troops were considerably discredited by this awful
fiasco, and there was in consequence no great anxiety
shown on the part of the authorities to allow us to
risk our lives in the field with the fellow-countrymen
of those cowardly wretches who had comprised poor
Baker's army.

That there was, however, already a different spirit
at work, soon commenced to be seen on the occasion
when the Bezinger blacks were being sent off to Suez
to join Baker. These had positively refused to go on

board the train at Cairo. Slade, however, who was superintending their departure, sent for Kitchener, the Engineer officer being then a major acting with the cavalry. He came down with a squadron to the railway station, and the yellow Egyptian cavalry, acting under the English officers, soon frightened the blacks into the train. Still, soldiers are not made in a day, and it takes a good deal of discipline to make fellaheen fight, although that they can be taught to fight, Englishmen have shown many times since the days of Baker's defeat.

As there were no Egyptian troops thought good enough to despatch alone to relieve Tokar, it was determined to send down a force of British under the command of Sir Gerald Graham, V.C. In the meantime, however, three of Wood's officers were ordered to Suakin at two days' notice to help to reorganise the remnants of Baker's forces. These three officers were Hallam Parr, Pigott, and myself.

We went down in a British man-of-war, H.M.S. Carysfort, which was crowded with marines, and arrived at Suakin a few days after Baker and his remnants had got back. There we found everything, as the saying is, pretty well "all up at Harwich"; but in a few days, Baker Pasha and his Staff having departed, we three had upon our shoulders the whole management and command of all the trash he had left behind him. Before he left, though, we were in a constant state of night alarms; and as, save for an earthwork which Harrington Bey, an ex-Rifle Brigade man, had made, and a few round detached redoubts spread in a semicircle about 1200 yards without the earthwork, Suakin was defenceless, the enemy might have rushed the place any night had they liked to try. Not, however, knowing their own strength, they contented themselves with coming outside the lines at night and firing into El Keff, the outlying part of Suakin where all the troops were encamped. On one of the nights I remember that Baker, who was, with Burnaby, standing by a wall close to myself, was nearly killed. A bullet struck the wall close to his head, the pieces of brick sprinkling his face all over. I nearly lost one of my own horses that night, a bullet passing through and nearly severing the rope of his head-stall. As both my horses had been wrecked on a rock in the Red Sea on their way down, and had only arrived on the previous day, it would have been hard luck to have lost a valuable Arab in this foolish way. But neither "The Squire" nor "The Parson" was doomed to die by the bullet, although many and many a time after that did they run the risk.

Suakin was a flat-roofed Arab town on an island enclosed by two creeks, which themselves ran out of a very narrow but deep inlet of the sea, which, widening opposite the town, made an excellent harbour. On one side it was connected to the mainland by a causeway, and the houses and huts beyond this causeway formed the suburb of El Keff. It was round the Keff that the earthworks had been thrown up, the creeks being supposed to be sufficient protection to the town of Suakin itself. Outside the Keff intrenchment, at about 1200 yards' distance, were situated the wells, protected by two earthworks joined by a high bank and called the right and left water-forts; while away to the left of the Keff was another earthwork, called the Tabiat el Foula, or Fort of Beans, from the Arabic word *foul*, beans. Within and forming part of the line of intrenchment round the Keff were two brick or stone flat-roofed edifices fit for occupation for Europeans; these were turned into forts, and named Forts Euryalus and Carys-fort.

Upon my first arrival at Suakin, the ground in the desert outside the Keff intrenchments was well culti-vated, with gardens of bananas and other vegetable produce; melons especially of various kinds grew in the desert soil in enormous abundance. By degrees, however, the risk to the natives of attending properly to these gardens became so great that they had to be abandoned. Moreover, the enemy had a playful way of descending upon these gardens and thoroughly raid-ing them at night whenever there was anything in them to raid.

The water-forts and the Foula, as they are now, are no longer mere earthworks, but two-storeyed octagonal towers—strong works, in fact, having three lines of fire for purposes of defence, from respectively the breast-work surrounding the forts, the first storey, and the roof. These forts were almost entirely built by my men of the 1st Battalion Egyptian Army, being all finished a year later than the period about which I am now

writing. When we first landed there, however, in
February 1884, neither the water-forts, the small round
redoubts, nor the earthworks round the Keff would
have been of any use against a resolute foe unless
strongly held by valiant troops.

The first duty that we three Egyptian officers were
told off to perform, by orders of Admiral Hewett,
was to take over Baker Pasha's troops of all sorts,
and to garrison all these places, with the exception of
Forts Euryalus and Carysfort, which were garrisoned
by marines; and my own immediate duty was to weld
into one trustworthy regiment about 900 blacks, they
being negroes who had formed originally members of
two separate regiments, consisting of Massowah blacks
and Bezingers respectively. The former with a little
training would soon have been of some use, but they
were then discontented and mutinous; the latter
were not only discontented and mutinous, but utterly
useless in every way, being, in fact, far more of a
hindrance than a help. These latter were the young
troops who had been raised nominally to serve under
Zobehr Pasha, but who had been instead sent off by
force to join Baker's army.

It may be imagined that with such untrustworthy
material, officered, by the bye, by the ordinary yellow
Egyptian officer, there was not much to be done.
However, I used to drill them all day, and then send
them out in detachments all over the place at night,
when they would often amuse themselves by firing off
their rifles in all directions, whether there was any

enemy in sight or no. I really believe that they sometimes did it for sheer amusement, as they found it dull
in the outlying forts; and the negroes, after all, were
cheery fellows, who enjoyed a joke of any sort, especially if accompanied by noise. They could not have
their hand-drums with them to play upon when on
outpost duty, so they let off their rifles instead.

But I did not enjoy the joke particularly myself the
first night after my arrival, when I had to make a
round of these outlying posts to see if the men were
on the alert,—a delightful proceeding in which I had
frequently afterwards to indulge, but which, on looking back now, seems to me to have been somewhat
useless. It was before I knew the ground, and a
pitch-dark and rainy night, and to find those tiny
redoubts in the dark would have been impossible if I
had not now and then seen the flash of a rifle in the
distance. I had no means of knowing whether these
flashes were caused by the fire of friend or foe. Indeed, as a matter of fact, there were some of the enemy
about, whom I saw just at dawn moving off from between two of the redoubts; but I do not believe they
fired a shot, though I must very nearly have tumbled
right in among them. I was out for hours that night,
accompanied only by an Egyptian cavalry orderly,
whom I had to thrash with a hunting-crop I carried
to make him go on and show me the way, so great was
his fear of the Hadendowah savage of the period.

I got round them all at last, finding the last redoubt
by daylight, after wandering about in the desert a

great deal, and successfully escaping all dangers from
friend and foe alike. But when the dawn had come,
I found myself for about the third time in the immediate vicinity of the two water-forts, whence, by the
bye, I had been challenged on several occasions during
my peregrinations by the sentries, who were all wide
enough awake. I then found that I had run the risk
of a more terrible disaster than that of merely being
shot, for I had ridden at least three times backwards
and forwards through a regular network of wide-
mouthed and deep wells, by any one of which I
might have been engulfed horse and all. As a matter
of fact, an Egyptian field-officer, going round one
night at a sharp canter, did actually ride into one
of these wells; but the pace at which he was going
threw him clear on the other side, his horse going
down the well. These very redoubts I am mentioning were the cause of the loss of two or three
soldiers' lives during the 1885 campaign, a year and a
half later, an idiotic order having been given that an
infantry corporal and a file of men were to patrol from
one to another by night. Thus a corporal's party of the
Shropshire Regiment was cut off and speared to death
by the savages.

What possible good could have been done by sending
a patrol of only three men by night from one of these
redoubts to the other, I can scarcely see, especially
when it was known that the bushes with which the
desert was in places thickly covered swarmed with the
enemy. However, it is a British tradition that a field

officer should go round the outposts by night, and
another that a patrol should visit the outlying sentries
of the outposts.   Therefore one can only imagine that
the Chief of the Staff who gave the order for those
patrols was mixing up in his mind outposts in the open
with fortified posts surrounded by strong parapets and
deep ditches; but in my humble opinion the officer
whose stupidity was answerable for sending those
wretched men to their death deserved to have been
tried by a court-martial and cashiered.

On arrival at Suakin, we three Egyptians were for
the time being sailors, borne on the books of H.M.S.
Euryalus, Admiral Hewett's flagship, whence we drew
our rations daily.   I had with me a civilian servant
named Alfred Thacker, who had, as stable-boy, groom,
and valet, served all his life with members of my
family in various parts of the world, with one of whom
he is indeed still serving at Tunis.   He was also enrolled as a sailor on the books of her Majesty's man-of-
war, and when he was not looking after the horses,
used to go backwards and forwards to the ship to draw
our rations for us, adding by his usefulness much to
our comfort.

A few days after we had landed, Baker Pasha and
his officers left, and then arrived the Jumna from India
with the 10th Hussars under Lieut.-Colonel Wood,
who took over the horses of the Egyptian cavalry.   As
Baker himself received permission to accompany the
British expedition to Trinkitat, he was able there to
meet this gallant corps, which he had formerly com-

manded, and the officers of which greeted him with
enthusiasm.

About the same time arrived in Suakin a battalion
of the 60th Royal Rifles, and all sorts of details were
landed, but only to stay for a few days; for Graham's
force for the relief of Tokar being constituted, all the
British troops and marines who had been landed re-
embarked and went off to Trinkitat, where General
Graham and his army arrived very soon.

When all the British troops were gone, we in Suakin
had nothing left but the rabble of Egyptian troops of
Baker's to work with; and Pigott having managed to
get off to take part in the relief of Tokar expedition,
Hallam Parr and myself had all the defence of the
place left on our shoulders. The men-of-war, it is
true, were sometimes present in the harbour; but they
were more often away down the coast at Trinkitat, and
had there been only the slightest attempt at any real
attack, the town must have fallen.

To the best of my belief, had Osman Digna sent only
100 men during the days that all British troops were
absent, with instructions to win or die, they would
have won, hands down, and all the dying would have
been on our side; for the spirit of mutiny among the
blacks spread and became rampant. One day they
actually deserted all the posts and came into Suakin to
drink a strong kind of native beer called *boosa*—a very
appropriate name, since they were undoubtedly soon in
a state of "booze." On this occasion I passed a pleasant
afternoon in the middle of 800 or 900 mutinous wretches

who were discontented with everything. The Bezingers, of course, were the worst; but neither of the two classes of negroes would listen to any kind of reason.

There was in especial one sergeant-major of Bezingers who was a regular sea-lawyer, such was the command of language with which he contrived to stir up all the rest. I had my hand on the butt of my revolver half-a-dozen times during the hours that I was in the middle of these howling excited semi-savages, and to this day I can see the exact point in the middle of that man's forehead in which, if the worst came to the worst, I intended to plant a bullet, although I well knew it would be the last shot I should ever fire.

I managed, after hours of heated argument, to get the Massowah blacks on my side, and at length gave them instructions to settle all the differences which existed between the two regiments among themselves. For it was jealousy between the two lots of blacks which was the principal cause of the riot. The Massowah blacks had got all their women with them; they had also annexed all the women of the other Massowah blacks who had been killed. The Bezingers had no women with them, and wanted some of the Massowah women, and could get none. Further, orders had been issued for the Bezingers, being worthless, to be sent back to Cairo, while the Massowah blacks, having already been five years in the Soudan, under Gordon part of the time, said that it was their place to be sent away first for a change to the delights of civilisation.

When I left them with a great assumption of indifference, which I by no means felt, I told them that if they wanted me again they were to send a deputation to fetch me, but not to come to my tent *en masse*. I got out of the crowd alive, and then they did a little fighting among themselves, which occupied them so well that they forgot to bother me until it was all over. Then when I found one man was killed and a few badly wounded, I went back to them to find them all satisfied; and the Massowah blacks having got the best of it, were so thoroughly pleased with themselves that they returned to occupy the outside forts without further trouble. As for the Bezingers, we carted them all off on two Khedivial steamships to Suez next day.

Graham's force meanwhile was landing down at Trinkitat. He had with him the 42d Black Watch, the 60th Rifles, the 75th Gordon Highlanders, the 19th Hussars, the 10th Hussars, a battalion of Marines, and other regiments—as far as I remember, a battalion of the Royal Irish Fusiliers (87th), and some of the York and Lancaster men (65th). There was a Naval Brigade, also some Gatling guns under naval officers. In addition there was an Egyptian battery of artillery under Wodehouse, with native gunners. These were the only Egyptian troops allowed to go to the scene of action; for it had been decided that Sir Evelyn Wood's offer of Egyptian troops was to be declined, much to the disgust of the British officers with his force. The management of the guns was taken over

by the Royal Artillery, however, in action. On some
pretence or other, though, my friend Chamley Turner
had also managed to get down with some men of his
Camel Corps to be employed in transport duty. He
bullied all the authorities in Cairo until they let him
go; indeed, although several times refused, he would
not take no for an answer, and in the end got there.
I may here make a remark *en parenthèse*.

The status of the Egyptian army in those days
was, that it was solely under the command of his
Highness the Khedive, and entirely independent of
the British General in command of the Army of
Occupation in Egypt. Considerable disgust was therefore felt when one day Lord Wolseley, then Adjutant-
General, sent a despatch to Lieut.-General Sir Frederick
Stephenson, commanding in Egypt, instructing him " to
make such use as he deemed fit of the Egyptian forces
of the new army." This was naturally looked upon at
the time as an insult to the Khedive, Sir Evelyn Wood,
and other Egyptian officials who had not been consulted,
and Moberly Bell, the very able ' Times ' correspondent
of those days, had much to say about it. Under the
most favourable aspect it was an uncalled-for blunder,
calculated to give offence most unnecessarily. The
Egyptian officers and troops were only too willing to go
and fight. The Khedive would gladly have accorded
the necessary permission; but since there was no protectorate in Egypt, it was a piece of bad taste on the
part of the English War Office to send such a despatch.

To begin with, we English officers of the Egyptian

army were not then even employed under the War
Office, but solely under the Foreign Office, through
which department of State all correspondence concerning our employment had to pass; and to continue,
Sir Evelyn Baring, the representative of the British
Government and of the Foreign Office, was not even
consulted before this extraordinary despatch was issued
by the gallant general of Tel-el-Kebir, Red River, and
Coomassie fame, who, good soldier though he has ever
proved himself, showed himself upon that occasion
lamentably deficient in the arts which make a diplomatist. Lord Dufferin might have given him a lesson
in the art of doing a thing politely had he only been
asked, but the brusque hand of the successful soldier
was too arbitrary and strong to ask for assistance from
the suave guidance of the diplomât. A little matter
like this, however, is hardly worth dwelling upon after
the lapse of years, so it may be dismissed after these
few reflections, especially as it is now time to end this
chapter.

CHAPTER X.

THE SECOND BATTLE OF EL TEB.

On Leap Year's Day, the 29th February 1884, Graham was ready to advance upon the foe. In the meantime the town of Tokar had capitulated, the governor having made friends with the enemy after Baker's disastrous fight, when he himself had made a sortie only to lose many men killed and wounded. It was nevertheless determined that Graham was to go ahead and crush Osman Digna if possible; accordingly at eight o'clock on the morning of Leap Year's Day he started to do so. The principal members of his Staff were Colonel Sir Redvers Buller, Colonels Herbert Stewart, Clery, Wauchope, and Taylor of the 19th Hussars. "Keggy" Slade of the Egyptian army was also on the Staff as assistant intelligence officer under Colonel Ardagh of the Royal Engineers. In addition to the actual officers of his own large force there were present with him several independent officers. There were Baker Pasha and Captain Harvey, late of the Black Watch, who had been present at Baker's disaster; while Admiral Hewett,

who was determined to be present to see the fun, and
Commander Crawford-Catlin of H.M.S. Sphinx, were
also present with General Graham throughout the
day.

The advance was guided by General Baker, who led
the force a few hundred yards to the right of his old
battle-field to avoid the men trampling over the corpses
which strewed the ground for miles, the sight and smell
of which, moreover, would not be likely to give much
stomach for fighting to the advancing troops. The
front was covered by a capital fellow, Lieutenant Humphreys of the Mounted Infantry. This gallant fellow,
after doing much good service, died an extraordinary
death on the Cairo race-course, where, as the result of
a fall when practising over a jump, he lay for eleven
days with his neck broken, or at any rate dislocated.
He never was moved from the spot where he fell, and
was sensible the whole time till his death, and able to
talk to officers who visited him in the tent erected over
him, and also to make his will. I knew him well, poor
fellow, as he, Pigott, and myself all messed together for
a time in an Arab house in Suakin.

Humphreys' Mounted Infantry scouts became engaged with the enemy after the force had been advancing for about two hours, and before long the enemy
were seen intrenched on a small hill where they had
got two Krupp guns in position, these guns having been
taken from Baker's force at the previous battle.

The enemy hid behind their breastwork and also in
holes in the ground, whence they put out the head and

K

shoulders to carry on a tremendous fire. The shell-fire was very heavy and very fairly accurate, the shells bursting inside the large square into which Graham had now formed his troops; but the enemy's rifle-fire was high. This was fortunate, as they had any amount of Remington rifles and boundless stores of ammunition at their disposal. Although the shells burst in the square, they did not do very much harm. Baker Pasha, however, was hit under the eye by a shrapnel-bullet from one of them, which lodged in the cheek-bone, but would only dismount to have the face bandaged after considerable persuasion, and remounted again at once.

At length, after the Artillery had been pounding back at the enemy's Krupps for a time, and silenced them, the square being halted, a fresh advance was made away to the left and right round to the rear of the enemy's position. Then a most deadly conflict commenced.

The enemy rushed out on all sides to encircle the square, while those in the various forts they had constructed poured in a heavy fire both with their rifles and Krupp guns. A lot of our men were hit at this period, and among them a splendidly athletic young naval officer, Lieutenant Frank Royds of the Carysfort. During my voyage out in the Carysfort he had every evening been the leading spirit among the officers in the way of athletic exercises—indeed his performances on the horizontal bar were almost up to professional form. He was one of the finest young fellows that I have ever known, as handsome as he was brave. But, alas! the ball that struck him was in the stomach, and the wound proved fatal.

As the enemy got near the square their men on the hill ceased firing; but for a change our Gardners and Gatlings got to work under the sailors, while the infantry-men, who were lying down and kneeling, were firing volleys and pouring a perfect stream of lead upon the advancing foe. They fell by dozens; yet not only did the remainder rush on, but even those who were shot down, if not actually dead, got up again and rushed on, brandishing their swords and spears. Some of them got right home to the square, and either stabbed a man or threw their spear before our men, now on their feet, finished them off with the bayonet.

After half an hour's fighting they were drawn off, and retreated, followed by the ringing cheers of our men, who now advanced to get nearer the works and forts. While, however, a halt was called in some broken ground to correct irregularities of distance and to serve out fresh ammunition, the rebels, apparently reinforced, made a fresh advance, and came dodging up behind hills, hillocks, and bushes as close as they could, when they would get up and make a rush at the square.

Luckily our men stood firm, and as the enemy were again driven off, the square advanced up to the fort, which was charged by some sailors under Captain Arthur Wilson of the Hecla, a company of the Black Watch, and some marines. Colonel Burnaby was with them, and it is here that he did so much execution upon the foe with his double-barrelled shot-gun, with which, loaded with slugs, he bowled them over right and left like snipe. This was after he had had his horse shot under him, and he thought that, being on foot, it was a good opportunity for wiping out a few old scores!

Captain Arthur Wilson, an old friend of mine in previous years, here earned the V.C. for a gallant rescue of a marine from a band of savages who were surrounding them. Although his naval sword broke short off in the body of one man, he went on at the rest in seaman-like fashion, striking them in the face with the hilt, and saving his man. Although Wilson and I made several attempts to meet later on at Suakin and elsewhere, it never has been our lot to do so since that day. Thus I have never been able to tell him that I have still in my posssession the original rough sketch drawn on the ground at the time by Fred. Villiers, the celebrated correspondent of the 'Graphic,' of his winning the V.C. What is more, I might have told him that afterwards, when Villiers and I were at Massowah together, I sacrificed myself for hours together in the cause of friendship; for Villiers, wishing to make a finished sketch for the 'Graphic' of Captain Arthur Wilson gaining the V.C., used to make me pose for an hour at a time with sword uplifted over the prostrate bodies of two savages at my feet.

After this first line and the guns were taken, there was another terrific fight to capture the enemy's second position near the village of El Teb, the principal fight being round a large brick factory in front of the village, which was full of the rebels, who were also in pits dug in the ground, and even three or four of them inside an iron boiler lying close by. From the boiler they crept out and attacked our men in the pluckiest way.

The Naval Brigade were chiefly responsible for clearing the factory, which was done by firing in through the loop-holes and windows; but even when the building was taken, the enemy, falling back to a third position, continued shelling our men from the rear of the village, which the Gordon Highlanders took after a bit of a fight among the huts, after which the enemy lost heart and fled in great numbers. As the Black Watch at the same time captured the enemy's last position, in which were found two Krupps, a brass mountain-howitzer, and some rocket-tubes, the second battle of El Teb might now be considered at an end.

The cavalry, under Colonel and Acting Brigadier-General Herbert Stewart, towards the last of the fight was very active in charging the enemy whenever possible; but unfortunately it seems only too probable that they suffered themselves more than the enemy, who stepped behind bushes as they approached, or, lying down behind mounds, jumped up suddenly and slashed and cut at the horses' hocks. When the rider was down, they jumped upon him and speared him. About thirty of their number who

were mounted even charged back at a squadron of
the 19th Hussars which was charging under Colonel
Barrow, and some three of them, after actually getting through Barrow's squadron unhurt, turned and
pursued them. Barrow himself was severely wounded
in arm and side by a spear which was thrown at
him, and there were many other cavalry casualties.
After Barrow was wounded, the squadron he was
with continued charging in the wrong direction; but
Stewart himself caught them up, getting three out
of the four orderlies with him killed or wounded.
The enemy carried with them a short stick curved
at one end. This stick was very heavy, and they
were skilled at throwing it with precision, and it
was the throwing of this weapon at the horses' legs
which brought some of them down.

Although on subsequent occasions we again tried
cavalry against these Hadendowah Arabs, it must be
confessed that they were never a success. They had all
that was required—bravery, skill, and discipline. The
small Arab horses that they had taken over from the
Egyptians proved, although brought into action without
being given a drop of water, that they were capable of
any amount of endurance; but all this was of no avail.
It was of no use to try to charge with cavalry an enemy
who had all the agility of acrobats—who could jump
about and bound from one side to another like an india-
rubber ball. I have myself, for fun, sometimes tried
my best to ride down members of the Amarar tribe
with whom we were friendly. The man I would

pursue would only be armed with a long stick instead of a spear. I have ridden right on to him, and only when actually under my horse's head would he spring to one side, striking me as I passed him with the point of his stick. And this is how our cavalry lost so many at El Teb without doing any harm to the enemy themselves.

The presence of the cavalry, however, was useful, as it overawed the enemy at the time of retreat, and no doubt prevented them from re-forming. Some of the best cavalry fighting was enjoyed by Lieut.-Colonel Webster, who with 100 men of the 10th Hussars, mounted on English horses, employed most of the day in various little actions of his own, being occasionally opposed to considerable numbers of the enemy's mounted men.

Among the cavalry losses were, killed, Major "Monte" Slade of the 10th Hussars, brother to our Slade; Lieutenant Freeman of the 19th Hussars; and Lieutenant Probyn of the 9th Bengal Lancers, who was attached to the 10th. With the exception of Royds of the Navy, the only other officer killed was the quartermaster of the 3d battalion Royal Rifles, Wilkins. But the list of wounded among the officers was a heavy one. There were in addition 24 men killed and 142 wounded, some of whom succumbed. Considering the toughness of the fight, nothing but the steadiness of the troops and the bad shooting of the enemy prevented the list of casualties from being far larger than it was. The enemy, of course, lost enormously.

The immediate effect of the battle was that the next day, March 1, the British troops advanced to the town of Tokar. A few shots were fired at them from outlying Arabs as they advanced, but there was no pretence at a fight. The whole population of the place and its defeated garrison, who were left at liberty by the prompt retreat of the Arabs occupying the town, rushed out to greet General Stewart as he rode forward to reconnoitre with the cavalry. Graham halted all his troops outside Tokar, where he relieved some 750 men, the remnants of the garrison, and many women and children. This, then, was the immediate effect; we have now to chronicle the subsequent results.

Gordon was at this time apparently arranging things in a satisfactory manner at Khartoum. Seeing that the only possible way to get on with the forces he had to contend with was to temporise, he first issued a proclamation to the effect that all domestic slavery would in future be allowed and in no way interfered with, and then sent a messenger to the Mahdi at El Obeid saying that he would be recognised as the Sultan of the province of Kordofan. This conciliatory spirit had for a time very excellent results, and when, on the top of it, the news reached Khartoum, as it swiftly did, of the British victory at El Teb, all the important Arab sheikhs in the neighbourhood came in to Khartoum to make friends with Gordon Pasha. He was in the meantime sending Colonel Stuart on various expeditions in armed steamers up and down the Nile, which expeditions met with little or no resistance. The General, however, knew for a certainty that the temporary quiet in his own immediate neighbourhood could not possibly last unless some other power were raised to counteract the influence of the Mahdi. And as Sir Samuel Baker had cried loudly for the establishment of Sheikh Hussein Khalifa, of Korosko, at the head of the desert tribes between Berber and Suakin, so did Gordon Pasha now begin to cry loudly for the appointment of Zobehr Pasha to the head of the government at Khartoum. This Zobehr was a Soudanese of great power and wealth who had formerly been a large slave-trader. He was, strange to say, a personal enemy of Gordon, who had formerly caught, on some slave-raiding expedition, Zobehr's son Suleiman and put him to death. Zobehr had gone to Cairo on a visit to the Khedive, and was there still at this time, not being allowed to leave, his importance being recognised and his loyalty distrusted.

Gordon, in his characteristic way, did not mind in the least about his being a personal enemy of his own: he felt assured that Zobehr was the only man with sufficient ability and firmness for the post of governor, and was convinced that his arrival in Khartoum would at once draw to his side all the odd tribes of rebels who were scattered without a definite head all over the Soudan. Therefore he kept wiring to Sir Evelyn Baring, "Send me up Zobehr, send me up Zobehr! Tell the Khedive's Ministers to send me up Zobehr and put him in a grand position."

Gordon said that after Graham's victory a couple of

squadrons sent on to Berber would be enough to keep all the people in that part of the world quiet; that our Egyptian troops under Wood—according to the 'Times' he called them Wood's Invincibles—should be sent up the Nile to back them up; and that, further, 100 British troops might go up the Nile as far as Wady Halfa for a two months' picnic. Then he suggested he would himself be able, with the black troops in Berber and Khartoum, to open up the road on the Blue Nile to Sennaar, take out all the Egyptians still there, then leave Zobehr to succeed him, and to put his own men in those parts while the equatorial Bahr Gazelle provinces were evacuated. Zobehr, he said, would not care twopence for the blood-feud with himself, which, if only he were properly paid, would go for nothing. But he urged that something must be done at once, or Graham's victory would be of no use whatever.

But his prayer was not listened to, and Zobehr Pasha was kept under surveillance in Cairo and then sent to Gibraltar. It is evident that neither Sir Evelyn Baring nor the Egyptian Government shared Gordon's belief in the Ethiopian being able to change his skin, and it is possible that they were in the right.

Accordingly, when he went on "howling for Zobehr," just as one's partner at whist frequently meets a similar "howl" for trumps, so was Gordon met by his friends in Cairo and Mr Gladstone in England. They sent Zobehr Pasha off a prisoner to Gibraltar to be out of the way, and instead of following out their partner's plans, continued to play a feeble and vacillating little game of their own which was eminently futile. A vote of censure on the Government policy, moved by the Marquis of Salisbury, being defeated, proved of no use.

After the victory of El Teb, all the British inhabitants of Egypt began to cry out that now was the time to go on as we had begun, and march from Suakin to Berber, and so to Khartoum. Just at first it seemed as if the cry would be listened to, and hopes went up generally when Graham and all his force left Trinkitat and came to land in Suakin, where we were very glad to see him.

It was now for the first time that I realised what an enormous capacity the Egyptian fellah soldier has for manual labour, if not for fighting, and the skill that he can display in carrying out any works, even if pyramids, that he may be ordered to construct. Only a day before his troops arrived from Trinkitat, General Graham sent off for me to come to the ship in the harbour of Suakin upon which he had himself arrived, and asked me if I could build a pier out into the deep water of the creek to the south of the town which would be sufficiently strong and large to permit of the disembarking of his troops, guns, cavalry, and stores.

I had not the slightest idea how to build a pier, and I had no materials that I knew of with which to build one. I could therefore only reply to the General that I would do my best; and then going ashore, I got hold of Mahmoud Ali, the chief of the native police, a fine fellow, who was partly Turk and partly Hadendowah, and of an Egyptian gendarmerie sergeant-major whose name I forget. The Egyptian said it could be done in a satisfactory manner if only I could get the material; and as I had spotted a lot of square blocks of coralstone lying about ready for house-building purposes, I told Mahmoud Ali to impound me some boats to carry it across the creek, and, with any amount of Egyptians, I set to work to seize all this stone without asking "With your leave" or "By your leave" from anybody; and thus, in spite of great outcry from the rich owner of the stone, the pier was started. The Egyptians had no materials to work with, except little baskets in which to carry these stones and earth, with which materials alone I was going to construct my pier. My Egyptian sergeant-major, however, pointed out to me that something was required for binding purposes, and that seaweed would do excellently well in default of better material. So well did the men work with the seaweed, sand, and stones, that within twentyfour hours we had constructed right out into the deep water a splendid pier alongside which the largest steam-launches and boats were able to lie. Not only was the pier made solid, but we had strong posts and bulkheads firmly planted all round, to which the boats could moor. The troops were therefore able to commence disembarking at once, and the pier, which was strengthened afterwards by the Royal Engineers, is, I believe, standing to this day.

At the close of the 1884 campaign I saw that General

Graham had been kind enough to mention me in despatches for my services in building this wharf; but the real people who deserved all the credit for it were my sergeant-major and the fellaheen under him.

Apart from the personal satisfaction I had in being able to facilitate matters in this way for the landing of the troops, I had an additional satisfaction in seizing this stone when I found that it belonged to a wealthy sheikh, an old scoundrel, who was one of the headmen of the town, and who, I was perfectly certain, was an ardent sympathiser with the rebels.

This old man gave us a great deal of trouble later on when Colonel Chermside was Governor-General of the Red Sea littoral; for this gallant officer, although a very good diplomât, was always being humbugged by the old wretch, to whose representations on various points he was inclined to offer a too willing ear, even if it were to the disadvantage of the British officers serving under him. I well remember a case in point. The sheikh, on the strength of being the richest man in the place, used to allow his donkeys, of which he had many, to run wild and eat the Government *tibbin*, the chopped straw for the cavalry and Camel Corps. Pigott, who cared for no sheikh living, was for a short time in command of the cavalry, and finding the *tibbin* for his horses going too quick, he sensibly seized and shot one of these donkeys, a fact which Colonel Chermside considered to be fraught with "grave political contingencies," and which he said must not occur again. Therefore when, on a similar occasion, after Pigott had left, I merely

seized and imprisoned the sheikh's asses without shooting them, I imagined I was quite within my rights.
Not so thought Chermside Pasha. He ordered me to
release the "cuddies," and also to apologise to the
sheikh for having captured them, no matter how much
Government *tibbin* they might have digested. I let
the donkeys go, but refused to apologise to the Arab,
not seeing the advantage of diplomacy quite so much
as did the gallant Sapper.

But to get back to "our muttons." I got the sheikh's
stones, and so the army was landed.

After El Teb, Pigott still remained attached to the
British cavalry, while Hallam Parr and myself for a
while did the best in our power with the gendarmerie
troops, who were, however, being found "quite impossible," sent away to Egypt whenever an opportunity
occurred. By degrees we thus got rid of the most of
them, and as we found that there was going to be a
second expedition against Osman Digna, we asked the
Admiral under whose orders we were, and the General
Officer commanding, if we could not be taken on to the
British strength. There was not much difficulty about
this; but as there were so many Staff officers already
with Graham's force, the only billet open to Parr and
myself, and which we were obliged to accept, was with
the transport department of the British army. As far
as I was personally concerned, General Herbert Stewart
asked permission to take me on his personal staff as
his interpreter. For once, however, the knowledge of
Arabic was rather a disadvantage than otherwise; for,

purely on account of my knowledge of that heathen
tongue, I was condemned to remain with the transport
and look after all the native camel-drivers.

An advance being determined on to Tamai, and the
passing of stores, and especially of water, to the front
being very necessary, this billet kept us constantly on
the go before the troops advanced, especially as a half-
way post in the desert, called Baker's zeriba, had to be
stored before the advance took place. This zeriba,
which was occupied by a detachment of the Black
Watch, was about seven miles out from Suakin, part of
the journey to it leading through pretty open desert,
while the remainder led through high mimosa-bushes
capable of hiding any number of the enemy. The zeriba
itself was a high and very strong fence of thorny brushwood, which had originally been made with great care
by Baker's men, and it surrounded a wide open space
capable of holding a large camp. There was only one
gateway at the north side, which gate was never closed,
and which there were no preparations made for closing
—a curious oversight.

In addition to Parr and myself, a third Egyptian,
Chamley Turner to wit, was hard at work on the convoy service; and the odd thing was, that although our
convoys were continually sent out with no manner of
escort, no attack on them was ever made. As a matter
of fact, it was a very great risk to send out unprotected
convoys in this way; but the Admiral was in constant
communication with the sheikhs of the Amarar tribe,
who declared themselves our friends, and these people

represented to him that Osman Digna's men had received such a lesson that they would never fight again. This every one believed at first, so the convoys of camels, with water and stores, pranced every day gaily backwards and forwards through the desert entirely unprotected, and by good luck more than by good management were never attacked, for apparently Osman Digna was napping.

Osman Digna, who was the nominal general of the enemy, was by origin a man of no importance. He had, according to report, been a shoemaker in Suakin, and amassing a little money, had then gone in for the slave-trade from that post to the Red Sea coast at Jeddah. Osman had, however, been pretty nearly ruined by the capture of his slave dhows by British men-of-war's boats about the time of the commencement of the disturbances, when the Mahdi, whom he personally knew, delegated to him the organisation of the rebellion in the provinces of the Eastern Soudan. With the exception of the siege of Sinkat, where he was wounded, Osman Digna was never known actually to come under fire in any of the numerous engagements which took place around Suakin. He would, on the contrary, stay at a distance with a body-guard and pray for the success of the force whom he would despatch to fight,—an eminently successful proceeding as far as he himself was concerned, for although by rumour killed a hundred times, he is still alive and kicking. I have myself once or twice, while engaged with the Hadendowahs outside Suakin, seen Osman

Digna's praying brigade in the distance, but he never came within rifle-shot.

In spite of all the *pourparlers* in which Admiral Hewett indulged with the enemy, as Osman Digna declined to come in and surrender, the advance to Tamai was decided to be an absolute necessity. Much fighting was not considered probable, or indeed even possible, but it was thought necessary to make a show of strength.

The advance was made in a division of two brigades, one under that downright soldier Major-General John Davis and the other under Brigadier-General Sir Redvers Buller, their first night's march being out to the zeriba above-mentioned, the whole advance being covered by cavalry scouts. Well do I remember the moonlight night when, coming back with an empty convoy of camels from Baker's zeriba towards Suakin, I met the gallant Davis and his *kharkee*-coated warriors of the left brigade plodding out through the sand. I, from the eminence of a camel's back, saw them long before they saw us, our splay-footed beasts making no sound on the desert soil. I had one other officer with me, but no men except camel-drivers, and this officer wisely suggested that we should make a *détour* and avoid the advancing brigade, for fear of being fired at. The cavalry advance-guard extending hardly enough to the left, the ease with which I could have done this gave me at once an idea of how readily an enemy, especially if mounted, could have turned their flanks, and, by making a sudden flank-attack, created a panic, and themselves escaped unhurt.

L

I had, however, a message for General Davis from the officer in command of the zeriba, and so held straight on, although, when our camels were at length discovered, this circumstance was the signal for a general halt of the brigade.   Before the General rode up to me, I could easily in the silent air hear the excited remarks of the men to the effect, "There they are ! They're coming on !"   They were thoroughly disappointed to find it was, after all, only a friendly convoy, and that they were therefore unable to shoot at sight.   It is almost a wonder that they did not do so; for weird indeed must have been the sudden and silent appearance of a lot of mounted men on camels amidst tall and sparse bushes in the moonlight, in a country where every shadow might conceal a foe.

CHAPTER XI.

THE BATTLE OF TAMAI.

VERY nearly the same troops were concerned in the affair of Tamai as in that of El Teb; but I had the advantage of being personally present at Tamai, while when Teb was fought I was amusing myself by drilling the mutinous troops by day, and trying to dodge the wells on my rounds by night. General Graham was very kind to me, and told me that he would be glad to see me at the front should there be another engagement; but he shared frankly the popular opinion that the enemy were knocked out of time. When, however, he had marched out with his two brigades, and when I learned from Admiral Hewett himself that the enemy were going to make a stand, and that a battle was imminent on the morrow, I determined that, by hook or by crook, I would be present at it.

The Admiral backed my plans; and as water was a commodity which would be greatly required, I started from Suakin with a long convoy of camels laden with water the evening before the fight. Sir William Hewett and G. D. Giles, neither of whom was this time allowed to face the foe again, both rode out with me into the desert until after nightfall, the cheery old Admiral chaffing me most heartily all the time at the slow rate of progress I was making, owing to the constant falling off of the water-skins and *zamzamichs*, a peculiar tin arrangement used in Egypt for carrying water on mules or camels. Every time a load fell off the whole convoy had to halt, and it was frequently a difficult matter to stop the men who were going strong at the head when a rear camel either refused to proceed or the skins fell off his back. I had, however, a good aide-de-camp in the person of my only armed escort, my civilian servant Alfred Thacker, who, being mounted on a good horse of mine, and armed not only with a revolver but with a good hunting-crop, kept the unruly camel-drivers in the front in order if I was busy in rear, and *vice versa*.

At last the Admiral and Giles left me, and I struggled as far as Baker's zeriba, where I arrived an hour after nightfall. Here, halting all my camels outside, I went in and reported my arrival to General Herbert Stewart, who with his cavalry brigade was halted there, all the infantry having gone on early in the day for a ten-mile march to the front. There was, I remember, to my surprise, no guard at the gate.

The inside of that zeriba was on that evening a wonderful example of what work coupled with organisation can effect. Arranged in an oblong square, in the middle of the zeriba, were heaps of boxes of stores, sacks of corn, and bales of *tibbin*, all piled one upon the top of the other as neatly as if they had been arranged in peace-time in a barrack square in England. There were also capital water-troughs arranged for watering the mules, which, just as I arrived, were all fighting to get to the troughs at once as only mules will fight under such circumstances.

The senior officer of the Commissariat whom I found there, and who was worthy of praise for all this order and arrangement, was a man called Jessop. I do not know what has become of him since, nor whether he be alive or dead; but I can honestly say that, while doubtless an excellent commissariat-man, I found him a most disagreeable person to have anything to do with, so eaten up was he with red-tape and officialism. If he had had his way, he would have kept back all the water I had brought with me there at Baker's zeriba, and I should never have got to the battle, and there would have been no water for the army in front. But General Stewart wisely overruled his representations, and ordered him only to take a third of what I had brought, giving me instructions to march for the front, where water of course was most wanted, very early in the morning with the remainder.

When I had delivered over to Jessop, accordingly, all the water that he was to get, I asked him to be good enough to allow me a certain amount of water for my own two horses. This he refused, on the grounds of water not being sufficient even for English much less for Egyptian officers' horses, of there not being a proper "indent" made out in regular form, signed by the competent officer, and other foolish excuses of the same sort. I then asked my friend if, since water was so scarce, he would be kind enough to give me a ration of corn for my two horses. Would he? Not a bit of it! He said that all the corn was entered on lists, that rations were numbered, that he had not proper authority —in fact, made objections just the same as before.

Turning my back upon the gentleman of "the cart-train," as we used to call them, I called my servant Alfred. Showing him a soldier's discarded flannel shirt lying on the ground, I said, " Alfred, the Commissariat officer refuses to give us corn; do you think you could ' find ' some near any of those thousands of sacks ? "

" I think I can, sir," answered Alfred, with a twinkle in his eye, taking out his pocket-knife.

In a few minutes he returned with the shirt, the sleeves of which he had tied up, filled full unto bursting with the corn which he had "found."

In the meantime I had very easily settled the water question ; for, considering that the labourer was worthy of his hire, I simply unloaded one of my own camels and took as much water as I required. But for all the assistance I obtained from the Commissariat, my horses might have starved not only that night but all next day. I had no transport myself whatever, as it was as much as the camels could do to stagger along under their loads, and it was, letting courtesy alone, a matter of right for me to obtain water and rations both for man and beast under the circumstances.

The beasts got their feed all right, though, but my servant and I went to rest on the ground hungry and thirsty that night. For although I saw General Stewart and all his staff enjoying an excellent meal while I was talking to the General and making arrangements with him about continuing my march, I was left, like the thirteenth little pig of the sow that had only provision for twelve, without being asked to take either bite or sup.

What grieved and pained me most was perhaps seeing my brother Egyptian " Keggy " Slade, with a beautiful bottle of beer poured out in a long tumbler standing by his side and other bottles close at hand, while it never seemed to enter into his head for a moment that I might possibly be thirsty after my trying march, half of which had been passed in helping to lash water-skins on to the backs of refractory camels. Ah! if he had only known what my thirst was, as I stood by, I almost think that he would have asked me to take a drink. What a friend he would have made of me for life for one little bottle of beer! Thus are we all—creatures of the stomach!

Well do I remember that night, the 12th of March 1884, as one of the most beautiful nights I have ever witnessed on this earth of ours. What did it matter to us then, as, entirely without cover of any sort, with our heads upon our saddles, my servant and I lay by the camels, if the following night should find us dead? Our only wish was to be present in the fight; the contingency of death alarmed us far less than it would have done if assailed by some insidious disease which we knew to be fatal. The only fear we had was, as a matter of fact, lest in the brilliant moonlight we should be attacked, not by Arabs but by moonstroke. Alfred Thacker kept a diary which I saw later. In it he had made the following note: "The Major and me covered our faces with our handkerchiefs for fear of moonstroaks, which is very prevalent in these parts"!

I had found part of an old Soudanese straw basket, with which, as we met with so little hospitality inside the zeriba, we made two impromptu mattresses; and having seen to the camels, which I did not unload at all that night, we slept until 2.30 A.M., when we rose and made a couple of cups of cocoa from a tin in our wallets. Then we started on our march to an unknown front with no guide and no escort. My plan of action before saying good-night to Stewart had been definitely arranged; it was that I was to start at 4 A.M., to follow the gun-tracks in the sand, and to travel in a south-westerly direction, where he told me I should see after a time a certain hill, on which would be encamped our troops. He himself would, he said, start two hours later at the latest, probably sooner, and would then detach a squadron to find and join me, and bring me to the place where General Graham and his force were bivouacked.

Accordingly I started at 4 A.M. The moon being as bright as day, I had for some miles no difficulty in following the tracks of the gun-wheels in the sand, but after a time things became more difficult. There were horses' tracks everywhere, and going in all directions. Evidently the cavalry scouts had been out and had returned that way; the guns also had changed their line of march, and the wheel-tracks had been completely obliterated. We had after a time no idea of the exact direction in which to go, but, guided by the moon and the stars, managed to keep on pretty well on the line which we imagined to be the right one. And thus the day broke, and we expected momentarily to see the escorting squadron which had been promised to us; but no squadron came, and we were lost! The army at the front was left without water, and supposing we did not find it, might be, for all we knew, reduced to very sore straits for the want of that precious fluid. All this time my native camel-drivers were wanting to bolt; but Alfred and I showed them the revolver pretty frequently, and to this day I do not know how it was we did not blow out a few of their brains.

At length, an hour after daybreak, Alfred Thacker, who had particularly good eyesight, saw the cavalry far away to our right going at a sharp pace in the direction which we ourselves should doubtless have followed. There were, however, no signs of any squadron being detached to look after the water convoy. No; they were all so anxious to get to the front in time for the fight that such a simple detail as water for the combatants was altogether forgotten.

And then! suddenly a native, one solitary native, armed with spear, shield, and sword, rose up in front of us from amid the long grass and rough bushes.

There was instantly a stampede among the camel-drivers, who imagined that there were 100 or 1000 more hidden close by, as indeed there might have been. We stopped the flight of our camelmen and captured the native, for fortunately there were no more than one, and he, when captured and deprived of his arms, declared himself to be friendly. As he did no unfriendly action to us, possibly he was. I attached him to my staff, at all events, for the rest of that day, after which he disappeared, and I never saw him again. But I made a great deal of use of him while I had him under my own eye; and Alfred made use of him too, making him hold his horse whenever he wanted to dismount, or help to reload a camel which had cast its load. It was a lucky thing for us that he was the only native there, for had there been half-a-dozen only, there would have been no water in the front zeriba for the troops after the battle.

It was a glorious morning. The grass in the desert was green after recent rains, the mimosa and other bushes were all putting out their shoots. On one side, as we advanced, we saw scuttling away a group of gazelles; on the other would be seen flying off a flock of sand-grouse. Hares scampered about in every direction, partridges and guinea-fowls were calling on every side. There was such an exhilarating freshness in the morning air that one felt inclined to offer up a prayer to the Almighty Maker of all things, and to say, " O God, this is a glorious world; this is a day in which we should offer up thanks to Thee that we are allowed to live." And yet, although it was, as far as I remember, a Sabbath morn, it was a day devoted to killing and slaughter, and to nothing else.

As we advanced, presently we heard the report of a gun, then faintly came the detonation of the shell bursting, the smoke from which, like a fleece of wool, gently hung for a few moments along the side of a distant hill, and then faded as gently away. Then another gun and another, after which some very desultory musketry-fire in the distance.

It was nothing of importance, only that the Mounted Infantry and the enemy were firing a few shots at each other, while the Artillery were just despatching a shell or two to remind every one that, although nature was beautiful and worthy of admiration, the end of all nature is death.

We got the camels up in time before the troops started for the fight; and to show how plainly any distinctive badge is noticed in an army, long before I reached the troops I had noticed among them all the only three other officers of the Egyptian army who were not distinctly serving with the English army as Englishmen. These were Chamley Turner, Hallam Parr, and Pigott. They all wore, as I did myself, a bright red *puggaree* round their white helmets,—for we had in active service discarded the fez and taken to the helmet. Very pretty, too, I thought it looked, as I saw Pigott sitting grimly on his horse in front of a cavalry regiment, his one spot of colour relieving the whole tedium of a regiment in sad-coloured *kharkee*.

On entering the zeriba, which was, by the bye, a very poor and useless affair, made very hurriedly the night before, I at once met General Graham, who was very genial and cheery as usual.

"Hulloa, Haggard!" said he; "so you have got here after all! Well, I am glad to see you; but I am afraid that you are not going to see anything, for I fear they won't fight."

I then unfolded a special communication with which I had been intrusted for the General by the Admiral at the last moment, to the effect that the enemy were going to attack in force from a ravine.

"Oh yes," said the General; "I know all that already. Well, we shall see presently."

And we did!

Ten minutes later the two squares marched off, the left square being under Major-General Davis, and the right under Sir Redvers Buller. It was the left which got nearly all the fighting. As far as pluck goes, the enemy were just as brave as at El Teb. They smashed up the left square for a time and got inside it, and took, moreover, two of our Gatling guns from our blue-jackets. I never in all my life heard such a hellish din as that which prevailed for an hour or two at the battle of Tamai, and I never was under such a hellish fire as that which I was then under. For Parr, Chamley Turner, and myself being on the transport, were left with some details in the so-called

zeriba; and as the enemy attacked from several sides
at once, we not only got the enemy's fire, but also
much of the fire from the rear face of the left, General
Davis's square, and from the right, Buller's square, as
well!

Suddenly we were vigorously attacked ourselves by
quantities of the enemy, who came steadily on round
our flank, running and skipping, and exclaiming all
the time in hoarse guttural tones, "Allah! Allah!"

Parr then excited my admiration. There was a
certain amount of — what shall I call it? — astonishment among the few troops left in the zeriba; but
Parr quickly put the fear of God — not of the enemy
— into them. He rallied them, and by his coolness
soon disposed of this attack. Chamley Turner and I
were with him, and we three had a jolly good fight;
and although I may not always have approved of
everything that Hallam Parr subsequently did as regards Egyptian organisation, I would, after my experience of the battle of Tamai, never ask for anything
better than to go into action again under Hallam Parr.

CHAPTER XII.

MORE ABOUT TAMAI—WOUNDED ARABS SHAMMING DEATH—
A NIGHT SCARE.

WHILE we in the zeriba were being attacked, so also
was Buller's Brigade, which was in a good square away
to our right front; but although many of the enemy
got quite close to the square, they were all, if not
killed sooner, shot down within a distance of from
ten to fifteen yards. There was intense fanaticism
among them, and they advanced steadily, if only to
die. Among others there was a boy of only about
fifteen years of age who advanced armed with one of
the heavy curved sticks I have mentioned, which at
the battle of El Teb they threw at the horses. He too
had to be killed, for had he been spared he might have
knocked a man's brains out with his stick. In fact, one
of the first of our wounded was a naval officer who was
for a time knocked nearly senseless by a crack from
one of these sticks. He was, I think, a Lieutenant
Conybeare, but I cannot remember for certain; I only
recollect that the poor fellow looked most deadly sick.

We lost in the action 110 officers and men killed, and

either 99 or 100 wounded. The large proportion of
killed to wounded was caused by the enemy getting
inside the 2d Brigade square and coming to close
quarters with the men, stabbing and hacking with their
spears and frightfully sharp long swords like demons.
The way this came about was as follows.

The 2d Brigade were, under General Davis, advancing in a square, the front face of which was composed
of half a battalion respectively of the York and Lancaster Regiment and of the Black Watch. The sides
of the square were composed of the other half-battalions
of these regiments, while the battalion of Royal Marines
formed the rear face.

Suddenly, as the square approached the incline leading to the ravine about which Admiral Hewett had
sent the message by me to General Graham, an enormous number of the enemy appeared charging upon
the square. The left half front and left face of the
square, consisting of the Black Watch, were then, as
subsequent events proved rashly, ordered by General
Graham himself to charge in turn, and rushed forward
to do so, when the enemy, under cover of the smoke,
rushed round both flanks of the advancing line, getting
in behind them by the large openings left as they had
advanced. They then attacked the men of the front
line furiously both in front and in rear at once, when
the York and Lancaster men fell back behind the
Naval Brigade, which, with its Gardners and Gatling
guns, was just in rear of the left flank of the leading line.

There was considerable confusion—in fact an actual

panic—for a time, almost the whole Brigade, with exception of the Naval Brigade with its guns, rapidly retreating towards the zeriba, with the rebels after, around,
and among them.   The unfortunate sailors stuck man-
fully to their guns until they had three officers and a
number of men killed, when the remainder had to
abandon their Gatlings and retreat also.

During this temporary success of the enemy the
Black Watch and York and Lancaster men suffered
terribly.   This was before the zeriba was attacked.
Having fortunately unloaded in time all my camels of
their water-skins and emptied them into the canvas
water-tanks, I, having nothing to do, had ridden out
towards the left square a short way to see what was
going on.   Then I observed the tremendous commotion
caused by this terrific hand-to-hand combat, though, so
great was the smoke, I could not realise more than that
the tide of war was apparently sweeping the square
back to the zeriba.   In a very short time the whole
formation of the square was changed; the square had
indeed ceased to be a square, and looked to me more
like a long line.   Then suddenly I saw two companies
of the Royal Marines, with their bayonets flashing in
the sun, entirely detached from the rest and away to
the right by themselves, repelling in excellent order
the thousands of savages around them.   I shall never
forget the flashing of those bayonets in the bright sun
before, the rolling smoke in a few minutes hiding all
from my view, I went back to the zeriba, where all the
camelmen and the camels were just then running away

as hard as they could go. And then the right face of
the zeriba was, as described in the last chapter, immediately attacked itself.

So critical did things look at this time that Cameron,
who was the special war correspondent of the 'Standard,'
galloped back as hard as he could go to Suakin in order
to get in first the telegraphic news of a reverse. In
this action he was, however, a little premature, and he
got himself severely disliked in consequence by Sir
William Hewett, who refused a little later on to allow
poor Cameron, under any circumstances, to accompany
him on his mission to Abyssinia, although he had all
his kit ready to start. He in consequence lent me
his camp-bed, which I in turn lent to Fred Villiers of
the 'Graphic' at Massowah, who has it still, as poor
Cameron was afterwards killed at Abou Klea.

Had Cameron stayed a little longer, he would have
seen a great change in the position of affairs. For
Stewart, who with his cavalry brigade was halted away
to the left, selected this time to make a demonstration
against the right flank of the successful foe. With
drawn swords the cavalry charged, but profiting by
the lesson learnt at El Teb, the orders given to the
officers in command were not to press the charge home
among the bushes unless absolutely obliged to do so to
save the retreating infantry.

The sight of the cavalry advancing was fortunately
enough to frighten the enemy, who first paused and
then turned to fall back. Then Colonel Wood of the
10th Hussars dismounted a large number of his men,

M

and with their carbines they poured a heavy fire into the foe, in which they were seconded by the Mounted Infantry. This cavalry manœuvre saved the day as far as the 2d Brigade was concerned; for the few minutes' respite allowed their officers time to get the men together again, and advancing, they drove all before them, sweeping the enemy into the ravine and recapturing the lost Gatlings. The cavalry and the infantry, continuing to advance, took possession of the wells in the ravine, where there was a fairly good supply of water. Still driving the enemy before them, they advanced up the heights the other side of the ravine and took Osman Digna's camp in the village of Tamai, where the enemy tried to make a final stand. This village consisted of groups of mat huts and tents. These were burned and enormous stores of rifles and ammunition set fire to on the following day, when the whole of the troops except the sailors advanced again from their bivouac.

After an advance in the direction of the hills the troops all started to return to Suakin two days after the big fight, Osman Digna having eluded them, and being, as the Arabs said, "Zay kelb fil gebbel" (Like a dog in the mountains). That this was rather different from the position he apparently expected to have been in may be judged by the arrogant tone of a letter which he sent to the Admiral only three or four days before the battle of Tamai. It gives a good idea of the religious motives for the war from the Arab point of view, and began as follows:—

" In the name of the most merciful God, the Lord be praised! From the whole of the tribes and the sheikhs who have received your writings to the Commandant of the English soldiers, whom may God help to Islam. Know that the gracious God has sent His Mahdi suddenly, who was expected, the looked-for messenger for the religions and against the infidels, so as to show the religion of God through him, and by him to kill those that hate Him — which has happened. You have seen who have gone to him from the people and the soldiers, who are countless. God killed them, so look at the multitudes.

" You, who never know religion till after death, hate God from the beginning. Then we are sure that God and only God sent the Mahdi, so as to take away your property. And you know this since the time of our Lord Mahomed's coming. Pray to God and be converted.

" There is nothing between us but the sword, especially as the Mahdi has come to kill you and destroy you unless God wishes you to come to Islam. The Mahdi's sword be on your necks wherever you may go, and God's iron round your necks.

" Do not think that you are enough for us, and the Turks are only a little better than you. We will not leave your heads unless you become Mussulmans and listen to the Prophet and laws of God.

" So there is nothing for you but the sword, so that there will not remain one of you on the face of the earth." '

The foregoing is only a part of Osman Digna's arrogant letter. It sounded like a declaration of war in the time of the Crusades from some Saracen Sultan to the Christian leader of those days. But for all his boastings and invocations of the name of God, Osman Digna was now deserted by all his followers, and a price of $5000 was set upon his head, dead or alive.

Had it not been that orders came out by telegraph from home to Admiral Hewett to withdraw the offer of this reward, which order was a mere sop thrown by Gladstone to the Exeter Hall division, Osman Digna would soon have been nothing but a name of the past. The humanitarian scream against setting a price on that man's head was, however, entirely a mistaken idea. For owing to its being listened to, that one fanatic brute was allowed, it is true, to go free; but the preservation of his single worthless and mischievous life was the direct cause of the loss of thousands of other lives, both Mahomedans and Christians, during the twelve months which followed the withdrawal of the offered reward for his capture.

Before quite leaving the subject of the battle-field of Tamai a few remarks on various trifling details connected with it seem not out of place; for there are little things connected with a big matter which, if not put on record by one who knows, are lost for ever. The first of these is the great bravery and coolness displayed by General Graham himself. He rode about everywhere where the fire was the hottest, with a red flag accompanying him to denote his presence, as calmly as if he were walking his horse up Rotten Row. He even appeared quite unconcerned when an agile Arab, jumping up behind him on his horse and placing his arms round his waist, was his unwelcome fellow-traveller for some time. With his red flag over him, his tall figure was so conspicuous that I was forced, even in the heat of action, to think of Macaulay's lines—

> " And in they burst, and on they rushed,
>   While like a guiding star
> Amid the thickest carnage blazed
>   The helmet of Navarre."

After the bravery of our own General, the pluck of the Arabs was worthy of the highest praise. For instance, after the Arabs had captured the Gatlings, a couple of them quietly and calmly, under a tremendous fire directed on them, opened the box of a limber, found a bottle of oil in it, poured the oil over the limber, and set fire to it. After this they walked quietly away, untouched by the bullets and thoroughly well pleased with themselves.

There were several narrow escapes even after the battle was virtually over, and one or two deaths were caused by the horrible custom of the wounded Arabs of jumping up behind and killing some unsuspecting soldier who thought them, as they pretended to be, dead. A few lives were lost in this way at El Teb, and there was especially one smart sergeant of Engineers killed by one of these men "foxing dead" at Tamai. In consequence of these habits there were no prisoners made, for to go near a wounded man to help him or to

give him water was to run the risk of getting your
throat cut with a horrible curved knife which the
Hadendowahs wore fastened to the left arm. Owing
to this detestable habit the soldiers went round, in
some cases two together, and shot every wounded or
shamming man they found. The Arabs who were not
dead lay quite still with a sheet, which they usually
carried wound round their waists, drawn up over their
faces and bodies as if asleep, or like a corpse decently
covered. One "Tommy" would stealthily approach,
seize the end of the sheet and whip it off his face. Up
would jump the Arab, when the other "Tommy," who
was waiting with a loaded rifle, shot him.

This was a fairly safe amusement when indulged in
in couples, but not so safe when followed by one man
alone. For some time I watched through my glasses
one of the Black Watch who was going round by himself poking the apparently dead men with his bayonet.
If they jumped up he shot them. He was taking it
very easy as if he liked the job, and smoking. Ten
minutes later I rode over to where I had seen him last.
I found the Highlander lying quite dead beside a pretty
active savage who was only slightly wounded in the
leg. My servant, Alfred Thacker, who had been very
useful during the fight in various ways—among others
in rescuing Parr's horse—was by at the time. Being
a mere civilian, he was of a particularly bloodthirsty
nature where savages were concerned, and as far as
I remember, he avenged the Highlander by adding
that particular Hadendowah's scalp to his list, which

was, I fancy, already a pretty long one. For according to his own diary, which I have already once quoted, he had been doing a little slaughtering on his own account, as I well remember the following passage therein: "About this time there was a good deal of the enemy around, which I amused of myself with a-killing of a few of them"!

On the march of the troops back to Suakin I was witness to one of those extraordinary night-scares which sometimes occur among even the best-disciplined troops. I had brought out a large convoy of water from Suakin to Baker's zeriba, which was being made a half-way house for the wounded, and some short distance outside which on the south side were encamped for the night Buller's Brigade, the south side being the side farthest away from the gateway, which was, as I have before stated, the only entrance.

Having arrived early in the evening, I had, after unloading them, left my fifty camels with their drivers, and then, I remember, had shared a frugal meal of tinned soup and "bully beef" with Rainsford of the Commissariat, who was as kind and hospitable as a man could be, which was a pleasant change from my previous visit to the zeriba. The wounded officers and men were in hospital tents inside the zeriba, to the west side of the oblong of boxes piled up in the middle; and there was also encamped there a detachment of troops under a major of the Black Watch, to whom I had remarked that the fact of his having no guard upon the entrance of the zeriba would make it easy for an enemy to march in or out if they liked at night, even with camels, as I had done myself. "What's the use of tiring the men with extra guard duty," he replied. "The enemy are beaten; they will never try to rush the zeriba." It was no business of mine to say any more, or to suggest that any amount of commissariat stores might be pilfered by any one,—my own camelmen, for instance, just as I had helped myself to corn on the occasion of my own last visit,—that was his look-out.

After dinner and a smoke, Rainsford and I lay down on some blankets close to the boxes to get out of the brilliant moonlight. I had one blanket of my own on that occasion, and his servant, a capital "Tommy," I well remember, produced me another from somewhere. The only articles I removed were my sword, revolver, and spurs. I kept on my long brown boots, and I remember telling Rainsford he had better do the same, as it was as well never to remove one's boots on active service. He, however, poor chap, had not had his boots off for about a week, and considered that the presence of a brigade of the British troops close by justified him in for once indulging in the slight approach to comfort which their removal would procure him. We were soon sound asleep, his head being just by my feet, for we were wearied out with work. I do not know how long we had been sleeping, when suddenly we heard one or two rifle-shots from the direction of the men bivouacked outside. Then there was heard through the silent night a roar of voices as if it were the roar of the sea coming in with a tidal wave towards us.

All we sleepers jumped up, and the first thing I remember was hearing men saying, "The enemy are upon us! they are rushing the zeriba!" Half asleep, I jumped up to look for my revolver and sword, which I had laid on the boxes. Being quite dazed, I went to the wrong side of the boxes and could not find either. This was perhaps fortunate, for even as I did so I saw dark figures all around me, bounding and jumping over the high barrier of boxes, whom I was convinced were the enemy, and on whom I should certainly have fired. After a few moments, during which I remember congratulating myself that I had kept my boots on, I found my revolver, and by this time was able to see that it was our own men, soldiers and sailors alike, who were leaping over the boxes, having come through the tremendously thick face on the south side. I, of course, then imagined that the enemy had rushed the camp in front, and, as the commotion continued, thinking of my camels, I ran off to the place where I had left them outside the gate and brought the whole fifty in, for there being no guard any one could come and go as they liked. As I brought them in I found two blue-jackets outside the gate of the zeriba: they had bare feet full of thorns, having come in by a short cut and run out the other side. On stopping them and asking them what was up in front, the answer I got from one of them was, "I don't know nothing, sir; we was asleep, and waking up and seein' every one else a-boltin', we ran away too."

By the time I had got the camels safely in, with their legs tied, lying down in a row inside, the uproar had ceased. Then, as I went round to the hospital tents, I found that all the wounded, especially poor Prendergast, a doctor, who had a frightful spear-wound through his back from a blow delivered on him while attending a patient, had in their alarm run out of their tents and were in a sorry plight. I also saw two complete companies of a certain regiment, all of whom had come in through the terrible thorn fence, being formed up by their officers. I then for the first time learnt the meaning of it all. It was a pure scare, which, without any enemy at all to cause it, had alarmed the whole brigade. A sleeping man had had a dream, jumped up and discharged his rifle, some others near him had done the same thing, and then the whole mass of men, all half-asleep, had stampeded just like a stampede of horses or cattle. This night alarm was described by the correspondents in the papers as follows: "A slight scare took place among our troops last night." I remember thinking at the time that if only it had been some of our "Gyppies" who had bolted like this two days after a successful battle, the special correspondents would have had no words strong enough to describe "the horrible demoralisation of those cowardly Egyptians."

CHAPTER XIII.

AFTER the troops returned from Tamai to Suakin a pretence of an advance was made for a short distance on the Berber road through the mountains, a long chain of which run down parallel to the sea the whole length of the Red Sea coast. We had fought on the edge of these mountains at Tamai. The next thing done was to send out the cavalry, the Mounted Infantry, and a battalion of infantry to a native village called Handoub, twelve miles west of Suakin.

This Handoub was a native village of mat huts situated at the mouth of the *khor* or ravine through which the caravan-road to Berber passed. There were some wells at Handoub of rather brackish but still drinkable water, so it was possible to form a camp there, which was accordingly done. It would be tedious to relate in detail all the movements of troops for the following fortnight or so, for they resulted in very little.

Osman Digna was supposed to be at a village called

Tamanieb, so after advancing up the *khor* first to Otao and then to Hambuk, twenty-seven miles from Suakin, a move was made on this place Tamanieb, scarcely any trouble at all being found from the enemy throughout the movement. Thus, as Osman Digna had disappeared somewhere else, the troops returned to Suakin.

Now the road to Berber was virtually open, had it only been decided to go on, and some caravans of natives, non-combatants of course, arrived through it unmolested. But it was decided by the Government that the Soudan campaign of 1884 was now to be considered at an end, and the British troops withdrawn to Cairo.

Situated 241 miles from Suakin, Berber itself is nothing but a mud town on the right bank of the Nile; but it was very important as an objective point at that particular time, as to have advanced there would have placed us in direct steamboat communication with Gordon at Khartoum. It may be urged that there was not sufficient water on the road for the troops, and further, that at that time of the year the weather was too hot. That these statements are fallacious I think I can show. While admitting freely that there was not enough water for all the troops to be concentrated at once at any one spot along the road, that enough water was available for the cavalry and Mounted Infantry to push along in detachments will be seen by the following statements, which I take from my old notes made when an advance was expected.

There were wells at Handoub sufficient for 250 men

and 500 animals at one time; at Otao were wells for
250 men and 250 horses at one time, and good pasturage for camels. At Hambuk, wells for 200 men and
300 camels at once; at Es Sibil, two wells sufficient for
a small party; at Wady Haratri, seventy miles from
Suakin, two excellent deep wells, riveted with stone,
capable of supplying at a time enough water for 600
men and all their animals. At Bir Salahet, two excellent riveted wells with abundance of water. Between
Bir Salahet and Bir Abd el Hab, which is 105 miles
from Suakin, were several places where, by merely
scraping holes in the sandy bed of the *khor*, water could
be obtained; while at Bir Abd el Hab itself, and again
at Ariab, twenty-three miles farther, Lieutenant-Colonel
Stuart, from whose report these notes were taken,
mentions a fine supply, especially at Ariab.

It was at Ariab that the difficulty in the want of
water would have commenced, since for a distance of
fifty-three miles to Obak there was no water of any
consequence on the road itself, although springs were
reported in the villages in Jebel el Gharrad, the mountains to the right of the track. As there was also in
this neighbourhood excellent pasturage for camels and
goats, cattle even thriving, there was no reason why an
advanced camp could not easily have been established
at Ariab, whence convoys of camels with water could
have been sent on under escort to various points between Ariab and Obak.

At Obak were thirty wells, brackish but drinkable,
while thence to Bir Mahobeh, fifty-two miles farther

on, there was again no water. But Bir Mahobeh itself, 234 miles from Suakin, offered an excellent supply: as it was only two hours' march from the Nile, when once some advanced posts had been established along the route water-caravans could have been continually marching backwards and forwards from the Nile to assist the advancing force. It must be remembered that Berber, only seven miles from Bir Mahobeh, was still strongly garrisoned, that Gordon was not yet in danger at Khartoum, and that the Hadendowah and Bishareen tribesmen, living on this route, habitually lived by transporting large caravans up and down to the coast from Berber, thus showing that the water supply was by no means a difficult matter. In fact, the Berber route was that usually followed by Egyptian troops on their march to Khartoum.

Further, after the two tremendous defeats near the coast, the tribesmen would themselves have been peaceable, and for payment would have been only too glad to have done the water-carrying for us, if we had not sufficient transport to do it ourselves. For in those days the Mahdi's name had not yet become omnipotent, and many of the tribes only wished to be left at peace, while some of them, such as the Amarar tribe, openly declared themselves friendly. So much for the water-supply.

As regards the heat, it was at that time of the year by no means insupportable. In fact, throughout a great part of the distance the caravan-road led through the mountains, reaching in places an altitude of nearly 2000 feet. Here the disadvantage would rather have been the cold by night than the heat by day. But if we were to have gone on to Berber, we should have done so at once; and had we done so, Khartoum would have been relieved and Gordon saved without difficulty of any kind. The Government at home, however, determined that no such advance should take place. Thus was all the advantage to be gained from decisive victory in two pitched battles deliberately thrown away, all the blood of brave men, white and black alike, wantonly and for nothing shed on the sands by the Red Sea shores.

Further, the Government were laying up for themselves a rod in pickle of which the weight was to be soon experienced, while its smarting after-effects are plainly felt even unto this day.

About this time, and while the troops were making preparations to return to Cairo, I was told one day by Admiral Hewett that he had received instructions that I was to be sent to Massowah to report upon the fortifications of that post; and that further, in his position as Governor-General of the Red Sea littoral, he intended to appoint me Governor of this place, of which I had hardly even heard the name before. I opened my eyes a bit at this, but I only touched my hat and said, " Yes, sir ; most certainly I will be a governor if you like, and of any place you like." And then he asked me to dinner with him on board the Euryalus. Although, being still borne on the books of that ship, I continued to draw my rations from her, I much preferred eating my share of her Majesty's rations at the Admiral's table in a beautiful cool cabin to pigging it in a tent. I enjoyed that clean comfortable dinner very much; the ports being open, and the sea-breeze coming in, made the change from the hot parched shore most refreshing. The change from a tent to a ship made me appreciate the advantage the sailor enjoys in being able to live and to fight in his own house.

The gallant old Admiral was one of the kindest men living, and a good *raconteur*; and there was also present his flag-captain, Captain Hastings, a charming fellow, whose face it did one good to look at. During the dinner the Admiral related to me with considerable pride a story about his son, who was a sub-lieutenant on the ship, and who had been present with the Naval Brigade at the battle of Tamai. In the greatest heat of the action, just as the troops were being driven back, a Highlander of the Black Watch came up to this young fellow unarmed, having lost his rifle and bayonet in some way. Seeing that young Hewett, who was busy with his revolver, had also a sword, he saluted him and earnestly begged the loan of his naval officer's sword until after the fight, saying that he promised faithfully to return it then. The young sub hurriedly gave the Highlander the sword, never expecting to see the man alive again, especially as he saw him rush at the enemy and kill one man instantly. He did see him again, though; for at the end of the action the gallant member of the "auld Forty-twa," approaching the young sailor, held out to him his weapon, saying, " A've brought hit back, sir! She's a vara guid weepon, but a'm verra sorry, I fear she's just a wee bittie bent." Bent, indeed, was that sword, and all covered with blood too! for that Highlander had been carving away with a vengeance to make up for the loss of his bayonet.

When the Admiral showed me this weapon, which was a regulation tailor-made sword of bad steel, it looked far more like a sickle than the orthodox thing. The old gentleman was very pleased about it, and said he intended to preserve it as a trophy.

On saying good-bye to the Admiral he kindly told me that he was going to mention me in a special despatch for my services under his orders, which was a promise he did not forget to fulfil, for I have a copy of his despatch now, dated H.M.S. Euryalus, April 6, 1884, in which he spoke very flatteringly of Hallam Parr, G. D. Giles, and myself. We were, however, to meet again before long at Massowah, as Sir William Hewett was to make that seaport the starting-place for the embassy to King John of Abyssinia, on which he was shortly to proceed.

When I sailed for Massowah on the 23d March, on board the Khedivial steamship Mansurah, I had some interesting and pleasant companions. I also had my servant Thacker and a couple of horses on board the ship, the said horses being two particularly good, although small, cavalry horses, which I had obtained on the break up of Baker's force simply by signing, or rather sealing, a receipt which I gave to an Egyptian officer. An Egyptian official of any kind will give anything to anybody for a receipt which exonerates him from responsibility. Thus I had sealed my *wasla* and got two horses which were never required of me again. The subsequent fate of one of them, a very good grey, may be related here.

My companions on board were Captain Speedy, the celebrated Abyssinian traveller; Lieutenant Graham, R.N., flag-lieutenant to the Admiral, who had greatly distinguished himself at El Teb; and Fred Villiers of the 'Graphic.' Some time later, when Sir William Hewett arrived at Massowah, Villiers asked me for a horse to ride with the Admiral on his embassy to King John, promising, like the Highlander with young Hewett's sword, to return it to me when done with. Like that Highlander, he returned it — somewhat damaged! It fell out like this. One hot evening, some months later, I was back again in Suakin, when I met a bronzed stranger, burnt indeed by the sun almost black, in whom I with difficulty recognised my friend Villiers.

"Holloa! old fellow," said I. "Glad to see you back again. Where's my horse?"

"Here he is!" said Villiers, adding solemnly, "Will you take him?" holding up at the same time a stick, to the end of which was attached a considerable amount of grey horse-hair, thus making an excellent fly-whisk.

This was all that was left of my gallant grey! The excellent 'Graphic' correspondent had literally ridden his tail off in the mountains of Abyssinia. But now we must get back to an anterior period, and to the town of Massowah.

My fellow-passengers and I, also my staff officer, an Egyptian named Major Mustapha Effendi Ramzie, landing with our mules and horses, proceeded to the Governor's palace, a large domed edifice situated on the island of Talut outside the town. This palace was then the residence of Mason Bey, a capital fellow. He was a South American gentleman in the Egyptian service, who having had quite enough of the Soudan, had declined to remain any longer at Massowah, and whose successor the Admiral intended me to be. He was most hospitable, and after we had taken up our quarters with him we all went off to explore the town of Massowah, going in over a long causeway.

From Captain Speedy, however, we soon became separated; for no sooner was his stalwart form seen in the native bazaars than he was surrounded by all sorts and descriptions of natives—Turks, Egyptians, Arabs, and Abyssinians—who all greeted him with joy as their friend El Pasha Feliki; the word *feliki* meaning, like lightning, quick. Speedy was an excellent translation for the name of this officer, to rescue whom had been formerly one of the primary causes of the Abyssinian war against King Theodore, which war, as all will still remember, had ended in our capture of Magdala.

Leaving Speedy to his swarthy friends, therefore, Villiers and I made a thorough inspection of Massowah; and as it was my business to make a note of

all I saw, I have no difficulty in putting upon record
what it was like in those days. It was something
like Suakin, only probably worse. There were, as at
Suakin, white flat-roofed houses inhabited by Government officials, the better class Arabs, and a few
Europeans; and as at Suakin, crowds of filthy mat
or wooden huts in the native bazaars. As at Suakin,
again, the town was built upon an island, connected
with the mainland by a causeway, or rather two, one
connecting it with the island of El Talut, another
with the shore. It was surrounded by a sea which
sometimes remained at low tide for three or four
months at a stretch, leaving quantities of fetid mud,
of decomposing shell-fish, and all the refuse of the
town exposed to the rays of the tropical sun, without a breath of wind to disseminate the horrid odours
and steaming miasma rising constantly from this com-
bination of horrors.

As we walked through the native bazaars the whole
place seemed to be alive with flies, horrid little sticky
flies, smaller than the ordinary house-fly, but which
from their myriads covered the wayfarer from head
to foot. Head, eyes, ears, hands, neck—everywhere
they buzzed and clung to you. We soon got out of
the bazaars, and went to inspect the fort which
guarded the entrance to the harbour, and which was
garrisoned by black troops.

I had not at the first glance felt particularly
enamoured of my future governorate; but here I
was a little better reconciled to my fate, for I found

everything beautifully clean. The fort was a seven-sided masonry edifice, with a large courtyard and nine embrasures for artillery. It contained then eight Krupp guns in excellent order, as clean indeed as though they were on board a British man-of-war. When towards the end of that same year the Italians, with the connivance of the British Government, so calmly annexed Massowah, I suppose they also took possession of these excellent guns. The garrison of the fort lived outside it in long thatched huts of poles and matting. The hospital huts for the soldiers were of the same description, and very clean. Owing to the want of any green rations for the troops, the hospital was full of cases of scurvy.

On roaming about we also visited a fort on the island of El Talut, which protected the second cause-way, that to the mainland; it had a kind of bastion front, and was also armed with eight breechloading guns. I did not think that either of these forts was worth much, and it was a great disadvantage in any case that there were no barracks in either for the soldiers.

Before we got back to the palace again we picked up Speedy, who informed us that a Swedish mission-ary had been captured by an Abyssinian robber chief on the way to Senheit. This Senheit was a fortress held by Egyptians outside an Abyssinian village called Keren, in the former Abyssinian province of Bogos.

My programme included an immediate visit to Sen-heit, which was on the way to Kasala, then invested

by the rebels; but it did not look as if I had much
chance of getting there, as the brigand chieftain, Baramberas by name, commanded the mountain passes.
Mason Bey was especially facetious at my expense
on the subject that night, when we all dined at the
house of an Italian official named Marco Paoli Bey.
He said that he knew "old bully Baramberas" very
well; and that as he had got his wife safely in
custody in Massowah, he would bet ten to one that
if I did ever get through to Senheit, I should probably return minus my ears and eyes, if indeed I ever
got back at all.   His chaff was very funny, especially
to the others; but it was really meant in good part,
as he wanted to deter me from going.   For this robber
chief, an outlawed Abyssinian, had at least 800 men
under his orders, some being Abyssinians and others
Soudanese Arabs, all desperadoes apparently of the
deepest dye.

My business was, however, to find out all about the
road to Kasala and the fortress of Senheit; therefore
a day or two afterwards, after first interviewing the
captive Mrs Baramberas and other ladies, all Abyssinians and all pretty, and getting all their tender
messages for the robber chief, I arranged to go off
that evening on my journey to Senheit, which was reck-
oned as a four or five days' journey from Massowah.

CHAPTER XIV.

My departure for Senheit being determined upon, I arranged accordingly to start at once with fifty Bashi-Bazouks, who were about to form a post at El Ain, at about two days' journey distance. Mason Bey therefore telegraphed to Senheit for fifty Bashi-Bazouks to come down and meet me at a halting-place in the passes called Galamit; for as Baramberas had so many men— about 1000 more or less—the road was absolutely closed for unarmed parties. In the meantime, Lieutenant Crow of the Coquette sent out a letter to Baramberas, ordering him to come in and surrender to British authority, promising him safety and protection in Massowah if he would do so, and permission to live there in comfort with his womankind, on condition of his giving up the missionary unharmed.

At 4.30 P.M. I started for Senheit with Mustapha Effendi Ramzie and Alfred Thacker on horseback, taking with us four Bashi-Bazouks to carry guns, one mule to carry the light baggage, and one camel to take the forage for the animals, as nothing was to be obtained anywhere on the road. These Bashi-Bazouks were not Turks, as might be supposed from the name, but half Arabs, half Abyssinians. They moved at a sort of jog-trot, like the Hadendowah savages on the war-path, and seemed to be indefatigable. Five miles beyond the Massowah causeway we arrived at the village of Amkullu, where we inspected a fort on the slope of a hill. This fort was about 400 yards in length, and contained four mountain-guns. It was protected by the most enormous ditches I have ever seen in any fort, and these ditches were three feet deep. I concluded that they had been dug more as an object of occupation for the Egyptian garrison than for any other reason, as the fort was completely commanded from the hills on the left flank and rear. The place was very much under-garrisoned, the greater number of the blacks who had formerly been here having recently been killed at El Teb, or near Tamai, in Baker's and Moncrieff's ill-fated expeditions.

At this village we were joined by twenty-five of our Bashi-Bazouks, the remainder having gone on with camels and stores for the post at El Ain. We were received by the sheikh of the village, a very civil fellow named Abd el Rahim, who supplied us with luxuries in the shape of settees or *angarebs*, a table, and a lantern; also some milk, for he was a cowkeeper. But we had better have been without the lantern, for it attracted more flying bugs than it had ever previously been my lot to see.

Next morning, March 26th, we started at 5 A.M., just as dawn was breaking. The hyenas had been creating a lively music during the night, and just outside Amkullu we came upon a couple close to the track, which was a stony one. They were evidently a male and female, for the latter was carrying something in her mouth, which at first, in the dusk, we took for a sheep; but as we galloped after them we found it to be a young hyena. Ramzie, who was excessively impetuous, fired a shot at them, but missed, and we lost them in a nullah, and so continued our journey. The road lay through a country chiefly desert, although in some places there were plenty of green shrubs and some grass. We saw several gazelles and hares, of which latter my servant missed a couple. We also saw a couple of guinea-fowl, but Ali, one of my men, frightened them. We passed on the road plenty of natives armed with spear, sword, and shield, exactly the same sort of looking men we had fought at Tamai. Many of them belong to the "Zom Miriam" tribe. In the course of the morning's march we also overtook a very long caravan going to Kasala with merchandise, escorted by the very Hadendowah tribe of which Osman Digna's army was composed. We chaffed these fellows a little, and found them very good-natured and merry. We arrived at Amba, about twenty-three miles from Amkullu, in four hours and ten minutes from the time of starting—our Bashi-Bazouks having travelled at a jog-trot the whole of the way, although each carried a heavy Remington rifle and plenty of ball-cartridges. My pony was a most intelligent beast; he always exactly accommodated his pace to that of the Bashis running in front of him.

Amba was simply a place in a *khor* or sandy ravine, where there was water, plenty of which might be had by just grubbing up the ground in the bed of the *khor*. There was no shade under which to encamp save that of some thorn-bushes. However, by rigging up a rug and an enormous cloth sheet, which one of the natives unwound from his waist, we managed to get some shelter, under which we had a nap. Starting again from Amba at 3.30, we were just on the move when we saw eight wild pig close by coming down to the water. I tried to shoot one with a sporting rifle which I had borrowed from Hallam Parr, but to my great disgust it missed fire several times. The pig began moving off, so I blazed at them with a Remington rifle which I snatched from one of the Bashis; but I had lost my chance—they escaped. On the whole, it was as well that I should have learned thus early that my rifle was, owing to a broken striker, worthless, as I was going through a country full of lions; and that settled the question as to whether I should delay or not, on the chance of getting one of the kings of the forest. Directly afterwards I shot a hare, a curious beast, with perfectly hairless pink ears, through which the sunlight shone brightly.

Our route continued through scrub to a torrent-bed, now perfectly dry, where was a dry well. This place was called Kaufa. Crossing the ravine, we entered on the desert known as " El Shab," and a ghastly desert it was. For the first hour's march this consisted of loose, deep sand, through which struggled up a rough, bushy grass. Farther on the sand became firmer; there was no grass, but instead here and there a thorn tree. From the top of one of these I saw just at dusk three guinea-fowl flying away with a chuckling "come back, come back," which reminded me of a farmyard at home. We marched through this desert until two hours after dark, and then encamped on the bare sand at about 8 P.M., in a place where there was no water. The camels with the Bashi-Bazouks coming up, they carefully encamped to windward of where we were lying. The smell of combined savage and camel was by no means pleasant. However, I got inside my blanket-bag, and was soon asleep in spite of howling hyenas and camel-smells, my saddle making a capital pillow on this as on many other occasions.

At 2.30 A.M. we were again *en route*, for it was most important to avoid the heat of the day in this water-less desert. By the starlight I noticed, when not half asleep, that we passed a range of mountains, and that the desert continued to be of firm sand, from which sprang low and thorny trees with wide-spreading branches, which would make a fine shelter if nothing better offered. At about 5 A.M. the nature of the "Shab" changed. We entered on a stony country full of high bushes. On our left, at a short distance, was now a fine bold range of mountains stretching right into Abyssinia and the Soudan. We were soon at their base, when I shot a large fowl-like bird which was running in the bushes. I knocked over another of the same kind, but my attendant Mahomed did not realise that it might possibly get up and run, and wasted his time in getting a knife to cut its throat. By the time the knife was procured the bird had retired into the bushes. These two were the only birds I saw of this description during my journey— regular wild poultry as big as Cochin China fowls.

We now began to descend a steep incline into a valley, another range of mountains closing rapidly in on our right; and soon we saw, in the middle of the valley below us, a truly grateful sight, a clear running stream. We reached the bed, after five and a half hours' marching, at 8 A.M., and found the water clear, sparkling, and cool.

After a refreshing wash in a little pool down between two rocks, Alfred and I, accompanied by our favourites, Ali and Mahomed, followed up the course of the stream a mile or two, walking our horses in the shallow water and keeping a look-out for game. Although we heard guinea-fowl, we could see none; but there were number-less beautiful birds in this valley of " El Ain," and plenty of tailor-birds' nests hanging from the extreme ends of the slightest boughs of trees overshadowing the water. With the fresh morning breeze, it struck us, after the savage "Shab," as being indeed a most picturesque spot. We encamped in the shade of a charmingly thickly-leaved tree, and were soon engaged in watching the hare and the wild hen boiling together, Ali stirring the pot most diligently, while the stream

ran by at our feet, and the birds sang in the thick
branches overhead. With the exception of potted ham
and potted beef, we had had no food since leaving
Massowah; so the seething pot added considerably
to the poetry of the scene. Ramzie Effendi prepared
an onion and sardine salad, and Alfred started the
cocoa boiling. Altogether it was a bright spot in our
journey when we halted by the waters of El Ain.

Here there was a hut occupied by Bashi-Bazouks,
who kept the telegraph line in order. This line, which
went to Kasala and Khartoum, was still good as far
as Senheit. I sent for one of the men, and made
inquiries about the robber Baramberas, into whose
country we had now entered. He had not yet released
the missionary, and had on the previous day taken a
loaded camel from a passing caravan. It was evidently
necessary that I should write him a letter, as, if I
wished to get through comfortably or to set the missionary free, the best way was to see the robber personally, which I at once endeavoured to try and do.

I managed to get two emissaries, after a little trouble,
who undertook to try and find the robber chief for a
consideration. One of them was a man from the
telegraph repairing post, in Egyptian pay; the other,
another savage who was feeding a few cattle near the
water. They did not seem to like the job much, but I
think they knew that they personally would be quite
safe from the robbers, as they had nothing to fear.
I knew that Baramberas attached great importance to
letters being sealed, from two of his I had read before

leaving Massowah. I had therefore included in my light baggage, on starting, a couple of sheets of crested paper in case of eventualities,—the crest I pointed out to my messengers as my seal. By the spilling of a brandy flask in my saddle-bags the piece of paper I had to use was somewhat stained, but that did not matter. Any idea of my letter being understood was out of the question, but still the fact would remain that it was a letter, and that was enough, especially as it was sealed, which fact I carefully pointed out to the two bearers, while explaining to them the contents which they were to deliver as a message to the robber chief.

My letter was simple. I commenced it, "My dear Baramberas," and ended it, "Yours truly." It was also addressed simply, "Ras Baramberas Kella, Esq., &c., &c., &c.," which address was evidently the right one, for the letter came to hand, as the sequel will show.

After indulging in the luxury of a shave, we started from our leafy camp at 2.30 P.M., and marched for two hours up the same ravine or *khor* at the foot of which we were at El Ain. We had continued up the valley for a quarter of an hour when the running stream ceased to exist, and the mountains rapidly closed in on both sides of the path. The stream occasionally made its re-appearance in a much smaller form, trickling over the ground here and there for the first hour's march. Then the rocks closed in on both sides to a width of only twenty-five yards at the base. This was an apparently impregnable passage to force, but I found it was turned by a narrow and rough mountain-road, which was followed by Ramzie Effendi and most of my Bashi-Bazouks, while I myself, with Alfred, Ali, and Mahomed, followed the lower bed of the torrent. I had brought on all the Bashi-Bazouks, intending to keep them with me until I should meet the escort I expected down from Senheit, which would probably be at a point in the ravine some forty miles ahead, at the wells of Galamit.

As we proceeded, the road became at times excessively stony, and indeed dangerous: it was necessary to clamber over granite rocks which stuck up out of the bed of the ravine, and these were worn smooth with age and the action of water. Still, the extraordinary fact remains that the camels of the country, if not too heavily laden, are able to scramble over these obstacles in long strings, and that, too, in the dark. The most formidable part we had to pass through was a long defile called Awalid il Kird, or, "the place where the monkey was born." Here the rocks were very high, and were covered with quantities of red-sterned baboons, some of which were of great size. One of my men fired off a rifle at them, and it was a wonderful sight to see with what agility they fled shrieking along the nearly perpendicular rocks. Alfred shot a bird with an enormous curved serrated beak; each side of the upper mandible was marked with a broad yellow stripe: I took it to be a kind of hornbill. We afterwards saw plenty of these birds, some of which had red instead of yellow stripes along the upper part of the hill. This looked very handsome and striking.

After dark we halted in a broad part of the ravine, at a place where it took a large semicircular bend. The last hour's march had been an excessively trying one, the whole of the bottom of the defile having been wet and rocky. We were soon lying down on the bare sand, after starting fires on every side to keep off the lions, which here were numerous. The natives insisted, on account of these brutes, on our camping quite in the middle of the ravine, and not on the wooded sheltered side; and although there was a strong and cold wind blowing, they were undoubtedly right. There was a most marked change in the temperature that night, for we had been ascending the whole way from El Ain. I believe the native name of the spot we encamped in was Fatha.

Just before arriving at Fatha we met the Swedish missionary riding in on a camel, accompanied by four or five of the telegraph Bashi-Bazouks. Baramberas had apparently let him go, only keeping his mule; but why or where he had let him go, we endeavoured for some time in vain to make out. We tried the missionary in five languages without effect—Italian, French, English, German, and Arabic. He knew a few, a very few, words of all. However, as he appeared, if there was any choice at all, to be a shade best at Arabic, I stuck to that, although it seemed a curious tongue in which to be compelled to talk to a Swede. I conclude he made his conversions, when he did

make any, in Abyssinian. Eventually I gleaned that
his release was a result of the letter I had sent up the
pass earlier in the day to say I was coming. Owing
to more news of the Abyssinian robber having annexed
camels, Mustapha Effendi Ramzie amused us much
throughout this day's march by the considerable signs
of anxiety he could not help showing. Also, after
halting, he was very nervous about lions, although he
had previously told us that there was nothing he
enjoyed so much as hearing lions roaring round the
camp at night.

I determined to try him a little; and so, after he
was comfortably ensconced on the sand and ready for
the sleep he could always summon at two minutes'
notice, I said maliciously, "Ramzie, do you notice that
we are lying in a very dangerous position? There is
no fire on our side between us and the jungle, and you
haven't managed as usual to put the camels and Bashi-
Bazouks between you and the thicket. Besides, listen;
don't you hear something rustling and breaking the
bushes in there?"

He started up and listened, was convinced he did
hear something, and in a moment was up on his feet,
shouting for Osman Aga, the head Bashi, to place fires
and a guard between us and the jungle, and, in fact,
was quite prepared to turn the whole place upside
down. However, as I would allow no more fires or
guards, he was obliged to content himself by removing
his sleeping-place to the inside of mine and Alfred's,
protesting that he only did so that we might have more

room to shoot a lion if it came. A lion did come shortly after, and roared most lustily—and a fine sound his voice made, echoing through the rocks and hills; but I noticed that, in spite of his previously avowed predilection for this style of music, my staff officer Major Ramzie did not seem at all inclined for an *encore*. However, perhaps this was only because he was too tired after our long march. We were also disturbed that night by the howling of wolves and the chattering of monkeys: these latter, I think, had winded the lion, but they kept perfectly quiet when once he began to roar.

Next morning at 2 A.M. we started by starlight to continue our journey up the *khor*. When once we made up our minds to start, it always took us very few minutes to get under way, for I had distributed the duties among the Bashi-Bazouks, so that each man knew exactly what to do, and after the first day they never failed, either on coming into camp or leaving it. Mahomed and Ali looked after our guns and horses; an older man named Iddris always accompanied and loaded the little baggage-mule; while our fourth personal attendant, Hassan, was chief kitchen-boy, started the fires and got the water boiling for the cocoa, &c. We had no baggage, practically speaking—only a few cooking things and tinned provisions—so we were soon off at any time of day or night. We realised on this journey the immense advantage and comfort of travelling light.

This mountain journey of March 28th was the longest

and most eventful one we made. We traversed during the day sixty miles at least of the wildest country, and I had my first personal interview with Baramberas Kella, the robber chieftain. On starting it was very cold, but as we had no greatcoats we had to put up with that, as we plodded along silently in the night up this mystic and apparently interminable ravine. After about a couple of hours the ravine assumed quite a different character, becoming much wider—the sides not being so high and steep, but falling away with an easy slope to the base of well-clothed hills. We seemed to be near the top of the range, and for a long time were paddling along in water, having again encountered a shallow running stream. Towards dawn I found there was dense jungle on both sides, and the hills at each side again became lofty.

When within a couple of miles of Galamit, we got a few shots at guinea-fowl and partridge, as they flew off from their watering-places or ran across the path. These shots had the effect of bringing out a little party of Bashi-Bazouks to meet us, headed by a Turkish officer, their chief, whose title was the Sunga of Senheit. He accompanied us into his camp, where I was received by his troops, a hundred men of the very strangest description, with all the honours. The ranks were opened, arms were presented, and drums of the most outlandish sort beat the wildest of salutes.

The funniest part of it all was that the Bashi-Bazouk officers, who called themselves captains and majors, all had rifles as well as swords; and while drawn up in

their proper places at open order, three paces in front
of the line, these officers all presented arms with the
men.   As I passed down the line to inspect them,
and returned the salute, some of the men thought it
correct to salute me with one hand, while holding their
rifles still at "the present" with the other; and for
instructing this rabble to drill so well, the gallant
Sunga (Turkish Sanjak) had for many years been
receiving £45 a-month.   Such is the inequality of
pay in Egypt, that the Sunga of Massowah only got
£15 for undertaking exactly the same responsibilities.

The inspection of the "troops" concluded, the Sunga
conducted me with great ceremony to a seat on a car-
peted *angareb* or native bedstead under a tree.   Of
course coffee at once made its appearance.   This coffee
taught me that there is no forest too thick, and no
desert too wide, to prevent coffee being always ready
on the spot—good and hot and strong; and also I
found that, as a general rule, the most frightful-looking
savages made it the best.

Well, the Sunga Aga gave us coffee and water-melon
—this latter being the very best we ever tasted.   With
a little potted meat and biscuit in addition, we made
a most excellent breakfast at 6 A.M.   We did not get
another meal that day until 9 P.M., although we broke
our fast a little by eating raw cabbages and onions in
the Sunga's own kitchen-garden at Sabbab, seven miles
outside Senheit.   At Galamit we did not even off-
saddle; but after having watered and fed our animals,
we made a fresh start with our guard of 100 men,

leaving the old fifty who had come with us from Massowah to establish a post at Galamit until our return.
We heard here that Baramberas was somewhere in the
adjoining mountains, and that his sentries had been
seen on the hill-tops close by on the preceding day.
My two men with the letter had been seen to pass
through and plunge into the hills in search of him.

On leaving Galamit the route at once struck into a
dense jungle, and was covered with the most dreadful
loose stones of all shapes. We found it extremely
difficult for our horses; and as our friend the Sunga
had brought down with him from Senheit a horse and
two splendid mules, I was glad to accept his offer of
the latter for myself and servant. All his animals
were unshod, and scrambled over the rocks like a cat,
although in many places we had bare slippery rocks to
clamber over. The new Bashi-Bazouks went dancing
along in front, shouting their Abyssinian war-songs,
and moving at such a pace over the rough ground that
it was most difficult to keep up with them, although
the unshod animals moved over the boulders as if they
had never walked on anything else. When we had
been travelling through the forest several hours—finding it very hot, but in spite of the heat able to admire
the beautiful flowering cactus on all sides, and also the
numerous trees of the graceful Euphorbia candelabra
—suddenly there was a halt of our advanced-guard.
Glad of a little rest, I languidly inquired what was the
matter, thinking it was only a tree or an extra big rock
in the way. Nothing of the sort! Word was passed

back that the redoubtable Baramberas was himself in the neighbourhood, and that he wished to see me. Presently appeared my two messengers of yesterday, accompanied by a third person — a most villanous-looking one-eyed old savage, armed with a spear. This man, who was an emissary from the robber chief, was exactly like the pictures one sees of Old Nick, only without the horns. However, his grizzled, fuzzy wig was quite remarkable enough without any other Satanic accessories.

Old Nick informed me that Baramberas wished to see me and also the Sunga, but that we must leave all our soldiers behind, and meet him at a place an hour's march farther on in the mountains. The Sunga did not at all appreciate the honour of meeting Baramberas Kella Yasoos, and I felt that to do so I must put myself completely in his power, and trust to chance to get out of it all right; but seeing the importance of trying to open up the road, I decided at once to do as the robber wished, so ordered all the soldiers to halt where they were, while I went ahead with the Sunga, Ramzie Effendi, Alfred, and two Bashis to hold the horses. Old Nick preceded us to show the way; but before starting, in token of good faith, we exchanged weapons. He took my double-barrelled gun, which, as I forgot to withdraw the cartridges, was loaded, and I took his spear. I soon found we had a precipitous mountain-pass to cross called "Akabet Drinkalei"—a most dangerous place it was too. However, the Kasala caravans were able to pass it, I heard. This pass accomplished, we had a further

half-hour's journey into the mountains, and then turning off the track we soon came to a large bush, facing a
plain surrounded by rocky heights. This plain was
quite bare for several hundred metres to our front, then
wooded to the base of the hills, in the recesses of which,
Old Nick informed us, his master was at that time awaiting the report of our arrival. The old robber then left
us sitting by the bush, first, to my considerable surprise
and pleasure, returning me my gun. I had not relished
at all the idea of its disappearance into those grim-
looking retreats for which he was about to set out.

For some half-hour we waited patiently under the
bush, examining the mountains with our glasses, but
in vain, or nearly so; for, with the exception of a
black sentry, perched a mile away on a hill-top, we saw
nothing unusual. All this time the Sunga was in the
greatest state of fear of being shot or kidnapped.
Ramzie was a lion of courage compared to him, for
Ramzie did not believe that Baramberas would touch
an Englishman or his companions; but the Sunga, who
had begun the journey by expressing fears for my
safety, as the minutes passed now openly expressed
them strongly for his own. I verily believe that
nothing but my presence prevented his making a clean
bolt of it. While awaiting the chieftain's arrival, I
gave Alfred orders, in case of accidents, that should
there be any signs of foul play towards me, he was instantly to shoot that worthy himself through the head
with my revolver, which I handed over to his care. By
this means we should be sure of at least bagging one,

and that the principal one. It must be remembered that there had been no mutual promises of immunity, and therefore it was a complete toss-up how the whole thing would turn out.

At length we saw issuing from the bushes at the far end of the plain a little troop of armed men, one of whom was mounted. Being clad in a red toga, I rightly guessed that he was the chief. When the advancing party had got half-way across the open space, I advanced to meet them with only my hunting-crop in my hand. I was followed by Alfred and Ramzie; the Sunga took care to keep his distance under the bush near his horse. Somehow I thought the advancing party of bandits would act on the square, so I walked straight up to the robber's gang as if I had known them all my life. When the man in the red toga saw me coming, he dismounted, with the assistance of two of his followers, from the excellent mule he was riding, and came forward at the head of all his men. He was a fine-looking fellow of about forty; and a white flowing garment he wore from his shoulder flying loosely over the toga gave him a very picturesque appearance.

When we met we salaamed, and then shook hands heartily; and in our best Arabic, which was much on a par, we expressed our mutual joy at making each other's acquaintance. His Abyssinian Arabic sounded very strange to my ears: I wondered what he would think of mine. I turned to lead him across to our resting-place under the bush, when Baramberas himself insisted upon doing the honours of his mountains,

and conducting me instead. Putting one hand on my
shoulder in the most paternal manner, while holding
my hand with his other, he conducted me to a seat on
the Sunga's sheepskin saddle-cloth, which the bandit
ordered one of his men to take without any ceremony,
and where we made ourselves comfortable side by side.
The meeting between the Sunga and the chief was of
the very coldest description. The Sunga looked sulky,
salaamed, and said nothing, while the robber remarked,
"Neharak saeed" (Good day), and then took no more
notice of the leader of Bashi-Bazouks.

After seating ourselves I produced a flask of weak
whisky-and-water. After tasting it myself to show it
was not poisoned, I handed it to my distinguished
guest, who drank with great solemnity, and we then
had a pull all round, with the exception of the Sunga,
who, being a good Mahomedan, had religious scruples.
As for Ramzie, he was far too advanced an Egyptian
ever to have any scruples at all as to either what
he ate or what he drank.

I forgot to mention that while we had been coming
across the plain, Baramberas stopped his troop of
followers; but they were so picturesque, wearing
wreaths of lion's mane and capes of the same, that
I asked him to allow some of them to accompany
him. Four or five of them came: these were evidently
his superior officers — he called one his bimbashi or
major. These also were regaled with whisky-and-
water. They were well-armed fellows, carrying double-
barrelled guns and swords — most of the guns were

pinfire breechloaders. Among the troops were also men carrying Remington rifles. Most of the principal men bore a handsome Abyssinian shield, embossed with silver or brass, in addition to their other arms. After a little conversation on indifferent subjects, I told Baramberas I wished to speak with him apart. He immediately assented to this, and so we moved out from our bush into the sun with our sheepskin rugs; and there, for two mortal hours, in the hottest part of the day, the Abyssinian robber, Ramzie Effendi, and myself, sat and talked and argued.

I began by thanking him for releasing the Swedish missionary, but remarked that I understood that he still had his mule. He replied that he had only kept the mule for the use of an Abyssinian priest who was with Mr Bentsen when he had caught him, but that the priest would ride it into Massowah in a few days' time. I then went straight into affairs of importance, and asked him to give up his robbing habits and to come in with me to Massowah on my return to Senheit. I explained to him that the wisest thing he could do, in order to be at peace with both Abyssinia and Egypt, was to place himself in the hands of Admiral Sir W. Hewett, V.C., who was expected in Massowah in a few days' time on his projected journey into Abyssinia. I assured him of perfect safety if he would come in with me; told him that he would be allowed to live in perfect security in Massowah with his wife and family then retained there; and, moreover, pointed out that if he would come at once, the Admiral would arrange matters for him with King Johannes and with the powerful border chief, Ras Alula, in both of whose bad books he had been for a long time past. Indeed the latter was, according to the robber's own statement, his most deadly enemy and oppressor.

But I found Baramberas the most difficult man to deal with that I ever met. Nothing would induce him to consent to come to Massowah with me unless his family were first released and sent back to him to his home in the mountains. He said he believed in the English, but he did not care about his quarrel being made up with King Johannes; and then he proceeded to draw maps on the ground with his finger to show me the country in Hamaseen, of part of which he had been formerly chief, and which he said had been stolen from him by the king and given to his enemy Ras Alula. He further told me that another reason for his mode of life was the treachery that had been shown to him by the Egyptian Government, under whose flag he had taken shelter when driven from his native land. Raschid Pasha, he told me, had twice imprisoned him by treachery and put him in irons for long periods; and as he had already been previously in irons in Abyssinia for no wrong of his own doing, nothing should henceforward ever induce him to trust himself either in Massowah or Abyssinia without a letter placing him under British protection. This letter he required me to write, sign, and seal for him on behalf of the British Government. In return, he offered to give me a written declaration, signed and sealed, to the effect that he would quit the road, and would henceforth stop neither caravan nor traveller, be he European, Egyptian, Arab, or Abyssinian. But he added a rider, to the effect that if his wife were allowed to come out to him, and if the English would appoint a district for him to live in with his followers, then he would come into Massowah of his own accord. The point that he particularly dwelt on was that it would be considered shameful for him, a man and a chief, to go into Massowah before his wife had been returned to him. It would look, he said, as if he were going in for the sake of a woman. It would be unmanly, and he would be disgraced. He could not thus sacrifice his honour.

He repeated these objections over and over again, and to enforce his arguments held my hand the whole time, and kept on doubling down my fingers in succession at the second joint, in a manner that was by no means pleasant, to mark each point as he considered it established. When he had turned down all the fingers of the right hand, he continued doubling down those of the left; but as he had a remarkably strong and nervous grasp, he managed to squeeze one left-hand finger—on which I wore a ring—so hard in the beginning of his arguments that I took care to keep it behind my back for the rest of the interview, and only to surrender the right hand to his tender mercies. While talking away to the chief out in the sun, I suddenly saw a great commotion arise over by the bush where were still the rest of my party. Every one was on his feet at once, and I saw the little group of robbers with the lion-mane wreaths make a quick dash forward. Then I heard the old Sunga crying out, "It is his Excellency the Bey's mule; it is the Bey's mule, I tell you."

My servant Alfred informed me afterwards that a most laughable incident had occurred. A mule had unexpectedly poked his nose round the corner. It happened to be mine, coming on with the provisions. The robbers thought that here was a fine chance of an easy capture, and had made a bolt to seize it. When they heard it was mine, Alfred informed me, they slunk back again with much the kind of air that a dog has who, when wanting to follow his master, is told to go home! It was a sad disappointment to them, poor fellows!

Eventually I got completely tired of arguing with Ras Baramberas, and managed to get him to let me go, for I had heard over and over again all that he had got to say for himself. I told him that on arrival at Senheit I would telegraph into Massowah for instructions,—as, for a wonder, he had not yet cut the telegraph wire which traversed this wild district and formerly went on to Kasala and Khartoum. Before parting I arranged to meet him on the morrow at a place called Sennara. He said it was near Senheit. Of this I had my doubts,—I only knew it was about forty miles at least from the spot we were then standing on. The word "near" must be received with caution in a country where journeys are always talked about by the number of days, and miles are unknown.

The rest of that day's journey was very interesting.

For a long time we traversed the most beautiful forest, where guinea-fowl kept running into the bushes just a second too soon for us to shoot them, where partridges were heard calling at every step, and where the smell of lions and other *feræ naturæ* was as plain at times as in the "Zoo" in Regent's Park.

I am getting too old now ever to be surprised at anything, or I must confess I should have been surprised when, shortly after leaving Mr Baramberas, I suddenly came, in the middle of the jungle, upon a French bishop in full canonicals, wearing a gigantic cross round his neck, and riding a mule. He was accompanied by several armed blacks. We made friends, and I found he was Monseigneur Tovier of the French Mission at Senheit. We had a short chat in the middle of the dried-up watercourse. I told him I had just left Baramberas, who had promised to be a good boy; that Bentsen the missionary was loose again; and that the road was clear, the Abyssinian having gone away towards the depths of the mountains. The bishop was going to Massowah. He had heard by telegram that I had started, and he knew I had Bashi-Bazouks on the road, so he hoped to get through all right. We said farewell, and separated. By the bye, I was now travelling without my soldiers. I only had Iddris and the mule; but before leaving, I had sent back my two emissaries to Baramberas to inform the Bashis that they might follow on.

Shortly after leaving the bishop we came to a terrible place, a frightfully steep pass over a range of moun-

tains, which it crosses almost at the highest point.
It is known as the Akabet Mashalit. On the far side
we descended after an hour's ride into a *khor* or valley,
known as the Khor Ansaba, a famous place for lions.
We passed by a halting-place called Gabbana, where
there was water; but although we had still a four hours'
journey to Senheit, we determined not to stop, but to
ride on, for I was anxious to get on if possible that
night. We passed through a most pleasant and now
much more open country. Whenever we left the sandy
bed of the *khor*, which we frequently did to avoid its
windings, we traversed fields which had an English
park-like appearance. There was plenty of grass, which
was not yet very much burned up anywhere, and was
in some places as green as a tennis-lawn. This country
was full of partridges, and Alfred could not resist the
temptation of lagging behind occasionally to get a shot,
until I was obliged to stop his amusement, owing to
the delay it caused us. A frightful thunderstorm
now passed overhead, but luckily we got but little of
the rain, for we were not attired for wet weather.

Presently we came upon the traces of an Abyssinian
raid, for Ras Alula had been recently over the border,
and when he made a raid it was on the system of the
old English and Scottish Border raids. He burned,
scattered, ravished, and destroyed, drove off the cattle
and the women, and left a fertile country a desert
behind him. Where we now were he had completely
wrecked a caravan and killed a good many people. The
débris was still scattered along the road for miles—

rags, paper, broken bottles, boxes, bones, every imaginable thing, strewn about in every direction. Also there were a couple of small houses that had been occupied by European tobacco-growers, pulled down and burned, while their hedges and walls had shared the same fate. As for the gardens, or what once had been such, they were no longer worthy of the name. This showed me how absurd it was calling this country Egyptian territory; for outside the walls of Senheit, Egypt had always been utterly unable to protect the province of Bogos since it was annexed from Abyssinia thirteen years previously by an Italian Bey or Pasha, whose name I cannot now remember. I believe he afterwards perished in the Egyptian war with the country he had despoiled.

After passing through a ravine where the Khor Ansaba crosses through a mountain range called El Sabbab, we found ourselves in our friend the Sunga's vegetable garden at the foot of a hill crowned with an Egyptian fort, also called El Sabbab. Evening was now near, we were still seven miles from Senheit, and we had already been travelling sixteen hours!

The Egyptian fort here was meant to protect the defile of El Sabbab from the Abyssinian raiders; but when Ras Alula came down he carefully kept out of the range of the mountain guns which formed its armament. Although already dusk I dismounted, and, after a slight rest in the Sunga's garden, climbed the very steep hill to the fort. To my great surprise I

found the whole garrison of about 150 men under
arms turned out ready to receive me. This was the
more surprising, as I was not expected to arrive at
Senheit for another two days. I found everything in
most excellent order, and the fort itself was, I should
say, impregnable. The soldiers had built for themselves and their officers comfortable houses, kitchens,
magazines—in fact, everything that was wanted. And
all this never cost the Egyptian Government one single
piastre.

Upon my leaving the fort it was dark, and a beacon
light was hoisted to warn the people in the fort at
Senheit that I was coming. Looking back from time
to time during that last toilsome march of an hour and
a half's duration, wearily tramping over hill and ravine,
I thought, as I saw that blazing light, of the old tales
of Sir Walter Scott and the beacon fires of the Border
warfare times. At last, after stumbling along in the
dark by a track we could not see, until neither ourselves nor our animals had a kick left in us, we
struggled at about 8.30 P.M. into the fortress of
Senheit, having been on the journey since two in the
morning. The officers of the fort, warned by the light
at El Sabbah, were all collected at the gate to receive
me; and a hundred yards within the walls in front of
the Government House stood Khusru Bey, the governor
of the province and military commandant, who gave
us three weary travellers the kindest and most hospitable welcome it has ever been my lot to receive in
a foreign and thirsty land.

P

What a sleep we had that night in Khusru Bey's house on comfortable divans, in a nice cool climate! and how delightfully refreshing next morning to get a real tub, after having, for the first time for four days and nights, been able to divest one's self of one's long boots! We were all rather tired the morning after our arrival, but with a good honest healthy fatigue that did no harm My little Arab follower Ali, who, carrying a rifle and eighty rounds of ammunition, had accompanied me the whole previous day's march of about one hundred kilometres on foot, would not own to any fatigue; but Iddris and Hassan, who only turned up at about 5 A.M. with the mule, both looked rather done.

And now to describe Senheit. Looking out from the terrace in front of Khusru Bey's house—a most comfortable house, by the bye, built, like Sabbab, by the soldiers—I saw below me, inside the walls of the place, a quantity of wigwam-looking huts. These were the soldiers' quarters—the huts being built in the Abyssinian shape. Out beyond the walls, on the plain below, were more of the same huts, with here and there little square white houses. This constituted the bazaar. Again, at some little distance away to the left, another detached village of the same description. Here lived the wives and families of the soldiers, and the mixed Arab and Abyssinian population. Inside the fort and behind the governor's house on the hill were the second row of fortified lines, and within them the citadel, from the highest point of which had that day been hoisted

in my honour the large Egyptian flag, usually only
hoisted on Friday, the Mahomedan Sabbath.

The fort at Senheit was very large, and really from
4000 to 5000 men were required to properly man the
works. But at the time of my visit it only held about
900 men, the remainder of the garrison, chiefly blacks,
having been withdrawn a few months previously for
the Soudan war, near Tokar and Suakin, where they
had met a bloody and disastrous fate. The armament
consisted of mountain guns, which would only protect
the surrounding plain for about 3000 yards. This plain
surrounds the fortress on all sides, and it is in turn
surrounded by a high range of mountains. The only
noticeable gap in the hills is at a point about 1200
metres' distance, through which goes the road to Kasala.
The fort may be described as standing up out of the
plain like an isolated island in the middle of a rock-
bound lake. To the left of the pass leading to Kasala
were the buildings of the Roman Catholic French
Mission, and round these again a quantity of the
wigwam-shaped huts. These constituted the village
of Keren, while the fort and the buildings round it
were called Senheit; but the whole lot are as often
marked on a map by the name of Keren as by that
of Senheit.

After a comfortable breakfast in the English fashion,
I went down with Ramzie Effendi to the telegraph office
inside the fort to hold a conversation in Arabic by wire
with Mason Bey in Massowah. This telegraphic conversation lasted for an hour and a half, question and

answer succeeding each other with as great rapidity as if we had been in the same room. It seemed so strange to be able to do this sort of thing in Abyssinia, and it seemed the stranger from the fact that the distance that had just taken me four hard days' travelling could be talked across instantaneously. Mason Bey's definite instructions to me were: "Don't give Baramberas anything unless he consents to come in with you; but tell him to come in with all his men, and that you will be surety for him" (I had already promised him this the previous day, so I did not think it would be much use to reiterate it). Mason continued: "Promise him that all his followers shall be found and kept." As he had about 1000 men, I doubt if they would have cared to keep them long. I was also exhorted to try to get him to come to see the Admiral before he should go to Abyssinia, as it would be of no use his coming at all later. I had to show him he had all to gain and nothing to lose, and, in conclusion, to convey him Mason Bey's best thanks for releasing the Swedish missionary.

This telegraphic conversation ended, I strolled with Ramzie into the village, where I was received by every one with the greatest marks of respect and interest. I found a small store, kept by a young, bright-eyed Italian, who insisted upon treating us to some light German beer, which was capital. While in his shop, two Italian women, mother and daughter, came into the place to see me. The mother told me she had been settled in Sen-heit as a tobacco-farmer from a period three years previous to the time it had ceased to be Abyssinian ground.

She informed me there were several other European tobacco-growers there, but that the excessive duty placed on tobacco in Massowah made it very difficult to make tobacco-growing a paying trade. After visiting the bazaar I returned to the fort, of which I made a regular official inspection with Khusru Bey. I found that, in spite of the imposing appearance of its fortifications and its situation on a hill, there were several weak places in the defences, rendering it liable to capture by a resolute enemy. I was surprised to find what capital outhouses, magazines, bakeries, carpenters' shops, &c., there were on the premises. Even lime for building purposes—like everything else, made by the soldiers themselves—was present in abundance. I visited the hospital, and it was well enough arranged. As for the apothecary's shop attached to it, I never saw a better: it was beautifully clean and neat, with a capital store of drugs and medicines, many bearing English labels.

The inspection concluded, it was time for lunch. It was very hot outside, but inside Khusru Bey's house it was delightfully cool and pleasant. What we found particularly agreeable under this hospitable roof was that everything was served in European fashion, and therefore we were not called upon, as in most Egyptian establishments, to eat with our fingers out of a common dish.

At three o'clock that day I had to start to meet Baramberas near the Abyssinian church at Sennara, which I found to be six miles distant, at the foot of the mountains enclosing the plain. Just as we started our mules, a fine strong lad, one of the robbers, named Burro —whom I had remarked on the previous day, quite forty miles away, with his chief—approached me and delivered the letter which had been promised. It was written in Abyssinian, but sealed by Baramberas with an Arabic seal. It stated "that I was his father"! that he would cease all bad practices and come to Massowah if only his family were restored to him. I preserve this interesting document still, for I thought I had a very fine son!

On the way to Sennara we saw plenty of partridges and hares, but had no time for shooting. Before reaching the church, which was a small barn-like building, I sent robber Burro on to give notice of my arrival, and then followed, leaving the twenty Bashi-Bazouks, whom the Bey had insisted upon sending with me, under the shade of a tree in sight of the church.

I got the key of the church from an old Abyssinian living in a wigwam close by, and visited the church while awaiting the robber chief. It was just a simple little Catholic chapel, with neat little crucifix in the chancel, where also were the books and sacramental vessels in an unlocked box—all very tidy and clean. In a room at the other end of the building was a bedstead, fitted with mosquito curtains, where, I suppose, the officiating priest, who came from Senheit, slept occasionally. The only seats in the church were forms, one of which I had placed outside the church, on the shady side.

Presently arrived an advanced-guard of robbers, who all smiled most agreeably and kissed my hand. They all had on their lion-mane wreaths, and looked very smart and picturesque. When Baramberas, after having been informed by a messenger that the coast was clear, appeared in person, our meeting was quite cordial. On this occasion he was clad in a clean white toga, and he looked certainly a very fine fellow with a fine forehead. His hair, which, with the exception of one or two grey threads, was perfectly black, was laid back along the sides and over the top of the head in very neat little parallel plaits, fastened in a small knot at the nape of the neck. He was tall, sinewy, and strongly built, with a very dignified expression.

It is useless to recapitulate all the conversation we held during this second meeting. I need only mention that there was plenty of mutual swearing on the cross he carried on his rosary; and many were the appeals made to our common faith. I swore as to his personal safety, that I would answer with my life and liberty for it; he swore to perform all he had written me, but, as before, insisted upon having his family sent out to him before he would come into Massowah.

At one time he became very angry and said, when I could not promise this, "After all, if you won't give me my wife, what do I care? There are plenty of other women I can take, and that is what I shall do." For a few minutes all negotiation was nearly at an end, but I managed to pacify him; and afterwards, when in Massowah I again saw Mrs Baramberas, I took care not to tell her how faithless her lord and master had expressed his intention of becoming. Had I done so, I fancy, from what I saw of her very decided character, that when he eventually got his dearly loved wife back again, he would have had a rather rough time of it round his domestic hearth.

But to return. He made a concession. "Send me," he said, "only my wife, and keep my children and all the other women if you like." I promised to wire and ask for her, and to let him know the result by young robber Burro, who was to be temporarily attached to my person. My leave-taking was most tender. Baramberas kissed my hand and placed it on his head, and we further shook hands warmly, for I really felt a considerable respect for this fine fellow, who, however misguided, had certainly experienced considerable hardships both from the King of Abyssinia and his myrmidon Ras Alula, and again from the Egyptian local government. As he said, if he had taken to the road as a means of subsistence, it was only because his country had been stolen from him by the Abyssinians; and again, because, after having been employed for border warfare purposes by the Egyptians, he had been neglected and imprisoned as all his reward, whenever it had suited the policy of the time-serving ruler of that part of the Soudan to try and appear to the Abyssinian border chief, Ras Alula, as having no hand in the raids which Baramberas had been instigated to make over the frontier.

"How," he asked me, "can I live? My own country

I cannot live in, and Egypt will not have me. Am I and all of my followers to die of hunger? But I hope the English will do something for me, and settle a country for me to live in—either in Maria, or in Hall-hall or Senheit."

I have forgotten to mention several little incidents of more or less interest which took place on this occasion. One was that, when Baramberas ordered one of the robbers to give me his lion-mane wreath, on my making the robber a present of a dollar in return, the man refused to have it at any price. However, I got young robber Burro to persuade him to take it afterwards, by telling him it was to buy himself a present with in memory of me. Baramberas also insisted upon forcing on me at leave-taking a fine shield, embossed with silver, which I believe to have been his own shield, as his principal officer was carrying it. I had inadvertently admired it, when, taking it from the bearer, he forced me to accept it. In return, I gave him my hunting-crop and flask; but after having kept them for a minute, apparently not to hurt my feelings, he returned them to me, saying with a smile that he had no kind of use for them, and that all he wanted from me was— British protection!

Two more incidents may be mentioned in connection with this day's proceedings. The first was that he would hardly allow Ramzie Effendi to open his lips, even to translate for me when I became rather involved, shutting him up short by telling him he was only trying to put evil ideas into my head, and that he much preferred to hear anything I had to say from my own lips. Once he told him flatly, "You know I cannot believe a word you say, for you are an Egyptian, whereas the English don't tell lies." The second thing was, that my servant having gone strolling off partridge shooting during our talk, Baramberas became greatly alarmed on his firing a gun, saying the hills were full of his men, who might not understand it, but come down and cut his throat. Robber Burro was promptly sent to recall him, and the robber chief seemed equally pleased with myself to see him safe back.

When we left Baramberas it was nearly dark. On our way into Senheit we met a very nice-looking young priest, dressed as Monseigneur Tovier had been, in full canonicals. This was Père Picard of the French Mission of Keren. He engaged us to come and see the Mission of fathers, brothers, and sisters next day, which I did with the greatest pleasure; and much should I like to describe at greater length than my space will permit the Mission, the pretty and lively nuns, the coquettish well-built Abyssinian girls their pupils, the printing-press in Amharic type, the schools, church, and the evident amount of good done by these estimable people, from whom we met with the kindest reception.

CHAPTER XV.

ALTHOUGH I cannot describe at length the Mission at
Keren, the title of this book, 'Under Crescent and
Star,' would be incorrect or incomplete did I not give
some idea of the way in which, quite unmolested, a
Christian community was able to flourish under Mahomedan rule. For on the day of my visit to Keren,
the largest and finest flag floated proudly from the
citadel in the fortress of Senheit, the White Crescent
and the Star thereon representing the power of Islam,
glittering brightly in the morning sun against the
brilliant blue of the sky. It would, moreover, be un-
gallant and unkind on my part were I to pass over
entirely without mention the kind ladies who in such
friendly fashion received me in their convent.

As I was going to see ladies, I had to take pains
to make myself as neat and soldier-like as possible for
the credit of the British army. Travelling light as

I had been doing, I had not got much with which to make myself look smart; but I had managed to smuggle in among the provisions, on starting from Massowah, a pair of shiny black staff boots to replace my sand-brown service ones on state occasions such as this, and visiting the fort officially.

With clean gilt spurs, brightly polished brass helmet spike, and burnished steel sword scabbard, one looks something like a soldier after all, for *kharkee* clothing never looks dirty, and mine seemed rather to be improved by lying on the sandy beds of the ravines through which we had been travelling. My visit was made in state, attended by my staff officer Ramzie, and my henchman, Thacker, and I was received by several priests and lay brothers. After coffee had been served, as usual everywhere, the good priests took me over the establishment, where I must say I was lost in admiration at the excellent work they had by their perseverance been able to accomplish in that savage district. Their bookbinding establishment and their printing-press were a marvel. The printing type of the Abyssinian language which they were using had come from Trieste, and everything had been brought up from the coast piecemeal on camels. As there were 206 letters and compound letters in Amharic, the amount of type they required was considerable.

In spite of the disturbed state of the country, these priests and lay brothers did not bother themselves much about the hazardous position they were doubtless in, but quietly worked away at the book they were printing in Abyssinian, which was, I remember, 'The Imitation of Christ.'

The priests had a large school of Abyssinian boys, chiefly orphans, who were dressed in pretty blue and white striped jackets and white linen trousers. They had a pretty church which they had built themselves, with a domed roof which, with its thick walls, kept it cool. A very charming feature in the church was the altar. Over this had been trained green climbing creepers, giving a most cool and refreshing appearance.

When the priests had done their part of the entertainment, I was received by the nuns or sisters in their own part of the establishment. Although commonly called, by the Arab-speaking population around, the Saba Banāt, or seven virgins, these sisters were really nine in number. Nothing in that Eastern climate could have looked cooler and fresher than did these ladies in their large white caps and linen dresses. They were all particularly pleasant-looking, the Mother Superior, named Mère Lequette, and one other sister, only approaching to middle age. All the others were young and merry. One in particular, Sister Madeleine, was a Levantine with the most glorious dark eyes— a young lady who, with her frank and rather lively manner, would have attracted attention anywhere.

The nuns received myself and staff most hospitably. I was, although considerably embarrassed at the attention, forcibly enthroned in what I found to be Monseigneur the Bishop's chair at the head of the table, while the nuns all sat in front of me in a semicircle.

For about half an hour I had my work cut out for me
answering all the questions about the war and the outside world, the seven virgins especially inquiring for
Captain Speedy, who seemed to have left a very favourable impression at some previous period. The nuns insisted upon refreshing us with huge bumpers of claret
and sugar, a kind of claret-cup in fact; therefore I
managed to keep my throat moistened sufficiently to
tell them all I knew. Then they took me all over their
establishment, omitting nothing, and it was all most
delightful and interesting. I almost thought that if I
had such a pleasant convent to live in, and such interesting work to do, I should not much mind being
a nun myself—for a time!

The Abyssinian girls in the school, of a light copper
colour, with straight hair and shapely figures, were,
when about from fifteen to seventeen years of age,
very attractive and prettily dressed. They all spoke
French well, and were anxious to be talked to. All
Abyssinian girls are flirts almost from birth; and the
coquettish way in which these convent-reared young
women all ogled, laughed, and went on, might really
have proved rather dangerous to a young officer, had
he not been protected by a group of nine attractive
and holy maidens behind him.

The Mother Superior did not reprove them, as she
said it would probably be quite an event in their lives
to be able to say that they had talked to an English
officer; besides which, she wanted them to show off
their accomplishments and excellent knowledge of the

Gallic tongue, which most certainly did credit to their instructresses. She told me that the principal trouble they had with these precocious young things was that, just as they were getting on nicely with their work, they had a playful habit of eloping with some young man. As, of course, they did not ask the priests or Lady Superior for permission to do so, these elopements were indulged in without the formality of marriage. They would sometimes return after a time to school again, and then, after undergoing any penance they might be ordered to do, go through the ceremony of matrimony, provided always that the young man was at hand and willing.

These girls sang us both hymns and lively songs in French and in their native tongue, being accompanied on the harmonium by the sprightly Sister Madeleine; and then they spouted La Fontaine's fables, accompanying the recitation by all the gestures of an actress in the most entertaining way.

But the sisters had reserved to the last one of the little orphan boys of whom they also had charge. This little fellow was dressed up like a Zouave, and being trotted out, repeated in the most spirited manner a piece of poetry called "Le Soldat." In this he described a soldier's career from his start to his finish on the field of glory, from the cradle to the grave, every verse ending up with "*Le soldat! le soldat!*" It was most amusing to see this little Abyssinian, with head thrown well back, striking his breast as he talked away about *l'honneur et la patrie* in a style

which would have done credit to a French student
in the military school of St Cyr. The sisters had
really taught him splendidly.

At length I was obliged to say farewell to these
charming ladies. Both they and the priests insisted
upon coming out to the gate to see us off, and we
parted with mutual wishes that we might meet again
—a wish which was, in the case of the priests, but,
alas! not of the nuns, soon to be gratified. For, after
I had ridden back to the fort at Senheit, received
and got rid of a deputation of the European traders,
Italians and Greeks, who were in those days everywhere in the Soudan, no sooner had I, after a busy
morning, sat down to lunch with Khusru Bey than
up rode three priests on a return visit. It reminded
me of royalty, which always returns visits at once.
However, I thought it very kind of them to come
over in the sun at the hottest time of the day, especially as they brought me more parting salutations
from the delightful nuns.

I must own that I have always liked nuns! My
visit to those sisters in that convent at Keren reminded me strongly of previous visits paid, when
quite a youngster, to the nuns in the convent at
Aden. They were of several nationalities — French,
Italian, and one or two Irish; and once when they
wanted to get up a bazaar for the benefit of their
native school, I, as being supposed to be one of the best
hands at foreign languages in the King's Own Borderers
in those days, was sent over to see them and arrange

about our band going to play for them, and other
details. I was, on the occasion of my first visit, received by the Lady Superior, a quite young and pretty
Parisian with a brilliant complexion. I suppose that
she had put a fortune into the Church, to have become
"the boss" of a convent so young. I soon perceived
that, although she might have become a nun, she had
not forgotten that she was a *spirituelle* Frenchwoman
for all that. When I had been introduced into her
sanctum and given a cup of tea, she commenced to
chaff me.

"Why, monsieur, is it," she inquired, with a mock-
ing smile, "that you have never been to see us before?
Were you afraid that the nuns would eat you?"

For a second I was nonplussed; but as a boy I had
been brought up in a foreign school of diplomacy,
where a smart answer was considered to be the right
thing. I therefore rose to the occasion. Looking
steadfastly at her pretty face, I replied—

"Ah no, madame! it was not that. It was that
I feared—as I now find to be the case—that if once
I had the honour of beholding them, I should like to
eat the nuns."

She laughed most heartily, and we were always good
friends after that; and soon afterwards my friendship
for her, and hers for me, was the means of getting a
rather smart but naughty little French girl of fifteen
out of a scrape which, however ridiculous, seemed
likely to be serious.

She was the daughter of a hotel-keeper, and when

the bazaar came off, I, as master of the ceremonies, had installed her as post-mistress. For the sum of eight annas, or one shilling, she had to give to all who came for letters a letter written by herself in which was some amusing nonsense. Among those who applied for a letter and paid his eight annas was an Italian priest, Father Antonio by name, who used to look after our Catholic soldiers. He got his letter, but was horrified when he opened it, for he could not see the joke. On the contrary, the worthy Father rushed off at once furiously to the Lady Superior, and laying the letter before her, lodged a formal complaint against the little French girl. I was immediately sent for into the convent, where I found a great hubbub, one of the Irish nuns having read and translated the epistle, which was at once handed to me by the head lady, who thought it right to pretend that it was really "Schocking!" When I read it, I only roared with laughter; for this is what the scandalised priest had received from this little *ingénue*, "Kiss me quick, and go."

However, I soon smoothed matters over, and after we had all had a hearty laugh at Father Antonio, behind his back, I got the youngster off any further punishment than an apology made before us all, which took the rather ambiguous form of saying that she really did not mean it, as he was the very last person in the world whom she would ever dream of wishing to embrace.

Ah well! it was all good fun at the time, but the period of this life spent by the ordinary British officer in convents is unfortunately limited—he has usually more mundane matters to engross his attention. And such was my fate.

That same day, which had been a day of ceremonies, I had to start on my return to Massowah. I could not get rid of pomp and ceremony even then, for Khusru Bey, and every officer of the garrison who had a horse or mule to ride, accompanied me for a space on my way, each falling out and retiring by turn according to rank, as the distance increased from the fortress, —Khusru Bey, to whom I was really very sorry to say good-bye, being of course the first to retire. When every one else had gone, I was still pestered with a crowd of Soudanese soldiers and a rabble of Bashi-Bazouks. When the Soudanese had at length, to my great joy, halted, the Bashi-Bazouks still went on through the Khor Ansaba, where the lions were, and over the pass Mashalit. For there were rumours that Ras Alula was out again on the war-path; and also Khusru Bey suspected some treachery towards me on my way back on the part of Baramberas the robber.

I got through all right, though, seeing nothing of Baramberas, although two of his men joined me on the road with last messages from him, and attached themselves to my person. One of these was the excellent young robber called Burro, who became my handy man; the other was my old friend Old Nick, who was going in to look after Mrs Baramberas and the other copper-coloured ladies in Massowah, and to see if they were conducting themselves properly, which, as regards the latter, I very much fear that they were not.

Those confounded Senheit Bashis were a horrible nuisance on the way back, until I got rid of them at length, for the whole country swarmed with game, which they drove away by their antics. They indulged in strange wild songs and war-dances in front of me the whole way, never seeming to get in the least fatigued. I got rid of them at the wells of Galamit; but there I picked up those I had left on my marching up, who were just as bad. They went along dancing and singing, jumping and skipping, mile after mile. Crouching down at times behind their shields on the ground, they would suddenly bound up and rush upon one of their companions, who would in turn leap about in the most wild and fantastic manner, or perhaps in the exuberance of his glee fire his rifle into the air. They would discharge their rifles at anything, irrespective of distance; and the most wonderful, if "fluky," shot I ever saw was when a negro, firing at a tiny little dik-dik, or mouse-deer, killed it at about a hundred yards' distance as it bounded across a ravine, the animal being not much larger than a hare. We shot several of these animals on our way back, or rather Thacker did, for he used to go roaming off by himself into the bush away from our prancing escort. I was at times very much alarmed lest he should fall a prey to a lion or lose his way; but he had a happy knack of turning up again, and usually with something to eat.

Our journey back was, especially for the last part of the journey, particularly hard, for we ran short of water. I was saving some up in my water-bottle, but on my letting a negro have a drink he drained the lot! There were quantities of beautiful deer and gazelles about, within a few miles of Amkullu, but, barring a distant shot or two, we had no chance at them, both ourselves and our beasts being far too done for want of water to stalk them properly.

At length we reached Amkullu, where we drank gluttonously huge tin pots full of filthy brackish water, with which our old friend Abd el Rahim supplied us from a muddy well, and then, too tired to attempt to cook any dinner, we fell asleep on the string *angarebs*, with which the old man as before kindly supplied us. The next morning we got back to Massowah in safety.

On my return to Massowah I went to pay a visit to the wife of the robber chief, who, although referred to previously, deserves a little further mention. Mrs Baramberas was a very handsome and intelligent-looking woman of about thirty, with a somewhat Jewish caste of feature, and she was not only as intelligent as she looked but also very well bred. She was the daughter of a big chief, by name Wald Ankeld, who had formerly held the province of Hamaseen, adjoining that ruled over by her husband. Wald Ankeld was, however, both of higher lineage and greater importance than his son-in-law Baramberas. The pair were, notwithstanding, outlawed together and banished from Abyssinia, and their provinces given to the bloodthirsty General Ras Alulu. For some years they had settled near Senheit, until, for some reason or other, Gordon Pasha forbade Wald Ankeld any longer to occupy Egyptian territory. Hereupon the chief sent and asked King John to forgive him and to receive him back on Abyssinian ground. Forgiveness being granted, he returned to his native country, only to be treacherously seized, loaded with chains, and thrown into prison by the king. It was this conduct of King John's towards his father-in-law which naturally made Baramberas too suspicious of the king to care whether or not Admiral Hewett should, on his mission, speak in his favour.

To return to the outlaw's wife, she seemed to look upon matters in a somewhat different light, and informed me that she intended to write to her husband in his camp in the mountain-passes to beg him to come in and place himself under British protection, and so invoke the Admiral's aid before it was too late.

The next day the Admiral arrived at Massowah, and after I had made him a full report of the state of things, he decided to let the daughter of Wald Ankeld with her two children go out to rejoin her husband. As regards the other women, all younger and prettier, but not so refined looking, they were detained in Massowah for the time. Their status could not very well be understood, but it was thought just as well to retain them, a decision in which they willingly acquiesced themselves. For they were in no sense of the word captives, beyond being forbidden permission to leave

Massowah, where, as a matter of fact, one of them, a very graceful girl, told me that she infinitely preferred to remain rather than to be for ever living about in the mountains in the stronghold of an outlawed chief, subject at any moment to the onslaughts of Ras Alula, with its inevitable consequence of battle, rapine, and possibly sudden death.

I must now dismiss the robber and his wife in a few words. Although the former did not, as was hoped, give any assistance in the way of helping the garrison of Kasala to retire, he, for four months after my visit to him and the release of his wife, kept the promise which he had made to me to molest nobody travelling through the passes. Thus we were enabled to withdraw without bloodshed the garrison of Senheit. After this he was besieged by Ras Alula in a mountain stronghold, from which he and his wife escaped by descending a precipice with ropes—the latter, poor woman! owing to the rope being too short, getting a serious fall in the escape, and seriously damaging her personal beauty. After this he went off with all his men and joined the Mahdi's forces, and as to his subsequent history—it is unknown.

Before Admiral Hewett started on the mission to King John, several convoys were sent on with mules laden with presents, stores, and camp equipage under Kennedy of the Black Watch, commonly known by us as "Smiler" Kennedy; there being with him Graham, the flag-lieutenant, and another naval officer. And on the day that this expedition started the Admiral transmitted to me instructions he had received, to the effect that I was wanted back in Cairo to tell them all that I had found out about Massowah and the road to Khartoum *via* Kasala, and that therefore I was not to be the Governor of Massowah after all, —information at which I was overjoyed.

But my poor friend Mason Bey was as sick as a bear with a sore head, as he had to stay there as Governor himself, and thus could only send his messages to his beloved in Cairo through me. However, Mason Bey was taken up by the Admiral on his interesting embassy to King Johannes, when, although the king treated him with marked coldness verging on discourtesy,—for he hated and distrusted him as an Egyptian official,—he nevertheless invested Mason with a shield and robes of honour, which, if they served no other good purpose, gave my handsome American friend an opportunity of having a splendid photograph taken which, now suitably framed, hangs among my gallery of celebrities. Accordingly, when Sir William started on his delightful trip for the mountains of Abyssinia, I embarked on board that charming ship H.M.S. Sphinx, commanded by my friend Captain Crawford-Caffin, and sailed in her southwards to Aden, there to catch a mail-steamer to take me back the whole length of the Red Sea to Suez. And as I sailed from Massowah I reflected that I had, during those three months since I had left Cairo, passed, one way and another, through quite as eventful experiences as fall to the lot of most men in these prosaic days.

CHAPTER XVI.

I WAS treated most kindly on board the Sphinx as
Catlin's guest. In fact, to use my now, alas! late friend
Chamley Turner's favourite expression, the voyage was
"just ripping."

She was a paddle-wheel despatch-vessel, especially
designed for the comfort of some senior naval officer in
command on a tropical station; and as I was provided
with a large and cool state saloon—fit for an admiral at
least—I was very sorry when the voyage was at an end,
and I found myself once more in Aden, where, nearly a
decade previously, I had passed a year of my life. What
with lawn-tennis grounds and polo-grounds, however,
the change that I found in the place was so much for
the better that I did not much pity any one of those
officers whose fate it might be to be then serving in
that arid spot.

At all events, I managed to put in a day or two there

most comfortably. It may have been merely the change of scene that shed the glamour, but at all events, after such awful Arab places as Suakin and Massowah, a visit to the orderly towns of Steamer Point and the Camp, with their substantial buildings all beautifully kept under military government, was like suddenly arriving in London from an obscure Irish village.

Since leaving Suez some months before, it had certainly already been my luck to meet all sorts of interesting people of every class and kind, and, upon boarding the P. & O. steamship Sutlej, I found that again my luck had not deserted me. For I found that all the Australian cricket team were on board, and, owing to the crowded state of the ship, I was thrust into the same cabin with Spofforth, the celebrated "demon bowler." My first going on board, though, was amusing and delightful, for thereby I made a friend of a beautiful and charming young lady whose friendship I am glad to say I am fortunate enough to retain to this day.

I had, of course, after the recent campaign, only got with me my uniform, and on first gaining the crowded deck of the Sutlej with Crawford-Caffin, who came to see me off, I flung down the enormous straight cavalry sword that I was wearing at the first convenient spot, while we went off to interview the captain. On our return aft, to the spot under the awning where I had left my lethal blade, it was not to be found anywhere. I saw a group of ladies, and one or two evil-disposed men on the other side of the deck, in a circle laughing heartily at something, upon whom I, being suspicious and well supported by my naval friend, made a cautious advance, at first unperceived. What did I behold? A beautiful little lady, not very much taller than the missing weapon, decked with it, with the straps round her shoulders, while she was performing all sorts of pranks with my sword to an admiring crowd who were encouraging her to go on.

All the onlookers basely deserted her and fled at my approach, leaving a poor little woman, with drawn sword in her hand, all tied up in knots with straps which she did not understand and could not get free from, tripping about over a gigantic scabbard which would get between her dainty feet. Of course I had to release the fair robber, who was a bride of nineteen summers, and thus commenced a friendship which has already lasted for many years.

There was lots of fun on board the Sutlej. Among other diversions we had a fancy-dress ball, at which, I remember, my cabin companion Spofforth appeared with a black face as a Christy minstrel, looking more like a demon than ever. Then, after far too short a passage, I, with all my war spoils of spears, shields, and curious weapons of all kinds, had to say farewell and to disembark at Suez. But no! if I remember rightly, I did not come ashore with quite all the spoils of the Soudan with which I had embarked, for I fancy that a few of them are now in some of those cricketers' homes in Australia.

I found that Cairo was delightful for a while after my

return, as, although I passed a considerable part of my time daily either in the Intelligence Department of the Egyptian War Office drawing maps and writing reports, or else in being interviewed upon Soudanese matters by various bigwigs, from the Khedive and Sir Evelyn Baring downwards, I was not attached to any regiment for duty, and therefore had a good spell of enjoyment in that dear old caravanserai, Shepheard's Hotel, in practising some horses down at the race-course at Gezireh, and in amusing myself generally.

But good things do not last long in this weary world, and I had hardly been back a month before Sir Evelyn Wood sent for me and told me that I was either to go off at once on an expedition to Korosko, to find out about the desert routes to Khartoum and the state of native feeling ; or else I was to go back to Suakin, where Colonel Chermside, who was now Governor-General in the Admiral's place, was asking for me.   It was all settled in a few days.   Kitchener was sent off to Korosko, while I was sent down again to Suakin, to take over the command of the 1st Battalion of the Egyptian Army. This battalion had formerly been commanded by Chermside himself, but he, on promotion to the rank of Governor-General, had given over command to a newly appointed officer named Major Hare, who soon found that, knowing nothing of Arabic, he did not care for the Egyptian service at all.

Chermside's care and skill had already made this regiment one of the smartest in the Khedive's army ; therefore I much preferred becoming its commander

to any other billet that could have been offered to me,
not even excluding the governorship of Massowah. To
Suakin I accordingly went once more, and as my ship
dropped her anchor in the harbour on the 27th May
1884, a boat flying an enormous Egyptian ensign came
off to greet me with great ceremony. In the stern-
sheets of this boat sat David Gregorie, Lieutenant in
the 18th Royal Irish Regiment, Yuzbasha or Captain in the Egyptian army, junior staff officer to
Colonel Chermside, and one of the best young soldiers
who ever lived or drew a sword. All the British
soldiers had gone away, and Suakin was now garrisoned solely with Egyptian troops, and there had been
already one attack upon the town a few days before
my arrival.

Upon getting ashore I went and took up my billet
in the quaint flat-roofed old building known as the
Muhafiza or Governor's house, where so many men
whose names were historical, most of them having been
mentioned already by me, had slept before us, if but
for a short space of time. I could not take over my
regiment quite at once, as Hare was still present in
command; I therefore became for a time Chermside's
senior staff officer. We were very good friends, and
I rugged down on a settee in the extraordinary room
where he transacted all his business by day and slept
by night. I call it extraordinary because of the
wonderful amount of litter there was about it. It was
very large, and really one of the only habitable rooms
in the place at that time—that is, for Europeans—

and consisted chiefly of windows, the shutters of which
were studded with bullet-holes, the result of the recent
attack. The litter in the room consisted of all the
Governor-General's kit, his boots, breeches, plates, canteen, &c., and also of endless documents in Arabic,
French, and English, which were frequently blown
about by the wind in every direction at once.

After a frugal meal to which he entertained me
at an Italian café in the town, Governor-General
Chermside and I rugged down respectively upon our
divans, and had just got comfortably to sleep when we
were awakened pretty quickly by a very lively fusil-
lade from across the adjacent creek, which had the
result of making a few more holes in the shutters, and
literally of making us "sit up" pretty quickly. For,
no doubt in honour of my arrival that day, the enemy
had arrived in force, and were attacking the town on
several sides, and altogether making things lively.
We were not long in getting off to the post most
nearly attacked, which was what we called the Camel
post, and there and at other points in the lines we
passed an hour or two with plenty to keep us occupied,
for the young Egyptian soldiers were not very much
trained in musketry in those early days. The enemy
came very close to us and were in large numbers, and
the fortifications were not at all calculated to keep out
a really resolute foe. But fortunately our exertions
in making the soldiers aim low had a satisfactory
result, for they actually killed some of the attacking
force dead on the spot; and as others got wounded

they went away towards dawn, when we returned to snatch an hour's rest before the daily work, which, in the East, always begins early.

We had just got up for our morning coffee and were discussing it, when a disagreeable sight was presented to our eyes. Being informed that a native wanted to see him, Colonel Chermside ordered him to be shown in. In came, not one native, but two. One of them instantly produced from a cloth the horrible and bloody head of one of the men whom we had killed a few hours previously—he said he had slain him himself; while the other, in the same way, produced a brown hand and a nose: the hand was, I remember, particularly disagreeable, being whitish inside.

The men who brought these disgusting trophies wanted "backsheesh." Naturally they did not get it; but as it was important to have the people who lived with us inside the town and at El Keff on our side against Osman Digna's people, the bearers of these grisly spoils were treated quite courteously, but at the same time asked to take them somewhere else. In fact, they were diplomatically and airily given to understand that if any funds had been available they no doubt would have been the recipients thereof, but that unfortunately the "Miri"—that is, the Government—were very parsimonious, and really could not be induced just as yet to advance money for heads and fingers, but no doubt they would do so in time when they saw the error of their ways. With which we went back to our coffee, which, however, seemed to have a disagreeable flavour after the unpleasant interruption.

In addition to the 1st Battalion E.A., there was also in Suakin then the 5th Egyptian Regiment, which was entirely officered by natives, from the Bey, or Lieutenant-Colonel, downwards. A great many of these officers were, however, very good and smart, notably the Adjutant Major, by name Abd el Effendi Ghani, who had been before promotion a captain in one of the British battalions. This rank of adjutant major, or Sagh kol Aghassi, as they called it in the vernacular, was a kind of intermediate one between a captain and a major, and upon the "right column leader," as the literal translation is, depended in a great measure the efficiency of the regiment.

My own adjutant major at first was Mustapha Effendi Sādik, rather a lackadaisical sort of a personage, given to lolling about on the backs of chairs and picking his teeth. He was for all that a good enough officer, who might always be relied upon to look after the discipline of the regiment properly. On first taking over command of the 1st Battalion E.A. there were five other British officers borne on its strength, the army having recently been augmented by a new batch of English officers just out from home. These were Majors Tapp and Hawtayne, Captains Gregorie, Drummond Wolff, and Barttelot. Of these only one of the five now remains living, that is Hawtayne, who is employed in West Africa.

Tapp, my second in command, was a most amiable

and remarkably handsome fellow—he was, poor chap, afterwards killed at Suakin ; Gregorie, after being under fire literally hundreds of times, was killed playing polo at Suakin ; Drummond Wolff and Barttelot, who were both reverted to the British service about the time I took over command, died, one in England and the other under Stanley in Africa, where he got shot in an altercation with the natives. To my great friend Chamley Turner also I had said good-bye for the last time on coming back to Suakin, for on going up the Nile to buy camels he was drowned in the river.

There was present one more officer, of whom I saw a great deal in those days, and that was Galbraith, who was our surgeon-major at Suakin. He too is dead! —he died of fever in Cairo.

As I write these lines and think of all my brother officers with whom in those days I was hail-fellow-well-met—think, too, how we fought together, drank together, had together good times in Cairo, and rough yet cheery times in the Soudan—it does indeed make me sad. There was not one of them much above thirty when he died, and most were between twenty-five and thirty.

It is indeed on looking back like this to the jolly companions with whom one served, that one is forcibly reminded of Moore's beautiful verses :—

> " When I remember all
>   The friends so linked together
> I've seen around me fall
>   Like leaves in wintry weather,

R

> I feel like one
> Who treads alone
> Some banquet-hall deserted,
> Whose lights are fled,
> Whose garlands dead,
> And all but he departed."

And then again recur to my mind Lamb's equally striking lines:—

> "I have been laughing, I have been carousing,
> Drinking late, sitting late, with my bosom cronies—
> All, all are gone, the old familiar faces."

For, alas! even one more has gone since I commenced penning these lines, for on Thursday, the 16th May 1895, passed away at Algiers that generous and kind-hearted man, William Alexander, Duke of Hamilton and Brandon, who, leaving all his honours behind him, has now gone to join his friend Chamley Turner in the happy hunting-grounds of another world. And let us hope that they have found one and all of them either plenty of sport or plenty of fighting in the halls of Valhalla. Chamley Turner, for one, cannot possibly rest in peace without either one or the other.

Before saying farewell to him, I must put on record his last exploit at Suakin. It was two or three days after the battle of Tamai, when all the troops were back at Suakin and as we were sitting round a camp-fire together, that he suddenly exclaimed—

"Confound it all! I've lost my knife. I left it on the ground under a bush on the battlefield at Tamai. I shall have to go and fetch it to-morrow."

"And who," I asked sarcastically, "do you propose

to take out as your escort for those nineteen miles to a battlefield where the enemy are probably hanging about in hundreds just now burying their dead?"

"Escort be d——d, and enemy be d——d," retorted he, with a loud guffaw. "I'll get on my camel at daybreak, and just take my orderly with me on another, and I'll be back here with my knife in my pocket for breakfast by ten o'clock to-morrow, or else I'll eat my hat."

And he kept his word. I saw him start, and I saw him come back with the knife. What a pity that a man like that should be lost to the service by being drowned in the Nile!

In addition to the two infantry battalions, we had at Suakin a squadron of Egyptian cavalry, some of the Camel Corps, and some Artillery men to fight the Krupp guns and mountain howitzers, most of which had been recaptured from the enemy by us at El Teb, and which we had now in position on the line of fortification.

Pigott soon came down to take over command of these mounted troops, while Wodehouse also arrived to take supreme command of the Artillery. The former, however, only remained a very short time, owing to what we may call a little misunderstanding upon a certain occasion, when his own undoubted bravery was, in the opinion of the senior officers, greater than his judgment.

The enemy having come down in force one night, were firing gaily into the town from some bushes beyond a plain a few hundred yards from the parapet.

Pigott, with his usual dash, thought it would be rather a good thing to go out suddenly and charge them in the dark ; but when they got to the edge of the bushes the young soldiers of the Gyppy cavalry, who could not see either the enemy or where they were going, turned round and charged the other way—that is, back into the lines. There were a few court-martials after that and some heavy punishments, but Pigott thought that all the officers at least, if not all the men also, ought to be shot at once for cowardice. This was a view of the case in which, under the circumstances, Sir Evelyn Wood and General Grenfell could not concur. Therefore Pigott left us, and the Egyptian service lost a brave officer, who since those days has considerably added to his laurels elsewhere.

Looking at the thing dispassionately however now, considering that some of the infantry had also showed slight elements of scare on the occasion of the first night attack—that which had taken place a few days before my return—it must be owned that this bolt on the part of Pigott's men was a little discouraging. Indeed it hardly looked just at first as if the policy of garrisoning Suakin by Egyptians alone was likely to turn out a success. But we who had been with them from the beginning were mostly sanguine of the future, as we remembered that none of them had more than about a year's service, while half of them had not got more than six months' service.

And what can one expect from a lot of quite young recruits of even one complete year's service, when, unaccompanied by any older soldiers to steady them, they suddenly find themselves under a heavy fire for the first time? That squadron of cavalry had not, moreover, in those days even been instructed in the use of their breech-loading carbines; so, had they been dismounted, as the 10th Hussars were at Tamai, and told to act as mounted infantry, they would have been useless. Nor could they have protected themselves by fire if rushed. Chermside, Wodehouse, and myself, at all events, thought that if only they had a little time and experience, we should find the troops behave well enough in the future; and so they did, for they were soon as cool under fire as any veterans, taking no more notice of bullets than if peas were flying about.

These were very busy times at Suakin, and we, as the poet says, "Never found the sun came a wink too soon, or brought too long a day," for we got up at four, drilled, or else practised field firing with ball cartridges, for two hours every morning, worked at building the fortifications in the lines and the water-forts outside all day long, and then we fought at nights. For regularly every night for months we were attacked, and especially on Sunday nights we used often to have a big fight,—on several occasions, indeed, the enemy very nearly got into the place.

As time went on, though, the shooting of our men improved so much that the enemy, who used at first to rush right up to the walls and the gateways, now kept a little farther off, and would lie down behind walls and bushes to fire into us an enormous number of bullets, which were as a rule very badly directed. Our losses, therefore, were not very heavy, though occasionally a few men were killed and wounded.

Those who really suffered more than the soldiers were the people who lived in the mat huts of El Keff, —several poor Abyssinian women who led a loose life there being, I remember, shot from time to time, and many others. The natives who lived in the masonry-built town on the creek-surrounded island beyond the causeway hardly ever suffered at all. The houses were too close together and the windows too small; thus they protected one another, all except Government House, which was very exposed to fire from the stone quarries on the south side just beyond the creek.

There were from time to time several ships of war coming and going at Suakin, but it was very seldom that they were engaged with the foe. They lay, as a rule, outside the line of fire, where they were neither struck by the bullets nor in a position to shell the attacking forces by night with much effect. But there was an island called Quarantine Island, connected at low tide with the mainland, and inside this, in shoal water, my gallant friend Captain Lloyd of the Briton, who was for a long time senior naval officer, used nightly to detach a boat with a good big gun to try to take the enemy in flank. It was not, however, of much use, being too low down, although the bluejackets fired it off on every possible occasion.

Captain Lloyd was, however, one night dining on shore with Chermside, Wodehouse, and myself, when I re-

minded him of the fact that he had a big gun in his
own cabin which exactly commanded a post, one of the
little round forts built by Baker outside the lines, known
as H Redoubt, only 900 yards from our lines, which,
as we did not occupy it ourselves for want of men, used
to be nightly occupied by the rebels. From its shelter
they kept up a heavy fire upon El Keff, and upon a
work we were making at the right-hand corner of the
lines called Tabiat el Yamin. We had a Krupp gun
in Tabiat el Yamin, and a mountain howitzer also on
the roof of a small house which we had enclosed and
strengthened within the fort. We had, besides, a fine
breastwork for infantry fire, but the ground falling
away behind the little redoubt where the enemy used
to go, we could not nail many of them, shoot as much
as we liked; for they were too cunning to remain
inside the redoubt after the first volley or two. They
would skip out and lie down behind it, on the ground
sloping away from us.

Lloyd, although a very good fellow, was not particularly inclined to turn the whole of his pretty cabin
upside down by manning the big gun with a lot of
brawny sailors and banging it off, filling the place with
smoke, only for the sake of three or four shots. Wodehouse and I, however, who always lived together in
the Caravanserai, which held also all the infantry,
gave him the very best dinner we could manage under
Alfred Thacker's superintendence. After we had caused
him to consume as much as, in fact more than, could
possibly be good for his health, of sweetish champagne

bought from Greek traders, which was all we could get, we tackled him on the subject—not for the first time— for we wanted him to let off that gun particularly.

We found him very recalcitrant indeed, but at the last moment he yielded, and promised us faithfully that he would do so if the enemy should come on that side on that night only, as he was not going to bind himself for the future. However he said, as we all saw him off in his steam launch, that he thought there was not much chance of having to keep his promise: the enemy would probably give us a night's rest, or else try the other side of the town for a change.

That was exactly where he made his mistake! No sooner had the screw of his launch commenced to make her first revolutions than heavy firing began from three sides of the town at once, the two biggest attacks being on the side of Tabiat el Yamin. We roared out some chaff to him, and then rushed off to get our horses and gallop out to the lines at once, a matter which never took long.

Wodehouse and I both went to the right fort, where the fighting was, while Chermside, who soon joined us there, whilst I was directing the infantry fire, went up on the low roof of the building with Wodehouse to fire the howitzer. Here, as I could hear and see all that went on, even above the roar and the racket of the Krupp gun below and my own regular musketry volleys, I was amused vastly to witness a regular row between the two scientific branches of the service, represented by my two friends on the roof, as to which was the proper way to lay that gun. The Engineer officer maintained that the Gunner knew nothing about the proper angle of elevation. The Gunner replied that the Sapper might be Governor-General, but that he had better stick to that, for how could a Sapper be expected to fire a gun? And so they fired it by turns, both very badly, and we remained under a very heavy fire ourselves, getting one or two men hit.

Just as the Gunner was getting too exasperated to have anything more to do with the howitzer at all, and was leaving it to the Sapper in disgust, there boomed forth from the seaward the sound of a very heavy gun, and there flashed in front of us a shell through the darkness of the night. Our friend Lloyd had kept his word, and had sacrificed his cabin comforts according to promise. Another shell from the Briton, and yet another! All burst beautifully exactly behind II Redoubt, in a spot where, try they ever so hard, neither Chermside nor Wodehouse could possibly have planted a shell. When the morning came the enemy's loss on that side amounted to nineteen dead, to say nothing of the wounded they had carried away. Bravo, Lloyd!

CHAPTER XVII.

THE ALBACORE'S SEARCH-LIGHT—A GOOD DEAL ABOUT MINES—
A DISASTROUS FLOOD.

IT would be a difficult matter, nor would it prove interesting, were I to attempt to give in detail an account of the siege, or rather land blockade, of Suakin in 1884; but still there is a good deal that is interesting with reference to this phase of Eastern warfare, and therefore I shall give a slight description of certain affairs connected with that period, selecting here and there from my old diaries events which, although perhaps not really of great importance, seem worthy of record.

The enemy were not easily to be scared in those days, for all the hammerings they had received at El Teb and Tamai; but they did get a good scare the first time that they saw the electric light suddenly turned upon them.

It fell out like this: H.M.S. Albacore, which was furnished with two powerful electric search-lights, had, on the 29th May, hauled right up into the narrow

creek on the south side of the town, near the post
where we kept the camels, when that evening the
enemy suddenly appeared in force in several directions
at once, being especially strong on the left of the town,
where they got behind some old houses and partly completed earthworks. From these protected points they
fired very heavily, while we in return fired a few sharp
volleys and shells. Then the Albacore's light was
suddenly turned on, and very weird did the travelling
circle of light look, as gradually it threw its zone of
brilliant radiance into the most obscure spots, showing
up everything, bushes, houses, earthworks, enemy, all
as clear as day. The effect was instantaneous! Not
another shot did the foemen fire, but they all disappeared with the most wonderful rapidity, and although we remained on the look-out for the rest of
the night we never saw them again.

The next morning at dawn we found how precipitate
had been their flight, for we picked up fifty-two pairs
of sandals, many spears and swords, and quantities of
ammunition, which they had left behind them as they
ran. And not only this, but in the mimosa bushes
were found quantities of their clothing also, which in
their eagerness to escape they had cast away.

I well remember the next morning, as furnishing an
example of Osman Digna's cruelty, for two Amarars of
the friendly tribe under old Mahmoud Bey Ali came
in horribly mutilated. These poor fellows had been
caught by the enemy in the bush, their right hands
were cut off at the wrist, and they were sent in with

them tied round their necks, as a warning and example to the rest of their tribe, who, rightly or wrongly, were all suspected of being spies. On the following night another batch of the Hadendowahs appeared, and these were again greeted by the electric light, with much the same result. We heard that they attributed it to our friend " El Sheitan "—that is, Satan or the devil himself.

They soon, however, got thoroughly accustomed to his Satanic majesty's powers of illumination, and it mattered not how much light the Albacore might turn on, for they would get into the stone quarries beyond the creek, and pour in, some nights, a terrific fire by the hour together. It used to be very tiring, as we hardly ever got any rest, being up night after night until 2 or 3 A.M.

When things had got almost beyond all bearing, the naval officers set to work to set mines in all the places within reach where the enemy used to ensconce themselves, in the hopes that by blowing up a few the others would be frightened, and some rest become possible for the garrison.

These mines were of various sorts: some were made to explode automatically, others were connected with an electric battery by a long insulated wire enclosed in gutta-percha covering. It was for a long time all of no use. The Arabs had eyes like cats, and they had the courage which can only be inspired by a most implicit faith in religion. They used to cut and carry away hundreds of yards of insulated wire, then dig up the mines, which they always found, no matter how well concealed, and in some extraordinary way remove them without themselves sustaining any injury whatever.

It was a most extraordinary thing, for so gingerly were some of these mines set that dogs occasionally exploded them. On one occasion even, a mine consisting of a large quantity of gun-cotton was exploded by a hare, whose only visible damage was that he had the tip of his nose blown off.

This occurred close to the right water-fort, which at that time was occupied by marines under Lieutenant Campbell, and I well remember a good deal of fun about it; for Colonel Chermside being then, as he often was, away at Massowah, I was at the time commanding officer on shore. When I rode out to the post at dawn, expecting to find many corpses about, Campbell had just discovered the only corpse, that of the hare! I urged that in my capacity of commanding officer all dead hares killed by mines belonged to me. The gallant marine, on the other hand, represented that he had found the noseless hare, and that he had the right of possession; and further, that there was no established precedent to show that all hares killed by gun-cotton mines within 1000 yards of the vicinity of a post did not belong to the officer commanding that post. So we settled the matter by having him cooked at once, and eating him together for breakfast; and as the shock of the explosion had made him tender, most uncommonly good he was.

Campbell frequently got most capital shooting, both sand-grouse and wild duck, outside the right water-fort, for a large quantity of water used, especially after a little rain, to stand against a huge bank, upon each end of which the water forts were built, and here these birds would come in quantities, it being the only fresh water obtainable.

In the same way, later on, when we were erecting an octagonal stone tower, like the water-forts, at the old earthwork fort of El Foula, I used to get plenty of shots at both duck and sand-grouse in the large hole, almost amounting to a pond, made by the men excavating mud wherewith to make mud bricks for the outside parapets or for other building purposes. The ducks did not mind the men working a bit, but would dabble about quite close to them. They soon, however, found out what a gun meant.

To this day the Foula Fort bears a superscription cut in beautiful Arabic letters on a stone tablet over the door by one of my men, a cunning mason and stone-cutter, which inscription states that the fort was erected by Andrew Haggard Bey, with the date in both the Mahomedan and Christian eras. It was while super-intending the work there one evening that I picked out one of the most intelligent Egyptians I ever had any-thing to do with. I had my gun with me, and shot and hit hard a duck of an unknown species. It flew straight away across the desert, when a soldier, working half up to his waist in water, declared that he had seen it fall far away among the bushes, and that if I would let him go he was sure he could retrieve it. He was a very black-skinned man from Upper Egypt, and I knew these fellows to have good sight, yet I could hardly believe it possible that he could find it.

" What is your name?" I asked.

" Ahmed Mahomed, ya Bey."

" Well, Ahmed Mahomed, if you can retrieve that duck I will make you a *wakeel onbashu* (lance-corporal) and my extra *murasalah* (orderly)." For I knew he must be a smart chap to do it.

He was off like an arrow from a bow, and in ten minutes' time returned, as fast as he had gone off, with the duck.

Ahmed Mahomed's name appeared accordingly in the order book next day as being promoted to the rank of lance-corporal and orderly. He never gave me any trouble except in one way. I used in that hot climate to be very fond of eau-de-Cologne, which was sent me from Cairo, and it began to disappear at an enormous rate. I knew that my other orderly, by name Lance-Corporal Mahomed Omar, had never touched it, so I was after a time more than ever convinced that it was my friend Ahmed Mahomed who was drinking it, as I had heard that ladies do sometimes in England. I liked the man, but nevertheless sent him to prison for seven days just to stop this custom, which he denied vigorously.

When he had done his seven days he came out, and then made humble confession, saying that he had drunk the " colognia " because he liked the smell so much, but, if only the Bey would forgive him and take him back as orderly, he would never offend again. The Bey did

forgive him, and he afterwards did capital service. A
year or two ago I saw him for the last time, when I,
coming home invalided from India, was on a visit to
Egypt. I was driving along in the most crowded part
of the Mooskee in Cairo, when suddenly from amid the
crowd a smart sergeant-major of police started rushing
after my carriage and yelling to the driver to stop. I
thought that the driver had at least committed some
offence against the police regulations. Nothing of the
sort! Before I knew what was happening, I found my
hand being alternately vigorously kissed by the police
sergeant-major and then laid on the top of his head
in token of respect, while many blessings were being
poured upon my head in rapid Arabic utterance. Lo
and behold! the police sergeant-major was none other
than my old swarthy friend Ahmed Mahomed, now in
the police service, who had commenced his career by
being made lance-corporal for his skill in retrieving
a duck! Although it is not a method followed in
the British service, it seems to me as good a mode of
selection as any other.

To get back to the mines, we did eventually catch
a batch of the enemy with a mine which was laid
outside II Redoubt, which I have already mentioned
as the spot on which Lloyd fired his big gun with
such success.

It was, I think, a naval officer named Talbot who
arranged this mine on a clever system, which he was
confident would defeat the ingenuity of the enemy in
removing these engines of destruction. I was speci-

ally interested in the laying of that particular mine in that exact spot, for among the enemies in general who came there, I had distinctly a personal enemy, whose tongue used frequently to annoy me night after night. For this ruffian would roar out in Arabic personal abuse directed at myself and at my female relations in words which were anything but fit for ears polite. And my officers and men did not like it; moreover, I did not like it myself. No matter how many volleys we fired, he never got touched, but would go on gaily all the same, shouting frightfully opprobrious terms at the top of his voice. It was becoming monotonous, as Bret Harte's miner said when the mule fell through the roof of his hut for the sixth time.

And then came the night of Talbot's mine. It consisted of a cask of gun-cotton arranged to explode automatically if moved out of the perpendicular. There was some arrangement with a tube of mercury: if the tube of mercury ceased to be quite straight the mine went off. They were horribly dangerous things to set, these mines, as I will show later on; but this one was successfully buried in the coral rock and sand behind the redoubt, where it was meant to be found by the enemy, who, even in the night, could always see where the ground had been disturbed.

That night, rather late, the enemy suddenly appeared opposite Tabiat el Yamin, the usual direction. They fired two or three volleys into the lines, then all

S

was still. I was watching with my native officers, standing behind the parapet of Fort Yamin.

"Now they are digging up the mine," I said. "I wonder if it will go off."

"*Ya salaam!*" and "*Al-hamd-ul-lillah!*" exclaimed the officers, holding up their hands. "The pigs have been caught this time, thank Allah!"

For even as I was speaking, the bright flash of the flame had shown us the mine exploding with a tremendous flare in the middle of a group of the enemy, the roar of the report only reaching us after all had again become dark. And after that, all was still and silent in the desert around; but we knew that some human souls had been released from their earthly trammels with an awful rapidity.

I must honestly own that our one and only sensation was a feeling of delight; for they had harried us too long. At the first faint streak of dawn I stood upon the spot where the mine had exploded, and noticed all the bodies and fragments of bodies scattered about in a circle around, the largest portions being at a distance of about sixty yards, though some were lying as far as three hundred yards away. One man, although his legs had been blown off below the knee, had not been fired away to a distance like the others, but had fallen close to the hole, and was lying on his back. He must have had hold of the cask, actually lifting it, when it exploded. He was a very handsome man indeed, and exactly like the pictures one sees of Jesus Christ. The natives of

Suakin recognised him, and also some of the others, and knew them all by name: he was the man who used to shout out the abuse at me.

There was, oddly enough, very little blood about; and although I saw a man's liver with a large stone firmly embedded in the middle of it, it looked quite dried up. It must have been the excessive scorching heat of the explosion which, even as it blew the poor wretches to pieces, had dried up their blood. Their rifles and other weapons were torn and twisted into the most extraordinary shapes, not one of the rifles having left on it one atom of the woodwork of the stock.

As an example of what extraordinary sight these men must have had, I may mention that in one detached hand I saw an object which I removed without difficulty, the hand being quite limp. I found it to be the wooden fuse out of one of the shells from the boat gun, which, as I have described, used to be fired whenever the sailors got a chance. It had not been fired at all that night, so the savage warrior must have seen the fuse in the dark and picked it up as a curiosity a minute before the explosion which had sent him to kingdom come!

That explosion did us a tremendous amount of good, for we got afterwards two months' absolute peace by night, although the enemy used occasionally to come down with their horsemen and camelmen by day and make a raid on the camels and on cattle feeding in the desert just outside the water-forts, and especially outside Fort Foula. Then Wodehouse, who was the quickest man at turning out that I ever knew, would dash after them with the cavalry, the water-forts and Foula would fire a few guns, a few men would be brought in wounded, one or two would be killed, and that would be the end of it.

At any rate, we got our sleep at nights; and then Wodehouse went off to Cairo to go up the Nile under Wolseley, and so I lost my chum. A native officer called Mustapha Helmi remained in command of the cavalry; but young Gregorie used every morning of his life to go out with a patrol of about twelve men, in order to protect the front of the lines, the marine camp, and the railway works, from any sudden attack in force from the enemy. For while Chermside and I had been building fortifications, other changes had taken place in Suakin as the summer had passed into autumn. A good number of marines had, as the year rolled on, been accumulated there, some living in a house in the town under command of Colonel Ozzard, others in an intrenched camp outside II Redoubt, where we blew up the savages.

A good number of Royal Engineers also, under Lieutenant-Colonel Wood, had been for some time encamped on Quarantine Island on the north of the town. They had built a causeway to the mainland, and were making a start at a railway, which had already got as far as the Marine Camp, and was dignified by the name of the Suakin-Berber Railway. Also we had now a General in the place, in the shape of a distinguished Guardsman,

Major-General Lyon Fremantle, who, although accompanied by his two staff-officers, Lieutenant-Colonel Kelly, Royal Sussex, and Captain Fred Stopford of the Guards, had absolutely no troops to manœuvre, except perhaps the marines and the sappers.

However, we Egyptians had, by arrangements in Cairo, now, for fighting purposes, come under a kind of British control, and therefore had to do what the General wished.   It must be owned, however, that General Fremantle was as kind and considerate as a man could be under the circumstances, and, beyond an intimation of what he would like done if it could be arranged, never interfered in the least in the Egyptian interior economy, either of any particular corps or of the whole brigade in Suakin.

All the year we had occupied ourselves with building barracks in each separate fort and the fortifications of the town, in our own way with our own men.   We cut stone ourselves, made our own bricks, just like the Israelites of old, of mud without straw, or of mud with chopped straw when we could get it; then as an improvement we burnt them in home-made brick kilns, where they often turned out a ghastly failure, all crumbling away to nothing.   We even made our own lime from the coral rock so plentiful in the place.

And then, after months of labour, just as we had got some nice barracks and some splendid walls built up of mud brick, there came one day a deluge of rain, when an enormous river formed out at the water-forts and poured towards the town.   It was arrested for some

considerable time by our walls, thus filling the plain
with water to a considerable depth outside. And then
it burst through them in one place in an enormous
river, and, carrying dead cattle and sheep with it,
traversed the lines and poured itself into the sea.

Some of Chermside's best barracks, built of mud
brick, in a fort called Ansari, were also that day
levelled with the ground. But he was away at Massowah at the time, and before he had got back again
I had built some new barracks, and built them on a
new plan of my own, and of stone. And although I
was not a sapper, but only an unscientific infantry
officer, those barracks were very highly commended
by Lieutenant-General Sir Frederick Stephenson when
he came down on a tour of inspection. But he was
never informed that they were my work, and I was
rather sore about it then, as one often is about little
things that seem mean at the time, but do not affect
one in the least a few years later.

But this is a point of no importance; what was
really important was that all the walls for the whole
circumvallation of El Keff had to be built over again.
And as the water stood for weeks and weeks outside
them and the ditches were filled to the brim, this could
never have been done were it not for the native
Egyptians' wonderful facility of puddling in mud and
water, as indeed shown by the way they irrigate their
fields. But they soon baled out the ditches, built
little walls to hold all the water back on to the surface
of the desert, and then, having at length got all the

base of the old walls dry, went at it again with a will. And thus, to cut a long story short, during the interval of comparative peace which the enemy left us after the mine burst, we fortified the town very strongly, and that, too, in spite of enormous difficulties in the way of procuring proper materials.

One strange thing, noticeable in even the most sandy and previously driest parts of the desert just after this rain, was that the ground was covered with toads of all sizes. But these toads disappeared again as quickly as they had come. I could not find one four days after the downpour. They must therefore either have come down in the rain or else up out of the ground, whither, I presume, they again retired to wait for the next flood, to come out once more for a few more days' enjoyment of life and liberty.

CHAPTER XVIII.

As mentioned before, Colonel Chermside being Governor-General of the Red Sea, and having, therefore,
to be constantly backwards and forwards either to
Massowah or Cairo, I often had all the command of
the Egyptian troops and all the interior economy of
the town thrown into my hands, under, of course,
General Fremantle's general supervision. In the
position that I then occupied I had soon an opportunity of finding out what a really excellent officer
David Gregorie was, whether in the office or the field,
as he was my own staff-officer. His was a nature full
of quiet observance, of dogged determination, slightly
opinionative certainly, but full of fun.

As, when I was in command of the Brigade, he was
always, as I have said, my staff-officer, he had, of
course, to write all the letters and to sign them "By
order" on my behalf. He therefore sometimes, when
I had got out of the Brigade Office and back to my

regimental orderly-room, used to manage to score me off in an amusing way. When present with my own regiment, I was of course only the "Officer Commanding the 1st Battalion Egyptian Army," and no longer "Officer Commanding Egyptian Troops." So he would send down by an orderly a regular snorter, in both English and Arabic (all our correspondence being in two languages), signed "By Order" and containing some perfectly justifiable complaint made by the Officer Commanding the Egyptian Troops (that was myself), of the conduct of the Officer Commanding the 1st Battalion E.A. (also, of course, myself) on some matter or other, and would in my name, as Officer Commanding the Troops, request information as to why certain orders had not been complied with.

I would then, as Officer Commanding the 1st Battalion, have to direct my second in command, Major Tapp, or my Adjutant Major, to write a humble reply to the Officer Commanding Egyptian Troops expressing deep regret that the orders had not been complied with, and promising to offend no more, which reply would also, of course, be sent in Arabic. It was then great fun when I got back again to the Brigade Office, and young Gregorie, putting the correspondence before me and complaining of the Officer Commanding the 1st Battalion, would make me write myself another "wigging." Although this sounds absurd, he was usually in the right in all official matters. As we had become very great friends, my junior officer enjoyed being able to go at me in this way, through myself. And in the field there was never a better soldier, though a little too rash, than was David Gregorie.

A little example of the way that Gregorie used to behave may be given by simply jotting down an extract taken at haphazard from my diary. Before transmitting it, I may mention that on every Tuesday we had field-firing for the whole of the garrison, making every man fire fifteen rounds of ammunition at various ranges from 100 to 1000 yards, the points selected to aim upon being those where the enemy were chiefly wont to appear at night. My entry for one Tuesday runs as follows :—

" To-day we had only field-firing on the left, so that, in case there should be any attack on the cavalry picket as on last Tuesday, there should be no inconvenience to our own men from the fire of the forts, &c.

" The cavalry picket did become engaged with the enemy. Captain Gregorie was with them. I went out with the remainder of the cavalry, and we ran the enemy nearly into Handoub, skirmishing all the way through the bushes.

" The formation I put the cavalry in was: one section, in extended order, forward in echelon on the right; one section in same order extended on the left. The remainder of these respective troops both in line at an interval of nearly a hundred yards apart. The G.O.C. [General Fremantle] rode out with a riding-cane in his hand and joined us; he was very pleased with the way that the cavalry went at their work."

Below this I have added a footnote which runs as follows :—

"This was the day that David Gregorie pursued the enemy alone, being only followed by an Egyptian orderly, with whose carbine he carried on a spirited fire long after the rest of us had fallen back, much to my alarm for his safety. I asked the General, when he eventually reappeared unhurt, to administer to him 'considerable snuff,' which he did.

"Askwith of the Royal Engineers also joined in during this fight to see the fun. The G.O.C. asked him if Colonel Wood did not require his services at the works going on at Quarantine Island. Askwith replied that he had leave from Wood to come out and see the fighting. General said, 'Oh! under those circumstances, all right ; but spectators are, as a rule, best at a distance.'"

Thus runs my entry. And as poor Askwith's name is mentioned, I may as well note here that he, poor fellow, was the man who some time after almost blew Tapp and myself to pieces with a dynamite box, called a land-torpedo, which worked with a spring and a cap, and subsequently did actually meet his own death through its explosion.

He was placing it in a new sandbag redoubt we were then making, from which the enemy used to steal the sandbags nightly. Suddenly he exclaimed, "Holloa! I've lost the run of this thing. I am only holding up the hammer now by sheer force : if I let go it will go off!"

"Hold tight, old chap!" we said with fervour; and when he had successfully fixed it, we said we would go torpedo-laying with him no more, as it was not in our line. That night the enemy took away the sandbags again; they also dug up the land-torpedo, which did not explode, but they left it where it was, lying in the redoubt,—they did not try to carry it away with them.

Next day poor Askwith, trying to set it again, blew himself into a thousand pieces. I heard the explosion, and on riding out saw the poor chap's remains being picked up. It was literally a case of "an engineer being hoist with his own petard."

He and I were very good friends, and it was a great shock to me. To show the extraordinary action of the dynamite, I myself picked up the pocket of the serge coat he had been wearing, which was lying entirely apart from anything else, quite uninjured, simply looking as though the stitches had been unripped with a knife at the seams.

After Askwith's death some very brave deeds were performed by Lieut.-Colonel Elliott Wood, and also by Lieut. Graham Thompson, both of the Royal Engineers.

Now, as a soldier, I objected particularly to Wood, for, as the English gradually gained a certain amount of power in Suakin, he was always complaining to the General that I and my men did not build causeways, or walls, or conduits, or wells, or something or other, in exactly the approved sapper Chatham style. I, being an entirely independent, and perhaps a bigoted, infantry officer, one moreover belonging to a foreign army, looked upon these complaints as being a sign of his ignorance of etiquette, and also of narrow-mindedness, begotten by that extraordinary sapper training which seems often to make a man think he knows everything three times as well as any other soldier belonging to every other department of the service.

I also objected, but only in a friendly way, to Graham Thompson, and for a very good reason. He, on two successive days at our Suakin races, riding his own horse, an old racer from Malta—Sunbeam was, I think, the brute's name—defeated me on my " Parson." He thrashed me all to pieces in a flat race, and next day just won the steeple-chase from me, although I was catching him up at the time, and would have beaten him had there been only one more jump. And, alas! I had built all those jumps myself, had put out pickets of my own regiment during the racing to keep the enemy off, and done all that a prudent commanding officer could do. It was too hard altogether to be beaten by the scientific branch of the service after all!

Nevertheless, after poor Askwith was dead, both Wood and Graham Thompson did deeds worthy of the V.C., so I will freely forgive them all the annoyance that they caused me. They went groping about in the sand, down on their hands and knees, by the hour together, feeling for hidden land-torpedoes in unknown places, concealed by their poor dead comrade, to save others from the risk of a death of which they ran an

imminent risk themselves; for even a touch to the
hidden infernal machines might have sent them to
blazes! But they found them all in the end, and were
not killed in the process. I saw them at it myself, and
it made me shudder to watch them. To do in cold
blood a thing of that sort is far braver than to do a
plucky thing in the heat of action—at least that is my
idea, and I think that others will share it.

But having now cursed and blessed my friends the
sappers, I must for the present leave them severely
alone.

As that year of 1884 wore on at Suakin, by degrees
the natives outside thought that they might perhaps be
able to take the town after all. Lord Wolseley had
started on his expedition up the Nile, and as no very
favourable reports were received of his progress, the
rebels, as we called them, forgetting the mine episode,
commenced anew to make themselves extremely unpleasant. They made numerous raids upon our cattle
and camels, and often caught a fair number, although
there was always a fight and a few killed on both sides
in these raids. And then they took to coming down
and firing on us again at nights, especially from the
quarries on the south side of the town, across the narrow
creek.

To get the better of them, we sent to the Citadel at
Cairo for some of those antediluvian weapons—mortars; and what fun we had experimenting with those
mortars! No one knew how to use them. There
were no properly loaded shells, no proper fuses, in

fact nothing! But, making a mortar battery down in the town with an Egyptian gunner officer and artillery-men in charge, I used to practise that mortar day after day, to the very great risk of the inhabitants of Suakin. For although we sent our mortar shells, like a cricket ball, high up into the air, and although they used on falling to burst on the other side of the creek, some of the fragments of the huge round shells often came straight back towards us again and into the town, causing thereby consternation among the natives. But we went on with the practice.

A night came, however, when all our dangerous manœuvres, which General Fremantle used to chaff me a good deal about, did not prove in vain, for everything comes to him who waits.

I had a mortar arranged on a battery at the ferry over the creek, exactly opposite to the quarries. We had been practising in the morning and adjusting the fuses, with the native artillery captain left in charge, and I thought we had got the fuses accurately disposed at last. Some very heavy firing took place that even-ing on the town from two sides at midnight, fire being especially heavy from the quarries. As usual we turned out instantly, and moved off men to occupy the roofs of houses and reply with rifle fire; but I per-sonally went off to my pet toy, the mortar. The very first shot that Captain Helmi fired was a success! The enormous shell, after flying up in the air, as I said before just like a cricket ball, dropped straight down into the middle of the quarries, and then, instead of waiting with the fuse fizzing, as most of our mortar shells did, long enough to allow every one to get out of the way, it burst instantaneously, killing and wounding a number of men.

We never had another attack from the quarries all the time that I remained in Suakin. They were frightened to death at the very name of the mortars after that; but that we should never have got in another shell so well I am convinced, had we tried for years. The scene in the quarry next morning was horrible to behold, for the shell had burst right in the middle of a crowd, and there was blood everywhere. I remember that night well.

In those days the marines under Colonel Ozzard were living in a large newly built house in the town near the creek, the roof of which they manned when the attack came on that side—first, however, making a parapet of their kit bags. They also had a Gardner gun on the roof, which, with their rifles, they began to play on the enemy, clearly seen in the moonlight as, terrified at the mortar, they sprang out in swarms from the quarries and ran back to where they had a large reserve with camels a few hundred yards in rear.

I had instantly thrown an inlying picket of thirty men of the 5th Egyptian Battalion on to the roof of a house belonging to an Arab sheikh named Mussalim Seyyid, which roof, as it was quite close to the quarries across the creek, we kept in a state of defence with sandbags.

These men and myself had moved down in double

time from the Caravanserai, where we all lived, and across the causeway, under the hottest fire I ever remember in the town, and they got to the roof just in time to slate the enemy well, as they showed themselves on the bare desert. I never knew a picket to turn out quicker and better in a sudden night attack than did those men of the 5th Battalion, who, like myself, must have all been asleep when the firing began. In fact, I remember poor Dr Galbraith, as we doubled past his window, all round which the bullets were spattering, leaning out and shouting to me, "Bravo, old boy! that's record time."

The enemy were not able that night, as they often did, to carry away their dead, but only their wounded, for the combined fire of the marines and the Egyptians in the clear moonlight was altogether too much for them; and moreover, although it was not really a hotter fire than their own had been before we "mortared" them out of the holes, it was far better directed. If those Arabs had only shot as well as they fought, what a terrible foe they would have been!

I never had a better opportunity of judging on this point than five days after the quarry fight, when, on Monday 8th December 1884, a determined attack was made by from 1500 to 2000 of the enemy just before daybreak, an ambush having been laid by them to catch Gregorie's morning patrol near the sandbag redoubt to the north of the town. Here there was a large fortified camp of marines close to the line of the little railway which was being run out from

T

Quarantine Island by the Royal Engineers under Wood. This camp and the head of the railway-works would probably have been rushed in the dark had not Gregorie with his twelve mounted men been too sharp for the enemy. He was advancing, as usual every morning, cautiously in skirmishing order through the bush, when he suddenly discovered them and drew their fire, when he fell back to the flank of the marine camp fighting, being followed by the enemy. To his astonishment the marines did nothing to assist him, but merely remained leaning on the parapet of their camp in their shirt-sleeves, looking on at the performance.

If, however, the officer in command of the marines thought it best to remain inactive, those commanding the ships in the harbour and forts did not that morning share his views, for as the dawn was just breaking every gun within range came into action. From the roof of the Caravanserai I could see that, protected by this fire, Gregorie with his patrol was still fighting, and being anxious about him, I, in consequence, took out the rest of the squadron of Egyptian cavalry, about eighty in number, to reinforce him—Freddy Stopford, General Fremantle's A.D.C., galloping out with me.

We found Gregorie still in touch with the enemy, who were falling back from the coast towards Hasheen, being evidently alarmed at the long-range gun on board H.M.S. Dolphin, which, from a range of three miles' distance, was dropping some shells near them. Indeed, as I joined Gregorie and took over the command, two of these Dolphin shells made it most unpleasant for us advancing, for their shrapnel burst with a scream exactly over our heads. To avoid a repetition of this, although thereby more exposed to the enemy's fire, I rapidly moved all the cavalry up on to a ridge bare of trees running towards the mountains at Hasheen, thinking that with their telescopes the sailors must surely see the white coats and red fezzes of the Egyptians. They fortunately did so, and stopped shelling us in consequence; what is more, on my return my servant, Alfred Thacker, and my English orderly-room clerk, Sergeant Rushin, both told me that from the roof of the Caravanserai they could with glasses often during the fight distinguish not only my great grey Arab " The Squire," but even clearly see the sun shining on my helmet spike.

I found at first on that ridge that we were exactly at the range most suited to the enemy's mode of firing high, so I advanced upon them, they retiring before me. We then fought a regular little battle; though, had I known what was seen from the masts of the ships, that there was an enormous reserve of camel-men in the bushes behind their fighting line, I don't think that I should have tried the "Gyppy" cavalry quite so highly, although they now knew perfectly well how to use their Martini-Henry carbines.

As the enemy gradually fell back into thick bush, where we saw them swarming, we followed them along the bare ridge until only at 150 yards' distance; we then dismounted half our men and opened fire. I sent one troop under Gregorie, which Stopford also accompanied, away to the right, into some low bushes one or two hundred yards away, whence they got a capital, almost direct, enfilading fire along the enemy's line, and with the other troop I fired direct at their front. Here the enemy stood firm, and we got a few men and horses hit; but their fire was chiefly high, whereas ours was, after just the first opening volleys, good. I can remember now with a smile how in my anger I threatened all the men with "confinement to barracks" for the rest of their natural lives, during those few first volleys, unless they made better practice, and how that terrible threat had a most excellent effect upon the dismounted firing squads of Egyptian cavalrymen, who really afterwards made excellent practice at the enemy, whom we could, so close were we, see falling fast. By making a squad of men fire at a low bush, behind which he was standing, we at length killed the man who, exposing himself all the time and shouting insults at us, appeared to be their chief.

Then their fire almost ceased, and after a confab with Freddy Stopford and Gregorie, who were both most truculent and would have liked to charge with the sabre, I came to the conclusion that it would be folly to try that game. Moreover, I knew that what General Fremantle would wish me to do would be to try to draw them back if possible under the fire of the guns. I therefore gave orders to retire at a walk, by alternate troops, moving well out to each flank so as to give the Dolphin a chance. This had a splendid effect, for no sooner did we commence our retirement than the whole of their reserve, which we had never seen, rushed forward with their camels and commenced to pick up the dead and wounded. Right into the middle of this throng of men did the Dolphin land two shells most beautifully with dire effect, for they bolted. Just at that moment General Fremantle rode up, as usual with nothing but a riding-cane in his hand, when he was kind enough to say that we had fought this little action exactly as he would have wished.

Our loss was one sergeant and several privates killed and wounded, and several horses hit. If only, however, instead of merely standing firing at us, the brave Hadendowahs had charged, in their great numbers, down upon us sword in hand, they must have caught our dismounted men, and then the victory would have been all the other way. By our getting so close, how-ever, they fired chiefly over our heads, and fortunately all went well.

The enemy, who owned to 108 men killed in this affair, were in fact awfully ashamed of themselves for not having charged. For we were, through our native so-called allies the Amarars, in constant communication with them, and we heard all about it that very same evening. They gave as an excuse for not charging, that, seeing the three English officers in white helmets, they thought that, although the Egyptians wore red fezes, they were really British soldiers in disguise, for they had never known Egyptians to stand so firm in the open before. This was a great feather in our caps, for it showed what the effects of discipline could do with the fellah soldier.

Talking about cowardice among the Egyptians was, indeed, after this scrimmage, far less rarely indulged in by any of the British naval officers and others, for it could not but be owned that they had done well. As regards cowardice, I never saw men behave better when wounded than did these men. They never complained, even when horribly hit, as was a certain Sergeant Redwan, who was shot in the neck during this action. When I went to speak to him as he lay there holding his gaping wound together with his hand, he exclaimed simply, "Oh, *Maalesh!* it is nothing; and now that the Bey has come to speak to me I shall soon be all right." By Galbraith's skill this plucky fellow was eventually rescued from the very jaws of death.

Another time, when the enemy got very close indeed during a heavy night attack on Tabiat el Turk, two of my men got shot in the head from behind by some of the marines under Lieut. Townshend, who were, until stopped by Chermside, firing rather wildly from the top of a house inside the lines. Neither of these men lost consciousness, and both of them refused to be removed to hospital until the attack was repulsed. One of them died before it was over.

Another time, when firing was going on, a man's Remington rifle burst at the breech and the breech block blew into the soldier's forehead, where it lodged in the bone, being only removed by sheer force by the captain of his company, Captain Mortadda Effendi. This man also refused to leave the firing line, and he too died. These few instances will, I think, show that there actually is some good heart among many of these men when trained, in spite of all the cowardice shown by Baker's miserable crew.

There may perhaps have been some justification in the enemy's remark with reference to our fight on the 8th December, that they thought the mounted men were Englishmen, for we had some months earlier organised some British mounted infantry from the marines under Townshend, who thus became literally "Horse Marines" for the time.

Townshend, who was a very plucky and smart young officer, was out with them pretty often, but they were far too few in number, and, not being good riders, were hardly a success. At last one day, when he and his men were out scouting, they were cut off by the enemy from Suakin, and only just saved themselves by riding for their very lives to get round the flank of the savages, who were also some of them mounted on horses and camels. Townshend got in by the skin of his teeth, though with some slight loss among his men, and after that the mounted marines returned to their infantry duties. He himself left the marines and got appointed to the Central Indian Horse, and in the recent Chitral campaign the name of Captain Townshend will have been noticed as one of the gallant defenders of the Chitral fort throughout the long siege, which was pushed by the enemy with such terrible vigour that it was almost touch and go with the garrison half-a-dozen times over. It is a source of great delight to me that he has been neither killed nor wounded in that arduous conflict, but lived to be promoted and given the C.B., which he well deserved.

In spite of this repulse, the enemy became more than ever active throughout that whole month of December, coming now far more often to attack us with camel-men and horsemen in some force in the daytime, while resuming also their nightly firing. Thus the cavalry and camel corps were out day after day, and it was indeed seldom that many consecutive hours passed without the roar of big guns or the rattle of musketry being heard.

At this period, and for long before this, Commodore, now Sir Robert More Molyneux, was the senior naval officer on the station. He had taken up his abode upon my old friend Crawford-Caffin's ship, the Sphinx, and was very kind in the way of asking us off to see him. Very jolly, too, it used to be to be able at times to get off for an hour or two of an afternoon or evening from the hot and fly-ridden beleaguered town of Suakin, to loll in comfort under an awning in the fresh sea-breeze on the beautifully clean deck of a man-of-war.

We had from time to time other distinguished visitors in the naval line who, for a short period, took up their residence in Suakin harbour. Among these was Admiral Lord John Hay, who asked Colonel Chermside, General Grenfell, who was down among us for a few days, and myself out to dine on his despatch-vessel the

Helicon. He was most hospitable, but there was something very strange in the taste of the champagne which he had kindly set before us. We all drank it in solemn silence, with the exception of our gallant Governor-General, who was not only particularly thirsty, but who also had the courage of his opinions. With upturned eyes, as though merely considering the flies upon the ceiling or the adornments of the cabin, he ventured to remark—

"May I ask, Lord John, if you would kindly allow me to ask for a bottle of soda-water?"

"Soda-water! why, what's the matter?" answered the Admiral, somewhat testily; "don't you like your champagne?"

"Oh, it's not that," answered Chermside, mendaciously, " but "—after a pause—"I always think, you know, that soda-water *brings out the flavour of champagne so!*"

Nobody who went out to see the Admiral again after that ever got anything stronger than champagne-cup! General Grenfell, however, who loved a joke, never let this one drop; and owing to this little incident, of which he made a good story, during the rest of the time that I was in Egypt nobody ever drank soda-water with champagne without its being invariably called " bringing out the flavour."

The end of the year 1884 went out with rather more fighting than usual; even the very last night of it there was a good deal of blazing and bloodshed.

On the 1st January 1885, Governor-General Chermside was again off on one of his periodical trips to Massowah; but we had present with us for a few days General Sir Frederick Stephenson and his staff, under whose patronage we brought off, on New Year's day, the first race-meeting ever held in Suakin, accompanied by all sorts of sports for the marines and bluejackets. This was a brilliant success in every way, the obstacle race for the sailors particularly filling all the natives with astonishment. I am not surprised at it either, for it was wonderful even to white men to witness their extraordinary agility in climbing poles, sliding down ropes, or darting, head first, through barrels. It was a strange experience, having to bring off a Gymkhana meeting like this with heavy pickets out to keep off the enemy in case of attack. Fortunately, however, they did not spoil the day's amusement by putting in an appearance.

Sir Frederick Stephenson was anxious to find out from me if any of the Egyptian cavalry and artillery then present were willing to volunteer to remain longer in Suakin than the year for which they had been originally sent down there. I accordingly inquired from the native officers of these corps, who told me that Egyptians did not understand volunteering, not having yet been trained up to that pitch, but that, if ordered to remain, all the men would remain cheerfully for six months or a year longer than the stipulated time, supposing they got a little present to do so. For they were quite happy in Suakin, getting good pay, clothes, and rations.

I told the Lieutenant-General and General Fremantle the result of my inquiries on this matter, but no decision was come to at that time.

General Stephenson went back to Cairo, and as it was now more than probable that there would be before long another campaign from Suakin with European troops, we had to work harder than ever at all sorts of things, especially at filling up holes within the lines and building a military road across the spongy seashore, which was often covered with water, to a gateway the sappers were making in the lines near the right fort, called Tabiat el Yamin.

During this period both Lieut.-Colonel Kelly, the Brigade Major, and Lieut.-Colonel Wood, R.E., were particularly active in getting the General to stir me up to do things in faster time than it was possible they could be done, the former being especially so after he had, when riding, himself fallen into a hole which I had already had filled up once. This place looked quite solid, but owing to the percolation of the sea-water, was really a kind of quagmire underneath, proving a veritable pitfall. As he was not hurt, I was rather amused than otherwise at this incident, as Kelly thought it all the fault of "those blessed Egyptians."

So I went quietly along, working with all the men I could get, in my own way; and when Wood insisted that I was not making the road, for which I had to find stones where I could, and in spite of great native opposition, in the way that the sappers would make a road, I merely smiled, and said that his gallant sappers were not making the gateway to which it led half so well as the "Gyppies" could do it, for it was far too narrow for guns and carts to pass through. And here, although at the time by measurements I proved to the engineers making it that I was right, I in turn was not listened to; but, to my great joy, I triumphed later on when the English troops began to disembark, for they had to pull down that gate and widen it after all. Score off the sappers!

All this time I was also building a new fort near the quarries, on the other side of the town, to keep the enemy out of them, for which I had to blast the stone, and also other work on hand; so it was no wonder if, with so much to do, the days in Suakin passed quickly.

It was while excavating coral rock one day from the deep ditch we were making to "A" Redoubt out in the desert to the right of this new quarry fort, that an extraordinary thing happened to me. For, on a soldier breaking with a pickaxe a piece of rock, what looked like a fossil whelk-shell fell out from its interior. I picked it up, and Gregorie and I, seeing it was covered with white lime, were both convinced that it was the fossil of a hermit crab in a whelk-shell. I was carrying it about when, some ten minutes later, I felt a tickling in the palm of my hand, and then a slight nip! On looking at it, lo and behold! the crab had pushed out an antenna and a claw, and was not a fossil at all, but alive and well, after thousands of years of imprisonment in that coral rock!

Plenty of people, including Mr Augustus Wylde, a well-known Suakin merchant, and the late Hon. Guy Dawnay, saw the little crab, and urged me to send it in a bottle of alcohol home to the 'Field' newspaper, or else to the British Museum; but I said No, it had been imprisoned in a living death already long enough, and should now have a chance of life. So that night I took it down to the creek near Adam's restaurant, where we all used to meet before dinner, and let it gaily run off into the salt water, which did not seem to disagree with it a bit, although it probably had never tasted it since the creation of man! My thus finding a hermit crab alive in a rock is on a par with the toads which have been found in coal mines, and is certainly equally extraordinary.

Firing went on, and various little day attacks as well, for every night of January 1885. In the meantime we got a telegram on the 20th that the 1st Battalion Berkshire Regiment, one squadron of the 19th Hussars, and two Royal Horse Artillery guns were coming down to our reinforcement; and then on the 22d we heard of General Stewart's victory at Abou Klea, in which the English loss was 9 officers and 65 men killed and other 9 officers and 85 wounded.

At noon on the following day all the guns in Suakin were discharged in a salvo together, and then three guns fired in succession in each fort from one end of the lines to the other, in honour of Stewart's victory. The band then played "God save the Queen," and the Khedivial hymn, in front of the Muhafiza (Government

House), and all was jubilation in Suakin. At night-time the ships fired rockets and burned blue-lights.

On the 27th and following days the Berkshires and the other expected troops arrived and encamped, we Egyptians rendering them every assistance in our power in the way of helping them to disembark, and giving them all our available transport to carry their camp-equipage out to the desert on the north of the town, where they instantly set to work to intrench themselves in a thoroughly workmanlike manner. Their arrival, however, made no difference in the tactics of the enemy.

General Fremantle accordingly, who was thoroughly tired of inaction, determined to make a little move at once, now that he had got a few men at his back; and what he did shall be related in another chapter.

CHAPTER XIX.

It was noon in Suakin. Outside in the hot sun all
was still except for the screaming of the kites wheeling
overhead, but inside Government House a council was
being held in a low tone.

"To-morrow," said the General to me, "I am thinking
of going to beat up the rebels at Hasheen before daylight. They have harassed us here long enough; we
will go and see what forces they have got out there. I
want your Egyptian cavalry and Camel Corps; they
will be under the command of young Gregorie. The
squadron of the 19th Hussars under Apthorp, and the
two 16-pounder Royal Horse Artillery guns under
young Fanshawe, will be the remainder of the attacking, or rather of the reconnoitring line, the whole of
which will be under Kelly. The 49th Berkshire Regiment and some of the Marines will be a reserve.
Colonel Wood, you, and Stopford will accompany me
personally. Don't tell a soul or warn any one until

about 2 A.M. to-night, and have all your men ready out at H Redoubt by 4 A.M."

My bosom friend and staff-officer, David Gregorie, and I were glad. He, poor fellow, has, as already related, now gone to that bourn whence no traveller returns; but enough has been said already to show what a brave young soldier he was. Talking over the matter together quietly in our office, I remember his saying to me—

"Well, old fellow, I hope we shall both be back here again at this time to-morrow transacting the ordinary business of the day; but I wish we could go straight at it at once, don't you? Don't you like a fight better which comes upon you quite unexpectedly, than one for which you are prepared beforehand?"

"Yes, old boy, indeed I do," I replied; "but we must just go about to-day nursing this secret, and talking to the other fellows and the native officers, while looking all the time as if nothing unusual were going to take place; but, please God, we will be talking it over here to-morrow after all. Meanwhile I'd better just finish up my outstanding correspondence in the office in case of accidents."

"Right," answered David Gregorie; "in case we either of us get knocked on the head we must leave things all square, so that when 'Chermy' comes back he will find that his 'Station Staff Officer' and 'the Bey' have kept the ball a-rolling all right in his absence. And then we'll go to tiffin."

Long before daylight on the following morning the

Egyptian cavalry and some of the Camel Corps had wended their way out through the gateway by Tabiat el Yamin, and joined the other troops quietly assembling in the starlight outside the camp at II Redoubt. Nothing was to be heard except the occasional growl of a camel or the neigh of a horse. The cavalry and two guns moved silently off in line, the Egyptian cavalry on the left, and the tall weird figures of the Camel Corps in the centre, looking ghostlike in their white uniforms through the darkness. The splendid Berkshire Regiment in square, under the gallant Colonel Huyshe, waited for a time, and then followed along a broad shingly ridge clear of bush which led straight in the direction of the hills at Hasheen, some seven miles away. In the centre of the square were the ambulance corps and water-carts, and also the detachment of Marines.

The General and we three officers of his staff accompanied the infantry square for a time, and very impressive was the tramp of the advancing body of red-coated soldiery in the darkness, for they wore red serge by order, so as the more to impress the enemy.

At last dawn faintly broke, when the General halted the square at a nice open place at the end of the ridge. Then he and his staff rode on to join the advanced line, where all was still silent, we using files of the Camel Corps men as flankers, and also as connecting-links with the infantry in rear. The General had just expressed his fears to me that we were not going to find the enemy after all, when, just as we joined the long-extended line of mounted troops, they all became engaged, and were instantly hotly engaged at close quarters. They had just reached a kind of valley behind two detached hills, on the far side of which was the village of Hasheen.

The guns were on the right front, on the village side of the right hill, and opened at short range at the enemy, who appeared very numerous; in fact we estimated their number at 7000. They were howling loudly in thick bush on the opposite slope. As the General and we, his staff, surveyed the scene from the summit of one of these hills, we could see the shrapnel fired across our front tearing in among them in the bushes close to us, and the savages falling before the shells in crowds. But they were not all dead by any means; half of them were only throwing themselves down to elude the fire, and in order the better to creep to the sides so as to make a counter-attack on the guns and dismounted troopers who were firing.

This we observed, and the General soon sent Stopford to order the guns to fall back from within the hills to the plain outside. I, being sent at the same time with some similar order to the Camel Corps on the left, was run away with by "the Squire," who was very fresh, and bolted gaily through large numbers of the fuzzy-wuzzies in the bushes, but far too quick for them to get a cut at me. Luckily he had a sand-crack, and eventually hurt it on a stone, when I got him in hand, and so got back again in safety to the knoll after delivering the order.

Stopford also returned saying that the guns were already falling back of their own accord, having found it getting too hot for them, and the position they were in too enclosed in the hills to be tenable. Meanwhile Gregorie was firing away hard on the far left in the bushes. I could soon see that the enemy were getting very close to us as we stood on our knoll, the front base of which was clothed in brushwood, and began to think that the General was running too much risk of his own safety, when Elliot Wood told him so straight out, suggesting that he was in too dangerous a position to remain any longer, now that the guns and 19th Hussars on our right and the Camel Corps on our left had all commenced to fall back.

"Oh, all right," said the General; "then I suppose we too had better go." And it was not a minute too soon; for no sooner had we scrambled our horses slowly down the rocky hill into the more open ground in rear than the summit of the knoll was crowned by a crowd of shouting and yelling savages, who commenced firing at us at a very short range. One man amused us vastly, as he went down on his knee and, resting his elbow upon the other, in the most approved Hythe position, sent in rapid succession in about a minute four or five bullets from his breechloader whizzing between our heads, all very close, but not quite close enough!

"Just look at that fellow!" said General Fremantle, smiling. "We shall have some good news for Tapp," he added, sarcastically but good-humouredly, "to the

effect that all his labour has not been thrown away."
For my second in command had taken a great fancy
to passing his spare time in teaching musketry to our
friendly (?) allies, the Amarars, so it was easy to see
how and where this savage warrior had got his instruction and excellent form. Poor old Tapp! he dropped
his musketry instruction at once after that.

As the savages now manned the crests of both the
hills in very large numbers, and were also getting among
the bushes on our flanks, the whole mounted line fell
back in the direction of the infantry square; at least
we thought that the whole line was falling back, but
we were vastly mistaken, for Gregorie, as usual, without conforming to the movement of the rest, had, as
I found afterwards, remained where he was, away on
the left, still fighting a battle of his own with the
cavalry. He had gone out for a fight, and he meant
to get it!

A very plucky action was done about this time by
an Egyptian cavalry corporal, who, whether as an
orderly to Kelly or for some other reason, was present
on the right flank as the squadron of the 19th Hussars
retired. A sergeant in that regiment had got his horse
shot, and was left behind helpless in the bushes with
the enemy coming up all round him fast. The Egyptian
corporal, seeing this, galloped back, and putting him on
his own horse with himself, just saved his life in the
very nick of time. For this act of bravery I am glad
to say he was awarded the British Distinguished Conduct medal.

Hoping to draw the enemy after us on to the fire of the Berkshire square, we continued retiring slowly for a while; but as apparently the sight of the red-coats in the distance had made them cautious, we halted the line for a short time, while we played at long-bowls with our guns at the masses of the enemy visible on the crest of the highest hill, whence they were keeping up a useless fire.

It was during this halt that I discovered for certain that Gregorie and his men were not with us, being nowhere to be seen. I informed the General of this fact, when Stopford asked the General if he should go to look for him and recall him, which he prudently refused to allow his A.D.C. to do.

At last my anxiety for my friend became so great, that, noticing that the General's attention was fully taken up in watching the fire of the guns, I, without asking his permission, sneaked off quietly by myself into the bushes on our left, and once there, rode away as hard as I could go towards our left front, where I could now distinguish some firing. And when at length, to my great relief, I eventually found my staff-officer falling back, fortunately with only two or three wounded men and horses among his troop, I, for once in my life, "came the senior officer over him" most thoroughly, and went down his throat, boots, spurs, and all.

He was very much aggrieved at my doing so; and as, when I reported his return to the G.O.C., he got, at my especial request, another rowing, he felt himself very much hurt indeed. But it was really simply and solely for his own good that we tried to curb his rashness, for the General thought as highly of him as I did myself, and simply did not want him to get shot uselessly in some of his adventures.

Among the few casualties that day on our side, one of the artillery horses got killed, and Colonel Kelly lost his charger, which included the loss of a fine new military saddle, and of his field-glasses and flask, which were in the holsters. Fortunately Mahmoud Ali, the chief of our native police, who had accompanied him as guide, upon being requested to do so, nobly surrendered his own horse to the commandant of the fighting line, trusting to his heels, or the limber of a gun-carriage, to get out of action safely himself.

As the enemy would not come on, the Berkshire square never came into action at all, and we were all back in Suakin to breakfast by 8.15 A.M., having successfully accomplished our reconnaissance and found out the enemy's strength at Hasheen to be far greater than we had expected.

It was on the day after this fight that the Italians showed themselves for the first time on the Red Sea coast. For they, with two men-of-war laden with troops to occupy a wretched town down the coast called Assab, arrived in harbour with an Italian admiral on board. There was a great firing of salutes and counter-salutes, and I sent a guard of honour of the 1st Battalion to receive him on landing. The troops with him were Bersaglieri, who wore black Tyrolean hats with drooping cock's plumes, by no

means a suitable head-dress for the Soudan! I believe
that our British authorities eventually gave them a lot
of soldiers' helmets. Poor fellows! many of their
bones, not long after, lay whitening the sands outside
Massowah, at which place they on February 9 landed
and took it by a show of force from the Egyptian
officer in command, giving him a written statement
that he had only yielded to compulsion. His name
was Mustapha Effendi Sadik, and he was my own late
adjutant-major, whose promotion to the rank of major
I had managed after some trouble to get the Sirdar to
confirm, although I remember well that the Sirdar
wrote me a doubtless well-deserved scolding, on the
subject of the amenities of official correspondence, with
reference to this officer's promotion. For as Mustapha
Effendi had been promised his promotion, and it had
been for some time, in spite of my representations,
withheld, I forwarded, through Chermside, an official
letter saying that the Sirdar had made "a distinct
breach of his promise" in the matter, which remark
he thought just a little bit too strong. Sir Evelyn
Wood was then up the Nile, as Chief of the Staff to
Lord Wolseley; but by the field-telegraph he wired
from the front to Chermside about the matter, I believe
reproving him also for having forwarded on my rash
communication. But in any case, if I got the scolding,
the officer got his majority, so I did not care. At the
time that the Italians came to Massowah almost all
the reliable troops at Mustapha Effendi's command
consisted of a very large so-called Discipline Company.

This was termed in Arabic the *Bolouk el Musnibeen*, or company of prisoners, and it was formed altogether of deserters and suchlike offending persons. They were really very good soldiers, and gave no trouble at all, but were hardly to be expected to be able to resist the might of two large men-of-war whose guns could have blown the whole place into the sea.

When, therefore, the Italians appeared suddenly at Massowah and ordered him to surrender the place to them, although he at length yielded to force, Mustapha Sadik at first refused to do so, saying that he had no instructions from Governor - General Chermside, who had left the port only a day or so before. For such was the extraordinary nature of the compact which had been made between the British Government and the Italians, that it had not even been thought necessary to inform the Governor-General of the Red Sea littoral of the proposed handing over of one of his towns to a foreign Power. It was a foolish way of doing things; for had Chermside been there himself, he would have been perfectly justified had he put down and exploded mines or torpedoes in the harbour to prevent the Italians from landing, — which, in fact, is what he probably would have done!

However, as all the world knows, they took the place, and have now got a holding in Abyssinia proper, also the province of Bogos and fortress of Senheit, and have even captured Kasala from the Mahdi's troops, into whose hands it had fallen after a long and gallantly defended siege, during which no effort had been made on the part of either England or Egypt to relieve the brave defenders.

Notwithstanding the strange political jugglery which landed them in Massowah, whatever the Italians have done since their landing there has probably been an advance on behalf of civilisation in that part of the world; and I think that, supposing they could even succeed in pushing on to Khartoum on the one side and capturing the whole of Abyssinia on the other, the civilised world at large would be distinctly a gainer by their success.

When, however, on February 2, 1885, the Italian admiral landed at Suakin under many salutes, not a soul in the place had the remotest idea of what was in the wind.

The very same day about noon Chermside himself returned from Massowah, where in the Governor's palace he had left some cases of champagne and other articles of his which he never got a chance of going again to fetch. His return was a signal for more salutes and counter-salutes all round. For he was on board an Egyptian ship, the Mukhbar, and we Egyptians on shore, having unlimited gunpowder, saluted him with nine guns, the Mukhbar replying. The Italians then saluted him in turn, with more gunpowder in reply from the Egyptian vessel, and the whole day was passed in visits and counter-visits of ceremony from the ships to the shore.

The whole thing was, looking back now, rather a farce, and an amusing one too! Here was Chermside, a captain and brevet-major in the British Royal Engineers, being treated with all this ceremony as if he were really, as an Egyptian colonel and Governor-General, a man of very great importance and power. Yet what were really the facts? We had on the one side a British General in the place who, although he certainly did firmly believe in Chermside's undoubted powers of diplomacy and management, was nevertheless now perfectly able, had he so chosen, to act without reference to him in all matters. On the other side we had an Italian admiral on board a ship who, while blazing off his guns to Chermside in a salute, had all the time up his sleeve a secret known neither to him the Egyptian official, to the English General, nor to any one else. And this is how history is made!

CHAPTER XX.

THE day after the Italians had visited Suakin was witness to a considerable misfortune which befell our
troops. The young troopers with the squadron of the
19th Hussars having had no experience in scouting,
orders were given for one troop to go out and practise
scouting in the direction of Handoub. Gregorie with
one troop of Egyptian cavalry accompanied them, Stopford and the adjutant of marines also riding out as well.
The officer in command of the 19th, a young captain,
finding all clear before him, instead of going merely in
the direction of Handoub, thought it would be a good
thing to push on all the way to this hostile village, a
distance of twelve miles, and if possible there to water
his horses, which were chiefly Russian horses of not
much stamina, at the wells.

They reached Handoub all right, the few of the
enemy they saw there flying before them into the hills;
but, after burning and looting the place, they fell into

the dreadful error of staying a considerable time to rest. All the time the enemy, coming down from Hasheen, away on the left, had been laying a trap for them and quietly lining the high bushes about a couple of miles from Handoub, at the edge of a large open plain which the cavalry would have to traverse, so as to cut them off from the sea-coast.

On their return the two troops of cavalry, the English being on the left and the Egyptians on the right, were driving along a few captured camels, and advancing with all military precautions, when, as their advanced files had just reached the trees, a most awful fire was suddenly opened upon them along a tremendously long front. The enemy were evidently there in thousands, and bent upon revenging themselves for the dressing we had given them a few mornings previously at Hasheen.

The only means of escape was to turn to the left and gallop to the northward, so as, if possible, to get round the flank and on the seaward side of the enemy. The Hadendowahs, however, who were very fleet of foot, and who also were many of them mounted on camels, kept running in the same direction, thus constantly overlapping and prolonging their own right flank, making escape a matter of great difficulty. Eventually, leaving many empty saddles behind them, the troops got round and made good their retreat into the town. Gregorie, with his men, having been on the right, was of course last to get round the enemy's flank. Once he was between the Arabs and the sea, he pluckily halted his troop to cover the retreat of the rest, only falling back by degrees before the enemy, while firing volleys for a long time and bringing his men in eventually in good order.

Before achieving this he had undergone extraordinary experiences, and certainly deserved the Victoria Cross quite as well as many a man before him who got it. The Hussars, being in the first instance on the left, had the best chance of escape to begin with, but they were nearer the bush on the first discharge, and so lost several more men. As they galloped off to the left, Gregorie, who was last of all, seeing a dismounted hussar, dismounted himself, picked him up, and put him on the saddle of his sturdy pony behind him. The man was apparently wounded, and after a short distance fell off the horse, grasping the young officer firmly round the waist and dragging him with him. In this fall David Gregorie lost his pony, and also his sword, which fell out of the scabbard. He then commenced running, when an English trooper in turn picked him up and carried him for a time. Then an Egyptian corporal, having captured Gregorie's pony, gallantly rode back with it to his commanding officer, after which Gregorie picked up a second hussar, whom he eventually brought safely out of danger. Stopford and several of the Egyptians also brought off a man apiece behind them.

Our total loss was eight of the 19th Hussars and eleven horses killed, three Egyptian cavalry and seven horses killed; one or two more Egyptians were wounded, and several of the Hussars' horses died of the effects of their gallop and wounds.

After this disastrous affair the enemy were seen burning huge bonfires in the desert in celebration of their triumph, and on the following day we received the dreadful and sad news that Khartoum had fallen and that Gordon was lost!

This, then, was all that the British Government had gained by the folly which, strongly against General Stephenson's advice, had induced it to choose the Nile instead of the Suakin-Berber route. All the blood of a year's fighting had been wasted for nothing—absolutely for nothing!

A vote of censure was moved on the Government in both the Commons and the Lords. In the former it was only rejected by a majority of fourteen, while in the latter it was passed by a large majority. But whether it passed or not, it could not bring back to life the hundreds lost in the Soudan.

But there was much more bloodshed in store; for even in those days troops were commencing to arrive daily for another campaign under General Graham, while also we soon received news of that fine fellow General Earle's death while leading his troops at the successful battle of Kirbekan. In that battle, by the bye, the guns used belonged to an Egyptian battery under Captain Crawford, who had been for a short time at Suakin, and they did most excellent service. It was a hard day on the senior officers, as, in addition to Earle, Colonel Eyre of the South Staffords and

Lieut.-Colonel Coveny of the Black Watch were killed, while Lieut. - Colonel Wauchope, also of the Black Watch, was severely wounded.

It was now settled that with General Graham's new expeditionary force, which was to consist both of British and Indian troops, there was to be a Brigade of Guards, consisting of the 1st Coldstreams, the 1st Scots, and 1st Grenadiers, and of this Brigade General Fremantle was to take command. In the meantime, as the troops kept on arriving, he went away for a few days' well-deserved change of air and scene to Cairo.

In addition to all the other troops, a new departure in British warfare was inaugurated in this campaign, owing to the colonists of Australia sending a contingent to fight beside their brethren belonging to the mother country.

Before Graham came down to assume command, an enormous staff, with Major-General Sir George Greaves as its chief, had arrived, Sir George being, of course, in command of all the troops.

By his orders, as they arrived, regiment by regiment, these occupied all kinds of detached camps, dotted about the plain, without, it must be owned, much regard for military precautions, whereby several valuable lives were lost almost nightly. For General Greaves started by committing that common fault of despising his enemy. The very headquarters-camp itself, wherein resided no less than twenty-five staff-officers, was pitched in an open plain without at first any intrenchment round it, and having for protection only a guard furnishing a few sentries.

Riding out there the day of his arrival to see my old friend Colonel "Robbie" Gordon, who had been brigade-major of the Highland Brigade at Tel-el-Kebir, and was now Provost-Marshal to Graham's army, I was surprised to find the absolute want of defence arrangements made for the camp, and urged him for the sake of his own safety to represent to General Greaves the habits of the enemy of making night attacks, and that the staff camp was most insecure. Old Gordon smiled grimly as he replied—

"I dare not speak to the General about it, but, by Jove! *if the enemy do come they will get a good bag.*"

Gordon was engaged to come next morning and breakfast with me at the Caravanserai, but failed to turn up. Later on a messenger arrived with a note to explain his non-arrival, and this is what it said: "I am very sorry that I cannot come, but the fact is that, just as you said, the enemy did come and run 'amuck' through our camp. They speared one or two men sleeping in their tents, among whom was unfortunately my groom, and they have also stolen my horse." Poor Gordon died of fever before the end of that campaign, —another life lost among many.

Night after night after this the enemy repeated these tactics of rushing through the camps and spearing men, sometimes for a change attacking the guard-tents and killing the sentries. The result was a perfect scare among the men of some regiments, notably one cavalry regiment, who, upon the cry being raised at night, "They're on us!" used to seize their carbines and blaze away in the dark in every direction, the bullets flying through the tents of their comrades and being far more dangerous to their friends than their unseen foes. At length this state of things became unbearable, and a proper arrangement of the camps on a system of mutual defence was made.

I am not going to describe at any length the 1885 campaign, as, beyond these opening phases, I saw nothing of it, being ordered with my regiment back to Cairo, while Gregorie and the 5th Egyptian Battalion remained behind, the former being taken on the staff of the General Officer commanding the cavalry.

I was offered a staff billet myself, and once again under Naval auspices; for Captain Fellowes, C.B., R.N., who was Principal Naval Transport Officer, asked me to accept the post of his disembarking officer. As, however, I had received information that there was a probability of my regiment, the 1st Battalion E.A., being shortly sent on active service up the Nile, I declined this kind offer, recommending in my place my friend Major Hare, the old commandant of the 1st Battalion, who got the post, and did most excellent and arduous service throughout the campaign.

As I was with my officers and men slowly steaming out of Suakin harbour on board the Queen, a strange thing happened. For on passing a transport, the Deccan, coming in crowded with troops, I heard my Christian name loudly shouted by an officer in a red coat standing out in one of the ship's boats swinging at the davits. It was my own brother, Lieutenant Arthur

Haggard of the Shropshire Regiment, the 53d, my chum Turner's old corps. He was going on active service just as I was leaving it. We only had time to exchange a hurried greeting when the two ships passed clear of each other, and for all we brothers knew, it might have been our last meeting on earth. Fortunately, however, my ship, the Queen, ran firmly aground at the entrance of the harbour, and after all efforts on the part of two men-of-war to remove her had proved futile, Commodore More Molyneux very kindly took me off on his steam-launch and put me on board the Deccan, where I passed a jolly night with my brother and his brother officers, many of them old friends.

The next morning very early the Commodore came and fetched me off again ; and as we managed to drag the Queen off the reef I bade farewell to him and Suakin for ever, landing in a few days at Suez, and proceeding at once with my regiment to Cairo, where we met with a most hearty welcome from the officers and men of other corps still there. And thus ended my year's fighting at Suakin, to which I look back as one of the happiest periods of a not wholly uneventful life.

CHAPTER XXI.

ON our return to Cairo we found, as both Sir Evelyn
Wood and General Grenfell were away up the Nile
with Lord Wolseley's expedition, that Watson, who was
a major-general in the E.A., was acting Sirdar. He it
was accordingly who held a review of the 1st Battalion
on their return from active service, and thanked them
on behalf of his Highness the Khedive for their war
services in Suakin. The parade terminated by the
regiment cheering the Khedive in the usual way—that
is, by shouting out three times in unison the Turkish
words "*Effendi miz chok yasha*" (May our lord live for
ever). This is a very impressive salute when roared
out by upwards of a thousand men at once, especially
as the band plays eight bars of the beautiful Khedivial
anthem between each salute, thus forming a contrast to
the volume of voices which is somewhat remarkable.
The commanding officer, whether of a regiment, brigade,

or division, always cries out this salute first alone, throwing up his arm with his drawn sword, and then, in the same way as the responses are heard in a church, all the other officers and men on the ground shout the same words after him in chorus. The effect of the sudden roar is somewhat startling to those who hear the *Effendi miz* salaam for the first time.

The next day we got a very kind telegram from General Grenfell at Korti congratulating the regiment on their services. We English officers of the 1st Battalion also received a message from the Khedive to come and see him. When, accompanied by my two majors, Tapp and Hawtayne, I arrived in the royal presence, Tewfik Pasha was most kind and conversational. After warmly thanking us for our services, he spoke most enthusiastically of the improvement that he noticed in the troops to what they used to be in former days. He detailed to us some of his unfortunate experiences with his own personal guards, whose condition and comfort he had done everything in his power to improve; and then taking us to the window of the palace at Abdeen, where we then were, contrasted them, very much to their disadvantage, with our own men, who were at the time forming the guard at the palace gate. He said that he found our men so smart, and that he saw in their faces a pleasant, open, and soldierlike expression compared to those of his old army. He dilated at some length on the gendarmerie and police, and said that he hated the idea of our men ever being drafted into either of these corps, as had just been proposed by Lord

Northbrook, for that he disliked thoroughly both gendarmerie and police, and considered them "simply horrible." The Khedive further told us in detail how some of his own guards had betrayed him at the time of Arabi Pasha's rebellion. It was very gratifying to see how he believed in the new army, disciplined and organised as it had been for two years only by British officers.

It was on this day of our visit to the Khedive that we learned that Sir Evelyn Wood was resigning his position as Sirdar, and that General Grenfell was to succeed him in the command on the 1st April, but only to receive £2500 yearly instead of the £5000 which had been paid to his predecessor.

This also was the day when, down at Suakin, a smart fight resulted in the occupation of Hasheen, our killed being Lieutenant Dallison, Scots Guards, and 21 men, 17 being Indians; our wounded being Major Harvey, 5th Lancers, Robertson of the 9th Bengal Cavalry, Surgeon-Major Lomand, and 42 men, of whom 18 were Indians. Again, as in former fights, the cavalry (chiefly Indian) lost heavily while charging in the bush.

The following day saw the celebrated fight of Tofrek or M‘Neill's zeriba, a short description of which may not be out of place.

On March 22, 1885, the Berkshire Regiment, a battalion of Royal Marines, the Indian infantry, a squadron of cavalry, a Gardner battery under the Naval Brigade, and a detachment of Royal Engineers, all under the command of Major-General Sir J. C. M‘Neill, went out in two squares to make a zeriba on the road to Tamai. After a slight zeriba had been made, and while the men were many of them in their shirt-sleeves and still working, or else dining, the enemy made a sudden attack in large force. The cavalry outposts had only just hurried in with the news that the enemy were coming when the enemy appeared at their heels. They rushed at the zeriba, and many got in at one corner, where was situated the naval Gardner gun, but all who got in were eventually killed.

At last the enemy were repulsed with enormous loss, but the camels and mules stampeded before the enemy's rush, knocking down and trampling on many of our men, while numbers of the animals got killed by getting between our fire and the enemy, who speared and hamstrung them by the hundred.

Our loss in this fight was 5 officers and 51 men killed and 170 wounded. Two of the officers killed were personal friends of my own, Lieutenant Seymour of H.M.S. Dolphin and Lieutenant Swinton of the 49th Berkshire Regiment.

The behaviour of the Berkshire Regiment in this action, in which they lost 10 killed and 17 wounded, was so conspicuously gallant that they were created The Royal Berkshire Regiment as a reward for their splendid steadiness, which more than anything else helped to save the day. For it was a terrible fight, and one that, from the suddenness of the attack upon men unprepared to receive it, might easily have resulted in a defeat.

Exactly whose fault it was that the enemy got so close to the zeriba without warning, when they had been seen passing in front of the heights at Hasheen towards M'Neill's halting-place for the greater part of the morning, is a question that has never yet been satisfactorily solved. Although I have heard many stories bearing on this point from those who were there, not having been on the spot myself I should not dream of venturing an opinion on the matter. I may, however, be allowed to make a reflection, which is, that if it be true, as stated by some, that a very superior officer refused to allow the heliograph at Hasheen to be made use of to warn General M'Neill that the enemy were approaching him in large numbers through the bush, he fell into a very grave error. For even supposing that this superior officer imagined that the cavalry outposts would prove infallible and warn the working troops in rear in time to prevent a disaster, he might surely have remembered that the bush was not only thick, but also in most places too high to be seen over by a mounted trooper.

With these remarks we may dismiss the battle of M'Neill's zeriba, which had, however, proved once again what discipline and skill in the handling of the rifle could do in the face of a vastly superior and equally courageous force.

About this period many of the wounded from the battles of Abou Klea, Gubat, and Metemmeh were by degrees arriving at Cairo, and the lounges in front of Shepheard's Hotel were constantly occupied by wounded officers who had in some marvellous way survived the terrible hardships and agonies of the homeward march across the desert in *cacolets* on the back of broken-down and sore-backed camels. There were old friends among the daily arrivals; but, alas! there were also many old friends who never came back at all. Stewart was gone, Burnaby was gone, Walter Atherton was gone, and how many others!

It was strange to get away at length from all these wars and rumours of wars, and to find myself back to England in the middle of the London season, the greater part of which was, however, lost to me—a serious operation, which had been too long delayed, confining me to my bed for some weeks. When, however, I was just beginning to get about, it seemed odd at first to notice how absolutely unmissed were all those who were still away, and how very little was known or thought about Egypt among those one met. As for having been personally missed oneself, that would be out of the question. On meeting a man he would say, "Hulloa! old chap, I haven't seen you the last week or two: where have you been?"

"Oh, I've been in Massowah and Suakin and other places in the Red Sea for the last two years."

"Massowah and Suakin! never heard of them: what took you there? What, fighting is it? Oh, I thought that was up the Nile. Well, come and take a turn in the Park and see Lady A. Do you know, by the bye, that she's going to be married for the third time?"

This was the sort of thing I experienced on my return, and I suppose that hundreds of others did the same. But before I was quite well enough to go about, to my great joy one day there was shown into my room David Gregorie. He was looking as fit as a fiddler, and had come through the last campaign with no other mischance than a smack on the back from a ricochet bullet, which, being fortunately flattened out, had not even cut the skin, although it had left an enormous bruise and made him very stiff for some days. I only saw him once, as he was off to the country, and before long we were both out in Egypt again, although we never met until at the very end of the year, on the battle-field of Ginness on the Nile.

For neither all the blood shed in two campaigns at Suakin nor all the fighting up the Nile had damped the ardour of the Dervishes (*Darawesh* in Arabic), as the followers of the Mahdi now universally styled themselves; and they, before long, commenced making themselves so obnoxious up the Nile that it was evident more fighting would be necessary to quell them, Lord Wolseley not having apparently inflicted upon them a sufficiently severe lesson in his "campaign for the relief of Gordon."

By degrees troops began to be pushed up the Nile in small quantities; but for all that, there were plenty of soldiers left in Cairo to make the place lively, while crowds of visitors thronged in from across the blue Mediterranean. Thus fun and flirtation were in October and November of that year once more for a while the order of the day, and many were the soft nothings whispered in the moonlight at the base of the Sphinx or under the splendid sycamore-fig tree in the garden of Shepheard's Hotel, under which tree the French General Kleber had been assassinated in the beginning of the century.

Among the regiments of the Egyptian army which were already away up the Nile in garrison at Assouan or Korosko was the 3d Battalion, to the command of which my friend and second in command, Major Tapp, was now appointed. I was very sorry to lose him, for his was, as all who knew him can testify, a singularly sweet and charming nature ; in fact his disposition was as good as his personal appearance was handsome, which is saying a good deal. However, I was delighted at his promotion, and knew he would make an excellent commanding officer for his new regiment, as indeed he did, until, poor fellow, his valuable life was cut short a year or so later by the spears of the enemy at Suakin, where he died in a sortie, receiving no less than thirteen wounds.

Towards the end of November my own regiment was once more under orders for active service. Hostilities were almost daily expected at our advanced posts in the province of Nubia, and the 79th Cameron Highlanders were with some black troops occupying certain forts which they had constructed on both banks of the Nile at Kosheh. This place in the Nubian desert was about eighteen days' post from Cairo, by train, steamboat, and camel, being a long camel-ride south of Akasheh, a village which was made the advanced base of the new operations.

Gregorie was already up at Kosheh with the black regiment, which was the 9th Battalion of the E.A., commanded by Archibald Hunter, a splendid fellow, and which had been raised during the past year entirely from Soudanese negroes, many of them being those who had been sent back from Suakin, while others had come from Khartoum. Great doings were expected from these negroes, when once properly disciplined, for they were a bloodthirsty lot to whom cutting throats came quite naturally. As all their women had been sent up the Nile with them, and encamped close at hand on the banks of the river, they were perfectly happy. After a short time, however, the noise and quarrelling to which these women gave rise, owing to the frequency with which the blacks would change wives, or else steal some girl from an adjoining Nubian village, became so intolerable that a change had to be made in the arrangements. All the women were therefore deported from the shore of the river to a large island in the middle of the stream. Here at night-time they could be heard quarrelling among themselves, jabbering, dancing, and drum-beating continually, and they were allowed to be visited by their lords and masters only when the latter were off duty. This arrangement worked much better than the other.

The 1st Battalion marched from Abbasiyeh to embark on barges and be towed up the Nile on 24th Nov. 1885. We left all our recruits behind, therefore our strength was 200 under what it had been in barracks, the total marching-out strength being 2 English officers, 22 native officers, and 541 rank and file.

As the regiment marched through Cairo to the place of embarkation, Shepheard's Hotel was passed. On the celebrated verandah, which was crowded, were gathered together many familiar faces; and as the ladies waved us their hasty adieux, and friends, many of whom were never to be seen again, ran down the steps to exchange a last hearty hand-grip, our band, now proficient in European music, played in return "Auld Lang Syne" in token of farewell.

The Khedive happened that morning to be holding a levee at the Abdeen Palace, and I received an intimation by an aide-de-camp that his Highness wished the regiment to march round the square under the windows of the reception-room. This was done, the battalion maintaining its formation in fours and "shouldering arms" as it passed.

The Khedive, who was attired in full dress and wearing a gorgeous new decoration which he had just received from Mukhtar Pasha, the Sultan's envoy, stepped out on to the balcony and repeatedly waved his good-bye to the officers and men. The latter greeted him in return with the royal salute, cheering lustily and heartily. This action of Tewfik Pasha's was a capital way of increasing the loyalty of the Egyptian soldier. Never before had he been thus taken notice of by his Sovereign when going away on active service; but Mahomed Tewfik was showing an interest in his small army which no previous Khedive had ever done.

The regiment embarked, just above the Kasr el Nile bridge, on a steamer called the Damietta, towing several large flats or barges on which the men and some horses and camels were packed as tight as herrings, and we expected to reach the first cataract at Assouan in about three weeks' time. The overcrowding in the boats did not matter so much, owing to the habit on the Nile, already referred to, of always halting and making fast to the shore for the night, thus giving the men an opportunity of going ashore and stretching their legs.

Every morning and evening a parade used to take place on shore for the purpose of medical inspection, thus allowing time for the flats to be washed and to get dry, the orderly officers being responsible that all was *en règle* before starting afresh. When the evening parade was over the men were allowed to amuse themselves as they liked within a certain boundary marked by sentries. Cooking operations were got under way on shore as soon as ever the boats stopped, and, after the first few days, it was wonderful to see how soon the big fires were merrily blazing and the large caldrons seething above them.

On the third night of our voyage we made fast to an island in the middle of the Nile opposite the town of Beni Soueff, where I had formerly had such a pleasant time at the Mudir's hospitable table, as related in the earlier chapters of this book. The boats were made fast on the side of the island farthest away from the town, and some officers were sent stumbling across the island, in the dark, to a ferry on its farther side, by which they crossed the wider branch of the river and so gained the town of Beni Soueff. There they made arrangements with my old friend the Governor of the province to supply by the following morning sufficient fresh beef for the whole regiment. Next morning early the requisite number of beasts arrived alive.

Owing to the time taken in slaughtering and cutting up the animals the boats could not, naturally, get away as soon as usual. The interval of time thus lost many of the troops employed in washing their clothes, but others made use of it in a different manner. Eluding the sentries—an easy matter in the high *dura* which was growing all round—they made off to Beni Soueff to see their relations. The consequence was that when the parade fell in for commanding officer's inspection, eight non-commissioned officers and men were found missing. Here was a go, indeed! but we could not possibly go on up the Nile without them. Thus pickets, accompanied by buglers, had to be sent off to the mainland to sound the recall in every direction and hunt for the absentees.

CHAPTER XXII.

IN vain for a time the steamer whistled its shrillest note; in vain the bugles sounded. At last, however, the absentees reappeared, brought in by the pickets from the mainland, but not until our little flotilla had been delayed in starting for several hours. As our object was to get to the front as soon as possible, and we had many a weary mile of Nile to traverse, it was evident that this sort of thing must be stopped, for there were plenty more towns before us on the way up where the same game might be played. To prevent its recurrence, therefore, all the delinquents were brought on board the steamer and tried during the course of the day's journey by court-martial. On the boats halting that night their respective punishments were promulgated and carried out. A triangle was rigged up in the centre of the regiment, formed into square, and twenty-five lashes apiece, well laid on by a couple of stalwart sergeant-majors (for we had company sergeant-

majors), took away from any of their comrades any
desire to go and do likewise. With one exception
there were no more absentees for the rest of the
voyage.

That night, which was that of 27th November 1885,
was indeed a remarkable one at the little village of
Minet-el-Gir (the "Town of Lime"), and, as I have
since heard, over many other parts of the world as
well. As soon as it was dark, which was about 5 P.M.,
a few shooting-stars were noticed, but more was to
follow. When just finishing dinner, a shrill voice—
that of Sub-Lieutenant Ibrahim Effendi Fehmy, the
interpreter to the battalion—was heard crying down
the hatchway in agonised tones, "Colonel! Colonel!
all the stars are falling down!" Naturally a rush on
deck ensued in the hope that one might be a personal
witness of the wonders described in the Revelation of
St John.

Wonderful, indeed, was the sight revealed to our
astonished gaze. North, south, east, and west, stars
were shooting about, some of them leaving a beautiful
after-glow quite as good as that of a first-class rocket.
It is only natural to conclude that they were all shooting at the same object, and perhaps they hit it, for
their direction was always the same—i.e., from west
to east. At the same time we noticed a comet
stretching all across the Milky Way, between the
constellation of Aquila and the star Vega in the constellation of Lyra. This comet was, more strictly
speaking, nothing but the tail of a comet; for al-

though we examined it carefully with a very strong binocular, we could see no nucleus or head.

Now, what follows is remarkable. At 7.25 we went below to finish our dinner. On our reappearance on deck twenty minutes afterwards, the comet had disappeared! *"Credat Judæus!"* one feels inclined to remark; but it is a fact all the same, and from that day to this, with the exception of the other two Englishmen on board that steamer with me, I never met any one who saw that comet at all. I must here put on record a remark made by Ibrahim Effendi Fehmy when the stars were shooting about at their thickest. In awe-struck tones he remarked, "I think, sir, that God is changing all the stars!" Indeed, it looked like it. As they still continued falling about, a sentry was put on duty specially to watch the stars and report when they had stopped their vagaries. He woke us up at about two o'clock in the morning, to say that they had quite done; and we were glad to hear, after so much shooting, that no casualties had occurred!

The journey up the Nile was not remarkable for anything until we got to Assiout, unless it was for the enormous quantities of water-fowl which we constantly saw in every direction. Literally tens of thousands of pelicans, cranes, geese, ducks, and other birds would sometimes be seen, sitting on low mud-banks in the centre of the river or on the shore. However, they generally kept a long way off the steamers and barges, and when they did fly over them it was at a great height. Now and then we had a shot into the crowd of them with a Martini-Henry rifle at a range of 600 or 700 yards, when, as the bullet went ricochetting along among them, they would get up and darken the air by their numbers, while the noise of their wings was like thunder.

On arrival at Assiout we heard the news that there had been a skirmish far away up the Nile at Kosheh, in which a couple of English mounted infantrymen and one Egyptian soldier had been lost. This was the first fighting to take place since that of the previous spring at Suakin; but even now, years later, fighting still goes on from time to time on both frontiers.

The day after passing Assiout we picked up the *dahabeah* Cheops. It was still travelling about from place to place carrying the Special Recruiting Commission, under the presidency of that fine old Circassian Yusouf Pasha Schudi. Of this Commission, as previously detailed, I had recently been a member, and the Pasha and the two other members—one a Scotchman, with a grand capability for whisky—were my best friends. It was therefore with mutual joy that we encountered the Cheops, and for the next two days, as there was no wind for them to sail, we were able to do them a good turn by towing the *dahabeah* up the stream. When we parted at a place called Sohag, it was with the greatest regret on both sides. However, we had made the best use of our time, and passed altogether the two jolliest evenings it had ever been our lot to enjoy. Just one little note here in a whisper—The Scotchman had taught the Pasha how to drink whisky!

After leaving the *dahabeah* Cheops behind, we passed Ekhmim, celebrated for its mummies, where, by the bye, I myself at a subsequent period became the happy possessor of a mummy which was popularly supposed to be that of Potiphar's wife. Anyhow, she now reposes quietly in Norwich Museum. Potiphar's wife or not, she was quite a lady, and never created any disturbance except once, when she was distinctly heard one night by the wife and servants walking about the house of an eminent novelist, a near relation of my own who has told the world plenty about mummies. She was probably looking for Joseph, poor thing!

A little beyond Ekhmim we found a man missing one night. He left his clothes and money on the bank, and went out to bathe in the thin shirt and drawers which form part of the Egyptian soldier's kit. He never returned, and as he was a hundred miles above his own province, we therefore pitied him and thought he was drowned, for in the then cold weather we did not think it was likely he had deserted in such light clothing. He had though, and we caught him afterwards. One man who got left behind at Assiout by his own carelessness ran the whole day along the banks until he was able to join the boat again in the evening. We saw him, and let him run as a warning to the others; besides, it was difficult to stop in the heavy current.

On the fourteenth day of our voyage we arrived

at Keneh, a coaling-station. The coaling-wharf was exactly opposite the ancient temple of Dendera, which we could see about three-quarters of a mile inland. As we were obliged to stop to coal, we determined to visit these magnificent relics of antiquity. Although Murray describes the carving on the walls and pillars, which date chiefly from the time of the Roman emperors, as being in a debased style, I think the writer would have changed his mind if he had visited, as we did, two series of underground chambers which had only recently been discovered. If not, then it was perhaps owing to our inexperience that we, one and all, English officers and Egyptian officers, were delighted with the beauty and symmetry of the carvings on the walls in these underground passages, the ceilings of which were decorated throughout with a universal star pattern. Some of the female figures portrayed were beautifully finished and positively handsome; and several of the animals, also, were delineated with the greatest accuracy and grace. Nothing, for instance, could have been more lifelike than some of the foxes; one especially, lying down on the top of a chest with his brush hanging down to the ground behind, looked as if he only required a "View holloa!" to set him scampering off across country at full speed.

We had a couple of guns with us when visiting Dendera, and bagged nine couple of pigeons going to and returning from this gigantic temple. Coming back, especially, we might have fired hundreds of cartridges had we had them, as flocks of the blue-rocks passed overhead continuously. Unfortunately we very soon had nothing left but cartridges loaded with No. 1 shot, intended for the geese on the sandbanks.

In the evening we paid a visit to the Mudir, or Governor, of Kench, getting donkeys for the purpose of proceeding to the town. Some of the donkeys had high-sounding names, such as Mehemet Ali Pasha, Hassan Effendi, or Mrs Langtry! They were capital beasts, but their saddles had an amusing knack of turning round just when one least expected it. When I say amusing, of course I mean amusing for the other people whose saddles did not happen to turn round. The Mudir, Arif Bey, received us very kindly; but he had no news to give us from the front, although he had, I remember, several big sheikhs of the Bishareen and Ababdeh tribes present in the town, and the men of their tribes were then watching, in the Egyptian and English interests, the desert route to Kosseir on the Red Sea side, and from Assouan to Dongola on the west bank of the Nile, respectively.

Having cleaned boilers at Kench, we made a very good run up the river next day to Luxor, nearly forty-four miles. As a rule, we only made about thirty miles daily. We arrived at Luxor before sunset, so were able to admire in passing the gigantic ruins of Karnac, which looked very fine from the river. We had no sooner made fast to the shore and got our chain of sentries out round the boats, than two American gentlemen, both wearing revolvers, turned up and immediately proceeded to make friends with us, insisting on our coming to dine with them at the Luxor Hotel. The names of these gentlemen were Dr J. Browning and Mr Yelden Blodgett, both of New York. They were making the tour of the world, and had just come down from Assouan, so were able to give us the latest news from the front. Two such hospitable fellows as were these ought never to be forgotten, and I never intend to forget them either. From them we learned that it was rumoured that a company or so of the Cameron Highlanders were then cut off and surrounded at Koshch, our extreme post, and had been so for a few days when they had left Assouan two days previously.

As for a long time previous some such move as this on the part of the enemy had been expected, we were not astonished, but only hoped that the Dervishes might be made soon to clear out. Browning and Blodgett said they had been entertained most hospitably by the English officers at Assouan, and that on leaving that place they had registered a vow to repay that hospitality as soon as ever they got the chance, and especially to English officers in the Egyptian service. They spoke in the highest terms of my now, alas! late friend, Major Martin, formerly of Hicks Pasha's Soudan Field Force, who was commonly known, on account of his enormous size, as "Baby" Martin. He seemed to have "done them remarkably well." They certainly kept their vows as far as we were concerned; for nothing that the excellent

Luxor Hotel could produce was, in the opinion of
our friends, good enough for us. Browning's admiration of "Baby" Martin, which was well deserved,
was rather amusing. All through the evening he
would now and then remark, à-propos de bottes, "If
you see Martin, tell him he is the best fellow that
ever lived;" or, "If you see Martin, mind you give
him my love." After dinner we went round to the
British Vice-Consulate in the ruins of Luxor, where
we found Ahmed Effendi, the son of the equally well-
known Mustapha Aga, waiting to show us some
curiosities.

Talking about curiosities, one of the greatest curiosities in Luxor was the visitors' book kept there.
What hundreds of well-known names we saw in it!
The Prince of Wales's name occurred twice, the second
time being accompanied by that of the Princess; and
there besides were registered the names of very many
British officers, written down when going, as we were,
into the Soudan. Among them was the undying name
of Gordon, written when passing through on his last
ill-fated journey to Khartoum. Even then, in the end
of 1885, one could not look over those names without
emotion; for many of those who had written them
were old schoolfellows or old comrades, whose bones
were already bleaching on the sands of the Soudan.
Alas! for those good fellows whose hands we can
never now hope to clasp again.

The curiosities seen, and the book duly signed by
ourselves and all our native officers, who too had strolled

up to look at the ruins by moonlight, we took leave
of the hospitable Dr Browning (nephew of the poet
Browning, as I forgot to say he had announced himself when he first introduced himself to us).

Browning's last words were, "If you see Martin, tell
him he's the best fellow that ever lived." Blodgett,
however, arranged to come with us early next morning
to have a hasty glimpse of the wonderful temples
and columns of Karnac under the tutelage of Ahmed
Effendi. Next morning, accordingly, as soon as the
sun was up, mounting some kicking donkeys, we rode
down and saw what are probably the most magnificent
relics of antiquity the world possesses; and then re-
gretfully leaving Karnac, its grand hieroglyph-covered
hall of 134 columns and its granite obelisks, we started
in good time to resume our journey up the Nile.

As we steamed past the ruins of Luxor we saw
Ahmed Effendi in front of the British Consulate. He
had two myrmidons with him, bearing in their hands
dilapidated flags, one of which looked like a Union-jack.
These colours he lowered to the regiment as the boats
passed by, and we dipped our flag in return. On
passing in front of the Luxor Hotel, a little higher up
the river, we saw our American friends getting into
a boat, they being about to cross the river to go and
see the ruins of the city of Thebes opposite Luxor.
As we passed we mutually waved our adieux, and
Browning shouted out something which sounded like,
"If you see Martin, give him my love!"

That same evening, steaming until after dark, we

reached Esneh. There we saw the temple by torch-light, and a very grand temple it is. There were plenty of, to us, new kings and queens, gods and goddesses, cut in the stone on its walls and columns, all wearing uncomfortable-looking hats—I beg pardon, crowns—to represent the sovereignty they held over Upper and Lower Egypt. The cartouches, or oval figures, in which are cut in hieroglyph the seals or names of their long-deceased owners, covered every inch of stone and were beautifully carved. The extraordinary thing to us was that, in such an enormous mass of hieroglyphic writing, one could not see the sign of one single mistake, error, or correction ever having taken place. Thinking about this since, I seem to have heard somewhere that whenever a mistake or slip of the workman's tool occurred, the whole of the enormous block of stone upon which he was engaged, and had probably been engaged for years, was rejected, and he had to begin all over again, after probably being well flogged by the thonged whips of the task-masters, which the workmen themselves had not forgotten to portray. Time was no object, apparently, in Egypt two or three thousand years ago. But how wonderful it is to look at these relics now, and to think that men like ourselves were able to elevate and place in position such wonderful pillars and masses of stone about 2500 years before the age of steam!

Again, on revisiting the Pyramids of Gizeh, eight miles from Cairo, this thought forced itself upon me more vividly than ever. Why! the very conception of beginning such a work as the Pyramid of Cheops is beyond our greatest engineers of the present day! But the men who did these things in former days not only did them, but left their names and histories behind them, carved in figures more lasting than brass, to tell us, of the later age, who and what they were, and when they lived and died! But I must now get on to Assouan, where we arrived on the nineteenth evening of our voyage, and found the great "Baby" Martin himself awaiting us on the bank.

On arrival at Assouan, we disembarked at once and pitched our camp for the regiment close by the landing-place. This was by the railway stopping-place or terminus known as the North End—I cannot call it a station. This railway only runs a distance of about seven miles through the rocky desert behind the town of Assouan to Shellal, which is the re-embarking place, opposite the island of Philæ and its ruins. At the head of the first cataract we found that General Grenfell, now newly become Sirdar of the Egyptian Army, who was also then commanding the whole F.F.F., or Frontier Field Force, had gone on to Wady Halfa, leaving instructions that the 1st Battalion was to encamp for a few days and then follow him up the river as soon as transport could be provided for us. We got news of two or three little fights up the river: one, in which the 9th Egyptian Battalion, supported by the Cameron Highlanders, had cleared a palm wood at Kosheh of the rebels in capital style; and another, at a place called Mograkkeh, which we ourselves were to know well afterwards. In this Mograkkeh scrimmage half of the 3d, now Tapp's, Egyptian Battalion had, under Besant, driven off in most gallant style large numbers of the rebels who had attacked them. Hearing of these fights and other little skirmishes as well, we did not at all fancy being left doing nothing at Assouan.

All the officers, non-commissioned officers, and men of the battalion represented to me that they wished a telegram sent to the Sirdar up at Halfa to the effect that the 1st Battalion was anxious to proceed at once to the front. Accordingly I sent off a telegram in every one's name, respectfully requesting permission to start. By the bye, I remember that this telegram had to be franked by poor " Baby " Martin himself. Most assuredly, also, we did not forget to deliver to him the oft-repeated messages of goodwill from our American friends.

After everything was squared up in camp, we rode our horses into town to take some of the stiffness out of their legs, and we dined that night on board the Assouan Club. It may seem odd to talk of dining on board the club ; but it was literally true, for the club-house in question was a most comfortable and roomy *dahabeah* moored near the shore. Here in the club we met several old friends—soldiers of various sorts, Stuart Wortley, Romilly, and Colonel Colville amongst them.

The next morning we got an answer from the Sirdar's military secretary, and it ran as follows: " The Sirdar is much pleased with the good spirit evinced by the unanimous desire of the 1st Battalion to come to the front. It will be sent on immediately after the Staffords." Now, the Staffordshire Regiment (38th) was starting that very day for Shellal, and the same evening we too got orders that headquarters and 310 men of the battalion were to go up by train to embark early next morning in two stern-wheel steamboats and barges. We were to be allowed *only ten trucks to carry everything — tents, baggage, ammunition, officers and men.* But we managed it all right, with the men in heavy marching order, all packed tight on top of the baggage, like sparrows perched on a wall, and we got to Shellal, for a wonder, without any one falling off. There was, we found, one sort of a carriage which rejoiced in the possession of seats, and which we made use of for the officers. On it some wag had painted " First Class," which amused us much. I should just like to see what the ordinary British third-class traveller would say if he was offered anything like it.

My old friend Oliver-Bellasis of the 20th Hussars rode up to see us off, and was vastly amused at the appearance our train presented. He rode alongside our train for a little way, which he could easily do without going out of a trot, and appeared still more amused when suddenly I stopped the train by causing a bugler on the nearest truck to sound " the halt" when my orderly, Mahomed Omar, who had been sent into Assouan to fetch the washing, appeared suddenly on the scene, riding a mule and carrying a large bundle in front of him. We had resigned ourselves to the idea of losing this man and the linen until the rest of the battalion should follow us up-country, but he himself had no intention of being left behind. He had, therefore, had the sense to hug the railway on the way out from Assouan to North End. When he met the train he slipped off the mule, turned its head in the direction of the camp, gave it a kick behind, and started off running after the train with his bundle. So we sounded the halt, took on board the orderly and the washing, and shouting to an Egyptian cavalry officer, who happened to be riding by, to look after the mule for us, we sounded the advance and resumed our journey. But, alas! alas! what was our grief when we discovered that the linen, although washed, was not starched! We had hoped, after our nineteen days' voyage, to get just one lot of linen done up smart for the last time before penetrating into the Soudan. But we were sold.

At Shellal we found the Staffords on board the boats, but not yet started. They had, to their great disgust, been waiting for twenty-four hours for their camp equipment, which was being brought up the river for them by the Essex Regiment. We found Lieutenant Mann of the 46th, and Lieutenant Jackson, R.A., who were respectively "Water Transport Officer" and "Commandant at Shellal," most kind. The barges they could give us were small, and nothing like the flats we had come up in from Cairo; but we crammed the men by nineties into three of the barges, the remainder going wherever they could on the horse-boat and stern-wheel steamers.

We took up with us nine horses belonging to the

Staffordshire Regiment, and my English second in command and myself managed by the greatest luck to get the three we had on board as well, although I was very nearly having to leave one of the two valuable Arab chargers I then possessed behind me on the bank. My English servant Alfred, who was with me as usual, and myself were delighted at getting both these horses on board this time; for all sorts of misfortunes, terminating in shipwreck on a reef in the Red Sea, had befallen them previously. Never, if it can be avoided, leave a horse behind anywhere, is my motto. But, unfortunately for us on this occasion, I had to leave behind at Assouan all my regimental transport, consisting of six magnificent camels and twelve first-class mules.

The names of the stern-wheelers were the Aurora and the Water-Lily. The latter was the first to start, after having lashed one barge on each side—not towing them behind, as had been done by the Damietta from Cairo to Assouan. We ourselves embarked on board the Aurora, having as travelling companions, in addition to one-half of the native officers, an English officer of Hussars and some non-commissioned officers. We in the Aurora had to wait fretting several hours for the return of the chief engineer, who had gone into Assouan on the drink. But this loss of time proved in the end really a gain, for a telegram arrived just before starting to say we were to travel by night as well as by day. Luckily there was a moon.

The day after leaving Shellal, although we had to stop for three hours to repair machinery, we in the

Aurora overtook and passed the Water-Lily. That
night, about ten o'clock, as we were passing the barren
post of Korosko, we heard frantic shouts from the
shore, and saw lights flashing repeatedly; so we concluded we had better stop, which we did, with a secret
foreboding that we might perhaps be stopped altogether. We were not very far wrong, for Colonel
Leach, V.C., R.E., Commandant, wanted to know if we
were the 1st Battalion E.A., and said he had received
instructions on the previous day that we were to stop
there. But we declared that we were to do nothing of
the sort, but to go on to Wady Halfa as fast as we could
go. "Have you written instructions?" he asked. No,
we replied, but quoted the telegrams before mentioned.
Good fellow that he was, although the case was doubt-
ful, he gave us the benefit of the doubt and let us go
on. After we had all pledged him and the two officers
who had come on board with him in a friendly glass,
with hopes to meet again at the front, we were off again.
We felt that a great danger had been avoided, and so we
one and all went on our way rejoicing; for we had no
wish to share the fate of half a battalion of the 19th
Yorkshire Regiment, which had been stuck for months
and months at Korosko, and was there then still.

From the fellows who came on board here we learned
that there had been more fighting at Kosheh on the previous day, and that Hunter, commanding the 9th Egyptian Battalion, was severely wounded, and poor young
Cameron (son of General Cameron), of the Cameron
Highlanders, had been wounded too, it proved mortally.

Captain Chalmers, of the same regiment, also was wounded in the hand. It appeared also that the enemy had got between Akasheh, which was the last point on the desert railway from Halfa, and a post of ours at Ambigol Wells, and torn up some three miles of the railroad, having bent the rails by burning the sleepers under them exactly in the way described as how to do it in Lord Wolseley's 'Soldier's Pocket-Book.' The estimated number of the enemy was 7000 men. From Assouan up to Wady Halfa the scenery on both sides of the Nile consists of nothing but rocks and sand, with in some places merely the narrowest strip of cultivation of only a few yards in width on the river-bank. In some places, certainly, in this part of the district of Nubia, there are a few palm-trees and a miserable village or so; but in others there is nothing but yellow sand right down to the water's edge.

It is difficult to understand, now that all the rest of the Soudan, and all the fertile part of the province of Dongola to which it belongs, have gone, what is the good of keeping this large piece of desert land which yields nothing and supports nothing. Strategical reasons must, I suppose, be the reply. There are some very remarkable ruins on the west bank at Dekka and Abou Sinbal: the latter especially, consisting of colossal figures and deep inscriptions cut on the face of the rocks round the entrance to two underground temples, are most magnificent and wonderful. A tombstone at the foot of these statues now marks the spot where lie the remains of Major Tidwell, of the Royal Dragoons,

who died coming down from the previous Nile expedition.

We arrived at Halfa, just below the second cataract,
on 7th December 1885, and disembarked early next
day, pitching our camp and settling down very soon.
We were informed, as soon as our camp was pitched,
that if only certain Commissariat camels and mules
came in from the front, we were to start by march route
that very afternoon for Akasheh, distant about ninety
miles. However, we waited two or three days in vain
for the camels; so our orders were altered, and we were
told to hold ourselves in readiness to proceed to Akasheh
by train, by the second desert railroad up the Nile. The
train service at that time between Halfa and Akasheh
was very poor, as it was found, owing to the bad condition of the engines, only possible to get through to
Akasheh three trains in every two days, arrangements
being made so that in case the enemy again cut the
line, there should always be one train left at the Wady
Halfa end. As these trains were only capable of drawing ten trucks at a time, a considerable difficulty was
always being felt in sending sufficient stores and forage
to the front, and also in forwarding the troops.

At this time the enemy were continually keeping up
a fire upon our small number of troops at Kosheh from
their own strong position in a village close by called
Ginness. They fired regularly with both shell and
rifles, and there were daily losses on our side in killed
and wounded either on the east or west bank of the
Nile, for we had thrown up earthworks on both. That

z

on the west bank, a strong parapet surrounded by
thorns, was called Borrow's zeriba—Borrow of the Black
Battalion having constructed it — and was occupied
chiefly by black troops under English officers. Gregorie,
who was there for five weeks, told me the enemy used
to make it very hot for them with their shell-fire;
while to cross the river, here 1000 yards wide, to
obtain provisions from the fort at Kosheh, was almost
an impossibility by daylight, and on account of the
rocks it could not be done quite in the dusk. The
whale-boats, therefore, used to start whenever they
thought the firing was at its slackest, and if the boats
were lucky they would get half-way over before a hail
of bullets began to fall all round them, smashing oars
and dropping men occasionally also.

About this time Major Hassan Redwan, a very plucky
fellow, of the Egyptian artillery, was wounded very
severely. This officer had distinguished himself a few
days previously, when a small party of English were
surrounded by a large party of the enemy, who had a
gun with them, at a small sand-bag post at Ambigol
Wells on the railway. Major Hassan Redwan, having
with him Lieutenant de Lisle, a young officer in the
Durham Light Infantry, and a few men mounted on
camels, had broken through the enemy's lines and ridden in to assist in the defence. I believe both the
Egyptian and the English officer were afterwards the
recipients of the Distinguished Service Order for this
smart little affair.

Meantime we were, with many others, waiting at

Wady Halfa, keeping the men well occupied with plenty of parades, especially practising the attack formation, and passing men to the front by small numbers on Commissariat camels, or on the trucks perched on the top of the baggage, whenever we could get a chance. General Grenfell was responsible for all the excellent arrangements at the front, in his capacity of Commandant of the Frontier Field Force, until Sir Frederick Stephenson arrived at Halfa and took over the command on the 19th December. By degrees in the meanwhile we got also a good many men to the front on camels escorting herds of oxen. The Egyptian infantry soldier requires no training to ride a camel; he has only to get on his back to become an efficient camelry-man at once. These parties were therefore always started by us in correct mounted-corps style — scouts out, in front, flanks, and rear. A week after arriving at Halfa, I was enabled to send on one English officer, Major Frith, and 70 men of the right half battalion with him to Akasheh by train, and also sent on one native captain, one subaltern, and 50 men of the left wing to occupy the Sarras post. When Christmas Day arrived we had altogether 150 on to the extreme front, and had also marched our horses forward across the desert to Akasheh.

CHAPTER XXIII.

CHRISTMAS DAY — AKASHEH — THE DESERT RAILWAY — ACROSS THE DESERT BY DAY AND NIGHT — SARKAMETTO — FIRKET — MOGRAKKEH.

ON Christmas Day we had a very good dinner in our tent, and drank to our absent friends' health in some excellent champagne, which Hawtayne, the English officer remaining with me, had discovered in a successful forage a few days previously among the Greek *bakkals*, then settled in Wady Halfa. Really most useful fellows were those Greeks, and most enterprising. Wherever our armies have been in the Soudan, some of them have accompanied them. As for the turkey and plum-pudding for our Christmas dinner, the former had accompanied us up the river all the way from Beni Souell; the latter had been brought by my servant Alfred, tinned, from Cairo, with a view to keeping Christmas properly when the time came. On Christmas Day General Grenfell and his staff moved on from Halfa to Akasheh. The Yorkshire Regiment (19th) also came up the river from Korosko, and went on next day, taking all the available trucks.

This was a great disappointment to us, as we had been promised two trucks that day. However, I managed somehow to squeeze in three men and a corporal to go on to Akasheh, and also to forward a month's dry rations of beans, biscuits, and lentils for our detachment at Sarras by the same train as the Yorkshire. We never lost a chance of forwarding even a single man or a biscuit.

On Christmas night, when we were at dinner, a telegram was received by us from General Grenfell forwarding one from the Khedive, which ran as follows: " I wish all my officers up the Nile a merry Christmas and a happy New Year." I suppose that that was the first time a Mahomedan potentate ever sent such a message to the Christian officers of his army.

On the morning of 28th December 1885 we at last got off with the remainder of those of the battalion who were to go on. Hawtayne, who had barely recovered from dysentery, had, by orders received, to remain at Halfa with two companies, much to his disappointment. We also took with us Ternan, of the Egyptian Army, and twenty men of the 9th or Negro Battalion, who had just turned up from Cairo under his command, he too being most anxious to get to the front in time for the expected fight. We packed the men in the trucks, at the rate of thirty men to a truck, on the top of the baggage. They did not look very comfortable, but they declared they were when asked. I always found Egyptian soldiers capital fellows for never grumbling. For the officers there were very comfortable first and second class carriages on this line. The latter were marked "Midland Railway," the others all appeared to have belonged to some lines at the Cape. This was a much higher class of railway altogether than that which turned the first cataract from Assouan to Shellal.

This eighty-seven miles of railway from Wady Halfa to Akasheh, after turning the second cataract just south of Halfa, passes through the most awfully sterile country it is possible to conceive—nothing but rocks and stones the whole way, the former looking like mountains of burned coal more than anything else. After skirting the river for some way, the railway winds—now, I suppose, I should say used to wind—in and out along the *wadys* or valleys which separate the mountain-chains in that awful country, which certainly struck me as being the abomination of desolation itself.

At various intervals we passed stations with little forts held by some of the Staffordshire Regiment (38th) or by our own Egyptian soldiers. The best constructed of these forts seemed that at Ambigol Wells, which was the one which had recently been besieged for several days by the enemy, with a gun to hammer it with, from a neighbouring hill. The train went slowly, but we arrived at Akasheh after our hot desert journey at six in the evening. There we found our detachment, consisting of the men we had sent on from time to time, drawn up on the platform, if such it could be called, waiting for us. Our horses, too, were already saddled; for we found that the instructions were that we were to march at once across the desert to Sarkametto, sixteen miles distant. We had unloaded the train and were off in an hour, having left all our knapsacks and extra ammunition, also all stores, behind under a small guard, only taking on a few days' rations for the men on the transport animals which had been provided for us. Being the last to arrive at Akasheh, we naturally found the worst animals left for us. Major Frith, my acting second in command, had been told to get camels where he could, and had literally been obliged to do so by getting thirteen camels out of the sick-lines, nearly every one of them with sore backs.

Luckily, however, we got the temporary use of some decent mules belonging to the Black Battalion, of which we were taking up the twenty men, and which battalion itself was now at Kosheh. With these mules we made the best of a bad job and started. In accordance with utterly absurd instructions I had received from Owen Quirk, who had now blossomed into a very fussy staff-officer, to leave absolutely *everything* behind, Ternan, Major Frith, and I were all nearly committing the egregious folly of leaving our most absolute necessaries at Akasheh. This staff-officer, who belonged to our Egyptian Force, had, I found out afterwards, two very fine camels for his own gear and stores which had been already loaded ready to start before our arrival. Luckily at the last moment I thought I would have my kit-bag with me at any price; for it held everything I wanted, and could be easily slung on a mule's pack - saddle. Very glad I often was afterwards that I did take it, and so were the other fellows, who stuck to their kit-bags too. I would give this piece of advice to any young officer on a campaign: Only take a kit-bag and a canteen with you; but take these if you can. As long as you have them, you can always be more or less comfortable, and you can generally manage to get them through somehow.

We had just been armed with the Martini, and the men on this night march carried eighty rounds of Martini-Henry ammunition apiece; also two blankets and a greatcoat rolled up over their shoulders, and with their rifles and bayonets a precious weight it all was! It was a most toilsome march. There was no moon, and we stumbled on over loose rocks, through narrow defiles and through deep sand, up hill and down hill, hour after hour. It seemed interminable. The sick baggage-animals, too, were constantly getting behind or falling down, causing great delay.

Well do I remember that weary and anxious march. It was a bitterly cold night, for it can indeed be cold in the desert; and we never knew but that every rock which loomed in the starlight might conceal a horde of fanatical savages, ready to pour a volley into, or charge upon, our weary men as they toiled along, in a constantly lengthening line, through the rocks and sand.

Of course we marched with the greatest military precautions, and I well remember a trait in Ibrahim

Effendi Fehmy's character which pleased me. This young lieutenant, the battalion interpreter, who has already been mentioned, came to me and said, " Please sir, may I go with the advanced guard ? " His was not the company detailed, but knowing his great intelligence, I detailed him too, with orders to go with the most advanced party. " Thank you, sir," said the youth; " I should like always to be on advance-guard." I did not forget the good spirit shown by the lad when the time came for sending in names for special mention after the fight.

At one place that night the track we followed hit off the Nile just above the furious rapid known as the Dāl cataract, and skirted the river for hundreds of yards, leading over sloping and very slippery and smooth slabs of rock. One of the worst of these places it was, where the path was only a yard or two wide, that my horse, a spirited Arab stallion, who had been playing the fool the whole night, selected as being the most appropriate for performing a kind of war-dance, nearly landing him and myself in the river, which really appeared to be the object he had in view. Indeed he managed while performing his *pas seul* to slip down to the very brink several times. As he had already been roaring and shrieking the whole of the march, thereby considerably increasing our risk of letting any possible enemy know our whereabouts, and as I knew he was simply going on in this way out of spite, because temporarily separated from his stable companion, " The Clerk," I felt at last inclined to get off and kick "The Parson" into the Nile for a lesson in manners before he took me in with him. It was in my mind also several times that night to put a bullet through his head, or else cut his throat, which would have been a less noisy proceeding, to keep him quiet. It often puzzles me why people call horses intelligent animals. It seems to me that they are frequently excessively foolish and unreasoning, and this was a case in point. Now, a dog, a cow, or any other animal, would have had far too much sense than to caracole about on a sloping rock, overhanging a roaring cataract, however inclined to indulge its exuberance of feelings. A noisy horse can do any amount of harm on service, and is a cause of irritation to his rider and every one else near him. I remember a similar case occurring early in that same year (1885) at Suakin, when we were trying to surprise the enemy at dawn at Hasheen. In fact it was on the occasion of the reconnaissance in force which I have fully described. On that occasion the General's horse it was that played the fool and screamed. The consequence was that he and his staff-officers, one of them myself, had to keep ever so far in rear for fear of alarming the enemy, until just as dawn broke and the front line had become actually engaged, when noise did not matter, for there was plenty of it.

But to return. At last we got to Sarkametto, which was simply a low breastwork and zeriba on a plain near a village overlooking the Nile. The zeriba we found perfectly empty, and therefore we occupied it at once. It was then two in the morning, and although the men

were dead-beat, not one had fallen out. Considering
that most of them had been up since three the preceding morning loading and unloading trucks, and considering also the weight they had had to carry, this was
more than creditable. We posted our sentries, bivouacked, and went to sleep; but not before I had had the
pleasure of finding out that a bag containing the head-
stalls, the heel-ropes, and blankets for my two horses
had fallen off a mule and been lost in the desert. Pleasant, indeed, this at the commencement of a campaign,
and when such articles could not possibly be replaced!
Next morning, to my great surprise, it being in an
enemy's country, my Egyptian *syce* was very anxious
to go back a mile or two and look for the lost bag.
I gave him an escort of a couple of men on mules
and let him go, and fortunately it was discovered
before we resumed our march at 9 A.M. I then
found out why he had been so keen to go back.
It was simply because all his own tobacco was in
the bag!

At daybreak we heard the old familiar boom of the
guns, which reminded us all of Suakin. They were
commencing the daily cannonade at Kosheh, thirteen
miles away; but in the clear morning air it sounded
as if fighting was going on quite close by. From Sarkametto we marched on to Firket, along the banks
of the Nile, about seven or eight miles. At Firket
we found a number of British troops were encamped,
but ready to move. We halted outside, and General
Grenfell and his staff came out to meet us and give

us orders. We were to leave fifty men at Firket, and march on to Mograkkeh, to be incorporated there in the 2d Brigade under that gallant officer, the late Colonel Huyshe, C.B., commanding the Royal Berkshire Regiment (49th), as our Brigadier. The battle was to take place on the morrow. I only had actually to leave ten men behind me at Firket, as I had forty men, mounted on camels, under a very smart young officer named Ismail Effendi Mukhtar, who were to arrive that morning from Akasheh, so left orders for them to stay at Firket on arrival. I was very sorry to lose young Mukhtar's services in this way; but it was better for me not to diminish the number of men I then had, now only 300 all told. The march on between Firket and Mograkkeh, under a mid-day sun, chiefly through loose sand bordered by burning rocks, was very trying, and especially so after the fatiguing march of the previous night. However, it was best to push on at once, so as to give the men a chance of a good rest in camp in the afternoon. We accordingly struggled on—greatcoats, blankets, eighty rounds of ammunition, and all — until, passing the mud fort of Mograkkeh, where poor Tapp came out to greet us, about a mile and a half farther on, we arrived at the camping-ground of our brigade, about 1000 yards north of the camp at Kosheh, and near the river-bank, which was fringed with palm-trees. Firing was going on heavily in front at Kosheh, and a few of the enemy's bullets fell about among us, having been fired at a very high elevation.

CHAPTER XXIV.

THE country was more fertile all about Kosheh, and we
bivouacked in square on a wheat-field. While comply-
ing with my orders, which were to encamp in rear of
the Yorkshire Regiment, which was also just moving
in, I managed to get a piece of ground where the
wheat was young, too young to be spoiled, instead of
some long vegetation about knee-deep, and wet with
irrigation, which was first pointed out to me by a staff-
officer as our camping - ground, and which we should
have utterly destroyed. This was Owen Quirk again,
the same clever staff-officer who had told us to leave
all our kits behind at Akasheh.

That afternoon was a pretty busy one for us, making
preparations for the morrow's fight. However, at last
we had got all our orders, posted our outposts, with
the line of sentries in connection with the outpost

sentries of the Yorkshire Regiment, foraged about until we had got sufficient fuel from a neighbouring village to cook all the men a meal of rice before they would start next day, made all the arrangements about water, reserve ammunition, &c., &c., and then at last were able to sit down and partake of a frugal meal of "bully beef" and biscuit and smoke the pipe of peace. Firing was going on all this time, and in spite of the distance two men in the 2d Brigade were wounded in our camp by the enemy's bullets.

The composition of the Anglo-Egyptian force that evening was roughly as follows: The Cameron Highlanders (79th) and part of the Egyptian Black Battalion were in Fort Kosheh, on the right or east bank of the Nile, 600 yards from a ravine, which ravine ran down to the Nile between a large black rock and a small village surrounded with palm-trees, very strongly occupied by the enemy. Another part of the Black Battalion was in the previously-mentioned strong work on the left bank of the Nile, called Borrow's zeriba. This work was just about 1200 yards from the celebrated "black rock" which always afforded the enemy such excellent cover, and was, as I mentioned already, for weeks previous to the battle continually engaged in an artillery duel with the enemy in the village, to say nothing of a perpetual interchange of musketry-fire with the enemy on both banks; for a large party of the Dervishes, although not the main body, had established themselves on the west bank also. Gibb of the 9th Battalion commanded in Borrow's zeriba during the fight, and drove off a large attacking force of the enemy.

After the action we found that the black rock resembled a target, almost every inch of it being covered with the ringed marks of our rifle-bullets. For some time beforehand every morning, on the bugles and bagpipes in Kosheh sounding *réveillé*, fire used to commence by one of the enemy, whom the men nicknamed Peter, because his stand was on the rock, firing the first shot. Peter used to rise slowly, stretch his arms while yawning portentously, then settle down into a comfortable position behind the crest and discharge his rifle at the soldiers in Fort Kosheh, the bullet being invariably very well aimed. The men always replied with a volley, but they never bagged Peter. Both of these corps in Kosheh—that is, the Camerons and the Blacks—belonged to the 2d Brigade, the remainder of which was composed of the Yorkshire Regiment, of my 300 Egyptians of the 1st Battalion, and a company of the Egyptian Camel Corps. An English mule-battery and a squadron of Egyptian cavalry joined the Brigade before going into action on the following morning. Lieutenant-Colonel Stanley Hebbert, R.A., an able and brilliant officer, commanded the artillery with the whole force.

The 1st Brigade, under Brigadier-General Butler, C.B., consisted of the 1st Battalion Berkshire Regiment (49th), the West Kent Regiment (50th), and the 2d Durham Light Infantry (106th). This Brigade was accompanied by the 20th Hussars, a company of

mounted infantry, a battery of Egyptian artillery
under Lieutenant - Colonel Wodehouse, and the 1st
company of the Egyptian Camel Corps under Major
Marriott. All the mounted troops were under the
command of Colonel Blake, 20th Hussars. I must
not forget to add that the next morning, that of
the battle, about half a company of the 3d Battalion
Egyptian Army was detached from Fort Mograkkeh
under Besant, and served as escort to Wodehouse's
guns with the 1st Brigade.

Early—that is, before daylight—on the morning of
December 30th the troops were in motion. The 1st
Brigade moved off at 4.30 A.M. by starlight, and took
up a position about three miles away, on a range of
rocky hills opposite to the enemy's principal encamp-
ment, which camp was situated beyond the long
straggling village of Ginness, buried in palm-trees
along the bank of the river. The 2d Brigade, with
the exception of the Cameron Highlanders and the
Blacks at Kosheh, were on foot directly afterwards,
and, also moving in a southerly direction for about
two miles, took up a position on the hills, about 900
yards from the detached part of the village of Ginness
—that is to say, the hamlet behind the ravine which
was directly opposite the fort at Kosheh This fort,
after we had come into position, was about 1500 yards
to our right front, while the village was directly between us and the river.

It is a very solemn and weird sight this starting of
troops in the dark before proceeding into action. In

spite of all attempts at silence, a sort of continued murmur seems to rise into the cold night air; vague forms are seen moving along, which prove perhaps to be the camels; a dull tramping is heard—it is a regiment moving off; a rattling and clanging of chains next attracts your attention — the guns are passing! And no one says a word, no matches are struck, no pipes are lighted; orders are given in a low tone, and passed on quietly from company to company. The dust rises and heavily fills the air, while through that dust is somehow felt to be moving a grim resistless force of men, going on to death or to glory, controlled solely by the love of honour and the iron hand of discipline. Looking back now to the various occasions upon which I have seen troops moving forward to the attack under cover of the darkness, I feel, even as I write these words, that the sensation felt upon those occasions was a grim and peculiar sense of subdued excitement—a sensation which completely dies away after the first shots are fired or the first blows struck, but a sensation well worth having lived to have experienced, because it is like nothing else in existence.

Having first crossed a ravine, the 2d Brigade crowned the rocky heights above mentioned just as daylight was faintly beginning to dawn. The guns had been brought up the steep slope from the ravine with a rush, and had just been got into position with one half battalion of the Yorkshire in column on their right, one half on the left, and our Egyptians, also in column, in rear, when suddenly a heavy fire opened upon us from the village below.

2 A

When the fire opened upon us from the village, the mule-guns instantly replied with shrapnel, and the two half battalions of the Yorkshire, deploying respectively to the right and the left of the guns along the ridge, also replied with volleys. As all the infantry were ordered to lie down, and the mounted troops told to remain just behind the crest of the hill, no damage was done by the enemy's fire at this time, although the bullets were kicking up the dust all around and among the men, or whizzing thickly just overhead. General Sir Frederick Stephenson, K.C.B., commanding the troops in Egypt, and Major-General Grenfell, C.B., Sirdar of the Egyptian Army and Commandant of the Frontier Field Force, were with the 2d Brigade during this opening phase of the action, and I well remember the latter bidding me a cheery good morning and re-marking, casually and coolly as if we had been meeting in the street, that it was a very cold day, just as the fight was beginning.

My old friend "Wortles," who had some months previously brought the two boats safely down from the wrecked steamers returning from Khartoum, was also present. He was supposed to be in Cairo, in what we soldiers call a "soft billet," as military attaché to Sir H. Drummond Wolff, but Stuart Wortley was not going to lose a chance of seeing more fighting if he could help it. I thought he looked superb, as, faultlessly attired with white kid gloves, and with rather more than his usual delightful swagger, he sat on his horse, and, with the utmost nonchalance, lighted his cigarette under a hail of bullets, while calmly discussing with me the prospects of our having "a good bag"!

It was a very pretty sight to watch the red flashes of the enemy's rifles just as dawn was breaking; and although, owing to the keen morning breeze, we had all previously been shivering with cold, we had soon forgotten to make any more remarks about the weather. Presently we saw some more flashes, not belonging to the enemy, away on our right front, and, as the light now became stronger, we saw that it was the rest of our brigade advancing from Kosheh to cross the ravine and storm the village among the palm-trees on the other side.

The sublime is near akin to the ridiculous. Just at this time, when we on the hill were forgetting that we ourselves were under fire as we watched our comrades advancing to the attack, a little incident occurred which made us all temporarily forget both these facts. A hare, which had been sleeping quietly on the mountain, suddenly got up, quite close to the right wing of the Yorkshire Regiment, and ran along the whole front, amidst the roars of Tommy Atkins and to the amusement of us all. I remember the temptation was too great for some of the soldiers, and many a rifle-bullet was sent whizzing after poor puss, who, however, escaped untouched, to fight and run away again another day. Since then I have read that at the battle of Wagram the hares were running about so thickly among the opposing forces that numbers were killed by the soldiers during the action, and that at the end of the day both conquerors and conquered dined freely off what would be called more appropriately potted than jugged hare. But since I am on the subject of hares in action, I may as well here just recall the extraordinary fate of the hare at Suakin, which was, as already mentioned, killed by the mine when that place was besieged by the enemy the previous year.

In the meantime, not having been equally successful in catching our hare at Ginness, we again turned our attention to the force advancing on the village. This force consisted of two very strong companies of the Egyptian Black Battalion, who were on the right of six companies of the Cameron Highlanders under that gallant soldier Lieutenant-Colonel Everett, then the second in command of this fine regiment. Colonel Everett was especially selected to command the regiment in action that day, his commanding officer, Colonel St Leger, being left in the fort at Kosheh with two companies. The Blacks were, owing to Hunter having been wounded, now under Borrow and David Gregorie, plucky fellows who were only too delighted when the Blacks under them were given the post of honour and of greatest danger on the right, of which they showed themselves to be well worthy. They it was who took the black rock and the village, as the Highlanders' line, stretching out into the desert to the left, although exposed to a heavy fire, did not come to hand-to-hand conflict with the enemy. The Cameron Highlanders afterwards presented the 9th Battalion with a set of colours in memory of this fight. While attacking the

village, the Blacks were under fire from both sides of
the Nile at once, and lost several men killed and
wounded before they drove, as they thought, all the
Dervishes out and passed through swiftly in pursuit,
among the straggling detached houses on the Nile
bank, capturing two of the enemy's guns as they did so.
That they had not really driven all the enemy out, or
else that some of them got back into the houses again
along the low bank of the river, unseen from the plain,
was shown later on.

During this attack by six companies of the Camerons,
with Lieutenant-Colonel Everett expressly selected to
command them, and the Blacks, the commanding officer
of the Camerons, Colonel St Leger, remained, as mentioned, with the other two companies of his regiment,
some gunners, and a detachment of the 3d Egyptian
Battalion from Mograkkeh, occupying the fort at
Kosheh. Of course, although the commanding officer is
not usually the one selected to be left behind in a fight,
some one had to stay to occupy the fort; but it was
hardly necessary for its occupants to fire shrapnel-
shells over its friends, as was done the whole time
the Blacks were advancing over the 600 yards of plain
to the black rock, one of which by the merest chance
escaped blowing them to pieces, it bursting just over
them. However, perhaps Colonel St Leger thought,
from his safe position in the fort, that a few shells
flying about among them would encourage them to get
among the enemy quicker, where they were intrenched
in the shelter of the palm-trees, as Gregorie told me it

most certainly did. A shell from one's own side bursting overhead is not at all a pleasant sensation. It was, however, not a new one for Gregorie; for he and I together had already once experienced it at Suakin the year before, when, as related, we were so nearly "landed" by the large shrapnel-shells from the long-range gun on board the Dolphin. However, there was an excuse then, for we were about three miles inland and easily mistaken for the enemy at that distance—a mistake, too, which was soon found out. Fortunately the troops were not demoralised on either occasion by this little *contretemps*.

From our position on the hill we soon began to see large bodies of the Dervishes retreating from the village across our front. They did not seem to hurry themselves, but retired leisurely along the river-bank before the advancing Blacks and Highlanders. Colonel Huyshe now advanced all our part of the Brigade across several ravines, marching diagonally away to the left to another ridge, where our volley-firing was continued. The enemy replying briskly, I saw the stretchers beginning to be carried about at this time, as the casualties commenced. We made a yet further advance, two of the companies of the Egyptians now prolonging the line to the left. Eventually, the advance continuing over broken ground, these companies fell back, after which, the whole battalion of Egyptians having deployed and prolonged the line to the right, we continued to advance in a south-westerly direction, keeping up a running fight on the flank of the retreating enemy. We were soon not far from their large camping-ground near the village of Ginness.

While the 2d Brigade was thus occupied, the 1st Brigade, under Brigadier-General Butler, away on our left, was closely engaged with the main body of the Dervishes, many of whom had advanced boldly to fight this brigade among the mountains. Streaming along up the numerous ravines with which the hills were everywhere intersected, they suffered to a certain extent from the heavy but too rapid fire to which they were exposed, but for a time they made a very plucky stand. They charged the Egyptian Camel Corps, commanded by Marriott, on the left, which, having dismounted, was firing upon them, when, as this little body of men was not supported, it had to fall back, after losing a man or two killed and six camels. However, the men of this company of the Camel Corps only fell back slowly upon the main line, and killed about a dozen of the Dervishes as they retreated. The Dervishes now threatened the Egyptian battery under Wodehouse, coming up to within sixty yards or so of the guns, whereupon Besant (of the 9th), with his little party of the 3d Egyptian Battalion, charged very pluckily down the hill into the midst of them, bayoneting some and shooting others, one of Besant's men being killed in the charge.

There is a good story told about Josceline Wodehouse in connection with this fight. Among us all there was no greater believer in the Egyptians than himself, and no one who resented more keenly any sneering words used concerning them by the English officers. In fact he, in

his honest partisanship, reciprocated very warmly the
jealousy which many of the English felt about us.
When, therefore, towards the end of the action, Wodehouse saw that the enemy were commencing to retire
leisurely across the front of the 1st Brigade, he performed the extraordinary manœuvre of charging them
with his guns, getting right through them into their
camp before any one else, but being almost immediately joined by Besant with his 60 men of the 3d
Battalion E.A. In the camp there was a quantity
of the enemy's standards, and these Wodehouse commenced to gather as fast as ever he could, tucking
them under his arms. When General Butler rode up
a minute later he found Wodehouse, looking like a
porcupine, with his *tarboosh* well on the back of his
head, and the ends of banners and spears sticking out
from him in every direction. At the same time he
was shouting wildly to Besant, " Don't let the English
get the flags! don't let the English get the flags!"

It was a bitter blow to the poor " Cornet," as he used
to be nicknamed, when General Butler mildly but
firmly insisted upon it that the English had, after all,
had something to do with winning the battle, and that
really, however excellently the Egyptian troops had
behaved, they were not entitled to quite all the trophies
of the fight.

All this time heavy firing could be heard going on
from Borrow's zeriba on the western bank; but after a
time that ceased, the enemy having vacated their position on that side. On the advance of the Black gar-

rison of the zeriba, under Gibb and Ternan, the enemy
retired, leaving about a score of their number dead
behind them. What now puzzled all of us with the
2d Brigade was, that although we had imagined that all
the enemy had retired from the village opposite Kosheh,
which we had seen being rushed by the Blacks and
Camerons, yet heavy firing could be heard still continuing in its vicinity. In fact the rolling sound of
independent firing never ceased round this hamlet,
although we could see the greater part of the Camerons
and the Blacks now marching towards us to join their
brigade, as we were still following the enemy, who
were streaming away before our advance. Colonel
Huyshe, our Brigadier, now sent his A.D.C. to find
out what was the reason of this continuous firing
behind us, and it was reported to him that there
were still some of the enemy clinging desperately to
the loop-holed houses, and that a company of the
Camerons and a small party of Blacks who had been
left behind for the purpose were unable to turn them
out. I was therefore directed to go back with my
Egyptians and eject these fanatics, and to order the
officer with the Camerons to rejoin his corps.

When getting near the village we met Gregorie,
who had dressed himself up smartly for the fight in
his best serge coat brightly adorned with medal ribbons.
This was the first time I had met him since seeing
him in London the previous spring. Short but cordial was our mutual greeting, meeting thus as we
did upon the field of battle; and then he informed

me he had just been reconnoitring the place, and
that I should find it a perfect impossibility to get
the enemy out without a gun. I therefore asked
him to inform the Brigadier, and went on. We
found the company of the Camerons lying down behind some cover about 150 yards from the houses,
and only replying to the enemy's fire by an occasional shot. The officer in command, Lieutenant
Macleod of Cadboll, told me that all the enemy were,
he thought, in one block of houses connected with
each other, and that there was, so far as he could
make out, only one entrance, a very small one, which
was firmly blocked. He, moreover, informed me that
he had had three men hit in trying to get in, and that
he thought we ourselves should find the getting in a
hard nut to crack. In this he proved quite right.
We tried in vain for some time to enter any of the
houses, although we went round on all sides of them.
Getting a party at first behind a little mud wall, within
ten paces of the small opening above mentioned, we
kept up a point-blank fire, blazing through the loop-
holes on the men inside, who in return kept up a
brisk fire on us. I think the party in this block
would have surrendered at one time on my challeng-
ing them to do so, as they replied to me and opened
the small doorway in order to come out. Unfortunately the small party of Blacks who had been left
behind here were without any officer, and were very
unruly. They had joined my Egyptians, but they were
so excited that it was impossible to restrain them from

firing, although without taking any kind of aim, when the enemy opened the door to surrender. Consequently the door was instantly closed again, and the chance was lost. Leaving the party behind the wall to watch this door, and posting men on two other sides of this block to keep down the fire from the loop-holes, we went round with a small party to the river-side to see if there was not another and a better opening.

Going round, to my great astonishment I instantly had a man killed from a fire opened upon us suddenly from a house which, from what the officer of the Camerons had told me, I had thought unoccupied. We found also that there was another entrance to the detached block of buildings besides the small door, but it was commanded by a loop-holed house on the flank occupied by the enemy. In fact, we found out that there were men in most of the houses, and that they could get about as they liked from one to the other. Now and then they made a bolt across from one door to the other in the open, when some of them got knocked over. A couple of mule-guns with English gunners came down to help us, and blazed shrapnel-shells into the village; but these shells did not seem to do much harm, as, the houses lying low, they passed through the upper part of the walls, which being of sun-dried mud bricks, the same effect was not produced as if they had been of ordinary brick or masonry. In fact, they usually passed through without bursting at all. One gun, too, soon became temporarily useless, and had to be left out of action. And, much to my

surprise, the young lieutenant in command declined
to bring the other gun close up and blow a door in
as I requested, saying that artillery was just as effec-
tive at a distance! Failing his assistance, we next
tried to effect an entrance to the loop-holed houses on
the river-side. Here we found no doors at all, but
plenty of small loop-holes, from one of which the officer with me, an Egyptian lieutenant named Mahomed
Hamdi, was shot dead at about fifteen paces' distance.
I nearly lost my own life too at this period in an
unexpected manner. A Dervish had poked out his
rifle from a loop-hole I had not noticed, within about
five yards of my head, and was covering me, when my
English orderly-room clerk, Private John Warburton
of the Durham Light Infantry (106th), saw it, as the
song says :--

> " Not too soon and not too late,
>   But *just in time*."

He gave me a tremendous shout, just in time to make
me jump aside and avoid the shot.

Leaving a section of men lining the Nile bank, under
good cover among palm-trees, to keep up a fire on the
loop-holes facing that way, we went to try another plan.
We now entered one or two detached houses, finding in
them some living, and some dead men who had been
killed by the Blacks before; but we left all dead behind
us, and got another man killed ourselves. An athletic
corporal, named Mahomed Daoud, showed himself
remarkably active with his bayonet among the Dervishes in these houses, jumping upon them instantly

and running them through before they had time to
cover him with their rifles. In spite of the disagreeable nature of the business still to be done, it had to be
accomplished. The main block had to be entered, and
enter it we did, from the side nearest to the ravine and
the fort at Kosheh. There was certainly just a little
hesitation at first; but once half-a-dozen men had got
in, the fellows all went at it with a will, going straight
at every low doorway and through the narrow passages
and rooms from nearly end to end of these connected
houses, shooting and bayoneting all they came across.
It was, owing to the lowness of the doors and the built-
up traverses across the passages, the most difficult place
to work one's way through, but the Egyptians did it
well.

Unfortunately, however, there were two fortified
rooms from which we could not dislodge the enemy,
although only a very small number of them were left
alive. One of these was the room from which Lieutenant Hamdi had been killed, and we could neither
bring the gun to bear on it, from a distance, nor get into
it from the other houses. However, Hamdi's body was
still lying outside the loop-holes of this room, and as we
could not leave it there, we had to go round to the river-
side again to fetch it away. While doing so, taking four
men with a stretcher, and Warburton and a couple of
Egyptians to try and keep down the fire from some loop-
holes opposite, we got another man killed. Private Warburton, too, who was most plucky and useful, standing
out in the open and keeping up a well-directed and rapid

fire on the loop-hole nearest our stretcher party, had a very narrow escape. While his own rifle was up at the "present," one of the enemy's bullets passed through his sleeve at the shoulder close to his head, but did not even touch the skin! We managed to get off poor Hamdi's body without any more loss. Indeed the enemy in the house had not even the satisfaction of knowing they had touched any of us, as the man who was struck did not fall at once when hit, but "ordered arms" quietly as if on parade, and then managed to walk back a pace or two to the river-bank. There, helping himself down by a palm-tree root, he lay down, poor fellow, never to rise again, as he died very soon, after having first said to me "*Maalesh*" once or twice, which means "It doesn't matter." I never yet knew an Egyptian wounded, whether mortally or other-wise, who did not say "*Maalesh*" with the greatest calmness and resignation. After this we fired a few more volleys through the various loop-holes, and pro-ceeded to knock down the walls and burn the roofs, getting on the top and setting fire to them. When we left, after nearly three hours' fighting round this place, there were about seventy dead bodies of the enemy lying around. Our own dead we buried at once in a Mahomedan cemetery within gunshot of the village; but the Blacks set fire to the clothes of the dead Dervishes, in the hope that, by burning their bodies, they would prevent their souls having a chance of entering heaven!

A few marksmen from the 3d Egyptian Battalion

were left to keep the few remaining enemy from bolting from the two rooms, being posted all round; and next morning, as they had been kept in all right, some guns were brought down, the houses were well pounded, and after a bit the poor wretches who still survived were bayoneted by some of the Camerons without any further loss on our side.

While the village-fighting previously detailed had been going on, the whole of the remainder of the enemy's position had been carried. The camp and the main village of Ginness were occupied, and the enemy was in full retreat south along the river-bank towards Amara. From some unfortunate mistake about the orders which had been given to the officer commanding the 20th Hussars, and in fact of all the mounted troops, to the effect that he was not to charge, the cavalry and other mounted troops omitted entirely to pursue the enemy. This was the more unfortunate as the Dervishes, when retreating, were, so to speak, "between the devil and the deep sea," for they had a high range of rocky hills on the one side and the wide and rapid Nile on the other. A crushing blow might therefore have been struck, without any charging at all, had the Dervishes only been followed up continuously and fired on with volleys from dismounted cavalry, mounted infantry, and Camel Corps men. The actual result was that far too many of them escaped. The infantry troops, and indeed also all of the mounted corps as well, were very indignant about this lack of pursuit. The enemy, therefore, calmly carried away

with them their wounded and the most important of
their killed, notably an Emir named Abd el Majid el
Saghair (or "The Little"), and buried them as they
went along. A great number of their wounded, too,
died as they fled, and were hastily buried by the river-
bank. Their total loss in this action was calculated,
but over calculated to judge from the corpses left, at
600 killed. The 1st Brigade under General Butler,
after a short rest, followed the enemy the same night
as far as Amara, but utterly failed to overtake any of
the fugitives.

Our brigade halted for the night and bivouacked by
the now burnt village of Ginness, and a bitterly cold
night it was. Fortunately my servant Alfred, to whom
I had given strict orders before the fight began "not
to get himself killed," had, after amusing himself by
seeing a bit of the fight, gone back to our previous
bivouac near Kosheh, and brought up the regimental
camels with everybody's (officers' and men's) greatcoats
and blankets. He had also been smart enough to
secure somehow a little forage for the horses, of which
they stood greatly in need. Although he was a civilian, I never knew any soldier who could beat him at
finding useful things on a campaign.

The Egyptian loss in this affair was twenty officers
and men killed. The British loss I forget; but I remember it was not very heavy, poor young Soltau of
the 49th being the only officer killed, or who died of
his wounds.

That evening—such is the advantage of the "field-telegraph "—congratulatory telegrams were received by the General from the Queen, the Khedive, the Duke of Cambridge, the Secretary of State for War, and from General Sir Frederick Roberts, Commander-in-Chief in India. The latter, I remember, wired as follows: "We soldiers in India congratulate you on your success." These telegrams were published in orders. The following is the text of a telegram sent by General Sir F. Stephenson to the Khedive the day after this smart little battle :—

"My sincerest congratulations to your Highness on yesterday's success and excellent behaviour of Egyptian troops. They were very steady under fire, and fought in line side by side with English, and on one occasion specially distinguished themselves, when a small number rushed at the enemy, engaged them hand-to-hand, and bayoneted some. The four guns captured were taken by Egyptians. Their conduct throughout the operations, including defence of railway, which was an arduous duty, has given me great satisfaction, and holds out high promise for future efficiency."

It was indeed very gratifying to us English officers, who had been serving for three years or so with Egyptian troops, during which time we had been accustomed to hear them continually abused as scoundrels of the deepest dye, that our men had at last been able to obtain from an English General of so high a character as General Stephenson the recognition that they were indeed well worthy of the name of soldiers. And yet, although they had been so continually "crabbed" or run down, they had already done good work both at Suakin and at Kirbekan; and so they have also in various actions on the frontiers since the battle of Ginness.

After the fight officers commanding corps were requested to send in the names of officers and men who had distinguished themselves. In addition to the names of some two or three Egyptian officers, one of whom was the little Egyptian interpreter who always wanted to be on advance-guard, Private John Warburton's name was sent in, and I am glad to say he was given the Distinguished Conduct medal. He well deserved it; for although he had never been in action before, he behaved during all that village-fighting with the utmost calmness, sense, and pluck, and was of the very greatest use in every way, just when a sensible and plucky fellow was most wanted.

The day after Ginness we Egyptians were ordered on up the Nile to Amara. After a good long march, on arriving there in a beautiful grove of palm-trees overlooking the river, from which the rear-guard of the 1st Brigade were just departing, I proposed to bivouac, especially as it was on the Amara cataract; and the principal reason of our move was, according to orders, to establish a portage at this place to transport stores in case the two stern-wheel steamers could not pass up it. Unfortunately we again had present the same staff-officer, senior to myself, who had told us on a previous occasion to leave everything we possessed behind at Akasheh. He now insisted, although my orders had been clear enough to remain at Amara, upon my marching the regiment on to join General Butler's brigade, now five miles farther south at Abri. Accordingly we marched the extra five miles through the heavy sand in the hottest part of the day, and on arrival this brilliant staff-officer went to report to General Butler that he had brought us on. The General thereupon replied, just what might have been expected from previous orders, that he did not require us in the least; so we had the pleasure of toiling back again five miles through the sand.

Again we reached our palm-grove at Amara, and led the column into it, intending this time at any rate to bivouac in the grateful shade of the date-palms. But once again I was reckoning without our gallant and intelligent Lieut.-Colonel Owen Quirk, who, although he had left us for a while, came back once more, just as we had halted, in order to say that we must not camp there, but move a few hundred yards farther on, and bivouac out in the desert where there was no shade at all!

His repeatedly turning up thus to interfere, with his unnecessary orders calculated to give every one discomfort, reminded me forcibly of a comic song which used to be sung with great success by Colour-Sergeant Mortimer, a gallant fellow now dead, who belonged to my regiment, "The Borderers." Mortimer's song had a refrain to every verse, which ran—

" When up comes Jones, just when he wasn't wanted !"

For " Jones" substitute the word " Quirk," and his song would have applied admirably to the situation.

Despairingly, for the second time we marched the thoroughly wearied men out of our cool retreat ; but fortunately for us, just as we had again got quite clear of the palm-grove, we met General Grenfell riding up, who, on being applied to, said that most certainly we were to encamp in the shade instead of bivouacking out in the sun on the sand. And as we remained in this jolly little camping-ground by the river, watching a desert road which led to Absarat, until the third or fourth day of the new year we were very happy. After that we marched on and joined the remainder of the troops at Abri, a place which, from its beautiful shingly beach, we used to call the Brighton of the Soudan. Here at Abri we found a little English cemetery, where lie the remains of some half-a-dozen poor fellows who had died in the preceding expedition up the Nile. The Dervishes, be it remarked to their credit, had never interfered with the crosses on the graves.

Although after this Marriott and Smith Dorrien, both Egyptians, pushed on with both the Egyptian and British Camel Corps and mounted infantry, and captured nine of the enemy's barges laden with arms and food, Abri was as far as the remainder of the troops went up the Nile. In fact, the advance on Abri ended the campaign.

CHAPTER XXV.

NO ADVANCE ON DONGOLA — GREGORIE STALKS GEESE — BAKER
PASHA VISITS US — MOGRAKKEH ABANDONED — RECONQUEST
OF SOUDAN, AIDED BY ITALY, DESIRABLE.

THE morning after the fight was the last day of the
year 1885, and after this success it was universally
imagined that an immediate advance would be made
in pursuit of the conquered Dervishes and the reoccu-
pation of Dongola carried out. The force which we
had defeated being the only force which the enemy
possessed in that part of the world, this would have
been a comparatively easy matter; for although water
transport was defective, the water in the Nile being
too low to get the armed stern-wheel steamer Lotus
except with great difficulty over the rapids or cata-
racts, there were sufficient camels available to carry
forward at once as much transport as would have
been required for the mounted troops, who could
have followed the defeated foe instantly and utterly
dispersed them, while more transport, whether of
camels, whale-boats, or the Nile boats called nuggars,
could have soon been got together along the banks of

the river. For there were many beautiful whale-boats still available from Wolseley's expedition lying at Kosheh, Sarkametto, and Dāl; these we eventually had to burn on our evacuation, while Montgomerie, of the Royal Navy, at great personal risk to himself, destroyed the Lotus and another stern-wheel steamboat by running them intentionally on the rocks in mid-stream when he had found it impossible to get them down the Dāl cataract. This destruction of boats was all a terrible waste of the country's money; but when we were told to clear out, as we could not take our shipping with us, we could not leave it to fall into the hands of Sheikh Abdullah, the Madhi's successor.

The climate at that period of the year, although hot in the middle of the day, presented no difficulty whatever to troops marching in the early morning or the evening. Thus there would have been no difficulty in the infantry following rapidly; for the transport service, admirably organised by Colonel Skinner, of the Army Service Corps, which had been sufficient to take the troops as far as Abri, would certainly have sufficed to take them farther still had only the advance been determined upon.

It was about this period that Abd el Kadir Pasha, who knew as much about the Soudan as anybody, expressed himself very plainly on the subject of our advancing or not advancing. He told Mr Moberly Bell, the remarkably foreseeing correspondent of 'The Times' in Cairo, that we might thrash these Dervishes as often as we pleased, but that if after each beating we gave them we always retired again, it would only be interpreted by them as a sign of weakness, and affairs on the frontier would never be brought to a satisfactory conclusion, but more trouble would be in store for us all before long.

Nevertheless, a shilly-shallying policy was once again adopted by the Government, and most of the troops were in a few days' time marched back northwards to Akasheh, and gradually to Wady Halfa, only a very small force being left at Ginness to form the extreme frontier guard. This force consisted of the 2d Battalion of the Durham Light Infantry under Lieut.-Colonel Coker, which regiment was encamped near the old fort at Kosheh, of my battalion of Egyptians, 300 men of which took possession of Fort Mograkkeh, the remainder being either with Hawtayne at Akasheh or on detachment under Frith at Sarkametto, of the Black Battalion now under Gibb, and a few details of British mounted infantry under a smart young officer named Tudway.

The 3d Battalion E.A., under Tapp, now marching northwards, Gregorie with a portion of the Blacks came to garrison the old mud fort at Mograkkeh with me, General Butler, who was left as Frontier Commandant at Halfa, having kindly acceded to my request to have this excessively smart officer once more with me as my staff-officer and general assistant, while I remained in command of all the details of Egyptian troops, both at the extreme front and at various detached posts between the front and Wady Halfa.

For about three months we occupied this advanced post at Mograkkeb, living in the horrible old fort, in mud huts full of flies, and only roofed in by parts of old tents. With the exception of some wild-dog hunting and some steeple-chasing we got up with the Durhams, when Tudway sometimes steered "The Parson" to victory, there was not much excitement, but still we always found plenty to do; for there was plenty of drill, or an occasional reconnaissance southwards, to help the days to pass, and Gregorie, who was an ardent sportsman, used to be particularly successful in stalking and shooting the beautiful Nile geese. The way he used to accomplish the destruction of these excessively shy birds was by disguising himself as a Nubian native. Then, clad in a filthy turban and dirty cotton dress, he would pretend to work the water-raising machine, called a *shadouf*, until the unsuspecting fowl approached near enough, when he would let go the *shadouf*, seize his gun, and let fly. He also occasionally in the early morning succeeded in stalking a gazelle or two, as these charming little creatures came down at dawn from the mountain-ranges to feed on the villagers' crops in the cultivated strip of ground near the river-banks.

The one real bit of excitement we had was when I obtained permission to proceed with Gregorie on a prolonged reconnaissance into the enemy's country, taking with us only about twenty Egyptian soldiers mounted on camels. We were away altogether for over a week, marching with all precaution southwards up the Nile,

and a charming trip we had of it. The only signs of
the enemy we found, however, were plenty of graves
of the dead, who had escaped from Ginness only to die
in their flight; and occasionally in some of the Nubian
villages we would come across a few of the wounded
men from the same action, who had been left behind
by their fellows. The absolute want of opposition to
our advance with such a small body of men showed
me how easy would have been at this time an advance
on Dongola.

It was not to be, however, and in the beginning of
April 1886 we received intelligence that not only was
all idea of any advance on Dongola quite abandoned,
but that our advanced posts were to be withdrawn, that
even Akasheh, at the head of the desert railway track,
was to be given up, and the railway track, eighty-seven
miles in length, to be left to its fate. All troops at the
front were to fall back on Wady Halfa, which place, on
the second cataract, was henceforth to be considered as
the boundary between Egypt and the Soudan. Thus to
Sheikh Abdullah, the successor of the Mahdi, was the
whole province of Nubia abandoned, and once again
had all the fighting and all the destruction of human
life, not only by the sword but by that fell disease
enteric fever, which caused the British dreadful losses,
been absolutely in vain.

Before we retreated from Mograkkeh, however, I
received there a visit from that distinguished officer
Valentine Baker Pasha. It was just after the trip
which Gregorie and I had taken southwards into the

farther parts of Nubia, and he came to see whether it would not, in my opinion, be possible for him to retain the greater part of Nubia by simply establishing a series of police-posts in the villages along the river. These police-posts were to be formed of black gendarmerie men, absolutely the same sort of men that we had in the 9th Battalion of the regular army, and armed in the same way. From what I had seen I believed the Pasha's scheme to be perfectly feasible at that time, but he was unfortunately refused sanction from Cairo to carry out his plan.

Baker Pasha came up accompanied by "Baby" Martin, both on camels, and arriving with a frightful thirst. They were both very heavy men, and as one of them, the Pasha, sitting on my camp-bed, to my great dismay broke it, while the other, Martin, taking possession of my only chair, smashed that to pieces likewise, we had the greatest difficulty in managing to seat them for the humble repast which Alfred Thacker, assisted by Corporal Mahomed Omar, my head orderly, had prepared for them. However, after a good deal of fun, we managed somehow to find seats for all; while as Gregorie had luckily killed a gazelle that morning and a wild goose the evening before, we had plenty to give them to eat.

As I said, they arrived with a most terrific thirst after their long camel-ride from Akasheh, and poor "Baby," who was tired, hot, and cross, was not at all contented with the absolutely flat soda-water, purchased from a Greek *bakkal*, which was at first all we had to

give him. I found out, however, that he had got a
store of soda-water of his own on a baggage-camel,
which he was reserving for the journey back, and as
I sent out surreptitiously and had some of this pur-
loined for his own use, he soon expressed himself as
being perfectly satisfied at his entertainment! Poor
fellow! he died very shortly afterwards of heat-apo-
plexy at Assouan; and Baker Pasha died not long
after him. Well! at all events it can be said of them
that they both did good and gallant service in their
time, and were both deeply regretted.

One can become attached to any place; and when,
having previously watched the Durhams, who had just
built some beautiful huts which they had to destroy,
march away to the northward, it came to be our turn to
pass out of the gates of Fort Mograkkeh for the last
time, it was after all with heavy hearts that we said good-
bye to the old place, or rather to its ruins. For after
having done all in our power to make the place as
strong as possible, we, before leaving, did all that was
possible to destroy the lofty mud-brick walls and parapets, and to utterly reduce the palm-thatched huts and
barracks within the enceinte to a burnt and shapeless
mass of rubbish-heaps. Nevertheless, as we marched
out, the band being accompanied by its three strange
pets—a black sheep, a black goat, and a small black
dog—which, as usual on parade, gambolled around the
musicians, neither Gregorie nor myself believed for a
moment but that the time would soon come for us to
view the old fort once more; for so vacillating had been

the whole policy of the Government of Mr Gladstone
from first to last in matters appertaining to the Soudan,
that it appeared to us as more than likely that an
order would be given when next the Nile was high for
an advance on Dongola after all.

Although the Government policy has never yet been
reversed since we left the Soudan, and although Mr
Gladstone has now retired from affairs of State, there is
still, nine years later, the same question remaining to be
solved: Is Egypt, aided by England with either men or
money, to reconquer the fertile province of Upper Nubia
and the town of Dongola, or is she not?

The Egyptian army has gradually been increased
during the last nine years both as regards cavalry and
infantry. The artillery, too, is in a thoroughly efficient
condition. In fact, against the 7000 or 8000 troops
which we had under Tewfik Pasha, the late Khedive, in
1886, there are now, under Abbas Pasha, the present
ruler of Egypt, upwards of 20,000 troops, all well disciplined by British officers. These men should be able
alone to advance to Dongola, Berber, and Khartoum;
and if only, now that the Government has taken over
the East African Company's Protectorate, a conjunc-
tion of forces could be made from Uganda by other
native troops, there is no reason why very shortly the
whole of the Nile valley should not be ours. One
thing is very certain. If Egypt, backed up by England, does not soon make some such move, some other
Power, either France or Italy, will.

As regards the former, her strength in the western

parts of the Soudan is already very great, and it is constantly increasing. Her jealousy and antagonism to Great Britain seem to increase rather than to diminish as the years roll on, for she has never forgiven herself the want of co-operation with our fleet before Alexandria in 1882, and never will. Therefore in France, England must always see a most formidable foe upon African soil, and the sooner that the position of Egypt and Great Britain combined is placed beyond the power of French interference in the Soudan the better. There is no time to waste.

With regard to the Italians, they are at present our sworn allies on African soil or elsewhere. With their assistance, especially now that they have taken Kasala, a town within striking distance of Khartoum, we might rapidly, and to the mutual advantage of the two countries, recover the whole of the Soudan, and an attempt to do so should be made without delay. In fact, if we do not do so, or let the Egyptians, backed by us, do so, it is quite probable that Italy, having got already such an excellent footing in the Eastern Soudan, may do all the rest for herself. Thus she may without external assistance become before long the holder of the Nile above and below the town of Khartoum, and may, moreover, capture and hoist the Italian flag over that town, which has been justly called the Key of Egypt.

All this, however, is a point for statesmen to decide upon; and as, looking at it from a mere soldier's point of view, statesmen seem to have done very little for

Egypt in the past, it seems almost hopeless to expect better things from them in the future.

While speaking of the present state of the Egyptian army, there is one important factor to be taken into consideration, which might, if not controlled, possibly seriously affect the future discipline and efficiency of the troops. This is the attitude taken up by Abbas Pasha, the present young Khedive, towards all British control in general, and towards the English officers of his own army in particular. Not so very long ago he publicly, on parade at Wady Halfa, grossly insulted Kitchener Pasha, the present Sirdar of the Egyptian army. How different is this attitude to that taken up by his father, Mahomed Tewfik, and how much to be deplored! A tight curb should be kept upon this young prince, who has been too much led away by the French press; and he should be speedily taught that, whether England has declared a protectorate over Egypt or no, she is, while perfectly prepared to support him if loyal, nevertheless quite strong enough, if he oppose her, to remove him and instal another and less captious ruler in his place. Fortunately, it seems probable that Lord Cromer has already taught him some such lesson. Yet does it not seem as if Kitchener Pasha is not, after all, sufficiently supported, for can any one imagine such an insult having been offered to Sir Evelyn Wood, when he was Sirdar, without an immediate protectorate having been proclaimed? It would never have been endured for a moment.

In 1886, however, there was no trouble with the

principal ruler of the State, Mahomed Tewfik being loyal alike to his English allies and to his English officers throughout. It was a pleasure to serve under him; and as for his personal courage, that it was undeniable he showed both by the way he refused to leave Egypt when he had lost almost everything in 1882, and again, when the cholera was rampant everywhere in the following year, by the fearless manner in which he visited all the hospitals, both of soldiers and civilians alike.

CHAPTER XXVI.

AFTER leaving Mograkkeh there is very little to chronicle as regards service on the frontier in those days. All the British troops being withdrawn, Wady Halfa became the frontier post, and was soon left entirely in the hands of Egyptians under Colonel Holled Smith as commander of the troops. It is true, though, that, for some extraordinary reason or other never explained, General Butler was kept up there also, being left with his brigade-major a sort of prisoner in Halfa for some considerable time after every man in his brigade had been withdrawn, and was thus forced to lead there a monotonous existence, having nothing to do.

There was nothing for our Egyptian troops to do there either but to build strong forts for the protection of the place against possible attacks in the future; and after a few monotonous months of this sort of thing, living under canvas in the hottest time of the year and getting bad water to drink, I found my health utterly giving way, and was thus at length forced to go down the Nile previous to retirement from the Khedive's service.

As an example of how great was the heat in Halfa in summer, it is worth recording that nine cocks and hens, which I had bought from poor old Tapp, who was a sybarite and liked little luxuries, on his regiment evacuating Fort Mograkkeh, after being conveyed by me to Halfa, all died in one day of sunstroke. Eggs were at a premium after that!

When, eventually, the time came for me to bid farewell to my officers and men, and embark on the stern-wheeler which was to bear me northwards, I found that it was a moment of considerable trial to leave the Egyptian regiment which, in war and in peace, I had come to look upon as my family. Fortunately, David Gregorie embarked with me to go down the river, for, after I had signed and sealed my farewell order in the regimental order-book, I do not think I could have stood alone the thronging around me of the officers and non-commissioned officers, the hand-kissing, and the exuberant blessings in Arabic which were showered upon my head by these swarthy sons of the Nile.

All the time, too, until at length it faded out of sight, the band kept on playing that confounded " Auld Lang Syne" till I wished to heaven that I had never had them taught the tune, or that all the instruments were at the bottom of the river. But everything has an end, and even this painful trial of parting was done with at

last, and I had, as its commandant, said farewell to the
1st Battalion of the Egyptian army for ever.

In my farewell order, published in Arabic and in
English, I made use of the words that I should never
forget the comrades with whom I had fought side by
side at Suakin and at Ginness, and said, moreover, in
conclusion, that while thanking all the officers for the
help they had given me, I hoped that the regiment
would ever retain its name for smartness, and continue in every sense of the word the *Bringi Orta* or
1st Battalion of the Egyptian army.

These hopes events since then have justified, for
under succeeding English commanding officers the 1st
Battalion has proved at the battle of Toski, a successful fight fought by Wodehouse with Egyptian troops
alone, and elsewhere, that all those who have filled
its ranks have, although swarthy in skin, yet been
well worthy of the name of soldier.

.   .   .   .

And now there is very little left to say of an English
soldier's experiences under Crescent and Star, for there
is but my leave-taking of the Khedive to be chronicled.

His Highness was very gracious to me, saying many
kind things which, even now that he is dead, modesty
forbids me to repeat. He also presented me with his
picture, and conferred upon me the Order of the Med-
jidieh of the third class. Both Gregorie and myself
had already received the fourth class of the Osmanieh,
which is a purely military order, for our services at
Suakin. Thus, as I, in common with all my brother

officers in the Khedive's army, had picked up a few
other decorations, I must honestly say that, from the
decorative point of view, the Egyptian service had
"done me remarkably well."

Mahomed Tewfik was particularly lively and full of
anecdote on that day of our parting interview. He
would, instead of his usual French or Arabic, talk to
me in English, in which language he had, by close
application, made immense progress during the last
two years, and of his proficiency in which he was
justly not a little proud. It was, indeed, strange how,
with all the affairs of State which constantly occupied
him, he ever found time to study and acquire fluently
a foreign language, yet he had done so.

I told him that I intended proceeding to England
via Turkey, when he exclaimed with animation laugh-
ingly: "Going by Turkey, are you? Then, by Allah!
Hajjard Bey, I must, although a Turk myself, give you
a warning. Beware of the Turkish women! Ah! they
are deceitful sirens if you like—pretty wretches, who
will laugh at you and smile at you just to lure you on;
but look out for them! and on no account trust them for
a minute, or try to speak to them, for all their wreathed
smiles. I had an experience of Turkish women myself
once, I can assure you, which was quite enough for me.
Shall I tell it you—for your warning?"

"By all means, your Highness; I should like to hear
it."

"Well," began the Khedive, "when I was a young
fellow I went over to Constantinople with my cousin,

Raschid Pasha, who was of my own age and very inflammable by nature.

"We went down one day together to the 'Sweet Waters of Europe,' where, among other handsome women assembled, we saw one lady in a carriage who was a perfect beauty. She wore only the thinnest of *yashmaks*, and I really think that she was the loveliest creature I ever saw in all my life. Immediately we saw her, this divine young being looked languorously at us out of her lustrous dark eyes, and, quite unabashed, smiled at us, with parted rosebud lips, in a way that was an invitation in itself.

I must confess that I was extremely taken with her myself, but as for my cousin, he instantly fell head over ears in love with her, and wanted to go up and speak to her to tell her so, from doing which I with difficulty restrained him. While we were watching her, and she continued still smiling sweetly upon us, to our surprise up came a handsome young Greek effendi to her carriage. Leaning over, he spoke to her familiarly, while she in return greeted him with the greatest cordiality of manner. In a few minutes he left, and then I could restrain Raschid no longer. 'Surely,' said he, 'if she will speak to a Greek effendi, a Christian, she will not refuse to enter into conversation with me, a Mussulman like herself.'

"As if to confirm his words, the beauty began laughing at us more entrancingly than ever, showing the most deliciously white little teeth, which were just like pearls in sheen. Quite reassured, Raschid boldly marched up to the carriage and made to the lady some complimentary remark. He was not long, though, before he regretted it, for her beaming face instantly changed to a look of intense anger, as she seized him by the collar of his 'Stambouli' coat, and, gripping it firmly, commenced to abuse him.

"'By Allah!' she exclaimed, 'that I should have lived to have been so insulted, you dog and you son of a dog! What do you take me for?—oh, you filthy descendant of a race of pigs! I will teach you to insult a Turkish lady, oh, you Sheitan (devil), you accursed Majnoon (maniac)!' And thus she went on, shaking him all the time like a rat, and screaming at him at the top of her voice like a veritable fury. Poor fellow! his plight was bad enough. As a crowd of other angry ladies and some few men had commenced to gather around, I could not desert my cousin; but as they indulged in all sorts of offensive remarks towards the pair of us, I was undergoing almost as bad a quarter of an hour as my unfortunate cousin himself.

"At length the beautiful termagant worked herself up into an acme of fury. Seizing his *tarboosh* from his head, she tore it right across, then, holding it by the tassel, struck him violently over the face with it. 'There, dog!' said she, flinging it at him, 'take that as a lesson to teach you how, unmasked, you may talk to Turkish ladies in the future.' Then she sank back in her carriage exhausted, while we made our escape the best way we could, like dogs with their tails between their legs.

"What do you think of that for a disagreeable adventure?" added the Khedive, laughing heartily; "and do you not think, seeing how we of the same race could be deceived, that I am doing you, my friend, in return for all you have done for me, a good turn in putting you on your guard against those deceitful she-devils the Turkish ladies?"

Most assuredly I did think that the hint was worth remembering; and when I too saw in turn, at the same "Sweet Waters of Europe," the pretty women smiling all around them at every man who came near, simply because, in their empty existences, they had nothing else to do, I thought of the Khedive's yarn and of Raschid Pasha's discomfiture. Thus forewarned, I was forearmed; and—as I must now do from these pages —I beat a speedy retreat.

With my late august master the Khedive's amusing story, I will bid farewell to the Crescent and the Star, to Mahomed Tewfik himself, and to my dear friend David Gregorie, whom, alas! I left in Egypt never to see again.

THE END.

PRINTED BY WILLIAM BLACKWOOD AND SONS.

Catalogue

of

Messrs Blackwood & Sons'

Publications

PERIODS OF EUROPEAN LITERATURE. Edited by
PROFESSOR SAINTSBURY.

THE FLOURISHING OF ROMANCE AND THE RISE OF ALLE-
GORY. (12TH AND 13TH CENTURIES.) By GEORGE SAINTSBURY, M.A.,
Professor of Rhetoric and English Literature in Edinburgh University.
Crown 8vo, 5s. net.

THE LATER RENAISSANCE. By DAVID HANNAY. Crown 8vo,
5s. net.

THE FOURTEENTH CENTURY. By F. J. SNELL. Crown 8vo.
[In the press.

THE AUGUSTAN AGES. By OLIVER ELTON. Crown 8vo.
[In the press.

The other Volumes are :—

THE DARK AGES . . . Prof. W. P. Kerr.	THE MID-EIGHTEENTH
THE TRANSITION	CENTURY . . . . J. Hepburn Millar.
PERIOD . . . . G. Gregory Smith.	THE ROMANTIC REVOLT Prof. C. E. Vaughan.
THE EARLIER RENAISSANCE.	THE ROMANTIC TRIUMPH . T. S. Omond.
THE FIRST HALF OF THE SEVENTEENTH	THE LATER NINETEENTH
CENTURY . . Prof. H. J. C. Grierson.	CENTURY . . . . The Editor.

PHILOSOPHICAL CLASSICS FOR ENGLISH READERS.

Edited by WILLIAM KNIGHT, LL.D., Professor of Moral Philosophy
in the University of St Andrews. In crown 8vo Volumes, with Portraits,
price 3s. 6d.

Contents of the Series. — DESCARTES, by Professor Mahaffy, Dublin. — BUTLER, by Rev. W. Lucas Collins, M.A. — BERKELEY, by Professor Campbell Fraser. — FICHTE, by Professor Adamson, Glasgow. — KANT, by Professor Wallace, Oxford. — HAMILTON, by Professor Veitch, Glasgow. — HEGEL, by the Master of Balliol. — LEIBNIZ, by J. Theodore Merz. — VICO, by Professor Flint, Edinburgh. — HOBBES, by Professor Croom Robertson. — HUME, by the Editor. — SPINOZA, by the Very Rev. Principal Caird, Glasgow. — BACON: Part I. The Life, by Professor Nichol. — BACON: Part II. Philosophy, by the same Author. — LOCKE, by Professor Campbell Fraser.

FOREIGN CLASSICS FOR ENGLISH READERS. Edited by
Mrs OLIPHANT. CHEAP RE-ISSUE. In limp cloth, fcap. 8vo, price 1s.
each.

Ready. — DANTE, by the Editor. — VOLTAIRE, by General Sir E. B. Hamley, K.C.B. — PASCAL, by Principal Tulloch. — PETRARCH, by Henry Reeve, C.B. — GOETHE, by A. Hayward, Q.C. — MOLIÈRE, by the Editor and F. Tarver, M.A. — MONTAIGNE, by Rev. W. L. Collins. — RABELAIS, by Sir Walter Besant. — CALDERON, by E. J. Hasell. — SAINT SIMON, by C. W. Collins.

In preparation. — CERVANTES, by the Editor. — CORNEILLE AND RACINE, by Henry M. Trollope. — MADAME DE SÉVIGNÉ, by Miss Thackeray. — LA FONTAINE, AND OTHER FRENCH FABULISTS, by Rev. W. Lucas Collins, M.A. — SCHILLER, by James Sime, M.A. — TASSO, by E. J. Hasell. — ROUSSEAU, by Henry Grey Graham. — ALFRED DE MUSSET, by C. F. Oliphant.

ANCIENT CLASSICS FOR ENGLISH READERS. Edited by
the Rev. W. LUCAS COLLINS, M.A. CHEAP RE-ISSUE. In limp cloth,
fcap. 8vo, price 1s. each.

Contents of the Series. — HOMER: ILIAD, by the Editor. — HOMER: ODYSSEY, by the Editor. — HERODOTUS, by G. C. Swayne. — CÆSAR, by Anthony Trollope. — VIRGIL, by the Editor. — HORACE, by Sir Theodore Martin. — ÆSCHYLUS, by Bishop Copleston. — XENOPHON, by Sir Alex. Grant. — CICERO, by the Editor. — SOPHOCLES, by C. W. Collins. — PLINY, by Rev. A. Church and W. J. Brodribb. — EURIPIDES, by W. B. Donne. — JUVENAL, by E. Walford. — ARISTOPHANES, by the Editor. — HESIOD AND THEOGNIS, by J. Davies. — PLAUTUS AND TERENCE, by the Editor. — TACITUS, by W. B. Donne. — LUCIAN, by the Editor. — PLATO, by C. W. Collins. — GREEK ANTHOLOGY, by Lord Neaves. — LIVY, by the Editor. — OVID, by Rev. A. Church. — CATULLUS, TIBULLUS, AND PROPERTIUS, by J. Davies. — DEMOSTHENES, by W. J. Brodribb. — ARISTOTLE, by Sir Alex. Grant. — THUCYDIDES, by the Editor. — LUCRETIUS, by W. H. Mallock. — PINDAR, by Rev. F. D. Morice.

CATALOGUE

OF

MESSRS BLACKWOOD & SONS'

PUBLICATIONS.

ALISON.
History of Europe. By Sir ARCHIBALD ALISON, Bart., D.C.L.

1. From the Commencement of the French Revolution to the Battle of Waterloo.
   LIBRARY EDITION, 14 vols., with Portraits. Demy 8vo, £10, 10s.
   ANOTHER EDITION, in 20 vols. crown 8vo, £6.
   PEOPLE'S EDITION 13 vols. crown 8vo, £2, 11s.

2. Continuation to the Accession of Louis Napoleon.
   LIBRARY EDITION, 8 vols. 8vo, £6, 7s. 6d.
   PEOPLE'S EDITION, 8 vols. crown 8vo 34s.

Epitome of Alison's History of Europe. Thirtieth Thousand, 7s. 6d.

Atlas to Alison's History of Europe. By A. Keith Johnston.
   LIBRARY EDITION, demy 4to, £3, 3s.
   PEOPLE'S EDITION, 31s. 6d.

Life of John Duke of Marlborough. With some Account of his Contemporaries, and of the War of the Succession. Third Edition. 2 vols. 8vo. Portraits and Maps, 30s.

Essays : Historical, Political, and Miscellaneous. 3 vols. demy 8vo, 45s.

ACROSS FRANCE IN A CARAVAN: BEING SOME ACCOUNT OF A JOURNEY FROM BORDEAUX TO GENOA IN THE "ESCARGOT," taken in the Winter 1889-90. By the Author of 'A Day of my Life at Eton.' With fifty Illustrations by John Wallace, after Sketches by the Author, and a Map. Cheap Edition, demy 8vo, 7s. 6d.

ACTA SANCTORUM HIBERNIÆ; Ex Codice Salmanticensi. Nunc primum integre edita opera CAROLI DE SMEDT et JOSEPHI DE BACKER, e Soc. Jesu, Hagiographorum Bollandianorum; Auctore et Sumptus Largiente JOANNE PATRICIO MARCHIONE BOTHAE. In One handsome 4to Volume, bound in half roxburghe, £2, 2s.; in paper cover, 31s. 6d.

ADOLPHUS. Some Memories of Paris. By F. ADOLPHUS. Crown 8vo, 6s.

AFLALO. A Sketch of the Natural History (Vertebrates) of the British Islands. By F. G. AFLALO, F.R.G.S., F.Z.S., Author of 'A Sketch of the Natural History of Australia,' &c. With numerous Illustrations by Lodge and Bennett. Crown 8vo, 6s. net.

AIKMAN.
    Manures and the Principles of Manuring. By C. M. AIKMAN, D.Sc., F.R.S.E., &c., Professor of Chemistry, Glasgow Veterinary College; Examiner in Chemistry, University of Glasgow, &c. Crown 8vo, 6s. 6d.
    Farmyard Manure: Its Nature, Composition, and Treatment. Crown 8vo, 1s. 6d.

ALLARDYCE.
    The City of Sunshine. By ALEXANDER ALLARDYCE, Author of 'Earlscourt,' &c. New Edition. Crown 8vo, 6s.
    Balmoral: A Romance of the Queen's Country. New Edition. Crown 8vo, 6s.

ANCIENT CLASSICS FOR ENGLISH READERS. Edited by Rev. W. LUCAS COLLINS, M.A. Price 1s. each. *For List of Vols. see p. 2.*

ANDERSON. Daniel in the Critics' Den. A Reply to Dean Farrar's 'Book of Daniel.' By ROBERT ANDERSON, LL.D., Barrister-at-Law, Assistant Commissioner of Police of the Metropolis; Author of 'The Coming Prince,' 'Human Destiny,' &c. Post 8vo, 4s. 6d.

AYTOUN.
    Lays of the Scottish Cavaliers, and other Poems. By W. EDMONDSTOUNE AYTOUN, D.C.L., Professor of Rhetoric and Belles-Lettres in the University of Edinburgh. New Edition. Fcap. 8vo, 3s. 6d.
        ANOTHER EDITION. Fcap. 8vo, 7s. 6d.
        CHEAP EDITION. 1s. Cloth, 1s. 3d.
    An Illustrated Edition of the Lays of the Scottish Cavaliers. From designs by Sir NOEL PATON. Cheaper Edition. Small 4to, 10s. 6d.
    Bothwell: a Poem. Third Edition. Fcap., 7s. 6d.
    Poems and Ballads of Goethe. Translated by Professor AYTOUN and Sir THEODORE MARTIN, K.C.B. Third Edition. Fcap., 6s.
    Memoir of William E. Aytoun, D.C.L. By Sir THEODORE MARTIN, K.C.B. With Portrait. Post 8vo, 12s.

BADEN-POWELL. The Saving of Ireland. Conditions and Remedies: Industrial, Financial, and Political. By Sir GEORGE BADEN-POWELL, K.C.M.G., M.P. Demy 8vo, 7s. 6d.

BEDFORD & COLLINS. Annals of the Free Foresters, from 1856 to the Present Day. By W. K. R. BEDFORD, W. E. W. COLLINS, and other Contributors. With 55 Portraits and 59 other Illustrations. Demy 8vo, 21s. net.

BELLAIRS. Gossips with Girls and Maidens, Betrothed and Free. By LADY BELLAIRS. New Edition. Crown 8vo, 3s. 6d. Cloth, extra gilt edges, 5s.

BELLESHEIM. History of the Catholic Church of Scotland. From the Introduction of Christianity to the Present Day. By ALPHONS BELLESHEIM, D.D., Canon of Aix-la-Chapelle. Translated, with Notes and Additions, by D. OSWALD HUNTER BLAIR, O.S.B., Monk of Fort Augustus. Cheap Edition. Complete in 4 vols. demy 8vo, with Maps. Price 21s. net.

BENTINCK. Racing Life of Lord George Cavendish Bentinck, M.P., and other Reminiscences. By JOHN KENT, Private Trainer to the Goodwood Stable. Edited by the Hon. FRANCIS LAWLEY. With Twenty-three full-page Plates, and Facsimile Letter. Third Edition. Demy 8vo, 25s.

BICKERDYKE. A Banished Beauty. By JOHN BICKERDYKE, Author of 'Days in Thule, with Rod, Gun, and Camera,' 'The Book of the All-Round Angler,' 'Curiosities of Ale and Beer,' &c. With Illustrations. Cheap Edition. Crown 8vo, 2s.

BINDLOSS. In the Niger Country. By HAROLD BINDLOSS.
With 2 Maps. In 1 vol. demy 8vo.   [*In the press.*

BIRCH.

Examples of Stables, Hunting-Boxes, Kennels, Racing Establishments, &c. By JOHN BIRCH, Architect, Author of 'Country Architecture,'
&c. With 30 Plates. Royal 8vo, 7s.

Examples of Labourers' Cottages, &c. With Plans for Im-
proving the Dwellings of the Poor in Large Towns. With 34 Plates. Royal 8vo, 7s.

Picturesque Lodges. A Series of Designs for Gate Lodges,
Park Entrances, Keepers', Gardeners', Bailiffs', Grooms', Upper and Under Servants' Lodges, and other Rural Residences. With 16 Plates. 4to, 12s. 6d.

BLACKIE.

The Wisdom of Goethe. By JOHN STUART BLACKIE, Emeritus
Professor of Greek in the University of Edinburgh. Fcap. 8vo. Cloth, extra
gilt, 6s.

John Stuart Blackie : A Biography. By ANNA M. STODDART.
With 3 Plates. Third Edition. 2 vols. demy 8vo, 21s.
POPULAR EDITION. With Portrait. Crown 8vo 6s.

BLACKMORE.

The Maid of Sker. By R. D. BLACKMORE, Author of 'Lorna
Doone,' &c. New Edition. Crown 8vo, 6s. Cheaper Edition. Crown 8vo,
3s. 6d.

Dariel : A Romance of Surrey. With 14 Illustrations by
Chris. Hammond. Crown 8vo. 6s.

BLACKWOOD.

Annals of a Publishing House. William Blackwood and his
Sons ; Their Magazine and Friends. By Mrs OLIPHANT. With Four Portraits.
Third Edition. Demy 8vo. Vols. I. and II. £2, 2s.

———— Vol. III. John Blackwood. By his Daughter, Mrs
GERALD PORTER. With 2 Portraits and View of Strathtyrum. Demy 8vo, 21s.

Blackwood's Magazine, from Commencement in 1817 to December 1897. Nos. 1 to 986, forming 161 Volumes.

Index to Blackwood's Magazine. Vols. 1 to 50. 8vo, 15s.

Tales from Blackwood. First Series. Price One Shilling each,
in Paper Cover. Sold separately at all Railway Bookstalls.
They may also be had bound in 12 vols., cloth, 18s. Half calf, richly gilt, 30s.
Or the 12 vols. in 6, roxburghe, 21s. Half red morocco, 28s.

Tales from Blackwood. Second Series. Complete in Twenty-
four Shilling Parts. Handsomely bound in 12 vols., cloth, 30s. In leather back,
roxburghe style, 37s. 6d. Half calf, gilt, 52s. 6d. Half morocco, 55s.

Tales from Blackwood. Third Series. Complete in Twelve
Shilling Parts. Handsomely bound in 6 vols., cloth, 15s.; and in 12 vols., cloth,
18s. The 6 vols. in roxburghe, 21s. Half calf, 25s. Half morocco, 28s.

Travel, Adventure, and Sport. From 'Blackwood's Magazine.'
Uniform with 'Tales from Blackwood.' In Twelve Parts, each price 1s. Handsomely bound in 6 vols., cloth, 15s. And in half calf, 25s.

New Educational Series. *See separate Catalogue.*

BLACKWOOD.

New Uniform Series of Novels (Copyright).

Crown 8vo, cloth. Price 3s. 6d. each. Now ready:—

THE MAID OF SKER. By R. D. Blackmore.
WENDERHOLME. By P. G. Hamerton.
THE STORY OF MARGRÉDEL. By D. Storrar Meldrum.
MISS MARJORIBANKS. By Mrs Oliphant.
THE PERPETUAL CURATE, and THE RECTOR. By the Same.
SALEM CHAPEL, and THE DOCTOR'S FAMILY. By the Same.
A SENSITIVE PLANT. By E. D. Gerard.
LADY LEE'S WIDOWHOOD. By General Sir E. B. Hamley.
KATIE STEWART, and other Stories. By Mrs Oliphant.
VALENTINE AND HIS BROTHER. By the Same.
SONS AND DAUGHTERS. By the Same.
MARMORNE. By P. G. Hamerton.
REATA. By E. D. Gerard.
BEGGAR MY NEIGHBOUR. By the Same.
THE WATERS OF HERCULES. By the Same.
FAIR TO SEE. By L. W. M. Lockhart.
MINE IS THINE. By the Same.
DOUBLES AND QUITS. By the Same.
ALTIORA PETO. By Laurence Oliphant
PICCADILLY. By the Same. With Illustrations.
LADY BABY. By D. Gerard.
THE BLACKSMITH OF VOE. By Paul Cushing.
THE DILEMMA. By the Author of 'The Battle of Dorking.'
MY TRIVIAL LIFE AND MISFORTUNE. By A Plain Woman.
POOR NELLIE. By the Same.

Standard Novels. Uniform in size and binding. Each complete in one Volume.

FLORIN SERIES, Illustrated Boards. Bound in Cloth, 2s. 6d.

TOM CRINGLE'S LOG. By Michael Scott.
THE CRUISE OF THE MIDGE. By the Same.
CYRIL THORNTON. By Captain Hamilton.
ANNALS OF THE PARISH. By John Galt.
THE PROVOST, &c. By the Same.
SIR ANDREW WYLIE. By the Same.
THE ENTAIL. By the Same.
MISS MOLLY. By Beatrice May Butt.
REGINALD DALTON. By J. G. Lockhart.
PEN OWEN. By Dean Hook.
ADAM BLAIR. By J. G. Lockhart.
LADY LEE'S WIDOWHOOD. By General Sir E. B. Hamley.
SALEM CHAPEL. By Mrs Oliphant.
THE PERPETUAL CURATE. By the Same
MISS MARJORIBANKS. By the Same.
JOHN: A Love Story. By the Same.

SHILLING SERIES, Illustrated Cover. Bound in Cloth, 1s. 6d.

THE RECTOR, and THE DOCTOR'S FAMILY. By Mrs Oliphant.
THE LIFE OF MANSIE WAUCH. By D. M. Moir.
PENINSULAR SCENES AND SKETCHES. By F. Hardman.
SIR FRIZZLE PUMPKIN, NIGHTS AT MESS, &c.
THE SUBALTERN.
LIFE IN THE FAR WEST. By G. F. Ruxton.
VALERIUS: A Roman Story. By J. G. Lockhart.

BON GAULTIER'S BOOK OF BALLADS. Fifteenth Edition. With Illustrations by Doyle, Leech, and Crowquill. Fcap. 8vo, 5s.

BOWHILL. Questions and Answers in the Theory and Practice of Military Topography. By Major J. H. BOWHILL. Crown 8vo, 4s. 6d. net. Portfolio containing 34 working plans and diagrams. 3s. 6d. net.

BRADDON. Thirty Years of Shikar. By Sir EDWARD BRADDON, K.C.M.G. With Illustrations by G. D. Giles, and Map of Oudh Forest Tracts and Nepul Terai. Demy 8vo, 18s.

BROUGHAM. Memoirs of the Life and Times of Henry Lord Brougham. Written by HIMSELF. 3 vols. 8vo, £2, 8s. The Volumes are sold separately, price 16s. each.

BROWN. The Forester: A Practical Treatise on the Planting and Tending of Forest-trees and the General Management of Woodlands. By JAMES BROWN, LL.D. Sixth Edition, Enlarged. Edited by JOHN NISBET, D.Œc., Author of 'British Forest Trees,' &c. In 2 vols. royal 8vo, with 350 Illustrations, 42s. net.

BROWN. A Manual of Botany, Anatomical and Physiological. For the Use of Students. By ROBERT BROWN, M.A., Ph.D. Crown 8vo, with numerous Illustrations, 12s. 6d.

BRUCE. In Clover and Heather. Poems by WALLACE BRUCE. New and Enlarged Edition. Crown 8vo, 3s. 6d. *A limited number of Copies of the First Edition, on large hand-made paper, 12s. 6d.*

BRUCE.

Here's a Hand. Addresses and Poems. Crown 8vo, 5s.
Large Paper Edition, limited to 100 copies, price 21s.

BUCHAN. Introductory Text-Book of Meteorology. By ALEX-
ANDER BUCHAN, LL.D., F.R.S.E., Secretary of the Scottish Meteorological
Society, &c. New Edition. Crown 8vo, with Coloured Charts and Engravings.
[*In preparation.*

BURBIDGE.

Domestic Floriculture, Window Gardening, and Floral Decora-
tions. Being Practical Directions for the Propagation, Culture, and Arrangement
of Plants and Flowers as Domestic Ornaments. By F. W. BURBIDGE. Second
Edition. Crown 8vo, with numerous Illustrations, 7s. 6d.

Cultivated Plants: Their Propagation and Improvement.
Including Natural and Artificial Hybridisation, Raising from Seed, Cuttings,
and Layers, Grafting and Budding, as applied to the Families and Genera in
Cultivation. Crown 8vo, with numerous Illustrations, 12s. 6d.

BURKE. The Flowering of the Almond Tree, and other Poems.
By CHRISTIAN BURKE. Pott 4to, 5s.

BURROWS.

Commentaries on the History of England, from the Earliest
Times to 1865. By MONTAGU BURROWS, Chichele Professor of Modern History
in the University of Oxford; Captain R.N.; F.S.A., &c.; "Officier de l'Instruction Publique," France. Crown 8vo, 7s. 6d.

The History of the Foreign Policy of Great Britain. New
Edition, revised. Crown 8vo, 6s.

BURTON.

The History of Scotland: From Agricola's Invasion to the
Extinction of the last Jacobite Insurrection. By JOHN HILL BURTON, D.C.L.,
Historiographer-Royal for Scotland. Cheaper Edition. In 8 vols. Crown 8vo,
3s. 6d. each.

History of the British Empire during the Reign of Queen
Anne. In 3 vols. 8vo. 36s.

The Scot Abroad. Cheap Edition. Crown 8vo, 3s. 6d.

The Book-Hunter. Cheap Edition. Crown 8vo, 3s. 6d.

BUTCHER. Armenosa of Egypt. A Romance of the Arab
Conquest. By the Very Rev. Dean BUTCHER, D.D., F.S.A., Chaplain at Cairo.
Crown 8vo, 6s.

BUTE. The Altus of St Columba. With a Prose Paraphrase
and Notes. By JOHN, MARQUESS OF BUTE, K.T. In paper cover, 2s. 6d.

BUTE, MACPHAIL, AND LONSDALE. The Arms of the
Royal and Parliamentary Burghs of Scotland. By JOHN, MARQUESS OF BUTE,
K.T., J. R. N. MACPHAIL, and H. W. LONSDALE. With 131 Engravings on
wood, and 11 other Illustrations. Crown 4to. £2, 2s. net.

BUTLER.

The Ancient Church and Parish of Abernethy, Perthshire.
An Historical Study. By Rev. D. BUTLER, M.A., Minister of the Parish. With
13 Collotype Plates and a Map. Crown 4to, 25s. net.

John Wesley and George Whitefield in Scotland; or, The
Influence of the Oxford Methodists on Scottish Religion. In 1 vol. Crown 8vo.
[*In the press.*

BUTT.

Theatricals: An Interlude. By BEATRICE MAY BUTT. Crown
8vo, 6s.

Miss Molly. Cheap Edition, 2s.

Eugenie. Crown 8vo, 6s. 6d.

Elizabeth, and other Sketches. Crown 8vo, 6s.

Delicia. New Edition. Crown 8vo, 2s. 6d.

CAIRD. Sermons. By JOHN CAIRD, D.D., Principal of the
University of Glasgow. Seventeenth Thousand. Fcap. 8vo, 5s.

CALDWELL. Schopenhauer's System in its Philosophical Significance (the Shaw Fellowship Lectures, 1893). By WILLIAM CALDWELL, M.A.,
D.Sc., Professor of Moral and Social Philosophy, Northwestern University,
U.S.A.; formerly Assistant to the Professor of Logic and Metaphysics, Edin.,
and Examiner in Philosophy in the University of St Andrews. Demy 8vo,
10s. 6d. net.

CALLWELL. The Effect of Maritime Command on Land
Campaigns since Waterloo. By Major C. E. CALLWELL, R.A. With Plans.
Post 8vo, 6s. net.

CAPES. The Adventures of the Comte de la Muette during the
Reign of Terror. By BERNARD CAPES, Author of 'The Lake of Wine,' 'The Mill
of Silence,' &c. Crown 8vo, 6s.

CARSTAIRS.
Human Nature in Rural India. By R. CARSTAIRS. Crown
8vo, 6s.
British Work in India. Crown 8vo, 6s.

CAUVIN. A Treasury of the English and German Languages.
Compiled from the best Authors and Lexicographers in both Languages. By
JOSEPH CAUVIN, LL.D. and Ph.D., of the University of Göttingen, &c. Crown
8vo, 7s. 6d.

CHARTERIS. Canonicity; or, Early Testimonies to the Exist-
ence and Use of the Books of the New Testament. Based on Kirchhoffer's
'Quellensammlung.' Edited by A. H. CHARTERIS, D.D., Professor of Biblical
Criticism in the University of Edinburgh. 8vo, 18s.

CHENNELLS. Recollections of an Egyptian Princess. By
her English Governess (Miss E. CHENNELLS). Being a Record of Five Years'
Residence at the Court of Ismael Pasha, Khédive. Second Edition. With Three
Portraits. Post 8vo, 7s. 6d.

CHESNEY. The Dilemma. By General Sir GEORGE CHESNEY,
K.C.B., M.P., Author of 'The Battle of Dorking,' &c. New Edition. Crown
8vo, 3s. 6d.

CHRISTISON. Early Fortifications in Scotland: Motes, Camps,
and Forts. Being the Rhind Lectures in Archaeology for 1894. By DAVID
CHRISTISON, M.D., F.R.C.P.E., Secretary of the Society of Antiquaries of Scotland. With 379 Plans and Illustrations and 3 Maps. Fcap. 4to, 21s. net.

CHRISTISON. Life of Sir Robert Christison, Bart., M.D.,
D.C.L. Oxon., Professor of Medical Jurisprudence in the University of Edin-
burgh. Edited by his SONS. In 2 vols. 8vo. Vol. I.—Autobiography. 16s.
Vol. II.—Memoirs. 16s.

CHURCH. Chapters in an Adventurous Life. Sir Richard
Church in Italy and Greece. By E. M. CHURCH. With Photogravure
Portrait. Demy 8vo, 10s. 6d.

CHURCH SERVICE SOCIETY.
A Book of Common Order: being Forms of Worship issued
by the Church Service Society. Seventh Edition, carefully revised. In 1 vol.
crown 8vo, cloth, 3s. 6d.; French morocco, 5s. Also in 2 vols. crown 8vo,
cloth, 4s.; French morocco, 6s. 6d.
Daily Offices for Morning and Evening Prayer throughout
the Week. Crown 8vo, 3s. 6d.
Order of Divine Service for Children. Issued by the Church
Service Society. With Scottish Hymnal. Cloth, 3d.

COCHRAN. A Handy Text-Book of Military Law. Compiled
chiefly to assist Officers preparing for Examination; also for all Officers of the
Regular and Auxiliary Forces. Comprising also a Synopsis of part of the Army
Act. By Major F. COCHRAN, Hampshire Regiment Garrison Instructor, North
British District. Crown 8vo, 7s. 6d.

COLQUHOUN. The Moor and the Loch. Containing Minute Instructions in all Highland Sports, with Wanderings over Crag and Corrie, Flood and Fell. By JOHN COLQUHOUN. Cheap Edition. With Illustrations. Demy 8vo, 10s. 6d.

COLVILE. Round the Black Man's Garden. By Lady Z. COLVILE, F.R.G.S. With 2 Maps and 50 Illustrations from Drawings by the Author and from Photographs. Demy 8vo, 16s.

CONDER.

The Bible and the East. By Lieut.-Col. C. R. CONDER, R.E., LL.D., D.C.L., M.R.A.S., Author of 'Tent Work in Palestine,' &c. With Illustrations and a Map. Crown 8vo, 5s.

The Hittites and their Language. With Illustrations and Map. Post 8vo, 7s. 6d.

CONSTITUTION AND LAW OF THE CHURCH OF SCOTLAND. With an Introductory Note by the late Principal Tulloch. New Edition, Revised and Enlarged. Crown 8vo, 3s. 6d.

COUNTY HISTORIES OF SCOTLAND. In demy 8vo volumes of about 350 pp. each. With Maps. Price 7s. 6d. net.

Fife and Kinross. By ÆNEAS J. G. MACKAY, LL.D., Sheriff of these Counties.

Dumfries and Galloway. By Sir HERBERT MAXWELL, Bart., M.P

Moray and Nairn. By CHARLES RAMPINI, LL.D., Sheriff-Substitute of these Counties.

Inverness. By J. CAMERON LEES, D.D.

Roxburgh, Peebles, and Selkirk. By Sir GEORGE DOUGLAS, Bart. *[In the press.*

CRAWFORD. Saracinesca. By F. MARION CRAWFORD, Author of 'Mr Isaacs,' &c., &c. Cheap Edition. Crown 8vo, 3s. 6d.

CRAWFORD.

The Doctrine of Holy Scripture respecting the Atonement. By the late THOMAS J. CRAWFORD, D.D., Professor of Divinity in the University of Edinburgh. Fifth Edition. 8vo, 12s.

The Fatherhood of God, Considered in its General and Special Aspects. Third Edition, Revised and Enlarged. 8vo, 9s.

The Preaching of the Cross, and other Sermons. 8vo, 7s. 6d.

The Mysteries of Christianity. Crown 8vo, 7s. 6d.

CROSS. Impressions of Dante, and of the New World ; with a Few Words on Bimetallism. By J. W. CROSS, Editor of 'George Eliot's Life, as related in her Letters and Journals.' Post 8vo, 6s.

CUMBERLAND. Sport on the Pamirs and Turkistan Steppes. By Major C. S. CUMBERLAND. With Map and Frontispiece. Demy 8vo, 10s. 6d.

CURSE OF INTELLECT. Third Edition. Fcap. 8vo, 2s. 6d. net.

CUSHING. The Blacksmith of Voe. By PAUL CUSHING, Author of 'The Bull i' th' Thorn,' 'Cut with his own Diamond.' Cheap Edition. Crown 8vo, 3s. 6d

DARBISHIRE. Physical Maps for the use of History Students. By BERNHARD V. DARBISHIRE, M.A., Trinity College, Oxford. Two Series:— Ancient History (9 maps); Modern History (12 maps). *[In the press.*

DAVIES. Norfolk Broads and Rivers ; or, The Waterways, Lagoons, and Decoys of East Anglia. By G. CHRISTOPHER DAVIES. Illustrated with Seven full-page Plates. New and Cheaper Edition. Crown 8vo, 6s.

DE LA WARR. An Eastern Cruise in the 'Edeline.' By the Countess DE LA WARR. In Illustrated Cover. 2s.

DESCARTES. The Method, Meditations, and Principles of Philosophy of Descartes. Translated from the Original French and Latin. With a New Introductory Essay, Historical and Critical, on the Cartesian Philosophy. By Professor VEITCH, LL.D., Glasgow University. Eleventh Edition. 6s. 6d.

DOGS, OUR DOMESTICATED : Their Treatment in reference to Food, Diseases, Habits, Punishment, Accomplishments. By 'MAGENTA.' Crown 8vo, 2s. 6d.

DOUGLAS.

The Ethics of John Stuart Mill. By CHARLES DOUGLAS, M.A., D.Sc., Lecturer in Moral Philosophy, and Assistant to the Professor of Moral Philosophy in the University of Edinburgh. Post 8vo, 6s. net.

John Stuart Mill : A Study of his Philosophy. Crown 8vo, 4s. 6d. net.

DOUGLAS. Chinese Stories. By ROBERT K. DOUGLAS. With numerous Illustrations by Parkinson, Forestier, and others. New and Cheaper Edition. Small demy 8vo, 5s.

DOUGLAS. Iras: A Mystery. By THEO. DOUGLAS, Author of 'A Bride Elect.' Cheaper Edition, in Paper Cover specially designed by Womrath. Crown 8vo, 1s. 6d.

DU CANE. The Odyssey of Homer, Books I.-XII. Translated into English Verse. By Sir CHARLES DU CANE, K.C.M.G. 8vo, 10s. 6d.

DUNSMORE. Manual of the Law of Scotland as to the Relations between Agricultural Tenants and the Landlords, Servants, Merchants, and Bowers. By W. DUNSMORE. 8vo, 7s. 6d.

DZIEWICKI. Entombed in Flesh. By M. H. DZIEWICKI. Crown 8vo, 3s. 6d.

ELIOT.

George Eliot's Life, Related in Her Letters and Journals. Arranged and Edited by her husband, J. W. CROSS. With Portrait and other Illustrations. Third Edition. 3 vols. post 8vo, 42s.

George Eliot's Life. With Portrait and other Illustrations. New Edition, in one volume. Crown 8vo, 7s. 6d.

Works of George Eliot (Standard Edition). 21 volumes, crown 8vo. In buckram cloth, gilt top, 2s. 6d. per vol.; or in roxburghe binding, 3s. 6d. per vol.

ADAM BEDE. 2 vols.—THE MILL ON THE FLOSS. 2 vols.—FELIX HOLT, THE RADICAL. 2 vols.—ROMOLA. 2 vols.—SCENES OF CLERICAL LIFE. 2 vols.—MIDDLEMARCH. 3 vols.—DANIEL DERONDA. 3 vols.—SILAS MARNER. 1 vol.—JUBAL. 1 vol.—THE SPANISH GIPSY. 1 vol.—ESSAYS. 1 vol.—THEOPHRASTUS SUCH. 1 vol.

Life and Works of George Eliot (Cabinet Edition). 24 volumes, crown 8vo, price £6. Also to be had handsomely bound in half and full calf. The Volumes are sold separately, bound in cloth, price 5s. each

Novels by George Eliot. New Cheap Edition. Printed on fine laid paper, and uniformly bound.

Adam Bede. 3s. 6d.—The Mill on the Floss. 3s. 6d.—Scenes of Clerical Life. 3s.—Silas Marner: the Weaver of Raveloe. 2s. 6d.—Felix Holt, the Radical. 3s. 6d.—Romola. 3s. 6d.—Middlemarch. 7s. 6d.—Daniel Deronda. 7s. 6d.

Essays. New Edition. Crown 8vo, 5s.

Impressions of Theophrastus Such. New Edition. Crown 8vo, 5s.

The Spanish Gypsy. New Edition. Crown 8vo, 5s.

The Legend of Jubal, and other Poems, Old and New. New Edition. Crown 8vo, 5s.

ELIOT.

Scenes of Clerical Life. Pocket Edition, 3 vols. pott 8vo,
1s. net each ; bound in leather, 1s. 6d. net each. Popular Edition. Royal 8vo,
in paper cover, price 6d.

Adam Bede. Pocket Edition. In 3 vols. pott 8vo, 3s. net ;
bound in leather, 4s. 6d. net.

Wise, Witty, and Tender Sayings, in Prose and Verse. Selected
from the Works of GEORGE ELIOT. New Edition. Fcap. 8vo, 3s. 6d.

ELTON. The Augustan Ages. 'Periods of European Literature.' By OLIVER ELTON. In 1 vol. crown 8vo. [In the press.

ESSAYS ON SOCIAL SUBJECTS. Originally published in
the 'Saturday Review.' New Edition. First and Second Series. 2 vols. crown
8vo, 6s. each.

FAITHS OF THE WORLD, The. A Concise History of the
Great Religious Systems of the World. By various Authors. Crown 8vo, 5s.

FALKNER. The Lost Stradivarius. By J. MEADE FALKNER.
Second Edition. Crown 8vo, 6s.

FENNELL AND O'CALLAGHAN. A Prince of Tyrone. By
CHARLOTTE FENNELL and J. P. O'CALLAGHAN. Crown 8vo, 6s.

FERGUSON. Sir Samuel Ferguson in the Ireland of his Day.
By LADY FERGUSON, Author of 'The Irish before the Conquest,' 'Life of William
Reeves, D.D., Lord Bishop of Down, Connor, and Dromore,' &c., &c. With
Two Portraits. 2 vols. post 8vo, 21s.

FERGUSSON. Scots Poems. By ROBERT FERGUSSON. With
Photogravure Portrait. Pott 8vo, gilt top, bound in cloth, 1s. net.

FERRIER.

Philosophical Works of the late James F. Ferrier, B.A.
Oxon., Professor of Moral Philosophy and Political Economy, St Andrews.
New Edition. Edited by Sir ALEXANDER GRANT, Bart., D.C.L., and Professor
LUSHINGTON. 3 vols. crown 8vo, 34s. 6d.

Institutes of Metaphysic. Third Edition. 10s. 6d.

Lectures on the Early Greek Philosophy. 4th Edition. 10s. 6d.

Philosophical Remains, including the Lectures on Early
Greek Philosophy. New Edition. 2 vols. 24s.

FLINT.

Historical Philosophy in France and French Belgium and
Switzerland. By ROBERT FLINT, Corresponding Member of the Institute of
France, Hon. Member of the Royal Society of Palermo, Professor in the Univer-
sity of Edinburgh, &c. 8vo, 21s.

Agnosticism. Being the Croall Lecture for 1887-88.
[In the press.

Theism. Being the Baird Lecture for 1876. Ninth Edition,
Revised. Crown 8vo, 7s. 6d

Anti-Theistic Theories. Being the Baird Lecture for 1877.
Fifth Edition. Crown 8vo, 10s. 6d.

Sermons and Addresses. In 1 vol. Demy 8vo. [In the press.

FOREIGN CLASSICS FOR ENGLISH READERS. Edited
by Mrs OLIPHANT. Price 1s. each. *For List of Volumes, see page 2.*

FOSTER. The Fallen City, and other Poems. By WILL FOSTER.
Crown 8vo, 6s.

FRANCILLON. Gods and Heroes ; or, The Kingdom of Jupiter.
By R. E. FRANCILLON. With 8 Illustrations. Crown 8vo, 5s.

FRANCIS. Among the Untrodden Ways. By M. E. FRANCIS
(Mrs Francis Blundell), Author of 'In a North Country Village,' 'A Daughter of
the Soil,' 'Frieze and Fustian,' &c. Crown 8vo, 3s. 6d.

FRASER.

Philosophy of Theism. Being the Gifford Lectures delivered before the University of Edinburgh in 1894-95. By ALEXANDER CAMPBELL FRASER, D.C.L. Oxford; Emeritus Professor of Logic and Metaphysics in the University of Edinburgh. Second Edition, Revised. In 1 vol. Post 8vo.
[In the press.

GALT.

Novels by JOHN GALT. With General Introduction and Prefatory Notes by S. R. CROCKETT. The Text Revised and Edited by D. STORRAR MELDRUM, Author of 'The Story of Margrédel.' With Photogravure Illustrations from Drawings by John Wallace. Fcap. 8vo, 3s. net each vol.
ANNALS OF THE PARISH, and THE AYRSHIRE LEGATEES. 2 vols.—SIR ANDREW WYLIE. 2 vols.—THE ENTAIL; or, The Lairds of Grippy. 2 vols.—THE PROVOST, and THE LAST OF THE LAIRDS. 2 vols.
See also STANDARD NOVELS, *p.* 6.

GENERAL ASSEMBLY OF THE CHURCH OF SCOTLAND.

Scottish Hymnal, With Appendix Incorporated. Published for use in Churches by Authority of the General Assembly. 1. Large type, cloth, red edges, 2s. 6d.; French morocco, 4s. 2. Bourgeois type, limp cloth, 1s.; French morocco, 2s. 3. Nonpareil type, cloth, red edges, 6d.; French morocco, 1s. 4d. 4. Paper covers, 3d. 5. Sunday-School Edition, paper covers, 1d., cloth, 2d. No. 1, bound with the Psalms and Paraphrases, French morocco, 8s. No. 2, bound with the Psalms and Paraphrases, cloth, 2s.; French morocco, 3s.

Prayers for Social and Family Worship. Prepared by a Special Committee of the General Assembly of the Church of Scotland. Entirely New Edition, Revised and Enlarged. Fcap. 8vo, red edges, 2s.

Prayers for Family Worship. A Selection of Four Weeks' Prayers. New Edition. Authorised by the General Assembly of the Church of Scotland. Fcap. 8vo, red edges, 1s. 6d.

One Hundred Prayers. Prepared by the Committee on Aids to Devotion. 16mo, cloth limp, 6d.

Morning and Evening Prayers for Affixing to Bibles. Prepared by the Committee on Aids to Devotion. 1d. for 6, or 1s. per 100.

Prayers for Soldiers and Sailors. Prepared by the Committee on Aids to Devotion. Thirtieth Thousand. 16mo, cloth limp. 2d. net.

GERARD.

Reata: What's in a Name. By E. D. GERARD. Cheap Edition. Crown 8vo, 3s. 6d.

Beggar my Neighbour. Cheap Edition. Crown 8vo, 3s. 6d.

The Waters of Hercules. Cheap Edition. Crown 8vo, 3s. 6d.

A Sensitive Plant. Crown 8vo, 3s. 6d.

GERARD.

A Foreigner. An Anglo-German Study. By E. GERARD. Crown 8vo, 6s.

The Land beyond the Forest. Facts, Figures, and Fancies from Transylvania. With Maps and Illustrations. 2 vols. post 8vo, 25s.

Bis: Some Tales Retold. Crown 8vo, 6s.

A Secret Mission. 2 vols. crown 8vo, 17s.

An Electric Shock, and other Stories. Crown 8vo, 6s.

GERARD.

The Impediment. By DOROTHEA GERARD. Crown 8vo, 6s.

A Forgotten Sin. Crown 8vo, 6s.

A Spotless Reputation. Third Edition. Crown 8vo, 6s.

GERARD.
　The Wrong Man. Second Edition. Crown 8vo, 6s.
　Lady Baby. Cheap Edition. Crown 8vo, 3s. 6d.
　Recha. Second Edition. Crown 8vo, 6s.
　The Rich Miss Riddell. Second Edition. Crown 8vo, 6s.

GERARD. Stonyhurst Latin Grammar. By Rev. JOHN GERARD.
　Second Edition. Fcap. 8vo, 3s.

GOODALL. Association Football. By JOHN GOODALL. Edited
　by S. ARCHIBALD DE BEAR. With Diagrams. Fcap. 8vo, 1s.

GORDON CUMMING.
　At Home in Fiji. By C. F. GORDON CUMMING. Fourth
　　Edition, post 8vo. With Illustrations and Map. 7s. 6d.
　A Lady's Cruise in a French Man-of-War. New and Cheaper
　　Edition. 8vo. With Illustrations and Map. 12s. 6d.
　Fire-Fountains. The Kingdom of Hawaii: Its Volcanoes,
　　and the History of its Missions. With Map and Illustrations. 2 vols. 8vo, 25s.
　Wanderings in China. New and Cheaper Edition. 8vo, with
　　Illustrations, 10s.
　Granite Crags: The Yō-semité Region of California. Illus-
　　trated with 8 Engravings. New and Cheaper Edition. 8vo, 8s. 6d.

GRAHAM. Manual of the Elections (Scot.) (Corrupt and Illegal
　Practices) Act, 1890. With Analysis, Relative Act of Sederunt, Appendix con-
　taining the Corrupt Practices Acts of 1883 and 1885, and Copious Index. By J.
　EDWARD GRAHAM, Advocate. 8vo, 4s. 6d.

GRAND.
　A Domestic Experiment. By SARAH GRAND, Author of
　　'The Heavenly Twins,' 'Ideals: A Study from Life.' Crown 8vo, 6s.
　Singularly Deluded. Crown 8vo, 6s.

GRANT. Bush-Life in Queensland. By A. C. GRANT. New
　Edition. Crown 8vo, 6s.

GREGG. The Decian Persecution. Being the Hulsean Prize
　Essay for 1896. By JOHN A. F. GREGG, B.A., late Scholar of Christ's College,
　Cambridge. Crown 8vo, 6s.

GRIER.
　In Furthest Ind. The Narrative of Mr EDWARD CARLYON of
　　Ellswether, in the County of Northampton, and late of the Honourable East India
　　Company's Service, Gentleman. Wrote by his own hand in the year of grace 1697.
　　Edited, with a few Explanatory Notes, by SYDNEY C. GRIER. Post 8vo, 6s.
　His Excellency's English Governess. Second Edition. Crown
　　8vo, 6s.
　An Uncrowned King: A Romance of High Politics. Second
　　Edition. Crown 8vo, 6s.
　Peace with Honour. Second Edition. Crown 8vo, 6s.
　A Crowned Queen: The Romance of a Minister of State.
　　Crown 8vo, 6s.

GROOT. A Lotus Flower. By J. MORGAN DE GROOT. Crown
　8vo, 6s.

GUTHRIE-SMITH. Crispus: A Drama. By H. GUTHRIE-
　SMITH. Fcap. 4to, 5s.

HAGGARD. Under Crescent and Star. By Lieut.-Col. ANDREW
　HAGGARD, D.S.O., Author of 'Dodo and I,' 'Tempest Torn,' &c. With a
　Portrait. Second Edition. Crown 8vo, 6s.

HALDANE. Subtropical Cultivations and Climates. A Handy
　Book for Planters, Colonists, and Settlers. By R. C. HALDANE. Post 8vo, 9s.

HAMERTON.

Wenderholme : A Story of Lancashire and Yorkshire Life
By P. G. HAMERTON, Author of 'A Painter's Camp.' New Edition. Crown
8vo, 3s. 6d.

Marmorne. New Edition. Crown 8vo, **3s. 6d.**

HAMILTON.

Lectures on Metaphysics. By Sir WILLIAM HAMILTON
Bart., Professor of Logic and Metaphysics in the University of Edinburgh.
Edited by the Rev. H. L. MANSEL, B.D., LL.D., Dean of St Paul's; and JOHN
VEITCH, M.A., LL.D., Professor of Logic and Rhetoric, Glasgow. Seventh
Edition. 2 vols. 8vo, 24s.

Lectures on Logic. Edited by the SAME. Third Edition,
Revised. 2 vols., 24s.

Discussions on Philosophy and Literature, Education and
University Reform. Third Edition. 8vo, 21s.

Memoir of Sir William Hamilton, Bart., Professor of Logic
and Metaphysics in the University of Edinburgh. By Professor VEITCH, of the
University of Glasgow. 8vo, with Portrait, 18s.

Sir William Hamilton : The Man and his Philosophy. Two
Lectures delivered before the Edinburgh Philosophical Institution, January and
February 1883. By Professor VEITCH. Crown 8vo, 2s.

HAMLEY.

The Operations of War Explained and Illustrated. By
General Sir EDWARD BRUCE HAMLEY, K.C.B., K.C.M.G. Fifth Edition, Revised
throughout. 4to, with numerous Illustrations, 30s.

National Defence ; Articles and Speeches. Post 8vo, **6s.**

Shakespeare's Funeral, and other Papers. Post 8vo, 7s. 6d.

Thomas Carlyle : An Essay. Second Edition. Crown 8vo,
2s. 6d.

On Outposts. Second Edition. 8vo, **2s.**

Wellington's Career ; A Military and Political Summary.
Crown 8vo, 2s.

Lady Lee's Widowhood. New Edition. Crown 8vo, **3s. 6d.**
Cheaper Edition, 2s. 6d.

Our Poor Relations. A Philozoic Essay. With Illustrations,
chiefly by Ernest Griset. Crown 8vo, cloth gilt, 3s. 6d.

The Life of General Sir Edward Bruce Hamley, K.C.B.,
K.C.M.G. By ALEXANDER INNES SHAND. With two Photogravure Portraits and
other Illustrations. Cheaper Edition. With a Statement by Mr EDWARD
HAMLEY. 2 vols. demy 8vo, 10s. 6d.

HANNAY. The Later Renaissance. 'Periods of European
Literature.' By DAVID HANNAY. Crown 8vo, 5s. net.

HARE. Down the Village Street : Scenes in a West Country
Hamlet. By CHRISTOPHER HARE. Second Edition. Crown 8vo, 6s.

HARRADEN.

In Varying Moods : Short Stories. By BEATRICE HARRADEN,
Author of 'Ships that Pass in the Night.' Twelfth Edition Crown 8vo, 3s. 6d.

Hilda Strafford, and The Remittance Man. Two Californian
Stories. Tenth Edition. Crown 8vo, 3s. 6d.

Untold Tales of the Past. With 40 Illustrations by H. R. Millar.
Square crown 8vo, gilt top, 6s.

HARRIS.

From Batum to Baghdad, *via* Tiflis, Tabriz, and Persian
Kurdistan. By WALTER B. HARRIS, F.R.G.S., Author of 'The Land of an
African Sultan ; Travels in Morocco,' &c. With numerous Illustrations and 2
Maps. Demy 8vo, 12s.

HARRIS.

Tafilet. The Narrative of a Journey of Exploration to the Atlas Mountains and the Oases of the North-West Sahara. With Illustrations by Maurice Romberg from Sketches and Photographs by the Author, and Two Maps. Demy 8vo, 12s.

A Journey through the Yemen, and some General Remarks upon that Country. With 3 Maps and numerous Illustrations by Forestier and Wallace from Sketches and Photographs taken by the Author. Demy 8vo, 16s.

Danovitch, and other Stories. Crown 8vo, 6s.

HAY. The Works of the Right Rev. Dr George Hay, Bishop of Edinburgh. Edited under the Supervision of the Right Rev. Bishop STRAIN. With Memoir and Portrait of the Author. 5 vols. crown 8vo, bound in extra cloth, £1, 1s. The following Volumes may be had separately—viz.:
The Devout Christian Instructed in the Law of Christ from the Written Word. 2 vols., 8s.—The Pious Christian Instructed in the Nature and Practice of the Principal Exercises of Piety. 1 vol., 3s.

HEATLEY.

The Horse-Owner's Safeguard. A Handy Medical Guide for every Man who owns a Horse. By G. S. HEATLEY, M.R.C.V.S. Crown 8vo, 5s.

The Stock-Owner's Guide. A Handy Medical Treatise for every Man who owns an Ox or a Cow. Crown 8vo, 4s. 6d.

HEMANS.

The Poetical Works of Mrs Hemans. Copyright Edition. Royal 8vo, with Engravings, cloth, gilt edges, 7s. 6d.

Select Poems of Mrs Hemans. Fcap., cloth, gilt edges, 3s.

HENDERSON. The Young Estate Manager's Guide. By RICHARD HENDERSON, Member (by Examination) of the Royal Agricultural Society of England, the Highland and Agricultural Society of Scotland, and the Surveyors' Institution. With an Introduction by R. Patrick Wright, F.R.S.E., Professor of Agriculture, Glasgow and West of Scotland Technical College. With Plans and Diagrams. Crown 8vo, 5s.

HERKLESS. Cardinal Beaton: Priest and Politician. By JOHN HERKLESS, Professor of Church History, St Andrews. With a Portrait. Post 8vo, 7s. 6d.

HEWISON. The Isle of Bute in the Olden Time. With Illustrations, Maps, and Plans. By JAMES KING HEWISON, M.A., F.S.A. (Scot.), Minister of Rothesay. Vol. I., Celtic Saints and Heroes. Crown 4to, 15s. net. Vol. II., The Royal Stewards and the Brandanes. Crown 4to, 15s. net.

HIBBEN. Inductive Logic. By JOHN GRIER HIBBEN, Ph.D., Assistant Professor of Logic in Princeton University, U.S.A. Cr. 8vo, 3s. 6d. net.

HOME PRAYERS. By Ministers of the Church of Scotland and Members of the Church Service Society. Second Edition. Fcap. 8vo, 3s.

HORNBY. Admiral of the Fleet Sir Geoffrey Phipps Hornby, G.C.B. A Biography. By Mrs FRED. EGERTON. With Three Portraits. Demy 8vo, 16s.

HUTCHINSON. Hints on the Game of Golf. By HORACE G. HUTCHINSON. Ninth Edition, Enlarged. Fcap. 8vo, cloth, 1s.

HYSLOP. The Elements of Ethics. By JAMES H. HYSLOP, Ph.D., Instructor in Ethics, Columbia College, New York, Author of 'The Elements of Logic.' Post 8vo, 7s. 6d. net.

IDDESLEIGH. Life, Letters, and Diaries of Sir Stafford Northcote, First Earl of Iddesleigh. By ANDREW LANG. With Three Portraits and a View of Pynes. Third Edition. 2 vols. post 8vo, 31s. 6d.
POPULAR EDITION. With Portrait and View of Pynes. Post 8vo, 7s. 6d.

JEAN JAMBON. Our Trip to Blunderland; or, Grand Excursion to Blundertown and Back. By JEAN JAMBON. With Sixty Illustrations designed by CHARLES DOYLE, engraved by DALZIEL. Fourth Thousand. Cloth, gilt edges, 6s. 6d. Cheap Edition, cloth, 3s. 6d. Boards, 2s. 6d.

JEBB.

A Strange Career. The Life and Adventures of JOHN GLADWYN JEBB. By his Widow. With an Introduction by H. RIDER HAGGARD, and an Electrogravure Portrait of Mr Jebb. Third Edition. Demy 8vo, 10s. 6d. CHEAP EDITION. With Illustrations by John Wallace. Crown 8vo, 3s. 6d.

Some Unconventional People. By Mrs GLADWYN JEBB, Author of 'Life and Adventures of J. G. Jebb.' With Illustrations. Cheap Edition. Paper covers, 1s.

JERNINGHAM.

Reminiscences of an Attaché. By HUBERT E. H. JERNINGHAM. Second Edition. Crown 8vo, 5s

Diane de Breteuille. A Love Story. Crown 8vo, 2s. 6d.

JOHNSTON.

The Chemistry of Common Life. By Professor J. F. W. JOHNSTON. New Edition, Revised. By ARTHUR HERBERT CHURCH, M.A. Oxon.; Author of 'Food: its Sources, Constituents, and Uses,' &c. With Maps and 102 Engravings. Crown 8vo, 7s. 6d.

Elements of Agricultural Chemistry. An entirely New Edition from the Edition by Sir CHARLES A. CAMERON, M.D., F.R.C.S.I., &c. Revised and brought down to date by C. M. AIKMAN, M.A., B.Sc., F.R.S.E., Professor of Chemistry, Glasgow Veterinary College. 17th Edition. Crown 8vo, 6s. 6d.

Catechism of Agricultural Chemistry. An entirely New Edition from the Edition by Sir CHARLES A. CAMERON. Revised and Enlarged by C. M. AIKMAN, M.A., &c. 95th Thousand. With numerous Illustrations. Crown 8vo, 1s.

JOHNSTON. Agricultural Holdings (Scotland) Acts, 1883 and 1889; and the Ground Game Act, 1880. With Notes, and Summary of Procedure, &c. By CHRISTOPHER N. JOHNSTON, M.A., Advocate. Demy 8vo, 5s.

JOKAI. Timar's Two Worlds. By MAURUS JOKAI. Authorised Translation by Mrs HEGAN KENNARD. Cheap Edition. Crown 8vo, 6s.

KEBBEL. The Old and the New: English Country Life. By T. E. KEBBEL, M.A., Author of 'The Agricultural Labourers,' 'Essays in History and Politics,' 'Life of Lord Beaconsfield.' Crown 8vo, 5s.

KERR. St Andrews in 1645-46. By D. R. KERR. Crown 8vo, 2s. 6d.

KINGLAKE.

History of the Invasion of the Crimea. By A. W. KINGLAKE. Cabinet Edition, Revised. With an Index to the Complete Work. Illustrated with Maps and Plans. Complete in 9 vols., crown 8vo, at 6s. each.

—— Abridged Edition for Military Students. Revised by Lieut.-Col. Sir GEORGE SYDENHAM CLARKE, K.C.M.G., R.E. In 1 vol. demy 8vo. [*In the press.*

History of the Invasion of the Crimea. Demy 8vo. Vol. VI. Winter Troubles. With a Map, 16s. Vols. VII. and VIII. From the Morrow of Inkerman to the Death of Lord Raglan With an Index to the Whole Work. With Maps and Plans. 28s

Eothen. A New Edition, uniform with the Cabinet Edition of the 'History of the Invasion of the Crimea.' 6s. CHEAPER EDITION. With Portrait and Biographical Sketch of the Author. Crown 8vo, 3s. 6d. Popular Edition, in paper cover, 1s. net.

KIRBY. In Haunts of Wild Game: A Hunter-Naturalist's Wanderings from Kahlamba to Libombo. By FREDERICK VAUGHAN KIRBY, F.Z.S. (Maqaqamba). With numerous Illustrations by Charles Whymper, and a Map. Large demy 8vo, 25s.

KNEIPP. My Water-Cure. As Tested through more than
Thirty Years, and Described for the Healing of Diseases and the Preservation of
Health. By Sebastian Kneipp, Parish Priest of Wörishofen (Bavaria). With a
Portrait and other Illustrations. Authorised English Translation from the
Thirtieth German Edition, by A. de F. Cheap Edition. With an Appendix, con-
taining the Latest Developments of Pfarrer Kneipp's System, and a Preface by
E. Gerard. Crown 8vo, 3s. 6d.

KNOLLYS. The Elements of Field-Artillery. Designed for
the Use of Infantry and Cavalry Officers. By Henry Knollys, Colonel Royal
Artillery; Author of 'From Sedan to Saarbrück,' Editor of 'Incidents in the
Sepoy War,' &c. With Engravings. Crown 8vo, 7s. 6d.

LANG.
Life, Letters, and Diaries of Sir Stafford Northcote, First
Earl of Iddesleigh. By Andrew Lang. With Three Portraits and a View of
Pynes. Third Edition. 2 vols. post 8vo, 31s. 6d.
    Popular Edition. With Portrait and View of Pynes. Post 8vo, 7s. 6d.
The Highlands of Scotland in 1750. From Manuscript 104
in the King's Library, British Museum. With an Introduction by Andrew Lang.
Crown 8vo, 5s. net.

LANG. The Expansion of the Christian Life. The Duff Lecture for 1897. By the Rev. J. Marshall Lang, D.D. Crown 8vo, 5s.

LAPWORTH. Intermediate Text-Book of Geology. By Professor Lapworth, LL.D., F.R.S., &c. Founded on Dr Page's 'Introductory
Text-Book of Geology.' With Illustrations. In 1 vol. crown 8vo. [*Immediately.*

LEES. A Handbook of the Sheriff and Justice of Peace Small
Debt Courts. With Notes, References, and Forms. By J. M. Lees, Advocate,
Sheriff of Stirling, Dumbarton, and Clackmannan. 8vo, 7s. 6d.

LENNOX and STURROCK. The Elements of Physical Educa-
tion: A Teacher's Manual. By David Lennox, M.D., late R.N., Medical Director
of Dundee Public Gymnasium, and Alexander Sturrock, Superintendent of
Dundee Public Gymnasium, Instructor to the University of St Andrews and
Dundee High School. With Original Musical Accompaniments to the Drill by
Harry Everitt Loseby. With 130 Illustrations. Crown 8vo, 4s.

LEWES. Dr Southwood Smith: A Retrospect. By his Grand-
daughter, Mrs C. L. Lewes. With Portraits and other Illustrations. Post
8vo, 6s.

LINDSAY.
Recent Advances in Theistic Philosophy of Religion. By Rev.
James Lindsay, M.A., B.D., B.Sc., F.R.S.E., F.G.S., Minister of the Parish of
St Andrew's, Kilmarnock. Demy 8vo, 12s. 6d. net.
The Progressiveness of Modern Christian Thought. Crown
8vo, 6s.
Essays, Literary and Philosophical. Crown 8vo, 3s. 6d.
The Significance of the Old Testament for Modern Theology.
Crown 8vo, 1s. net.
The Teaching Function of the Modern Pulpit. Crown 8vo,
1s. net.

LOCKHART.
Doubles and Quits. By Laurence W. M. Lockhart. New
Edition. Crown 8vo, 3s. 6d.
Fair to See. New Edition. Crown 8vo, 3s. 6d.
Mine is Thine. New Edition. Crown 8vo, 3s. 6d.

LOCKHART.
The Church of Scotland in the Thirteenth Century. The
Life and Times of David de Bernham of St Andrews (Bishop), A.D. 1239 to 1253.
With List of Churches dedicated by him, and Dates. By William Lockhart,
A.M., D.D., F.S.A. Scot., Minister of Colinton Parish. 2d Edition. 8vo, 6s.

LOCKHART.

Dies Tristes : Sermons for Seasons of Sorrow. Crown 8vo, 6s.

LORIMER.

The Institutes of Law : A Treatise of the Principles of Jurisprudence as determined by Nature. By the late JAMES LORIMER, Professor of
Public Law and of the Law of Nature and Nations in the University of Edinburgh. New Edition, Revised and much Enlarged. 8vo, 18s.

The Institutes of the Law of Nations. A Treatise of the
Jural Relation of Separate Political Communities. In 2 vols. 8vo. Volume I.,
price 16s. Volume II., price 20s.

LUGARD. The Rise of our East African Empire : Early Efforts
in Uganda and Nyasaland. By F. D. LUGARD, Captain Norfolk Regiment.
With 130 Illustrations from Drawings and Photographs under the personal
superintendence of the Author, and 14 specially prepared Maps. In 2 vols. large
demy 8vo, 42s.

MABIE.

Essays on Nature and Culture. By HAMILTON WRIGHT MABIE.
With Portrait. Fcap. 8vo, 3s. 6d.

Books and Culture. Fcap. 8vo, 3s. 6d.

M'CHESNEY.

Miriam Cromwell, Royalist : A Romance of the Great Rebellion. By DORA GREENWELL M'CHESNEY. Crown 8vo, 6s.

Kathleen Clare : Her Book, 1637-41. With Frontispiece, and
five full-page Illustrations by James A. Shearman. Crown 8vo, 6s.

M'COMBIE. Cattle and Cattle-Breeders. By WILLIAM M'COMBIE,
Tillyfour. New Edition, Enlarged, with Memoir of the Author by JAMES
MACDONALD, F.R.S.E., Secretary Highland and Agricultural Society of Scotland.
Crown 8vo, 3s. 6d.

M'CRIE.

Works of the Rev. Thomas M'Crie, D.D. Uniform Edition.
4 vols. crown 8vo, 24s.

Life of John Knox. Crown 8vo, 6s. Another Edition, 3s. 6d.

Life of Andrew Melville. Crown 8vo, 6s.

History of the Progress and Suppression of the Reformation
in Italy in the Sixteenth Century. Crown 8vo, 4s.

History of the Progress and Suppression of the Reformation
in Spain in the Sixteenth Century. Crown 8vo, 3s. 6d.

M'CRIE. The Public Worship of Presbyterian Scotland. Histori-
cally treated. With copious Notes, Appendices, and Index. The Fourteenth
Series of the Cunningham Lectures. By the Rev. CHARLES G. M'CRIE, D.D.
Demy 8vo, 10s. 6d.

MACDONALD. A Manual of the Criminal Law (Scotland) Procedure Act, 1887. By NORMAN DORAN MACDONALD. Revised by the LORD
JUSTICE-CLERK. 8vo, 10s. 6d.

MACDOUGALL AND DODDS. A Manual of the Local Govern-
ment (Scotland) Act, 1894. With Introduction, Explanatory Notes, and Copious
Index. By J. PATTEN MACDOUGALL, Legal Secretary to the Lord Advocate, and
J. M. DODDS. Tenth Thousand, Revised. Crown 8vo, 2s. 6d. net.

MACINTYRE. Hindu-Koh : Wanderings and Wild Sports on
and beyond the Himalayas. By Major-General DONALD MACINTYRE, V.C., late
Prince of Wales' Own Goorkhas, F.R.G.S. *Dedicated to H.R.H. the Prince of
Wales.* New and Cheaper Edition, Revised, with numerous Illustrations. Post
8vo, 3s. 6d.

MACKAY.

Elements of Modern Geography. By the Rev. ALEXANDER
MACKAY, LL.D., F.R.G.S. 55th Thousand, Revised to the present time. Crown
8vo, pp. 300, 3s.

MACKAY.

The Intermediate Geography. Intended as an Intermediate Book between the Author's 'Outlines of Geography' and 'Elements of Geography.' Eighteenth Edition, Revised. Fcap. 8vo, pp. 238, 2s.

Outlines of Modern Geography. 191st Thousand, Revised to the present time. Fcap. 8vo, pp. 128, 1s.

Elements of Physiography. New Edition. Rewritten and Enlarged. With numerous Illustrations. Crown 8vo. [*In the press*

MACKENZIE. Studies in Roman Law. With Comparative Views of the Laws of France, England, and Scotland. By Lord Mackenzie, one of the Judges of the Court of Session in Scotland. Seventh Edition, Edited by John Kirkpatrick, M.A., LL.B., Advocate, Professor of History in the University of Edinburgh. 8vo, 21s.

M'PHERSON. Golf and Golfers. Past and Present. By J. Gordon M'Pherson, Ph.D., F.R.S.E. With an Introduction by the Right Hon. A. J. Balfour, and a Portrait of the Author. Fcap. 8vo, 1s. 6d.

MACRAE. A Handbook of Deer-Stalking. By Alexander Macrae, late Forester to Lord Henry Bentinck. With Introduction by Horatio Ross, Esq. Fcap. 8vo, with 2 Photographs from Life. 3s. 6d.

MAIN. Three Hundred English Sonnets. Chosen and Edited by David M. Main. New Edition. Fcap. 8vo, 3s. 6d.

MAIR. A Digest of Laws and Decisions, Ecclesiastical and Civil, relating to the Constitution, Practice, and Affairs of the Church of Scotland. With Notes and Forms of Procedure. By the Rev. William Mair, D.D., Minister of the Parish of Earlston. New Edition, Revised. Crown 8vo, 9s. net.

MARSHMAN. History of India. From the Earliest Period to the present time. By John Clark Marshman, C.S.I. Third and Cheaper Edition. Post 8vo, with Map, 6s.

MARTIN.

The Æneid of Virgil. Books I.-VI. Translated by Sir Theodore Martin, K.C.B. Post 8vo, 7s. 6d.

Goethe's Faust. Part I. Translated into English Verse. Second Edition, crown 8vo, 6s. Ninth Edition, fcap. 8vo, 3s. 6d.

Goethe's Faust. Part II. Translated into English Verse. Second Edition, Revised. Fcap. 8vo, 6s.

The Works of Horace. Translated into English Verse, with Life and Notes. 2 vols. New Edition. Crown 8vo, 21s.

Poems and Ballads of Heinrich Heine. Done into English Verse. Third Edition. Small crown 8vo, 5s.

The Song of the Bell, and other Translations from Schiller, Goethe, Uhland, and Others. Crown 8vo, 7s. 6d.

Madonna Pia : A Tragedy ; and Three Other Dramas. Crown 8vo, 7s. 6d.

Catullus. With Life and Notes. Second Edition, Revised and Corrected. Post 8vo, 7s. 6d.

The 'Vita Nuova' of Dante. Translated, with an Introduction and Notes. Third Edition. Small crown 8vo, 5s.

Aladdin : A Dramatic Poem. By Adam Oehlenschlaeger. Fcap. 8vo, 5s.

Correggio : A Tragedy. By Oehlenschlaeger. With Notes. Fcap. 8vo, 3s.

MARTIN. On some of Shakespeare's Female Characters. By Helena Faucit, Lady Martin. Dedicated by permission to Her Most Gracious Majesty the Queen. Fifth Edition. With a Portrait by Lehmann. Demy 8vo, 7s. 6d.

MARWICK. Observations on the Law and Practice in regard to Municipal Elections and the Conduct of the Business of Town Councils and Commissioners of Police in Scotland. By Sir James D. Marwick, LL.D., Town-Clerk of Glasgow. Royal 8vo, 30s.

MATHESON.
Can the Old Faith Live with the New ? or, The Problem of Evolution and Revelation. By the Rev. GEORGE MATHESON, D.D. Third Edition. Crown 8vo, 7s. 6d.

The Psalmist and the Scientist ; or, Modern Value of the Religious Sentiment. Third Edition. Crown 8vo, 5s.

Spiritual Development of St Paul. Fourth Edition. Cr. 8vo, 5s.

The Distinctive Messages of the Old Religions. Second Edition. Crown 8vo, 5s.

Sacred Songs. New and Cheaper Edition. Crown 8vo, 2s. 6d.

MATHIESON. The Supremacy and Sufficiency of Jesus Christ our Lord, as set forth in the Epistle to the Hebrews. By J. E. MATHIESON, Superintendent of Mildmay Conference Hall, 1880 to 1890. Second Edition. Crown 8vo, 3s. 6d.

MAURICE. The Balance of Military Power in Europe. An Examination of the War Resources of Great Britain and the Continental States. By Colonel MAURICE, R.A., Professor of Military Art and History at the Royal Staff College. Crown 8vo, with a Map, 6s.

MAXWELL.
The Honourable Sir Charles Murray, K.C.B. A Memoir. By Sir HERBERT MAXWELL, Bart., M.P., F.S.A., &c., Author of 'Passages in the Life of Sir Lucian Elphin.' With Five Portraits. Demy 8vo, 18s.

Life and Times of the Rt. Hon. William Henry Smith, M.P. With Portraits and numerous Illustrations by Herbert Railton, G. L. Seymour, and Others. 2 vols. demy 8vo, 25s.
POPULAR EDITION. With a Portrait and other Illustrations. Crown 8vo, 3s. 6d.

Scottish Land-Names : Their Origin and Meaning. Being the Rhind Lectures in Archæology for 1893. Post 8vo, 6s.

Meridiana : Noontide Essays. Post 8vo, 7s. 6d.

Post Meridiana : Afternoon Essays. Post 8vo, 6s.

A Duke of Britain. A Romance of the Fourth Century. Fourth Edition. Crown 8vo, 6s.

Dumfries and Galloway. Being one of the Volumes of the County Histories of Scotland. With Four Maps. Demy 8vo, 7s. 6d. net.

MELDRUM.
Holland and the Hollanders. By D. STORRAR MELDRUM. With numerous Illustrations   In 1 vol. square 8vo.   [In the press.

The Story of Margrédel Being a Fireside History of a Fifeshire Family. Cheap Edition. Crown 8vo, 3s. 6d.

Grey Mantle and Gold Fringe. Crown 8vo, 6s.

MELLONE. Studies in Philosophical Criticism and Construction. By SYDNEY HERBERT MELLONE, M.A. Lond., D.Sc. Edin. Post 8vo, 10s. 6d. net.

MERZ. A History of European Thought in the Nineteenth Century. By JOHN THEODORE MERZ. Vol. I., post 8vo, 10s. 6d. net.

MICHIE.
The Larch : Being a Practical Treatise on its Culture and General Management. By CHRISTOPHER Y. MICHIE, Forester, Cullen House. Crown 8vo, with Illustrations. New and Cheaper Edition, Enlarged, 5s.

The Practice of Forestry. Crown 8vo, with Illustrations. 6s

MIDDLETON. The Story of Alastair Bhan Comyn ; or, The Tragedy of Dunphail. A Tale of Tradition and Romance. By the Lady MIDDLETON. Square 8vo, 10s. Cheaper Edition, 5s.

MIDDLETON. Latin Verse Unseens. By G. MIDDLETON, M.A., Lecturer in Latin, Aberdeen University ; late Scholar of Emmanuel College, Cambridge ; Joint-Author of 'Student's Companion to Latin Authors.' Crown 8vo, 1s. 6d.

MILLER. The Dream of Mr H——, the Herbalist. By HUGH
MILLER, F.R.S.E., late H.M. Geological Survey, Author of 'Landscape Geology.'
With a Photogravure Frontispiece. Crown 8vo, 2s. 6d.

MILLS. Greek Verse Unseens. By T. R. MILLS, M.A., late
Lecturer in Greek, Aberdeen University; formerly Scholar of Wadham College,
Oxford; Joint-Author of 'Student's Companion to Latin Authors. Crown 8vo,
1s. 6d.

MINTO.
A Manual of English Prose Literature, Biographical and
Critical: designed mainly to show Characteristics of Style. By W. MINTO,
M.A., Hon. LL.D. of St Andrews; Professor of Logic in the University of Aber-
deen. Third Edition, Revised. Crown 8vo, 7s. 6d.

Characteristics of English Poets, from Chaucer to Shirley.
New Edition, Revised. Crown 8vo, 7s. 6d.

Plain Principles of Prose Composition. Crown 8vo, 1s. 6d.

The Literature of the Georgian Era. Edited, with a Biographical Introduction, by Professor KNIGHT, St Andrews. Post 8vo, 6s.

MOIR.
Life of Mansie Wauch, Tailor in Dalkeith. By D. M. MOIR.
With CRUIKSHANK'S Illustrations. Cheaper Edition. Crown 8vo, 2s. 6d.
Another Edition, without Illustrations, fcap. 8vo, 1s. 6d.

Domestic Verses. Centenary Edition. With a Portrait. Crown
8vo, 2s. 6d. net.

MOLE. For the Sake of a Slandered Woman. By MARION
MOLE. Fcap. 8vo, 2s. 6d. net.

MOMERIE.
Defects of Modern Christianity, and other Sermons. By Rev.
ALFRED WILLIAMS MOMERIE, M.A., D.Sc., LL.D. Fifth Edition. Crown 8vo, 5s.

The Basis of Religion. Being an Examination of Natural
Religion. Third Edition. Crown 8vo, 2s. 6d.

The Origin of Evil, and other Sermons. Eighth Edition,
Enlarged. Crown 8vo, 5s.

Personality. The Beginning and End of Metaphysics, and a Necessary Assumption in all Positive Philosophy. Fifth Ed., Revised. Cr. 8vo, 3s.

Agnosticism. Fourth Edition, Revised. Crown 8vo, 5s.

Preaching and Hearing; and other Sermons. Fourth Edition,
Enlarged. Crown 8vo, 5s.

Belief in God. Fourth Edition. Crown 8vo, 3s.

Inspiration; and other Sermons. Second Edition, Enlarged.
Crown 8vo, 5s.

Church and Creed. Third Edition. Crown 8vo, 4s. 6d.

The Future of Religion, and other Essays. Second Edition.
Crown 8vo, 3s. 6d.

The English Church and the Romish Schism. Second Edition.
Crown 8vo, 2s. 6d.

MONCREIFF.
The Provost-Marshal. A Romance of the Middle Shires. By
the Hon. FREDERICK MONCREIFF. Crown 8vo, 6s.

The X Jewel. A Romance of the Days of James VI. Cr. 8vo, 6s.

MONTAGUE. Military Topography. Illustrated by Practical
Examples of a Practical Subject. By Major-General W. E. MONTAGUE, C.B.,
P.S.C., late Garrison Instructor Intelligence Department, Author of 'Campaign-
ing in South Africa.' With Forty-one Diagrams. Crown 8vo, 5s.

MONTALEMBERT. Memoir of Count de Montalembert. A
Chapter of Recent French History. By Mrs OLIPHANT, Author of the 'Life of
Edward Irving,' &c. 2 vols. crown 8vo, £1, 4s.

MORISON.

Doorside Ditties. By JEANIE MORISON. With a Frontispiece. Crown 8vo, 3s. 6d.

Æolus. A Romance in Lyrics. Crown 8vo, 3s.

There as Here. Crown 8vo, 3s.
  ** A limited impression on hand-made paper, bound in vellum, 7s. 6d.

Selections from Poems. Crown 8vo, 4s. 6d.

Sordello. An Outline Analysis of Mr Browning's Poem. Crown 8vo, 3s.

Of "Fifine at the Fair," "Christmas Eve and Easter Day," and other of Mr Browning's Poems. Crown 8vo, 3s.

The Purpose of the Ages. Crown 8vo, 9s.

Gordon : An Our-day Idyll. Crown 8vo, 3s.

Saint Isadora, and other Poems. Crown 8vo, 1s. 6d.

Snatches of Song. Paper, 1s. 6d. ; cloth, 3s.

Pontius Pilate. Paper, 1s. 6d.; cloth, 3s.

Mill o' Forres. Crown 8vo, 1s.

Ane Booke of Ballades. Fcap. 4to, 1s.

MUNRO.

John Splendid. The Tale of a Poor Gentleman and the Little Wars of Lorn. By NEIL MUNRO. Third Edition. Crown 8vo, 6s.

The Lost Pibroch, and other Sheiling Stories. Second Edition. Crown 8vo, 3s. 6d.

MUNRO.

Rambles and Studies in Bosnia-Herzegovina and Dalmatia. With an Account of the proceedings of the Congress of Archæologists and Anthropologists held at Sarajevo in 1894. By ROBERT MUNRO, M.A., M.D., F.R.S.E., Author of the 'Lake Dwellings of Europe,' &c. With numerous illustrations. Demy 8vo, 12s. 6d. net.

Prehistoric Problems. With numerous Illustrations. Demy 8vo, 10s. net.

MUNRO. On Valuation of Property. By WILLIAM MUNRO, M.A., Her Majesty's Assessor of Railways and Canals for Scotland. Second Edition. Revised and Enlarged. 8vo, 3s. 6d.

MURDOCH. Manual of the Law of Insolvency and Bankruptcy: Comprehending a Summary of the Law of Insolvency, Notour Bankruptcy, Composition-Contracts, Trust-Deeds, Cessios, and Sequestrations; and the Winding-up of Joint-Stock Companies in Scotland : with Annotations on the various Insolvency and Bankruptcy Statutes ; and with Forms of Procedure applicable to these Subjects. By JAMES MURDOCH, Member of the Faculty of Procurators in Glasgow. Fifth Edition, Revised and Enlarged. 8vo, 12s. net.

MYERS. A Manual of Classical Geography. By JOHN L. MYERS, M.A., Fellow of Magdalene College; Lecturer and Tutor, Christ Church, Oxford. In 1 vol. crown 8vo. *[In the press.*

MY TRIVIAL LIFE AND MISFORTUNE: A Gossip with no Plot in Particular. By A PLAIN WOMAN. Cheap Edition. Crown 8vo, 3s. 6d.
  By the SAME AUTHOR.
  POOR NELLIE. Cheap Edition. Crown 8vo, 3s. 6d.

NAPIER. The Construction of the Wonderful Canon of Logarithms. By JOHN NAPIER of Merchiston. Translated, with Notes, and a Catalogue of Napier's Works, by WILLIAM RAE MACDONALD. Small 4to, 15s.
  A few large-paper copies on Whatman paper, 30s.

NEAVES. Songs and Verses, Social and Scientific. By An Old Contributor to 'Maga.' By the Hon. Lord NEAVES. Fifth Edition. Fcap. 8vo, 4s.

NICHOLSON.

A Manual of Zoology, for the Use of Students. With a General Introduction on the Principles of Zoology. By HENRY ALLEYNE NICHOLSON, M.D., D.Sc., F.L.S., F G.S., Regius Professor of Natural History in the University of Aberdeen. Seventh Edition, Rewritten and Enlarged. Post 8vo, pp. 956, with 555 Engravings on Wood, 18s.

Text-Book of Zoology, for Junior Students. Fifth Edition. Rewritten and Enlarged. Crown 8vo, with 358 Engravings on Wood, 10s. 6d.

Introductory Text-Book of Zoology. New Edition. Revised by AUTHOR and ALEXANDER BROWN, M.A., M.B., B.Sc., Lecturer on Zoology in the University of Aberdeen. [In the press.

A Manual of Palæontology, for the Use of Students. With a General Introduction on the Principles of Palæontology. By Professor H. ALLEYNE NICHOLSON and RICHARD LYDEKKER, B.A. Third Edition, entirely Rewritten and greatly Enlarged. 2 vols. 8vo, £3, 3s.

The Ancient Life-History of the Earth. An Outline of the Principles and Leading Facts of Palæontological Science. Crown 8vo, with 276 Engravings, 10s. 6d.

On the "Tabulate Corals" of the Palæozoic Period, with Critical Descriptions of Illustrative Species. Illustrated with 15 Lithographed Plates and numerous Engravings. Super-royal 8vo, 21s.

Synopsis of the Classification of the Animal Kingdom. 8vo, with 106 Illustrations, 6s.

On the Structure and Affinities of the Genus Monticulipora and its Sub-Genera, with Critical Descriptions of Illustrative Species. Illustrated with numerous Engravings on Wood and Lithographed Plates. Super-royal 8vo, 18s.

NICHOLSON.

Thoth. A Romance. By JOSEPH SHIELD NICHOLSON, M.A., D.Sc., Professor of Commercial and Political Economy and Mercantile Law in the University of Edinburgh. Third Edition. Crown 8vo, 4s. 6d.

A Dreamer of Dreams. A Modern Romance. Second Edition. Crown 8vo, 6s.

OLIPHANT.

Masollam : A Problem of the Period. A Novel. By LAURENCE OLIPHANT. 3 vols. post 8vo, 25s. 6d.

Scientific Religion ; or, Higher Possibilities of Life and Practice through the Operation of Natural Forces. Second Edition. 8vo, 16s.

Altiora Peto. Cheap Edition. Crown 8vo, boards, 2s. 6d. ; cloth, 3s. 6d. Illustrated Edition. Crown 8vo, cloth, 6s.

Piccadilly. With Illustrations by Richard Doyle. New Edition, 3s. 6d. Cheap Edition, boards, 2s. 6d.

Traits and Travesties ; Social and Political. Post 8vo, 10s. 6d.

Episodes in a Life of Adventure ; or, Moss from a Rolling Stone. Cheaper Edition. Post 8vo, 3s. 6d.

Haifa : Life in Modern Palestine. Second Edition. 8vo, 7s. 6d.

The Land of Gilead. With Excursions in the Lebanon. With Illustrations and Maps. Demy 8vo, 21s.

Memoir of the Life of Laurence Oliphant, and of Alice Oliphant, his Wife. By Mrs M. O. W. OLIPHANT. Seventh Edition. 2 vols. post 8vo, with Portraits. 21s.
POPULAR EDITION. With a New Preface. Post 8vo, with Portraits. 7s. 6d.

OLIPHANT.

Annals of a Publishing House. William Blackwood and his Sons ; Their Magazine and Friends. By Mrs OLIPHANT. With Four Portraits. Third Edition. Demy 8vo. Vols. I. and II. £2, 2s.

A Widow's Tale, and other Stories. With an Introductory Note by J. M. BARRIE. Second Edition. Crown 8vo, 6s.

OLIPHANT.
Who was Lost and is Found. Second Edition. Crown
8vo, 6s.
Miss Marjoribanks. New Edition. Crown 8vo, 3s. 6d.
The Perpetual Curate, and The Rector. New Edition. Crown
8vo, 3s. 6d.
Salem Chapel, and The Doctor's Family. New Edition.
Crown 8vo, 3s. 6d
Chronicles of Carlingford. 3 vols. crown 8vo, in uniform
binding, gilt top, 3s. 6d. each.
Katie Stewart, and other Stories. New Edition. Crown 8vo,
cloth, 3s. 6d.
Katie Stewart. Illustrated boards, 2s. 6d.
Valentine and his Brother. New Edition. Crown 8vo, 3s. 6d
Sons and Daughters. Crown 8vo, 3s. 6d.
Two Stories of the Seen and the Unseen. The Open Door
—Old Lady Mary. Paper covers, 1s.

OLIPHANT. Notes of a Pilgrimage to Jerusalem and the Holy
Land. By F. R. OLIPHANT. Crown 8vo, 3s. 6d.

PAGE.
Intermediate Text-Book of Geology. Founded on Page's In-
troductory Text-Book of Geology. By Professor LAPWORTH of Mason Science
College, Birmingham. With Illustrations. Crown 8vo, 5s.
Advanced Text-Book of Geology, Descriptive and Industrial.
With Engravings, and Glossary of Scientific Terms. New Edition. Revised by
Professor LAPWORTH. [In preparation.
Introductory Text-Book of Physical Geography. With Sketch-
Maps and Illustrations. Edited by Professor LAPWORTH, LL.D., F.G.S., &c.,
Mason Science College, Birmingham. Thirteenth Edition, Revised and Enlarged.
2s. 6d.
Advanced Text-Book of Physical Geography. Third Edition.
Revised and Enlarged by Professor LAPWORTH. With Engravings. 5s.

PATERSON. A Manual of Agricultural Botany. From the
German of Dr A. B. FRANK, Professor in the Royal Agricultural College, Berlin.
Translated by JOHN W. PATERSON, B.Sc., Ph.D., Free Life Member of the Highland and Agricultural Society of Scotland, and of the Royal Agricultural Society
of England. With over 100 Illustrations. Crown 8vo, 3s. 6d.

PATON.
Spindrift. By Sir J. NOEL PATON. Fcap., cloth, 5s.
Poems by a Painter. Fcap., cloth, 5s.
PATON. Castlebraes. Drawn from "The Tinlie MSS." By
JAMES PATON, B.A., Editor of 'John G. Paton : an Autobiography,' &c., &c.
Crown 8vo, 6s.

PATRICK. The Apology of Origen in Reply to Celsus. A Chap-
ter in the History of Apologetics. By the Rev. J. PATRICK, D.D., Professor of
Biblical Criticism in the University of Edinburgh. Post 8vo, 7s. 6d.

PAUL. History of the Royal Company of Archers, the Queen's
Body-Guard for Scotland. By JAMES BALFOUR PAUL, Advocate of the Scottish
Bar. Crown 4to, with Portraits and other Illustrations. £2, 2s.

PEARSE. Soldier and Traveller : Being the Memoirs of
Alexander Gardner, Colonel of Artillery in the Service of Maharaja Ranjit
Singh. Edited by Major Hugh PEARSE, 2nd Battalion the East Surrey Regiment.
With an Introduction by the Right Hon. Sir RICHARD TEMPLE, Bart., G.C.S.I.
With Two Portraits and Maps. Demy 8vo, 15s.

PEILE. Lawn Tennis as a Game of Skill. By Lieut.-Col. S. C.
F. PEILE, B.S.C. Revised Edition, with new Scoring Rules. Fcap. 8vo, cloth, 1s.

PERIODS OF EUROPEAN LITERATURE. Edited by Professor SAINTSBURY. *For List of Volumes, see page 2.*

PETTIGREW. The Handy Book of Bees, and their Profitable Management. By A. PETTIGREW. Fifth Edition, Enlarged, with Engravings. Crown 8vo, 3s. 6d.

PFLEIDERER. Philosophy and Development of Religion. Being the Edinburgh Gifford Lectures for 1894. By OTTO PFLEIDERER, D.D., Professor of Theology at Berlin University. In 2 vols. post 8vo, 15s. net.

PHILLIPS. The Knight's Tale. By F. EMILY PHILLIPS, Author of 'The Education of Antonia.' Crown 8vo, 3s. 6d.

PHILOSOPHICAL CLASSICS FOR ENGLISH READERS. Edited by WILLIAM KNIGHT, LL.D., Professor of Moral Philosophy, University of St Andrews. In crown 8vo volumes, with Portraits, price 3s. 6d.
[*For List of Volumes, see page 2.*

POLLARD. A Study in Municipal Government : The Corporation of Berlin. By JAMES POLLARD, C.A., Chairman of the Edinburgh Public Health Committee, and Secretary of the Edinburgh Chamber of Commerce. Second Edition, Revised. Crown 8vo, 3s. 6d.

POLLOK. The Course of Time : A Poem. By ROBERT POLLOK, A.M. New Edition With Portrait. Fcap. 8vo, gilt top, 2s. 6d.

PORT ROYAL LOGIC. Translated from the French ; with Introduction, Notes, and Appendix. By THOMAS SPENCER BAYNES, LL.D., Professor in the University of St Andrews. Tenth Edition, 12mo, 4s.

POTTS AND DARNELL.
Aditus Faciliores : An Easy Latin Construing Book, with Complete Vocabulary By A. W. POTTS, M.A., LL.D., and the Rev. C. DARNELL, M.A., Head-Master of Cargilfield Preparatory School Edinburgh. Tenth Edition, fcap. 8vo, 3s. 6d

Aditus Faciliores Graeci. An Easy Greek Construing Book, with Complete Vocabulary. Fifth Edition, Revised. Fcap. 8vo, 3s.

POTTS. School Sermons. By the late ALEXANDER WM. POTTS, LL.D., First Head-Master of Fettes College. With a Memoir and Portrait. Crown 8vo, 7s. 6d.

PRINGLE. The Live Stock of the Farm. By ROBERT O. PRINGLE. Third Edition. Revised and Edited by JAMES MACDONALD. Crown 8vo, 7s. 6d.

PUBLIC GENERAL STATUTES AFFECTING SCOTLAND from 1707 to 1847, with Chronological Table and Index. 3 vols. large 8vo, £3, 3s.

PUBLIC GENERAL STATUTES AFFECTING SCOTLAND, COLLECTION OF. Published Annually, with General Index.

RAMSAY. Scotland and Scotsmen in the Eighteenth Century. Edited from the MSS. of JOHN RAMSAY, Esq. of Ochtertyre, by ALEXANDER ALLARDYCE, Author of 'Memoir of Admiral Lord Keith, K.B.,' &c. 2 vols. 8vo, 31s. 6d.

RANJITSINHJI. The Jubilee Book of Cricket. By PRINCE RANJITSINHJI.
ÉDITION DE LUXE. Limited to 350 Copies, printed on hand made paper, and handsomely bound in buckram. Crown 4to, with 22 Photogravures and 85 full-page Plates. Each copy signed by Prince Ranjitsinhji. Price £5, 5s. net.
FINE PAPER EDITION. Medium 8vo, with Photogravure Frontispiece and 106 full-page Plates on art paper. 25s. net.
POPULAR EDITION. With 107 full-page Illustrations. Sixth Edition. Large crown 8vo, 6s.

RANKIN.
Church Ideas in Scripture and Scotland. By JAMES RANKIN, D.D., Minister of Muthill ; Author of 'Character Studies in the Old Testament, &c. In 1 vol., crown 8vo, [*In the press.*

A Handbook of the Church of Scotland. An entirely New and much Enlarged Edition. Crown 8vo, with 2 Maps, 7s. 6d.

RANKIN.

The First Saints. Post 8vo, 7s. 6d.

The Creed in Scotland. An Exposition of the Apostles' Creed. With Extracts from Archbishop Hamilton's Catechism of 1552, John Calvin's Catechism of 1556, and a Catena of Ancient Latin and other Hymns. Post 8vo, 7s. 6d.

The Worthy Communicant. A Guide to the Devout Observance of the Lord's Supper. Limp cloth, 1s. 3d.

The Young Churchman. Lessons on the Creed, the Commandments, the Means of Grace, and the Church. Limp cloth, 1s. 3d.

First Communion Lessons. 25th Edition. Paper Cover, 2d.

RANKINE. A Hero of the Dark Continent. Memoir of Rev. Wm. Affleck Scott, M.A., M.B., C.M., Church of Scotland Missionary at Blantyre, British Central Africa. By W. Henry Rankine, B.D., Minister at Titwood. With a Portrait and other Illustrations. Cheap Edition. Crown 8vo, 2s.

ROBERTSON.

The Poetry and the Religion of the Psalms. The Croall Lectures, 1893-94. By James Robertson, D.D., Professor of Oriental Languages in the University of Glasgow. Demy 8vo, 12s.

The Early Religion of Israel. As set forth by Biblical Writers and Modern Critical Historians. Being the Baird Lecture for 1888-89. Fourth Edition. Crown 8vo, 10s. 6d.

ROBERTSON.

Orellana, and other Poems. By J. Logie Robertson, M.A. Fcap. 8vo. Printed on hand-made paper. 6s.

A History of English Literature. For Secondary Schools. With an Introduction by Professor Masson, Edinburgh University. Cr. 8vo, 3s.

English Verse for Junior Classes. In Two Parts. Part I.— Chaucer to Coleridge. Part II.—Nineteenth Century Poets. Crown 8vo, each 1s. 6d. net.

Outlines of English Literature for Young Scholars. With Illustrative Specimens. Crown 8vo, 1s. 6d.

English Prose for Junior and Senior Classes. Part I.—Malory to Johnson. Crown 8vo, 2s. 6d.   [*Part II. in the press.*

ROBINSON. Wild Traits in Tame Animals. Being some Familiar Studies in Evolution. By Louis Robinson, M.D. With Illustrations by Stephen T. Dadd. Demy 8vo, 10s. 6d. net.

ROSS and SOMERVILLE. Beggars on Horseback : A Riding Tour in North Wales. By Martin Ross and E. Œ. Somerville. With Illustrations by E. Œ. Somerville. Crown 8vo, 3s. 6d.

RUTLAND.

Notes of an Irish Tour in 1846. By the Duke of Rutland, G.C.B. (Lord John Manners). New Edition. Crown 8vo, 2s. 6d.

Correspondence between the Right Honble. William Pitt and Charles Duke of Rutland, Lord-Lieutenant of Ireland, 1781-1787. With Introductory Note by John Duke of Rutland. 8vo, 7s. 6d.

RUTLAND.

Gems of German Poetry. Translated by the Duchess of Rutland (Lady John Manners).   [*New Edition in preparation.*

Impressions of Bad-Homburg. Comprising a Short Account of the Women's Associations of Germany under the Red Cross. Crown 8vo, 1s. 6d.

Some Personal Recollections of the Later Years of the Earl of Beaconsfield, K.G. Sixth Edition. 6d.

Employment of Women in the Public Service. 6d.

Some of the Advantages of Easily Accessible Reading and Recreation Rooms and Free Libraries. With Remarks on Starting and Maintaining them. Second Edition. Crown 8vo, 1s.

RUTLAND.

A Sequel to Rich Men's Dwellings, and other Occasional
Papers. Crown 8vo, 2s. 6d.

Encouraging Experiences of Reading and Recreation Rooms,
Aims of Guilds, Nottingham Social Guide, Existing Institutions, &c., &c.
Crown 8vo, 1s.

SAINTSBURY. The Flourishing of Romance and the Rise of
Allegory (12th and 13th Centuries). 'Periods of European Literature.' By GEORGE
SAINTSBURY, M.A., Professor of Rhetoric and English Literature in Edinburgh
University. Crown 8vo, 5s. net.

SCHEFFEL. The Trumpeter. A Romance of the Rhine. By
JOSEPH VICTOR VON SCHEFFEL. Translated from the Two Hundredth German
Edition by JESSIE BECK and LOUISA LORIMER. With an Introduction by Sir
THEODORE MARTIN, K.C.B. Long 8vo, 3s. 6d.

SCOTT. Tom Cringle's Log. By MICHAEL SCOTT. New Edition.
With 19 Full-page Illustrations. Crown 8vo, 3s. 6d.

SELKIRK. Poems. By J. B. SELKIRK, Author of 'Ethics and
Æsthetics of Modern Poetry,' 'Bible Truths with Shakesparian Parallels,' &c.
New and Enlarged Edition. Crown 8vo, printed on antique paper, 6s.

SELLAR'S Manual of the Acts relating to Education in Scotland. By J. EDWARD GRAHAM, B.A. Oxon., Advocate. Ninth Edition. Demy
8vo, 12s. 6d.

SETH.

Scottish Philosophy. A Comparison of the Scottish and
German Answers to Hume. Balfour Philosophical Lectures, University of
Edinburgh. By ANDREW SETH, LL.D. (A. S. Pringle-Pattison), Professor of
Logic and Metaphysics in Edinburgh University. Third Edition. Crown
8vo.   [*In the press.*

Hegelianism and Personality. Balfour Philosophical Lectures.
Second Series. Second Edition. Crown 8vo, 5s.

Man's Place in the Cosmos, and other Essays. Post 8vo,
7s. 6d. net.

Two Lectures on Theism. Delivered on the occasion of the
Sesquicentennial Celebration of Princeton University. Crown 8vo, 2s. 6d.

SETH. A Study of Ethical Principles. By JAMES SETH, M.A.,
Professor of Moral Philosophy in the University of Edinburgh. Fourth Edition. Revised. Post 8vo, 7s. 6d.

SHARPE. Letters from and to Charles Kirkpatrick Sharpe.
Edited by ALEXANDER ALLARDYCE, Author of 'Memoir of Admiral Lord Keith,
K.B.,' &c. With a Memoir by the Rev. W. K. R. BEDFORD. In 2 vols. 8vo.
Illustrated with Etchings and other Engravings. £2, 12s. 6d.

SIM. Margaret Sim's Cookery. With an Introduction by L. B.
WALFORD, Author of 'Mr Smith: A Part of his Life,' &c. Crown 8vo, 5s.

SIMPSON. The Wild Rabbit in a New Aspect; or, Rabbit-
Warrens that Pay. A book for Landowners, Sportsmen, Land Agents, Farmers,
Gamekeepers, and Allotment Holders. A Record of Recent Experiments con-
ducted on the Estate of the Right Hon. the Earl of Wharncliffe at Wortley Hall.
By J. SIMPSON. Second Edition, Enlarged. Small crown 8vo, 5s.

SIMPSON. Side-Lights on Siberia. Some account of the Great
Siberian Iron Road: The Prisons and Exile System. By J. Y. SIMPSON, M.A.,
B.Sc. With numerous Illustrations and a Map. Demy 8vo, 16s.

SINCLAIR.

Mr and Mrs Nevill Tyson. By MAY SINCLAIR. Crown 8vo,
3s. 6d.

Audrey Craven. Second Edition. Crown 8vo, 6s.

SKELTON.

The Table-Talk of Shirley. By Sir JOHN SKELTON, K.C.B.,
LL.D., Author of 'The Essays of Shirley.' With a Frontispiece. Sixth Edition,
Revised and Enlarged. Post 8vo, 7s. 6d.

SKELTON.
>The Table-Talk of Shirley. Second Series. With Illustrations. Two Volumes. Second Edition. Post 8vo, 10s. net.
>
>Maitland of Lethington ; and the Scotland of Mary Stuart. A History. Limited Edition, with Portraits. Demy 8vo, 2 vols., 28s. net.
>
>The Handbook of Public Health. A New Edition, Revised by JAMES PATTEN MACDOUGALL, Advocate, Secretary of the Local Government Board for Scotland, Joint-Author of 'The Parish Council Guide for Scotland,' and ABIJAH MURRAY, Chief Clerk of the Local Government Board for Scotland. In Two Parts. Crown 8vo. Part I.—The Public Health (Scotland) Act, 1897, with Notes. 3s. 6d. net
>>Part II.—Circulars of the Local Government Board, &c.   [*In preparation.*
>
>The Local Government (Scotland) Act in Relation to Public Health. A Handy Guide for County and District Councillors, Medical Officers, Sanitary Inspectors, and Members of Parochial Boards. Second Edition. With a new Preface on appointment of Sanitary Officers. Crown 8vo, 2s.

SKRINE.   Columba: A Drama.   By JOHN HUNTLEY SKRINE, Warden of Glenalmond: Author of 'A Memory of Edward Thring.' Fcap. 4to, 6s.

SMITH. Retrievers, and how to Break them. By Lieutenant-Colonel Sir HENRY SMITH, K.C.B. With an Introduction by Mr S. E. SHIRLEY, President of the Kennel Club. Dedicated by special permission to H.R.H. the Duke of York. With Illustrations. Crown 8vo, 5s.

SMITH.
>Thorndale ; or, The Conflict of Opinions. By WILLIAM SMITH, Author of 'A Discourse on Ethics,' &c. New Edition. Crown 8vo, 10s. 6d.
>
>Gravenhurst ; or, Thoughts on Good and Evil. Second Edition. With Memoir and Portrait of the Author. Crown 8vo, 8s.

SMITH. Greek Testament Lessons for Colleges, Schools, and Private Students, consisting chiefly of the Sermon on the Mount and the Parables of our Lord. With Notes and Essays. By the Rev. J. HUNTER SMITH, M.A., King Edward's School, Birmingham. Crown 8vo, 6s.

SNELL. The Fourteenth Century. "Periods of European Literature." By F. J. SNELL. Crown 8vo, 5s. net.

"SON OF THE MARSHES, A."
>From Spring to Fall ; or, When Life Stirs. By "A SON OF THE MARSHES." Cheap Uniform Edition. Crown 8vo, 3s. 6d.
>
>Within an Hour of London Town: Among Wild Birds and their Haunts. Edited by J. A. OWEN. Cheap Uniform Edition. Cr. 8vo, 3s. 6d.
>
>With the Woodlanders and by the Tide. Cheap Uniform Edition. Crown 8vo, 3s. 6d.
>
>On Surrey Hills. Cheap Uniform Edition. Crown 8vo, 3s. 6d.
>
>Annals of a Fishing Village. Cheap Uniform Edition. Crown 8vo, 3s. 6d.

SORLEY. The Ethics of Naturalism. Being the Shaw Fellowship Lectures, 1884. By W. R. SORLEY, M.A., Fellow of Trinity College, Cambridge, Professor of Moral Philosophy, University of Aberdeen. Crown 8vo, 6s.

SPIELMANN. Millais and his Works. By M. H. SPIELMANN, Author of 'History of Punch.' With 28 Full-page Illustrations. Large crown 8vo. Paper covers, 1s.; in cloth binding, 2s. 6d.

SPROTT. The Worship and Offices of the Church of Scotland. By GEORGE W. SPROTT, D.D., Minister of North Berwick. Crown 8vo, 6s.

STATISTICAL ACCOUNT OF SCOTLAND. Complete, with Index. 15 vols. 8vo, £16, 16s.

STEEVENS.
>With Kitchener to Khartum. By G. W. STEEVENS. With 8 Maps and Plans. Seventh Edition. Crown 8vo, 6s.
>
>Egypt in 1898. With Illustrations. Crown 8vo, 6s.

STEEVENS.

The Land of the Dollar. Third Edition. Crown 8vo, 6s.

With the Conquering Turk. With 4 Maps. Demy 8vo, 10s. 6d.

STEPHENS.

The Book of the Farm ; detailing the Labours of the Farmer, Farm-Steward, Ploughman, Shepherd, Hedger, Farm-Labourer, Field-Worker, and Cattle-man. Illustrated with numerous Portraits of Animals and Engravings of Implements, and Plans of Farm Buildings. Fourth Edition. Revised, and in great part Re-written, by JAMES MACDONALD, F.R.S.E., Secretary Highland and Agricultural Society of Scotland. Complete in Six Divisional Volumes, bound in cloth, each 10s. 6d., or handsomely bound, in 3 volumes, with leather back and gilt top, £3, 3s.

. Also being issued in 20 monthly Parts, price 2s. 6d. net each.

[*Parts I.-XVIII. ready.*

Catechism of Practical Agriculture. 22d Thousand. Revised by JAMES MACDONALD, F.R.S.E. With numerous Illustrations. Crown 8vo, 1s.

The Book of Farm Implements and Machines. By J. SLIGHT and R. SCOTT BURN, Engineers. Edited by HENRY STEPHENS. Large 8vo, £2, 2s.

STEVENSON. British Fungi. (Hymenomycetes.) By Rev. JOHN STEVENSON, Author of 'Mycologia Scotica,' Hon. Sec. Cryptogamic Society of Scotland. Vols. I. and II., post 8vo, with Illustrations, price 12s. 6d. net each.

STEWART. Advice to Purchasers of Horses. By JOHN STEWART, V.S. New Edition. 2s. 6d.

STODDART.

John Stuart Blackie : A Biography. By ANNA M. STODDART. With 3 Plates. Third Edition. 2 vols. demy 8vo, 21s.

POPULAR EDITION, with Portrait. Crown 8vo, 6s.

Sir Philip Sidney : Servant of God. Illustrated by MARGARET L. HUGGINS. With a New Portrait of Sir Philip Sidney. Small 4to, with a specially designed Cover. 5s.

STORMONTH.

Dictionary of the English Language, Pronouncing, Etymological, and Explanatory. By the Rev. JAMES STORMONTH. Revised by the Rev. P. H. PHELP. Library Edition. New and Cheaper Edition, with Supplement. Imperial 8vo, handsomely bound in half morocco, 18s. net.

Etymological and Pronouncing Dictionary of the English Language. Including a very Copious Selection of Scientific Terms. For use in Schools and Colleges, and as a Book of General Reference. The Pronunciation carefully revised by the Rev. P. H. PHELP, M.A. Cantab. Thirteenth Edition, with Supplement. Crown 8vo, pp. 800. 7s. 6d.

The School Dictionary. New Edition, thoroughly Revised. By WILLIAM BAYNE. 16mo, 1s.

STORY. The Apostolic Ministry in the Scottish Church (The Baird Lecture for 1897). By ROBERT HERBERT STORY, D.D (Edin.), F.S.A. Scot., Principal of the University of Glasgow, Principal Clerk of the General Assembly, and Chaplain to the Queen. Crown 8vo, 7s. 6d.

STORY.

Poems. By W. W. Story, Author of 'Roba di Roma,' &c. 2 vols. 7s. 6d.

Fiammetta. A Summer Idyl. Crown 8vo, 7s. 6d.

Conversations in a Studio. 2 vols. crown 8vo, 12s. 6d.

Excursions in Art and Letters. Crown 8vo, 7s. 6d.

A Poet's Portfolio : Later Readings. 18mo, 3s. 6d.

STRACHEY. Talk at a Country House. Fact and Fiction. By Sir EDWARD STRACHEY, Bart. With a portrait of the Author. Crown 8vo, 4s. 6d. net.

STURGIS. Little Comedies, Old and New. By JULIAN STURGIS.
Crown 8vo, 7s. 6d.

TAYLOR. The Story of my Life. By the late Colonel
MEADOWS TAYLOR, Author of 'The Confessions of a Thug,' &c., &c. Edited by
his Daughter. New and Cheaper Edition, being the Fourth. Crown 8vo, 6s.

THEOBALD. A Text-Book of Agricultural Zoology. By FRED.
V. THEOBALD, M.A. (Cantab.), F.E.S., Foreign Member of the Association of
Official Economic Entomologists, U.S.A., Zoologist to the S.E. Agricultural
College, Wye, &c. With numerous Illustrations. In 1 vol. crown 8vo.
                                                        [*In the press.*

THOMAS. The Woodland Life. By EDWARD THOMAS. With a
Frontispiece. Square 8vo, 6s.

THOMSON.
    The Diversions of a Prime Minister. By Basil Thomson.
    With a Map, numerous Illustrations by J. W. Cawston and others, and Repro-
    ductions of Rare Plates, from Early Voyages of Sixteenth and Seventeenth Cen-
    turies. Small demy 8vo, 15s.
    South Sea Yarns. With 10 Full-page Illustrations. Cheaper
    Edition. Crown 8vo, 3s. 6d.

THOMSON.
    Handy Book of the Flower-Garden : Being Practical Direc-
    tions for the Propagation, Culture, and Arrangement of Plants in Flower-
    Gardens all the year round. With Engraved Plans. By DAVID THOMSON,
    Gardener to his Grace the Duke of Buccleuch, K.T., at Drumlanrig. Fourth
    and Cheaper Edition. Crown 8vo, 5s.
    The Handy Book of Fruit-Culture under Glass : Being a
    series of Elaborate Practical Treatises on the Cultivation and Forcing of Pines,
    Vines, Peaches, Figs, Melons, Strawberries, and Cucumbers. With Engravings
    of Hothouses, &c. Second Edition, Revised and Enlarged. Crown 8vo, 7s. 6d.

THOMSON. A Practical Treatise on the Cultivation of the
Grape Vine. By WILLIAM THOMSON, Tweed Vineyards. Tenth Edition. 8vo, 5s.

THOMSON. Cookery for the Sick and Convalescent. With
Directions for the Preparation of Poultices, Fomentations, &c. By BARBARA
THOMSON. Fcap. 8vo, 1s. 6d.

THORBURN. Asiatic Neighbours. By S. S. THORBURN, Bengal
Civil Service, Author of 'Bannú; or, Our Afghan Frontier,' 'David Leslie :
A Story of the Afghan Frontier,' 'Musalmans and Money-Lenders in the Pau-
jab.' With Two Maps. Demy 8vo, 10s. 6d. net.

THORNTON. Opposites. A Series of Essays on the Unpopular
Sides of Popular Questions. By LEWIS THORNTON. 8vo, 12s. 6d.

TIELE. Elements of the Science of Religion. Part I.—Morpho-
logical. Being the Gifford Lectures delivered before the University of Edinburgh
in 1896. By C. P. TIELE, Theol. D., Litt.D. (Bonon.), Hon. M.R.A.S., &c., Professor of the Science of Religion, in the University of Leiden. In 2 vols. Vol. I.
post 8vo, 7s. 6d. net.

TOKE. French Historical Unseens. For Army Classes. By
N. E. TOKE, B.A. In 1 vol. crown 8vo.   [*In the press.*

TRANSACTIONS OF THE HIGHLAND AND AGRICUL-
TURAL SOCIETY OF SCOTLAND. Published annually, price 5s.

TRAVERS.
    Windyhaugh. By GRAHAM TRAVERS (Margaret G. Todd,
    M.D.) Crown 8vo, 6s.
    Mona Maclean, Medical Student. A Novel. Thirteenth Edi-
    tion. Crown 8vo, 6s.
    Fellow Travellers. Fourth Edition. Crown 8vo, 6s.

TRYON. Life of Vice-Admiral Sir George Tryon, K.C.B. By
Rear-Admiral C. C. PENROSE FITZGERALD. Cheap Edition. With Portrait and
numerous Illustrations. Demy 8vo, 6s.

TULLOCH.

Rational Theology and Christian Philosophy in England in
the Seventeenth Century. By JOHN TULLOCH, D.D., Principal of St Mary's College in the University of St Andrews, and one of her Majesty's Chaplains in
Ordinary in Scotland. Second Edition. 2 vols. 8vo, 16s.

Modern Theories in Philosophy and Religion. 8vo, 15s.

Luther, and other Leaders of the Reformation. Third Edition, Enlarged. Crown 8vo, 3s. 6d.

Memoir of Principal Tulloch, D.D, LL.D. By Mrs OLIPHANT,
Author of 'Life of Edward Irving.' Third and Cheaper Edition. 8vo, with
Portrait, 7s. 6d.

TWEEDIE. The Arabian Horse: His Country and People.
By Major-General W. TWEEDIE, C.S.I., Bengal Staff Corps; for many years
H.B.M.'s Consul-General, Baghdad, and Political Resident for the Government
of India in Turkish Arabia. In one vol. royal 4to, with Seven Coloured Plates
and other Illustrations, and a Map of the Country. Price £3, 3s. net.

TYLER. The Whence and the Whither of Man. A Brief History of his Origin and Development through Conformity to Environment. The
Morse Lectures of 1895. By JOHN M. TYLER, Professor of Biology, Amherst
College. U.S.A. Post 8vo, 6s. net.

VANDERVELL. A Shuttle of an Empire's Loom; or, Five
Months before the Mast on a Modern Steam Cargo-Boat. By HARRY VANDERVELL. In 1 vol., crown 8vo. [In the press.

VEITCH.

Memoir of John Veitch, LL.D., Professor of Logic and Rhetoric,
University of Glasgow. By MARY R. L. BRYCE. With Portrait and 3 Photogravure Plates. Demy 8vo, 7s. 6d.

Border Essays. By JOHN VEITCH, LL.D., Professor of Logic
and Rhetoric, University of Glasgow. Crown 8vo, 4s. 6d. net.

The History and Poetry of the Scottish Border: their Main
Features and Relations. New and Enlarged Edition. 2 vols. demy 8vo, 16s.

Institutes of Logic. Post 8vo, 12s. 6d.

Merlin and other Poems. Fcap. 8vo, 4s. 6d.

Knowing and Being. Essays in Philosophy. First Series.
Crown 8vo, 5s.

Dualism and Monism; and other Essays. Essays in Philosophy. Second Series. With an Introduction by R. M. Wenley. Crown 8vo,
4s. 6d. net.

WACE. Christianity and Agnosticism. Reviews of some Recent
Attacks on the Christian Faith. By HENRY WACE, D.D., late Principal of King's
College, London; Preacher of Lincoln's Inn; Chaplain to the Queen. Second
Edition. Post 8vo, 10s. 6d. net.

WADDELL. An Old Kirk Chronicle: Being a History of Auldhame, Tyninghame, and Whitekirk, in East Lothian. From Session Records,
1615 to 1850. By Rev. P. HATELY WADDELL, B.D., Minister of the United
Parish. Small Paper Edition, 200 Copies. Price £1. Large Paper Edition, 50
Copies. Price, £1, 10s.

WALDO. The Ban of the Gubbe. By CEDRIC DANE WALDO.
Crown 8vo, 2s. 6d.

WALFORD. Four Biographies from 'Blackwood': Jane Taylor,
Hannah More, Elizabeth Fry, Mary Somerville. By L. B. WALFORD. Crown
8vo, 5s.

WARREN'S (SAMUEL) WORKS:—

Diary of a Late Physician. Cloth, 2s. 6d.; boards, 2s.

Ten Thousand A-Year. Cloth, 3s. 6d.; boards, 2s. 6d.

Now and Then. The Lily and the Bee. Intellectual and
Moral Development of the Present Age. 4s. 6d.

Essays: Critical, Imaginative, and Juridical. 5s.

WENLEY.

Socrates and Christ: A Study in the Philosophy of Religion. By R. M. WENLEY, M.A., D.Sc. D.Phil., Professor of Philosophy in the University of Michigan, U.S.A. Crown 8vo, 6s.

Aspects of Pessimism. Crown 8vo, 6s.

WHITE.

The Eighteen Christian Centuries. By the Rev. JAMES WHITE. Seventh Edition. Post 8vo, with Index, 6s.

History of France, from the Earliest Times. Sixth Thousand. Post 8vo, with Index, 6s.

WHITE.

Archæological Sketches in Scotland—Kintyre and Knapdale. By Colonel T. P. WHITE, R.E., of the Ordnance Survey. With numerous Illustrations. 2 vols. folio, £4, 4s. Vol. I., Kintyre, sold separately, £2, 2s.

The Ordnance Survey of the United Kingdom. A Popular Account. Crown 8vo, 5s.

WILKES. Latin Historical Unseens. For Army Classes. By L. C. VAUGHAN WILKES, M.A Crown 8vo, 2s.

WILLIAMSON. The Horticultural Handbook and Exhibitor's Guide. By W. WILLIAMSON, Gardener. Revised by MALCOLM DUNN, Gardener to his Grace the Duke of Buccleuch and Queensberry, Dalkeith Park. Cheap Edition. Crown 8vo, paper cover, 1s.

WILLS. Behind an Eastern Veil. A Plain Tale of Events occurring in the Experience of a Lady who had a unique opportunity of observing the Inner Life of Ladies of the Upper Class in Persia. By C. J. WILLS, Author of 'In the Land of the Lion and Sun,' 'Persia as it is,' &c., &c. Cheaper Edition. Demy 8vo, 5s.

WILSON.

Works of Professor Wilson. Edited by his Son-in-Law, Professor FERRIER. 12 vols. crown 8vo, £2, 8s.

Christopher in his Sporting-Jacket. 2 vols., 8s.

Isle of Palms, City of the Plague, and other Poems. 4s.

Lights and Shadows of Scottish Life, and other Tales. 4s.

Essays, Critical and Imaginative. 4 vols., 16s.

The Noctes Ambrosianæ. 4 vols., 16s.

Homer and his Translators, and the Greek Drama. Crown 8vo, 4s.

WORSLEY.

Homer's Odyssey. Translated into English Verse in the Spenserian Stanza. By PHILIP STANHOPE WORSLEY, M.A. New and Cheaper Edition. Post 8vo, 7s. 6d. net.

Homer's Iliad. Translated by P. S. Worsley and Prof. Conington. 2 vols. crown 8vo, 21s.

YATE. England and Russia Face to Face in Asia. A Record of Travel with the Afghan Boundary Commission. By Captain A. C. YATE, Bombay Staff Corps. 8vo, with Maps and Illustrations, 21s.

YATE. Northern Afghanistan; or, Letters from the Afghan Boundary Commission. By Colonel C. E. YATE, C.S.I., C.M.G., Bombay Staff Corps, F.R.G.S. 8vo, with Maps, 18s.

ZACK. Life is Life, and other Tales and Episodes. By ZACK. Second Edition. Crown 8vo, 6s.

www.ingramcontent.com/pod-product-compliance
Lightning Source LLC
Chambersburg PA
CBHW030042130726
47901CB00007BA/1699